FAREWELL THE INNOCENT

To Mike,
Best wishes and I hope
you enjoy the book.

STEVE PRINCE

Suite 300 - 990 Fort St
Victoria, BC, Canada, V8V 3K2
www.friesenpress.com

First Edition — 2016

ISBN
978-1-4602-0284-5 (Paperback)
978-1-4602-0285-2 (eBook)

1. Fiction, Historical

Distributed to the trade by The Ingram Book Company

Dedication

Dedicated to the memory of
all of the men and women,
North and South,
who struggled and fought and died
to transform a nation,
and to the families of the brave men
of the
Second Virginia Infantry Regiment,
"The Innocent Second"

Illustrated by Kris Prince

Maps by Steve and Kris Prince

Editorial reviews by
Bonni Hines

Acknowledgments

Thanks expressed to Vince Hackley for the terrific enlistment records of the Second Virginia, and for part of the inspiration for the character of Wil Harleck.

My greatest respect and appreciation, also, to all of the authors, historians, filmmakers, and pioneers who helped ignite the flame of passion for the Civil War in me and many others in a time when Civil War history was not cool.

Special thanks to my beautiful wife, soulmate, and best friend, Kris, who did the fantastic sketchwork, and helped me forge rough ideas into better ones, and to my entire family who lovingly and enthusiastically supported me through many hundreds of hours of research, writing, and editing over a span of ten years.

All thanks and glory to my Lord and Savior, Jesus Christ, in whom all things are possible, and without whom I can do nothing.

A Word from the Author

This is a novel about an ordinary soldier who might have been just about any soldier who lived and fought for the Confederacy in the great and terrible War Between the States. But this is not just another war story. It's a story of idealism and patriotism, of hope and faith and love, and of war and tragedy.

I chose to write the story in first person narrative, as if we were sitting with Wil Harleck around the fireplace after the war as he shared with us his memories, thoughts, feelings, and experiences. I suspect that a soldier who actually lived these experiences might be able to convey to us more of the fullness of the story in all its rich color and subtle detail, including the many different aspects of the war which are so often overlooked.

The officers, battles, events, and incredible experiences of the Second Virginia Infantry Regiment are real and based on actual historic records to the very best of my ability. The character of Wil Harleck, his family, friends, and the other private enlisted soldiers in the story are original (fictional) characters overlaid upon the historical backdrop with the necessary amount of artistic license applied to fill in the gaps where my research and/or the actual records are incomplete. Most of the dialog is fictional in order to tell the story as I imagine it might have happened, but wherever possible I have inserted actual quotes and factual information. For the sake of authenticity, I have endeavored to be true to the historic records to the greatest extent possible. However, there are some instances wherein a few historic records and accounts seem to differ from others. In these instances, I have done my best to present what I believe is the most historically accurate version. I have also placed a Glossary of Military Unit Structure and Composition at the end of the book as a reference, in case it might be helpful.

My hope is that, in reading this story, you might gain a greater appreciation of Civil War history in all of its color and depth and detail. May it inspire you to a deeper admiration of the war itself, and also of the people who fought, struggled, suffered, and persevered through it, and how they helped to form us into the nation we are today. Perhaps more importantly, may it deepen your appreciation of this great nation, and inspire you to help preserve it and keep it great.

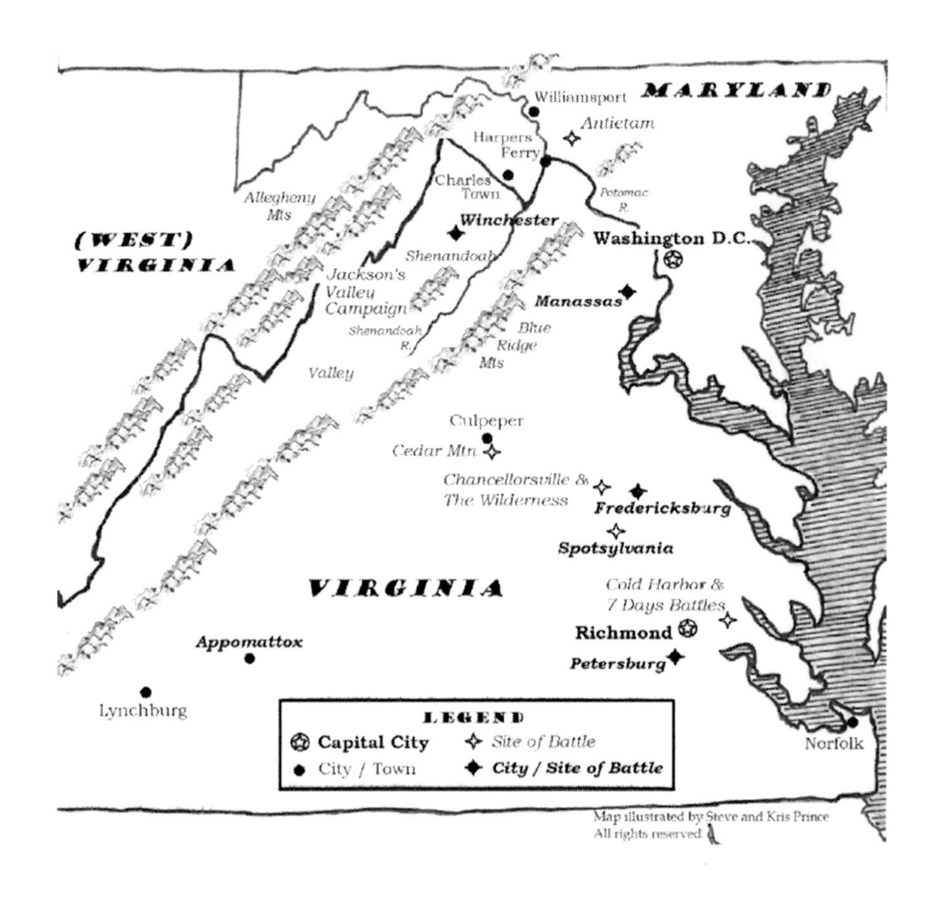
MARYLAND
Williamsport
Antietam
Harpers Ferry
Charles Town
Potomac R.
Allegheny Mts
(WEST) VIRGINIA
Winchester
Washington D.C.
Shenandoah
Jackson's Valley Campaign
Manassas
Shenandoah R.
Blue Ridge Mts
Valley
Culpeper
Cedar Mtn
Chancellorsville & The Wilderness
Fredericksburg
Spotsylvania
VIRGINIA
Cold Harbor & 7 Days Battles
Richmond
Appomattox
Petersburg
Lynchburg
Norfolk
LEGEND
Capital City
Site of Battle
City / Town
City / Site of Battle
Map illustrated by Steve and Kris Prince
All rights reserved.

Train Ride to Glory

Prologue
July 18, 1861

Three months after the surrender of Fort Sumter, Confederate soldiers of General James Longstreet's Brigade wait and watch from their positions on the banks of the Bull Run. They are the guardians of a crossing known as Blackburn's Ford, just a few miles northeast of Manassas, Virginia, on the road from Washington to Richmond. Longstreet's men are part of General P. G. T. Beauregard's Confederate Army of the Potomac, arrayed in defensive positions guarding the crossings along a six-mile stretch on the south bank of the Bull Run.

The Southerners watch in silence as a company of Union artillery deploys its four cannons along the hillcrest. Not long afterward, the peaceful air is shattered by the sharp report of the first federal gun. The Confederates brace themselves and wait for the impact, but the shell whistles by overhead, landing behind them not far from where the Southern artillery awaits. The impact of the twenty-pound solid shot projectile causes the ground to shake, and sends up a great plume of dust and dirt into the air. But to the inexperienced Confederates this is not just an ordinary artillery shell. It is the signal gun of something more ominous: the Union Army is coming.

For the next few hours, North and South will exchange deadly fire across the stream, and there will be numerous casualties on both sides. It is a sobering demonstration that the Napoleonic tactics employed this day have become woefully outmoded by the technology of late nineteenth century warfare. Standing shoulder to shoulder two rows deep in the open field, the Union soldiers are easy targets for the well-fortified Confederates hidden among the brush and trees on the south bank. Finally, late in the afternoon, the Northerners begin to fall back toward Centreville, where the rest of the Union force is gathering. The first meeting between the two great armies comes to a close.

For the Union, news of the battle is not well received. Although not a devastating defeat by any military standard, the loss threatens the already tenuous confidence of the green troops, most of whom are poorly trained three-month volunteers. The Confederates, however, consider it a great victory, and perhaps even a sign that God favors the South.

Such is the firm opinion of General Thomas J. Jackson. A staunch believer in the influence of divine providence, Jackson has every confidence that the Southerners' defense of their own homeland against the northern aggression is a just cause in God's sight. It is a cause he is fully committed to defend—indeed with his very life, if it should be God's will.

Still, though other men may delude themselves into believing that this war will end quickly, in his heart Jackson knows the North will not concede so easily. In fact, history will determine that the engagement at Blackburn's Ford will be all but forgotten in the light of events to come; dismissed as merely a footnote to preface the much more earnest and deadly battle that Jackson knows—perhaps even hopes—will come.

Even now, in the aftermath of today's action, General Irwin McDowell's Army of Washington D.C., 37,000 strong, is on the move near Centreville. Their target is Richmond, the new Confederate capital. To oppose them, the Secessionists have only 18,000 men entrenched on the banks of the Bull Run.

At Beauregard's urgent insistence, Confederate President Jefferson Davis has sent a telegram to General Joseph E. Johnston instructing him to move his Army of the Shenandoah from northwestern Virginia to Manassas to reinforce Beauregard with all dispatch. To accomplish this, Johnston must move his force of nearly 16,000 troops with all of their supplies and equipment a distance of sixty miles across rivers and mountains in less than three days. Upon his arrival, Johnston and Beauregard plan to strike the unsuspecting McDowell with their combined force of nearly 34,000 men before he is ready for battle, and thereby crush, once and for all, the northern hopes of compelling their southern brethren to rejoin the Union by force.

Now, Johnston, with a masterful slight of hand and the aid of a bold young cavalry commander named Colonel James Ewell Brown ("Jeb") Stuart, slips completely unnoticed away from a second Union force in the Shenandoah Valley and moves rapidly south and east to join Beauregard. Johnston has ordered Jackson's First Brigade to cross the Shenandoah River and march across the Blue Ridge to Piedmont Station, there to board trains to Manassas. The brigades of Bartow, Bee and Elzey are to follow quickly behind Jackson. It is the largest troop movement by rail in history yet written.

July 19, 1861

Prvt. W. A. Harleck
Army of the Shenandoah, near Parist

Dear Mama,

I am sorry if my writing is hard for you to read. I am writing this letter on a train. I am excited to be the first in our family to ride the railroad, and although I suspect the rail car in which I am riding is more suited for 20 hogs than for 50 soldiers, it is still a far cry better than walking. How marvelous to behold that the entire regiment can be moved the distance of a two days' march in such a short time and with such little effort. I would greatly prefer it if we could travel by train everywhere the army goes rather than by foot.

We camped just outside of the town of Paris last night after marching most of the way from Winchester across the Shenandoah and up into the mountains. The stockings you made for me have been most dandy, even when wet, as these army brogans are like hard, heavy weights and very unkind to the feet. My old shoes will be much better if you will send them. We had to send most of our belongings to Culpeper before we marched, along with many of those who have taken ill with the measles or some other dreadful ailment.

I reckon something surely is about to happen, as Captain Rowan was in quite a rush to get the Company on this train. I heard some of the boys say the Yankees have attacked General Beauregard's army near Manassas.

You musn't worry about me in the coming battle. I do not believe the Yankees have much stomach for fighting, and they will soon learn not to tangle with Virginians who are defending our homes. You remember, of course, that Colonel Allen fought in *the war with Mexico. He is a fine officer and the boys are fairly itching for a fight. I have no doubt we will give those northern boys a whipping they won't soon forget.*

Pray for me often. Tell Papa to visit the widow Mulholland, as her son Robby took ill with the fever and died last week. I think she's a Catholic, but since Charles Town is without a Catholic priest at the present, she might appreciate a visit from a man of the cloth.

All my love to Amos and Vanessa.

Your loving son,
Wil

Secessionitis

I'd heard stories about soldierin' from my brother, Joseph, before the war. Many a night we'd sit around by the fireplace, my little brother Amos and sister Vanessa and me, and we'd beg him to tell us again of the march to Harpers Ferry with the Jefferson Guards back in '59. He'd tell us how ol' John Brown had come down and seized the fed'ral arsenal there, stirrin' up trouble and tryin' to arm the slaves, and how the Jefferson Guards had marched from Charles Town to help put a quick end to all that tomfoolery. Somethin' about the way Joseph told those stories always had a way of makin' a boy wanna run right out and join up. I would've done just that too, but Pa said I was too young and had to wait a couple years 'til I was nineteen. I reckon he was hopin' I'd grow out of it by then, but oh, how I wanted to be like Joseph.

But that was before this whole secession business started. When folks started talkin' about breakin' away from the Union, Joseph's whole attitude changed. I remember that day in early April when he came home and made his big announcement.

"They say the Convention may vote on Virginia's ordinance of secession from the Union soon," he said as we were all sittin' down at the table for dinner.

Joseph was a mite taller than me, standin' just under six foot, and he was thin with brown hair parted on the side. He most times wore a friendly smile under the well-trimmed mustache. But on that day, the wrinkle between his dark brows and the look of concern in those deep eyes gave me the feelin' that he wasn't any too happy.

"I thought they already voted *not* to secede?" Vanessa replied.

"They did, Vanessa," Joseph said flatly, "but now they're talkin' about changin' their minds."

"Why?" she asked, her big brown eyes lookin' perplexed under the locks of wavy golden hair that hung down over her forehead.

"That's a mighty good question, little sister," he boasted, glancin' sideways at me. "Two months ago they were content to stay in the Union to keep the peace, but now, with all this fuss about Fort Sumter and all, they're afraid Lincoln wants to raise an army to stop more states from takin' up arms."

"Lincoln *is* raisin' an army, Joseph," I insisted. "You know that." I could feel myself losin' my patience and my voice gettin' higher, but I went on. "And he's fixin' on marchin' into Virginia—our own sovereign state!"

"That's right!" he shot back. "And we oughta be marchin' with 'em too! This whole secession business—well it just ain't right!"

"*Isn't* right," Mama reminded, settin' a platter on the table, and turnin' to walk back to the kitchen.

My Mama wasn't a very tall woman, and maybe she was a mite on the plump side, but she knew how to train up a child, and the four of us young'uns, well, we all pretty much treated her with rev'rence and awe. Maybe it was the streaks of gray in her brown hair all done up like a crown that made her look wise beyond her years, or maybe it was the kindness in her green eyes, even on the rare occasion when the rest of her face had to be strong and firm. But whatever it was, Joseph still gave heed to her, even though he was nigh on twenty-two.

"Sorry, Mama. *Isn't* right!" he corrected. Then, without battin' an eye, he got right back to the business of politics. "And I, for one, want no part of it."

"What are you going to do, Joseph?" Mama called back from the kitchen.

"Well, I'm not gonna pick up arms against my own countrymen. Of that you can be sure. There's somethin' just not right about Americans fightin' Americans, and I refuse to be party to it."

It felt like a knife stabbin' me right in the belly. "So, what are you sayin'?" I shot back. "You're quittin' the Jefferson Guards?" I knew what he was tryin' to say, but I didn't wanna hear it.

"That's exactly what I'm sayin', little brother." His words were cold and sharp.

I'll never forget that sick feelin' in the pit of my stomach. It was like eatin' Judas stew cooked with bitter root. Like all those years I'd looked up to him suddenly closed around my neck like a noose 'til I could scarcely breathe.

Doesn't he know how important this is to me?

But he just went on like nothin' was the matter. "Pa says there's a college up in Pennsylvania that'll take me on a scholarship if I decide to go into the ministry and if I get good grades," he said, speakin' up so Mama could hear in the kitchen.

Pa didn't say it, but I could see it in his eyes. The thought of Joseph goin' to seminary pleased him greatly. But it stuck in my craw how I'd idolized Joseph only to have him desert me like that just when I was finally old enough to join up. For two years I'd dreamt of goin' soldierin' with Joseph and all the adventures we'd have together, only to have it all go up in smoke in two minutes.

"Since when did you decide to be a preacher?!" I shouted. "You were plenty willing to take up arms against your own countrymen when it was just crazy ol' John Brown and his little band of hooligans! But now that it's an army comin', all the sudden you don't wanna fight anymore! Why you're just a coward! That's all you are! A yella-bellied coward!!" I was screamin' by then and tryin' hard to choke back the tears, but it was no use.

"Wil Harleck! You apologize to your brother!" Mama scolded from the kitchen doorway. And Pa shot me a look that said I was treadin' on thin ice. My Pa was a quiet man, and didn't say much, but he had a long stern face with deep eyes like Joseph that did a lot of his talkin' for him.

"Sorry," I muttered under my breath, lookin' down at the table and pickin' up my fork.

But Joseph just sat there and stared at me, and I could tell he wasn't havin' any of it.

I was mad as a wet hen and wanted to jump up and run right out of the house, but I didn't dare. Not without bein' excused from the table. My Pa would've made me go hungry the whole next day if I did that.

Mama sat down at the table and Pa said the prayer, but I didn't feel much like eatin' anymore. But I didn't wanna be rude to Mama, so I just ate my meal in silence.

Still, as the days went by, I couldn't get those stories out of my head. I wanted to be a soldier in the militia more than anything. Even without Joseph, I could hardly wait 'til it was my turn to march with those boys in the light blue uniforms and win a glorious battle. Turns out I didn't have to wait too long.

It was the seventeenth of April—ten days after my nineteenth birthday—when the telegraph arrived with word that the Legislature had voted to secede. The newspapers had stirred up a terrible fuss, and folks were all buzzin' around like a bunch of angry hornets. If you listened carefully to how they talked, you'd've thought ol' Abe Lincoln himself was personally leadin' a legion of demons to come and burn our homes!

Colonel Allen wasted no time callin' out the Second Virginia Volunteers, and Capt'n Rowan sent out word for Company A to muster in the Charles Town square on the very next day. On the mornin' of the eighteenth, I was one of the first to muster in, seein' as how I didn't have very far to go. The Market House was just down Church Street to Washington and around the corner a short ways. But I ran anyway.

There was excitement in the air on that crisp April day, and I felt a knot formin' in my stomach as I turned the corner onto Washington Street and the Market House came into sight. Men and boys came from all over the county that day. Most were about my age, though there were some younger, and some quite a bit older. Some came with brothers or friends; others by themselves. Robby Mulholland, one of my friends from the schoolhouse, came to sign up that day, along with Fredrick Ruyter, who worked with me at Mr. Jennings' wheelright and blacksmith shop. My best friend Tommy Johns and his older brother Arty were already there when I arrived, along with my friend Sean McAlister and several other boys I knew, and more than a few I didn't. Some, like Arty, were vet'rans of the John Brown affair. Others, like Tommy and me, we'd been too young back in '59, but we were finally old enough and we could hardly wait to put on the uniform like real men that day.

"Hey, Wil Harleck!" Tommy called out in excitement when he saw me comin'. "'Bout time you showed up!" he chided through a wide grin. I don't know if I can ever recollect seein' Tommy without that big grin on his face. It just seemed to go naturally with that head of wild shaggy brown hair and that youthful face that just made everybody love him.

"You didn't think I'd just let you go and have all the fun, did ya?" I answered with a smile and a brotherly hug.

"Hey, Wil, good to see ya," Arty chimed in, shakin' my hand. "Where's Joseph?"

But then the knot in my stomach turned sour when I remembered that Joseph wasn't comin' to join us.

"He isn't comin'," I confessed. "Said somethin' about not wantin' any part of this secession business." I tried to mind my tongue, but I was a good bit more frustrated than I was lettin' on.

"Oh . . . " Arty answered, lookin' a mite confused. "Well, ain't that somethin'."

I reckon the news took Arty by surprise too. He and Joseph were pert nigh as close as Tommy and me. He was more Joseph's height, with sand-colored hair and a thick bushy mushtache that came down around the corners of his mouth. And for just the briefest of moments, I thought I saw a flash of betrayal in those green eyes, but then he just shook his head and went on shakin' hands and greetin' the other fellas.

Fredrick arrived just after me. He was a fine strong boy; the biggest and strongest of us—me and my friends, that is—with a thick head of golden hair and blue eyes, on account of his Dutch side, likely as not.

"Sorry I'm late," he said, lookin' a little bedraggled. "Had to tend to some last-minute work at the shop. Didn't wanna leave ol' Jennings with more work than he could handle."

I felt bad about leavin' Fredrick to do more work for Mr. Jennings, but I hadn't known there was more work to be done. I was still searchin' for the words to say when Tommy answered back.

"Aw, that's alright," He said, still grinnin'. "I'm sure Wil here woulda helped ya, but he was too busy tryin' to get here first so's he could be sure and get all the best stuff before you got here!"

"Was not!" I protested without thinkin'. Then I realized Tommy was just havin' some fun at my expense, like always.

"Very funny, Tommy," Fredrick quipped in a deep voice, "but you forgot one thing . . . " He paused long enough for the grin to fade just a mite. Then when he was good and sure he'd gotten Tommy's attention, he went on. "Y'all might've got all the toy guns and kiddie uniforms, but I'm sure there's still plenty of real man-sized stuff left fer me!" Then he grinned and slugged Tommy playfully in the shoulder, just enough to make him blush just a little, but not enough to erase the grin.

We stood around for a little while longer, talkin' and jokin' and puttin' on a brave front while we waited for the others to arrive. We couldn't help but wonder at what tomorrow would bring, and our heads were full of visions of parades and glorious victory celebrations.

"Too bad Joseph's gonna miss out on all the action," Tommy bragged, stickin' out his chest and tuggin' on his suspender braces with his thumbs. "Yep. Guess I'll have to take his share of the glory when we get back. You know how the womenfolk love a man in uniform." The grin got even bigger, if that were possible. "I'm sure to get me a fine woman, now! Heck, maybe I'll get me two!" He was downright bustin' with pride at his own display of wit and it made him nigh intolerable.

Capt'n Rowan didn't waste any time. As soon as we signed the muster, Sergeant Robertson lined the new recruits up at the quartermaster's wagon to get our uniforms, and then told us to say our good-byes and be back before two o'clock. We had orders to march to Halltown and Harpers Ferry that very afternoon.

I can still remember the look on Pa's face when I came in wearin' the uniform with my pack slung over my shoulders. It was the look he always got when he knew somethin' bad was about to happen, but he couldn't stop it from happenin'.

I took a deep breath, put on my bravest face, and stood up tall with my shoulders back, but I still couldn't look him in the eye.

"I-Ive made up my mind, Pa. I'm joinin' the militia."

He stood there in the parlor not sayin' a word. I knew he was givin' me that disapprovin' look out from under those stern brows, but I didn't wanna look. So I just looked over his head at the wall behind and went on.

"We leave this afternoon for Halltown and Harpers Ferry. The Capt'n says the Fed'rals are raisin' an army to force us back into the Union and we're gonna need those guns at the arsenal there."

I reckon he'd known this was comin', but he still didn't take real kindly to it, what with Joseph bein' so against the war and all. The way I figured it, each man had to decide for himself the right thing to do, but I knew Pa wasn't too keen on me joinin' up to fight.

I tried again to convince him. "I know you don't approve of fightin', Pa, but a man's gotta do what a man's gotta do. It just wouldn't be right to just sit by and let some foreign army march right into our state and invade our homes."

But he wasn't buyin' what I was sellin'. He just looked at me with those deep eyes that could look right through to a man's soul and kept his peace. But I knew it was hard on him.

"Well . . . Good-bye, Pa," I said, lookin' down at my feet and tryin' not to be bothered that he couldn't even say 'good-bye'.

I turned and kissed Vanessa on the cheek and hugged Amos.

"Take care of Vanessa, okay?" I reminded him.

"I will. Don't forget to write. I wanta know everything that happens!" Amos and I were close—even closer than Joseph and I—and he wanted to sign up too. But even though he was almost seventeen, we both knew he wasn't old enough to convince Pa that he should go off to war just yet. And he wouldn't dare defy Pa.

I gave Mama a hug and a kiss, wiped the tears off her cheeks, and told her not to worry, then held out my hand to shake Pa's hand. I reckon he knew there was nothin' he could say to change my mind, so he never spoke a word. He just swallowed hard and shook my hand. But I thought I saw a tear in those deep eyes that day.

Then there was Maribel. At seventeen years old, Miss Maribel Nellis was the loveliest vision of an angelic being a boy ever laid eyes on. She was the daughter of a plantation owner, and probably the most eligible young lady in the whole of Jefferson County. How she ever came to like a simple preacher's boy like me the Good Lord only knows.

We met as children when her folks came to church. William and Grace-Anne Nellis weren't the richest folks in the county but they were close to it, and they had more class in one boot than most folks had in two. Seems they took a liking to good preachin', and my Pa had a special gift for good preachin'. Many a Sunday they'd invite us to dinner after church. When dinner was over, Joseph, Amos, Vanessa, and I would spend the warm summer afternoons playin' in the garden with Maribel, so it was only natural we'd become good friends.

As time went by, I grew real fond of Maribel and started makin' up excuses just so we could spend time together. In December of '60, it was, when I asked her pa for permission to court her, but we were already fallin' in love, as young folk have a way of doin'. My, she sure was the prettiest little thing though, and that smile of hers could melt fresh churned butter on a January day.

If sayin' good-bye to my family was hard, sayin' good-bye to Maribel was right near impossible. I knew her pa would be real proud to see me in the uniform, but I could scarcely stand the thought of seein' her cry. I thought about tryin' to explain it all to her, but a young lady oughtn't worry herself about such matters.

I practiced it over and over in my mind as I rode the old quarter-horse down the valley to her house. I told myself I'd be strong, bein' that she needed a strong man. After all, these were dangerous times. As I rode up to the house, I put on my best soldier face and slid down out of the saddle. But she'd seen the uniform and she already knew why I was there.

At first she just stood there on the porch frozen in place. In her eyes I could see the dread, as if she'd seen this day comin' too. Then she took a deep breath and stood up straight and tall, lookin' just like her mama, all prim and proper like a true southern lady.

"I suppose this means you're leavin' me," her voice trembled matter-of-factly, "and now you've come to say good-bye?" She was doin' her best to keep her composure, but I could tell she was breakin' inside.

I looked down at the porch steps under her feet, tryin' hard not to look her in the eyes, and all the words I'd practiced just blew away like the wind.

"That's right," I answered in a low voice, just loud enough for her to hear.

"Well . . . go ahead and say it then." Her voice sounded hurt.

"I don't wanna leave you, Maribel . . . " I looked up and tried hard to sound more sure of myself, but it was no use. " . . . but, a man has his duty."

She swallowed hard but stood her ground. But I knew she was just as loyal to Virginia as I, so I got up what courage I could and made my best appeal.

"Lincoln's gone and called up volunteers to force us back into the Union and, well, it just isn't right. What kind of man would I be if I didn't go?"

Along about then everything fell apart. All of a sudden she just ran down the steps, threw her arms around my neck, buried her face in my shoulder, and commenced to cryin'. I nearly broke right then and there. I had no earthly idea what to say next.

After a bit, she gathered herself together, and with all the grace and dignity she could muster, she stepped back, looked up into my eyes, and slapped me good across the face. I reckon that was for makin' a lady cry. If so, I surely deserved it. Then in her bravest voice she said, "You come back to me, Wil Harleck. You hear?"

"Yes, ma'am."

What else could I say?

I gathered her into my arms again and kissed her face, all streaked with tears. "Don't you worry. I'll be back just as soon as all this fuss is over."

A Soldier's Life

I wrote to Mama and Maribel as often as I could for the next few months, seein' as how we were never far from home. And they wrote back often too, especially Maribel. I always tried to keep my letters more on the pleasant side if I could. I reckon if Mama knew I'd had to leave behind my coat and that knit blanket she made for me, or how I often slept on (or sometimes under) my oilcloth on the hard Virginia clay instead of on a cot in a tent as some fancied, well, she'd just lay awake nights worryin'. No sense in both of us passin' sleepless nights.

The way I figure it, some aspects of soldier life oughtn't be uttered to those who've never had the privilege of sleepin', marchin', and drillin' in the hot sun and the cold rain, or eatin' army rations, or diggin' your own privy, or a hundred other disgraceful or demeanin' things soldiers have to live with every day. Most folks just wouldn't understand. So, most of the boys just kept to themselves about it. Better to keep quiet about such things than to be thought of as soft—or worse yet, a coward.

Joseph had told me about all the exciting parts of soldierin', but somehow he'd always managed to leave out the less appealin' details.

Or maybe it was just my boyish imagination that made his stories all seem so great, but it sure didn't take long to figure out that this soldierin' business wasn't all I'd figured it to be. Still, I reckon maybe it wasn't so bad. Not yet, leastwise.

Our outfit was one of the finest in the army in those early days at Harpers Ferry. If a soldier could want it, we probably had it. Most of the boys came with wooden trunks full of extra clothes, mountains of food, and a whole mess of other things from home we all thought we couldn't live without. Some even brought their own "boys" with 'em—slaves, mostly, which some called "darkies" or "niggs" or some other disparagin' reference—to cook and clean up after 'em, carry their trunks and gear, and tell 'em what great soldiers they were. Our mess—that's about twelve of us that cook and eat together—had two of 'em back then. And my-oh-my could those boys cook! But it wasn't long 'til all that changed.

I never much cared for ownin' slaves, myself, nor for havin' someone else clean up after me. Didn't much care for the way they were talked to or treated by some folk either. Maybe it was just the way my Pa raised me, him bein' a preacher and all, but somethin' about it just didn't feel right. But I knew lots of folks who showed their fair share of Christian charity towards the Negro. I don't rightly know if it's a sin for one person to own another person, but the way I saw it, the Good Book sure did have a lot to say about slaves and servants. I reckon if the Good Lord really felt that strong about it, He could've just made that the Eleventh Commandment: "Thou shalt not own thy neighbor," or some such thing. But sure as January was a-comin', some abolitionist folk like ol' John Brown were convinced that ownin' slaves was a grievous sin.

Still, I s'pose some other folks didn't take too kindly to the idea of losin' everything they'd worked for all their lives either. Seems to me, though, if everyone just took the Golden Rule to heart, there'd be nothin' to fight about. Me, I just thought the folks from Virginia oughta be the ones to decide what's best for Virginia. We didn't try to tell the folks up in New York or Massachusetts or Pennsylvania how they oughta live, and I didn't much care for them tellin' us how we oughta live. So I determined that I was fightin' for the right to decide for ourselves.

By late May the southern states had formed a new government, and we were to be called the Confederate States of America. A new gen'ral, Gen'ral Joseph E. Johnston, arrived to take command of all the army gathered there, which he called the Army of the Shenandoah. Our regiment was renamed as the Second Virginia Infantry Regiment, part of the First Brigade Virginia Infantry, C.S.A., Colonel Thomas J. Jackson, commandin'. Bein' that it was the third time we'd gotten a new name in just a few short weeks, some of the boys took to makin' bets about how soon we'd get the next one. I never was much for gamblin', but I thought it was amusin' anyways.

The Second Virginia was already one of the best equipped regiments in the army, and our uniforms were among the handsomest I'd ever seen. Even still, as soon as we were reorganized, Colonel Jackson ordered the whole brigade reequipped. It seemed like there was an endless stream of trains and wagons arrivin' every day full of new supplies for the army. We were issued knapsacks, bedrolls, shoes, stockin's, hats, shirts, britches, jackets, overcoats, and even new unmentionables, whether we needed 'em or not. Then they gave us haversacks, canteens, dippers, and even papers for writin', plus weapons, and plenty of ammunition, and the list went on and on. It seemed every other day we were linin' up to get somethin' else we didn't know we needed.

Of course all that changed too when Colonel Jackson started marchin' us to and fro all over the valley lookin' for the Yankee army. I remember that first slow march from Harpers Ferry to Winchester. We felt more like jackasses than soldiers that day: loaded down with so much gear we could barely march for an hour without rest. And all our wagons formed a line twice as long as the army, and twice as slow. I thought "Ol' Jack"—that's what we called him then (Colonel Jackson, that is)—was gonna up and die of too much blood in the face right there in front of us! We all knew he was a mite strange, but we'd never seen him so angry before. We thought he might just go mad and shoot one of those poor officers tryin' to get the wagons movin'!

It didn't take us long to reckon just exactly what we really needed and what was just extra weight to carry. Ol' Jack had had just about enough wagon train woes, so he went and ordered the wagon trains to carry only official army supplies and the officers' personal things. And that was that. The first things to go were the trunks and the extra clothes; especially the heavy coats and blankets. Not much use for coats and blankets in June in Virginia, anyway. The sheer weight of 'em is too much to carry on the march, even dry. Then when they got wet, the weight was doubled, and it seemed they'd never dry out, nor us with 'em.

The same went for my knapsack, canteen, and every other thing that could possibly be lived without. We knew the Yankees didn't wanna find us, seein' as how they surely could've if they'd wanted to. Everywhere we marched, we left behind a trail of discarded items that were no longer worth carryin'.

Tents were only a rare luxury. They mostly just stayed packed in the wagons some miles behind and were only unpacked when the army was stayin' in one place long enough to make 'em worth while, which wasn't very often. Even when we did use 'em they were crowded and hot. Unless it was rainin', some of the boys just preferred to sleep on their oilcloths, which were just dense cotton fabric coated with boiled linseed oil so as not to soak up water.

By early June, most of the boys had whittled their loads down to just the clothes on their backs, their muskets, and not much else, save a few small comforts that didn't add weight to the march. How a man could be expected to survive, much less fight, on such little fare I don't know. I still carried an oilcloth with me for sleepin', a haversack with a few necessary items, my dipper, and a pen and some ink and paper stuffed into my jacket. The boys from our mess took turns carryin' our skillet for cookin', and an axe for choppin' wood.

When it came to rifles our regiment was the envy of the army. Most of us were given brand new Harpers Ferry rifles saved from the arsenal fire. The '55 Harpers Ferry was a fine weapon—a soldier's weapon—a mite shorter and not as heavy to carry on the march as those old Mississippi Rifles, Musketoons, or farmer's muskets that most of the other boys had. They were also a good bit easier to take care of. They didn't seem to require all the fuss and bother the others did. A fine shootin' weapon too. After only a couple weeks of drillin',

I could hit a corn sheave at 200 yards just like the sun risin' in the mornin'. Some of the fellas got so good they became the talk of the Company. I'd swear Fredrick Ruyter could hit a jackrabbit on the run at fifty yards. Lord knows we practiced enough. Such a harsh task-master was Colonel Jackson when it came to drillin' and shootin', and he had such a peculiar way about him that some of the boys took to callin' him "Ol' Tom Fool."

In those early days, when ammunition was more abundant, we spent many a day shootin' at corn sheaves and straw men—a lot more than most of the boys from Alabama, Georgia, and Tennessee. By the time they arrived, most of the extra ammunition from Harpers Ferry had already been shipped to Richmond.

My First Train Ride

July the nineteenth found us at Piedmont Station, havin' just marched twenty-six miles the day before, which was a far sight further than those slow, early marches, to be sure. It was early in the mornin'—the sun just risin'—and about half of us from Company A were loaded into the first rail car. The rest of the regiment right behind us, and then the boys from the Fourth Virginia, in a big long line of train cars—the longest I'd ever seen.

None of us knew what the day would bring. Some said we were headin' to Washington. Others said ol' Beauregard had already won a major battle near Manassas, and we were goin' to finish off the Yankees once and for all and win the war for Virginia. Some even said the Yankees were marchin' on Richmond, but we reckoned that was more than likely not true. The Yanks hadn't shown any backbone for a fight yet. We figured they were all just full of smoke and talk, and weren't really gonna start anything 'til we came after 'em.

Still, we knew we were headed for a fight—our heads all full of dreams of glorious victory—otherwise the officers and sergeants wouldn't be in such a frenzy. Some of the boys were jokin' and laughin', and pretendin' not to be scared. Some wrote letters. Some nibbled on what vittles they had. Others were just quiet and kept to themselves. All were tired and hungry, but none could sleep.

The brigade had fought the Yankees before at Falling Waters when Gen'ral Patterson finally got up the nerve to come after us, but our regiment was held in reserve, so we didn't see any action. What a confusin' day that was. Colonel Jackson had just been promoted to Gen'ral. He was like a fox in the field that day, testin' the enemy line, then fallin' back just out of reach. The men wanted to attack and push the Yankees back into Maryland, but ol' Tom Fool wouldn't hear of it. Some said he was crazy; said he'd lost his backbone. Whatever it was, he sure kept us—and those Yankees—guessin'. Still, we were all sure we could whoop any army ol' Abe Lincoln could send against us.

The sound of the wheels on the tracks rattlin' up through the wooden floor of the rail car went on for more than eight hours, and we feared we might arrive too late. As the train rolled on, the clackin' of the wheels seemed to get louder and louder and the hard wood floor grew less and less tolerable, so we took to tryin' just about anything to get comfortable.

Tommy and Arty Johns and me, we'd been the best of friends for what seemed like forever. We grew up as neighbors and the Johns family had always been kind to us from the first day my family moved into Charles Town when I was just nine. Arty was eighteen months older than me, and Tommy was just three months younger. We went to school together, played together, hunted and trapped together, and even worked in Mrs Johns' garden together. Heck, I reckon we figured on growin' old together, all three of us. But none of us had ever been on a train before.

"Bet you never thought you'd be doin' this, huh, Wil?" Arty asked with a grin.

"Sure didn't," I said, stretchin' the stiffness out of my back. "Where do you reckon we're goin?"

"Place called Manassas, I heard tell," he replied, pullin' an apple out of his haversack and takin' a bite.

"Where's that?" I asked.

"Don't know. Never heard of it," he said, tryin' to chew and talk at the same time. "Somewhere near Washington, I reckon. Want some?" He held out the apple to offer me a bite.

"Sure. Thanks." Lookin' at that apple made me realize that I was a mite hungry too, and it looked mighty tasty.

He took out a small knife, cut the apple in half, and offered me the half he hadn't bitten into yet.

"Much obliged," I said gratefully as I took it from his hand and took a bite. It was just a bit on the tart side, but quite juicy. "Mmm. Mama could've made one swell apple pie with a mess of these."

"Do you think the Yankees are really comin'?" Tommy chimed in, soundin' a bit more excited than worried.

"Seems so," Arty answered confidently. "The Colonel says they already tried once yesterday, and he's bettin' they'll be back. I reckon they're in for a big surprise if they do come back, though. What with Beauregard's army and ours put together, we'll give 'em a right proper welcome to Virginia—if we get there in time, that is."

"I sure hope we get there soon," Tommy said, reachin' into his haversack and producin' his own apple, which started me to wonderin' where they got those apples and how I'd missed gettin' some for myself.

Sean McAlistair and Fredrick were there in the rail car with us too. Fredrick spoke up like he knew just what I was gonna say. "Where'd y'all get those?"

"Picked 'em from a farmer's tree just after we crossed the Shenandoah yesterday," Tommy answered cheerfully. "Want one?"

"You got more?" Fredrick asked.

"Heck yeah!" Tommy replied, grinnin' real big and reachin' into his haversack. He pulled out another apple and tossed it to Fredrick.

"Thanks!" Fredrick caught the apple and took a big bite with a loud crunch.

"Well if that don't beat all!" I said to Tommy, pretendin' to be put upon and tryin' to make him feel just a mite guilty. "Where was I when you found that tree?"

But Tommy just grinned and shot back, "Probably still wadin' across the river tryin' not to get everything you own wet!" Then they all had a good laugh on me. I reckon I deserved it, though, seein' as how I'd tried to be extra cautious crossin' that river in chest-deep water so as to keep my pack, cartridges, and rifle dry, but ended up slippin' on a stone and gettin' everything soaked anyhow.

"Y'all should be ashamed of yourselves," Fredrick joked back, lookin' right at Tommy with a grin while he patted me on the shoulder. "Don't worry, Wil. You see how I didn't get any apples either. They just didn't tell us about 'em so's they could keep more for themselves—leastwise 'til they got too heavy to carry anyway. That's when they finally decided to share." He took another bite of apple and his grin got even bigger.

Fredrick was always lookin' out for me, seein' as how we were both apprenticed to Mr. Jennings, and what with him bein' a year older than me and all. I reckon that's why we got along so famously. He was a good hunter too, and taught me how to load and shoot a rifle. And boy-oh-boy could he sing.

"You think we'll be gone long?" Sean asked, lookin' up at Arty, and tryin' not to look too concerned. But we all knew Sean lived with his grampa and gramma on the farm, and I wondered how they'd ever get by without him, seein' as how they didn't have any slaves and they couldn't afford to hire a hand. Sean was all they had.

Arty thought for a minute, lookin' at Sean's face and readin' it like a book. Arty was a smart fella, but it didn't take a smart fella to tell that Sean was worried about how his grampa and gramma would get by while he was gone away from home.

"Nah," Arty said, wavin' his hand in Sean's direction. "With any luck, we'll be back home in time to help bring in the crops."

Sean didn't say it, but he sure looked relieved to hear that.

Then there was Carlton Willis. Carlton was the town drunk, and I generally tried to avoid him as best I could. He was big too—a full six foot tall—and built like an ox. He had a reputation as a troublemaker back home, and he didn't take too kindly to me either. His face was mostly covered with a thick brown beard and mustache, and there was a scar under his left eye. He was missin' one of his upper front teeth, and the only time he ever laughed was when he was puttin' someone else down. When he was drunk he was just plain mean and most of the boys didn't much care for him. Still, we all reckoned he'd be handy in a fight.

Carlton had been in the Jefferson Guards even longer than Joseph and Arty. Sergeant Robertson knew all about his vice and usually kept an eye on him, but Sergeant Robertson wasn't in the rail car with us that day. Instead, Sergeant Kline, who was only twenty-six himself, was in charge of our rail car. But Sergeant Kline didn't know about Carlton, and Carlton had somehow gotten his hands on some whiskey, which usually meant trouble.

Somewhere about the end of the second hour, he'd had a snoot-full and was lookin' to start a fight. Tommy and I were just sittin' there next to the wall of the rail car, mindin' our own business and tryin' to write letters—which was no small feat in a movin' rail car—when Carlton up and took a fancy to the place where we were sittin'.

"You better move, preacher boy. That there's my spot."

When he was drunk, he took to droolin' when he talked, like his tongue was too big to fit in his mouth. I tried just ignorin' him, but he was bent on it.

"I said MOVE!" he shouted, and then kicked me hard, right in that soft spot in the back. No self-respectin' man oughta kick another man in the back when he's sittin' down. But Carlton Willis was no self-respectin' man.

When we didn't move, he started to cussin' and yellin'. I tried to stand up but the pain in my back persuaded me otherwise.

Then Tommy stood up. "Why don't you just keep to yourself and stop makin' trouble?" But that just made Willis mad.

"Why don't you just shut yer mouth, boy!" he shouted so loud as to make everyone in the rail car look up, then he shoved Tommy backward a step or two 'til he nearly fell over one of the other fellas.

When I finally managed to get to my feet, I looked around and saw Arty and Fredrick gettin' up too. I was sure Willis was gonna start swingin'. I didn't dare pick up my rifle. Willis would just take it away and use it as a club. I don't rightly know if I was more angry or more scared, but my fists were shakin' and my heart was beatin' like a jackrabbit.

Then I heard a voice boom from across the rail car.

"Willis! I'll clap you in irons!"

There was no man in the Company bigger than Carlton Willis but Sergeant Thomas Kline came the closest, and he was also younger and stronger than Willis. Carlton turned his head and the two glared at each other like two coyotes about to fight over the same chicken, but then Willis just waved his hand in the Sergeant's direction and turned to walk away. I guess he figured pickin' a fight with the Sergeant was more trouble than he was lookin' for.

After a few steps, he turned to look back at me and said, "Keep yer stupid spot ya little runt. I didn't want it anyway." Then he smiled that big toothless grin and mocked, "You probably pissed in it!" Then he just laughed in that irritatin' way that only a drunken idiot can, and stumbled off across the rail car barely able to stand up.

For a long while, we all just sat there together in silence listenin' to the clackin' of the wheels. I don't know how much time went by, but to my achin' back it seemed like hours, and we were startled when a voice finally broke the silence.

"A town!" It was Carlton again. He was standin' near the open door and pointin' enthusiastically. "We're comin' up to a town!"

Tommy and Arty and I and a few other fellas stood up and worked our way over to the door so we could see, tryin' not to step on anyone. The train slowed as we passed a crowd of people all cheerin' as we went by. Men in tall hats all waved their hands and hollered while the women and girls waved their hankerchiefs and blew kisses at us. We thought it was mighty nice of 'em to come out and cheer us on like that, and we forgot how uncomfortable we were for a little while.

That was when I realized that Carlton was no longer standin' there in the door of that rail car. He'd done tricked us into gettin' up out of our spot, and there he was, passed out on the floor in a pool of his own spit, right where we'd been sittin' just a few minutes before.

I was fumin' mad. As I stood there starin' at him, tryin' to calm myself down, and kickin' myself for lettin' him get the best of us like that, I wondered if it might be that even God looks on some men as bein' not worth savin'. Surely Carlton Willis must be one such man if ever there was one. I tried to find some measure of kindness toward him, but the pain in my back and my wounded pride only reminded me how much I loathed the man. After all, a man's honor can only abide just so much.

Dear God how I hate that man! I know you said I shouldn't, but I can't help it! I hate him!

In a way, I almost wished Sergeant Kline hadn't stepped in when he did. Almost . . .

Carolina Rabbit Stew

The train came to a stop at a small station, and we were allowed to get off and stretch our legs and use the necessary while the iron horse took on water for the steam engine—all but Carlton, that is. He just slept on through. Twenty minutes later, we were back on the train and rattlin' down the track again.

We thought the sun might bake us alive in that rail car before the train finally pulled in to Manassas Junction that afternoon. L'tenant Davenport appeared at the door and ordered us to move quickly off the train, which we were happily obliged to do, so it could be sent back for another brigade. We formed up, half soaked with sweat, and marched out of the town. It actually felt good to march a little, even in the hot summer afternoon sun. Before long, we came to an open meadow on a hillside not far from a small river. There we were told to bivouac for the night.

Colonel Allen placed the Second Virginia at the edge of the meadow near the trees. It was a hot July afternoon, but the trees offered a bit of shade and there was plenty of fresh water to be found. We had no tents and no food so most of us just had to forage for a meal.

Foragin' was a fine art that required a variety of skills to avoid goin' hungry. To be good at it, a fella had to be part hunter, part scavenger, part beggar, part thief, part farm hand, and part trapper. It usually involved scourin' the surrounding countryside for anything edible, shootin' any poor animal that had the misfortune of strayin' across our path, or relievin' the local farmers of a few extra vegetables or chicken eggs which the army had more need of than did the farmers. Every now and then, some of the local ladies would bake bread or pies for the boys, or some generous farmer would donate a couple of chickens or some produce to the cause, but more often than not we just had to make do with whatever vittles we could find until the supply train arrived.

We'd had just about all the rest we cared for on the train, and I was eager to put the whole affair with Carlton Willis behind me and stretch my achin' muscles and get some fresh air for awhile. So Tommy, Arty, Fredrick, and I set off into the woods nearby to see what we could find. We scared up a squirrel and Fredrick had it dead in his sights lickety-split, but decided not to shoot it. Our Harpers Ferry muskets were dandy for shootin' deer or boar, but they sure had a way of makin' a mess of the little critters. Besides, better he didn't shoot anyway, seein' as how there was no tellin' how close the Yankee army might be. So he let the squirrel go and we hiked on a bit further.

We came to the edge of a meadow and found a patch of ripe blackberries there just as we came out of the woods, so we picked a few to eat and gathered some more in our dippers for later. There was another regiment camped over yonder on the other side of the meadow, so we wandered over to talk to some of the boys there.

"Halt!" a picket shouted as we neared the camp. "Who are you?"

"Second Virginia," Fredrick shouted back. "Who are *you*?"

"Fifth North Carolina," the picket replied.

"Got anything to eat?" Fredrick asked.

"Depends," the picket answered. "Got anything to trade?"

"I've got some tobacco here," Arty said, takin' out his pouch and holdin' it up so as the picket could see, "and we found a mess of blackberries just over yonder."

"Got any coffee?" the picket asked.

"Sure!" Fredrick replied.

"C'mon over!" the picket said with a wave.

So we did.

The fellas from the Fifth North Carolina Regiment were part of Longstreet's Brigade. They seemed right friendly enough, and they told us all about how they'd been in the battle just the day before and pushed back the Yankee attack. Many a story was exchanged about the battle and how those boys from Massachusetts had been so surprised by how good those Carolina boys could shoot that they ran like rabbits from a hound! It did the heart good, and I completely forgot about my problems on the train.

We traded a little coffee and some berries and some of Arty's tobacco, and in exchange they filled our dippers with some rabbit stew which they'd made. It was mostly just carrots and turnips in a thick broth flavored with a small hare, but it sure beat anything the army ever gave us to cook, and we ate it right down, along with the last of the berries. After a while, we walked back to our camp talkin' and jokin' about all the things we'd heard.

"You think those Yankees'll come back after the whoopin' those boys gave 'em?" I asked.

"Don't know," Fredrick answered, "but if they do, we'll just have to whup 'em again!"

We all laughed, but we were mostly just puttin' on a brave act. Truth was, none of us had ever fired a shot in a real battle before, but we were sure we could lick those northern boys any day of the week. Leastwise we hoped we could anyways.

When we got back to camp, Sean came lookin' for me to ask if I'd help him write a letter to his gramma, which I did, of course, since he couldn't read nor write. My Pa taught me that a man who could use the pen with skill could go far in life, so I studied hard in school and learned to write well. Fact is, my writin' was a far sight better than my speakin'. I'd already written a letter to Mama on the train, so I thought it best if I took the opportunity to write to Maribel again too. Hardly an hour went by that I didn't think of her, and I had no way of knowin' what may come tomorrow. It might be days before I got another chance to write . . . or not at all. Then Sean and I, we went in search of the Colonel's aide to give our letters to the next mail courier.

After helpin' the other boys from our mess gather some wood to make a bivouac fire, I settled in to pass a restful night under the stars. Bein' from the mountains, we were used to bright starlit nights, but that night the heavens seemed even brighter. Such a beautiful night it was, and warm too. Somewhere off a little ways there were a couple of fellas playin' the gui-tar and the mouth organ, and singin' Just Before the Battle Mother, and Home Sweet Home. So confident we felt that I nearly forgot about the comin' battle and drifted off to sleep listenin' to the sounds of storytellin' and music and laughter.

A Stone in the Wall

July 20, 1861

Joseph E. Johnston's Confederate Army of the Shenandoah has begun to arrive in Manassas by train to reinforce Beauregard's positions along the Bull Run. Johnston's cavalry, under the masterful leadership of Jeb Stuart, has so effectively confused and deceived Patterson's Union army near Winchester that Patterson is utterly unaware that Johnston has escaped. Now, on July twentieth, Stuart's troopers simply vanish, moving quickly through Ashby's Gap to join Johnston and Beauregard. Patterson is helpless to follow.

Earlier that same morning, Colonel Francis Bartow's Second Brigade arrives in Manassas, followed in the afternoon by the Third Brigade under Brigadier General Bernard Bee. Behind them will follow Colonel Arnold Elzey's Fourth Brigade, temporarily under the command of Brigadier General Kirby Smith. By the morning hours of July twenty-first, Johnston, who is now in overall command of the Confederate forces in northern Virginia, has nearly 35,000 troops arrayed on the field to oppose McDowell's 37,000 Federals.

In a stroke of irony, both armies plan to employ the same strategy on the field this day: a sweeping maneuver around the enemy's left flank. Johnston, having only just arrived on the scene, largely defers to the flamboyant Beauregard, who is admittedly more familiar with the terrain. Beauregard, however, has adopted a plan far too ambitious for his untried army to execute effectively. His orders are confusing and frequently contradictory, and the resulting chaos allows the Union to gain the upper hand and strike first.

Marching in the early morning hours, McDowell sends three brigades of Tyler's division down the Warrenton Turnpike to a stone bridge crossing the Bull Run at the left end of the Confederate line. Tyler is to demonstrate in front of the Rebels to keep them from discovering McDowell's true intentions. Meanwhile, McDowell sends two divisions, nearly 10,000 men, under the command of Brigadier Generals David Hunter and Samuel P. Heintzelman, to cross the Bull Run at Sudley's Ford, two miles upstream to the left of the Confederate positions. McDowell intends to take the Rebels by surprise from behind and turn their left flank.

The left end of the Confederate line lies near the stone bridge where the Warrenton Turnpike crosses the Bull Run, directly across from where Tyler's brigades are now deployed. This position is held by a small half-brigade from South Carolina and Louisiana led by an audacious West Pointer named Colonel Nathan G. Evans.

By 8:30 a.m., Evans' scouts alertly spot a cloud of dust rising from the mass of Union troops moving to his left to get around behind his position. Evans realizes that he has been flanked and quickly divides his tiny force. Leaving only 400 riflemen to guard the stone bridge against Tyler's entire division, he races to meet the advancing Yankee columns, boldly hurling the balance of his small command at Hunter's leading brigades in a desperate attempt to slow their advance. With the lives of his men, he will buy precious time for southern reinforcements to be rushed to the scene. Incredibly, the gamble works. At Johnston's urging, Beauregard finally realizes the gravity of the situation, abandons his attack plan, and orders the brigades of Bee, Bartow, and Jackson to immediately reinforce Evans on the left.

July 19, 1861

Prvt. W. A. Harleck
Army of the Shenandoah, near Manassas Junction

Sweetest Maribel,

We arrived at Manassas Junction today courtesy of the railroad from Piedmont Station. I must tell you that it was quite a remarkable experience. In only a few hours, we travelled the distance of two days' march, and yet we arrived quite rested. I am well, and in good spirits, and pray you are well too.

We are camped here not far from a small river called the Bull Run, on the road from Washington D.C. to Richmond. The Yankee army has crossed into Virginia and seems intent upon invading our beloved State and marching upon Richmond, but they will not succeed. Only just yesterday, General Beauregard's army repelled them as they tried to cross the river not far from the very place where I am writing this letter now.

It appears we may be on the eve of a great battle, which we hope shall quickly give our northern friends a foul taste for this business of war. Surely never before has such a force of men been assembled on the field. There are thousands upon thousands of soldiers encamped for miles around us, and they say that if we prevail we may be home in time for the harvest.

Should you like, you may be able to send me another package of those delicious macaroons you make. They are still quite the talk of the Company ever since you sent the last box to me at Harpers Ferry in May.

I surely do miss spending the hours sitting with you on the porch, sipping lemonade, and talking, as we did last July. I can still see the sparkle in your eyes and the warm summer breeze teasing at your hair. I remember fondly the charming giggle in *your voice when we talked of our childhood Sunday afternoons spent in your father's garden. I greatly desire to see you again, and hope I may do so soon. Until then, I remain,*

Fondly Yours,
Wil

Gathering The Army

July the twentieth passed with much activity, but little action. We noted the arrival of Colonel Bartow's Brigade while we ate a meager breakfast consistin' mostly of what little remainin' rations we'd carried with us. They took up a position in the clearing on the hill behind us, and many a jeer and call went out from the edge of our camp upon their arrival. There was always some good natured pokin' and hecklin' that just seemed to come naturally between boys from different outfits.

Our boys would shout somethin' like, "Nice of y'all to come!"

Then they'd shout back somethin' like, "Thought you'd have all the fun, did ya?!" Or, "Y'all can just relax now, boys! The Second Brigade's here! We'll take care of them pesky Yanks for ya!"

We may've been jokin' and teasin' with 'em, but we were sure glad they were there. I reckon you can't have too many good men in a fight.

Right about mid-day, another train arrived with Gen'ral Bee's Third Brigade, and confidence in the camp was fast growin'. There was even talk of attackin' the Fed'rals and drivin' 'em back out of Virginia, but Capt'n Rowan said we'd surely have to wait for Gen'ral Johnston to arrive with Elzey's Fourth Brigade, Stuart's cavalry, and Pendleton's guns before mountin' an attack. So, we waited.

That afternoon, the cavalry arrived, along with a few of our supply wagons, so some of us had rations to eat for dinner, though they were no ways near as good as that cup of rabbit stew. But the rest of our supply train was still miles away up the road, and most of the boys had to forage for their suppers again that evenin'.

By nightfall, more of the wagons had arrived, and Colonel Allen, Capt'n Rowan, and some of the officers set up tents, as did a few of the men. But most of the boys just figured there wasn't much sense in settin' up tents now. We'd surely be movin' out as soon as the rest of the army arrived in the mornin'.

The night was clear and warm, and I drew the first sentry that night. Every private in the army knows what sentry duty is like. Not much to it, really. Most of the time it was just two hours of marchin' slowly back and forth in a straight line at the edge of the camp with the rifle on the shoulder. No talkin', no stoppin', and no foolin' around. Just marchin' and watchin', then turnin' around, shiftin' the rifle to the other shoulder, and marchin' back to where you started from.

One end of my patrol was near the top of the hill where Company A was camped. From there I could fairly see most of the countryside all around the camp. I can't recollect ever seein' such a sight before. Nor since, either. I imagined that the fields and the hillsides all around looked like great rollin' waves on a vast dark sea lit up by the light of a thousand small bivouac fires like golden moonlight sprinkled on the waves. And the stars above shone so brightly as to appear to be glimmerin' reflections of the landscape below, as if the Good Lord himself was holdin' up a great mirror so as we could see the magnificent sight as He saw it. Such a beautiful sight made even the dreariest of sentry patrols seem pleasant.

After my watch, I passed a restful but mostly sleepless night under the stars. I can't recollect ever feelin' so relaxed and peaceful on the one hand, and yet so nervous on the other, all at the same time, as I did that night. It was as if there was a battle already ragin' back and forth in my mind between thoughts of the comin' fight and the deep peaceful beauty of the night.

Early the next mornin', we were awakened before sun-up and told to break camp and prepare to march. Some said we were movin' to attack. One thing about army life though: rumors fly around the camp so fast and so often that a boy never knows which is the truth and which is just camp canard. We cooked a hasty breakfast of hard tack and bacon, which was a rare treat, seein' as how every mornin' since we'd left Harpers Ferry we just had to fry the biscuits in old bacon grease.

A couple of the boys from Company D came by to ask if we'd share some of our bacon with 'em. Their mess had been too late for the bacon at the commissary wagon. The army was funny that way. Sometimes you got plenty. Other times you got nothin'. We all thought it wasn't a bad idea to share some of ours, since we seemed to have plenty.

"I reckon there's plenty to go around," I said, startin' toward the mess table to retrieve some bacon.

But then Carlton Willis got up and stood in my way.

"Sure. You can have some of *our* bacon," he said, lookin' at the boys from Company D with that crooked toothless grin on his face.

We all knew that look. This was his idea of fun. The boys from the other mess, well, they didn't know Carlton like we did, so they didn't know what to think. They looked hopeful for just a brief moment, but then the look turned to confusion when they began to realize that Willis actually had no intention of sharin' the bacon with 'em.

Then came that ugly smirk that always made me wanna swear.

" . . . if you can take it away from *me*."

I fairly got my dander up watchin' him just stand there and stare at those boys while he slowly bit off a piece of the half-cooked bacon in his hand.

Why don't you say somethin', Wil? Don't just stand there and let him get away with this!

But the look in his eye persuaded me to hold my tongue. I looked around to see if Sergeant Robertson or Sergeant Kline or one of the officers might be about, thinkin' maybe I could appeal to them, but they were nowhere to be seen.

The boys from Company D looked at each other, then looked around at the rest of us to see if maybe we'd help 'em, but there was no help to be found. It was plain that Willis didn't care a lick about what we thought, and none of us cared to chance gettin' our mouths busted over a few strips of bacon.

Finally, one of the boys from Company D, an older fella with a thick mustache and glasses, waved his hand toward Willis and retorted, "Keep it." Then he just turned and walked away with no bacon, and the other fellas followed. That's when the smirk on Carlton's face grew into that mockin' laugh that meant he was drunk again and he'd just delighted himself by intimidatin' some poor unsuspectin' souls.

"Next time don't be late for the commissary wagon!" he mocked as they walked away.

It occurred to me that Carlton Willis might just be the most despicable creature I'd ever met. He indeed tested every ounce of Christian charity in me.

We finished our breakfast and packed up camp, which didn't take long, since there weren't many tents to take down or wagons to pack. But the marchin' orders never came. More than an hour went by and we began to wonder if Gen'ral Johnston had forgotten us. Then, at about half past six, way off to the north, we could just hear the faint sound of distant musket fire. I watched as Colonel Allen and some of the officers talked a short distance away. They clearly disagreed about somethin', and it was plain to see they didn't know what was happenin' either.

It was about that time that Gen'ral Jackson and his aides all came ridin' up the road on horseback with banners flyin'. They rode right up to Colonel Allen and the officers, who all saluted and waited for the Gen'ral to return their salute.

"Good morning, General," the Colonel called out in his usual pleasant voice.

"Colonel," the Gen'ral replied courteously, returnin' the Colonel's salute, "looks like we may have a fight in a little while. Are your men ready?"

"Ready as ever, General."

"Good. Very good." The brown charger the Gen'ral called Little Sorrel paced nervously and started to turn, but the Gen'ral brought him back around with a strong hand and continued. "Of course you know how I hate to fight on a Sunday. Seems akin to blasphemy. But it would appear the Yankees have no regard for the Sabbath." There was disdain in his voice, as if he was talkin' about eatin' somethin' unpleasant. "Well, there may yet be time for church services if we make haste. I've ordered my chaplain to lead Sunday prayers, and I'd like you to assemble your men just over yonder there in that grove of trees" he pointed with one gloved hand.

"Yes, sir!" Colonel Allen replied.

"Quickly, now, Colonel. Let's not offend the Almighty just when we may need Him the most!" he smiled widely, wheelin' the horse around to face the road.

"Yes, sir!" the Colonel said, salutin' again.

The Gen'ral saluted in return, spurred the horse on with a loud "Yah!" and galloped away down the road with his aides chasin' after him.

Church on the battlefield was nothin' like church back home, exceptin' the prayers were pretty much the same, and the musicians played Rock of Ages, which most of the boys seemed to know the words to. The chaplain read a few verses of scripture and said a few encouragin' words. Instead of dressin' nice and sittin' in pews in a church, we all just stood around in our uniforms or sat on the ground wherever we could. Somethin' just didn't seem right about havin' church with the sounds of muskets firin' off in the distance. Still, it was nice to have somethin' that felt a little bit normal in the face of the comin' battle. And the Good Lord knows we needed the prayers that day.

"Far cry from your Pa's church, huh?" Tommy leaned over and said in a hushed tone.

The chaplain was sayin' somethin' about Psalm somethin'-or-other and somethin' about dwellin' in secret places and abidin' in shadows that sounded vaguely familiar, but I couldn't really hear what he was sayin' very well.

"Whadaya mean?" I asked Tommy, not sure what he was gettin' at.

"I mean—"

"SHHHH," Arty hissed with a finger to his mouth. "I can't hear!" he whispered loudly.

"I mean this sure don't feel much like church back home," Tommy finished, whisperin' more quietly this time.

" . . . In the name of the Father, the Son, and the Holy Spirit. Amen," the chaplain droned a little louder so as to make sure everyone was awake for the response.

"Amen," we all repeated.

Then he sat down and the musicians started playin' Amazing Grace. Some of the fellas even sang along, what parts they knew anyways.

That's it? No sermon?

My Pa was known for his good preachin', but he was also known for his long sermons—a bit too long for a young boy by my reckonin'. But I thought it was mighty strange to be havin' church with no sermon at all.

Tommy's right. This sure is different from church back home.

"I'll say," I whispered back to Tommy, just loud enough to be heard over the music, "and a mite shorter too, I reckon."

'Twas grace that taught my heart to fear
And grace my fears relieved
How precious did that grace appear
The hour I first believed

It was Fredrick's voice, singin' loud and clear as a bell, that brought my mind back to the service, so I joined in the singin' too.

Through many dangers, toils, and snares
I have already come
'Twas grace hath brought me safe thus far
And grace 'twill lead me home

When we've been there ten thousand years
Bright shining as the sun
We've no less days to sing God's praise
Than when we first begun

Amen.

After the singin' was over, the chaplain gave the blessing, then Tommy, Arty, Fredrick, Sean, and me, we all made our way back to camp and made ready to march again. Another half hour went by, but still no orders came. Some of the boys wrote letters while we waited. Others cleaned their rifles again for the comin' fight, even though we'd already cleaned our guns earlier that mornin'. At least it was somethin' to do.

Fredrick and one of the other boys even took to tradin' punches just to break up the tension, bein' careful not to get too close to Carlton Willis while he was hung over, of course. It was all fine and good until Fredrick slugged the other fella just a bit too hard in the shoulder, then the other fella went after him, swingin' away like a mad man. Next thing we knew, they were in an all-out brawl, and from the looks of things, Fredrick was about to make the other boy look like a cougar who'd tangled with an angry mama bear. That's when Arty and I stepped in.

"Hey! Knock it off!" Arty shouted, runnin' to pull the two apart.

I jumped in to help hold the other fella while Arty pulled Fredrick off of him, wrappin' his arms around his chest real tight-like so as he couldn't swing.

By then, Sergeant Kline had come a-runnin' over too. "Save it for the enemy, boys!" he scolded, steppin' in between the two.

Fredrick and the other fella just stood there glarin' at each other for a while, but then they came back to their senses. Fredrick shrugged Arty's arms off and turned and walked away. I reckon we were all gettin' mighty anxious to get movin' and get into the fight.

Finally, we saw a courier ride up and hand a dispatch to Colonel Allen. He read it quickly, then turned to Capt'n Rowan and a few of the other officers and said, "Time to go, boys." The officers and sergeants made their way quickly through the camp rousin' all the boys to their feet. Then the bugler and drummer played Assembly, and the Second Virginia lined up to march.

This was the marchin' order for the First Brigade that day: The Fourth Virginia Regiment was the first in line, followed by the Twenty-seventh and Fifth. Then the boys from the Second fell in line behind the Fifth, with the Thirty-third behind us, and finally Pendleton's artillery.

Of all marches, I remember this one the most clearly. All together, there were more than 2,200 men and boys in the First Brigade, and what a sight to behold we were! Many of the regiments in the army had different colors and styles of uniforms. Some wore dark blue, some wore pale blue, some wore gray, some butternut, and even some bright red, so that when the army marched by, it looked like a brightly colored parade, all bristlin' with the gleamin' barrels of thousands of guns. But this was like no parade we'd ever seen before. On that hot Virginia summer day, for the first time since the brigade was formed, every soul marched with the knowledge that this day might be his last. Each man dealt with it in his own way, but none could escape it.

As for me, my mind was swimmin' with thoughts. *This here's the real thing, Wil Harleck. This is life or death, not some drill on a hillside in Harpers Ferry. Those boys out there, they aim to kill you. You might never see Mama or Pa or Maribel again. What're you gonna do?*

But I reckon it didn't really matter much what I thought. A man can't run from the angel of death when it's his time to go. So I set my face to it and marched on. It was like my feet were pullin' me forward, not on account of my own will, but as if compelled by some unseen power beyond my control.

Toward the Sound of Battle

It was a warm, clear mornin', and it didn't take long before I was covered with sweat and dust, though we'd only just begun the march. The column filed out of the field, turned right onto the road, and headed toward the sound of the battle. The drummers kept up a brisk tempo, but our progress was slower than molasses on account of bein' forced to stop every half mile or so to let someone else go by or wait for someone get out of the way. It was a disorganized mess, to be sure.

Gen'ral Bee's Brigade—mostly boys from Alabama, Mississippi and Tennessee—was the first to pass by as we waited. We saw the Gen'ral and his aides ride up to Gen'ral Jackson at the head of our column. It was obvious they were discussin' somethin' important, seein' as how there was a lot of pointin', gesturin' and noddin' of heads. Then they were off in a rush. Word swept back through the ranks, and we heard that the Yankees were flankin' us and tryin' to get around us on the left.

After that came Bee's artillery, then Bartow's Georgians of the Second Brigade. Then the road was finally clear again. By the time we got back on the road, the sounds of battle had slowed quite a bit, and we began to wonder what was goin' on. We marched up the road to the top of a wide plateau where we could see a ways farther. Ahead of us, the road led down into a wide trough between two hills: a larger wooded hill to the left, and a smaller one on the right. It was about half past nine by then. We marched down from the crest toward the trough, and there we saw the colors of Bee's Brigade on the road ahead. Just behind Bee we could see Bartow's boys nearin' the bottom of the valley too. Then our column halted again.

"We're stoppin' again?" Fredrick asked in a huff. "What for this time?" he asked, lookin' around to see if he could see what was causin' the delay. He and Arty were marchin' just ahead of Tommy and Sean and me in the ranks, and it was plain he was losin' his patience.

"Probably on account of some poor farmer's hens crossin' the road or some other such nonsense!" Tommy shot back sarcastically. "If we go any slower we'll be goin' backwards!" I reckon he was gettin' fed up too, which was a rare occasion indeed.

"I can't believe how hot it is here!" I complained. "Look at me. I'm soaked with sweat and my mouth's dry as a bed of ash. Anybody got any water left?"

"I do," Sean answered, holdin' out his canteen to offer me a drink, which I gratefully obliged. But it was almost empty and there was nary a well nor stream in sight, so I was careful only to drink a little.

"Rest now, boys. You'll get your chance to get at 'em," Capt'n Rowan said, walkin' up and down the line.

So we fell out of line and just sat by the side of the road tryin' to escape the scorchin' heat of the Virginia sun as best we could, but it was no use. I started thinkin' about Maribel, and I could feel my heart in my throat at the thought of what lay ahead. I wondered if I'd be able to keep my promise to her, and I thought about Mama and Pa, and Amos and Vanessa, and how they'd be most distressed indeed to find me listed among the slain. Mama and Amos especially. So I decided it might be best not to think on that too much. No one said much, but it was plain on their faces that my friends were thinkin' about the same things. Sean looked powerful worried, and the smile was even gone from Tommy's face.

Our rest was shorter this time. Bee's men quickly disappeared around behind the big hill to the left. Then the flags of Bartow's Brigade crossed the small stream, and the Georgians made haste to follow Bee around the hill and into the trees, and the road was finally clear for us to move ahead. Just before the First Brigade reached the small stream at the bottom of the valley, Gen'ral Jackson ordered a left turn and we began to wind our way up a narrow dirt road that climbed up the big wooded hill.

It was nearly eleven o'clock in the mornin' now, and we could hear Bee's artillery go into action just on the other side of the hill. The sharp reports of the guns shattered the air, and there was quite a bit more musket fire now too. From the sounds of it, the battle was growin' larger—and gettin' closer.

I could just see the boys of the Fifth Regiment just ahead of us up the narrow road. They turned off the road and started scramblin' up the hill through the trees to our right. Then, when our color bearers reached that place on the road, Colonel Allen dismounted his horse, drew out his sword, and stood in the middle of the road callin' out to the men.

"Quickly, now, boys. Up the hill!" he shouted again and again as each company reached the spot where he was standin' and turned to begin the wooded climb to the summit.

When we came to the edge of the woods near the top of the hill, we could see Gen'ral Jackson ridin' Little Sorrel quickly back and forth, shoutin' orders to the officers to post their colors and place the boys in line. Our cannon were in sight now, just over the crest of the hill, belchin' fire and smoke at the enemy somewhere across the valley. We watched as the Union shells burst all around 'em, and it looked to us like our boys were on the losin' end of the exchange. The fierceness of the Yankee bombardment made it hard to look away, but our boys stood their ground and fought on. The Company started movin' again to get into position, and I had to force myself to look away, but I found myself prayin' for that kind of courage.

We moved along in the edge of the trees up the back side of the hill toward the top. On the crest of the hill was a meadow of tall grass partly ringed by trees in a crescent shape around the back of the hill just below the top. On some other day it might've been a nice quiet spot for a picnic, but on this day it was a far cry from a place of tranquility or safety. Musket balls went buzzin' through the air above like angry hornets and rippin' through the leaves in the trees overhead. Occasionally, a fed'ral shell would fall nearby, explodin' with terrible effect. I reckon many a boy wanted to just run away, but none did that I could see.

There were a few minutes when the shellin' grew particularly intense. One shell exploded in a tree above our heads, and a large branch fell and struck Colonel Allen square on the head. The force of the blow knocked him to the ground and bloodied his face real good.

The Colonel was already mostly blind in one eye. Some said it was on account of a wound he'd received in the War with Mexico, but I heard another fella say it was from an accident when he was a boy. I don't reckon it mattered much, seein' as how the end result was the same either way. From what I could tell from where I stood, it appeared the branch must've struck him on the forehead, causin' a steady flow of blood to run down into his good eye, which fairly rendered him blind. One of the L'tenants and a couple of the boys helped him to his feet and guided him to a safer spot further back in the trees. We were too far away and there was too much noise to hear what they were sayin', but we could tell he couldn't see much by the way he walked with one hand held over his eye, and the other out in front of him.

What with the Colonel bein' out of action and all, things got a mite confusin' for a while, but we soon managed to get the regiment lined up. Still, somethin' just didn't feel right, and I wondered how in tarnation we'd ever be able to fight without the Colonel leadin' and doin' whatever it is Colonels do. Who'd tell us what to do and when to do it? But Capt'n Rowan didn't seem any too bothered about the matter so I reckoned he must know what to do.

The Thirty-third Virginia formed their lines to our left in a thick grove of pines. From there, the rest of the brigade spread out in a long line across the meadow in front of the trees. The Second was placed in line next to the Thirty-third, then the Fourth and Fifth Regiments formed the right end of the line. The Twenty-seventh was placed in reserve behind the line just in the edge of the trees on the opposite side of the meadow.

The sound of the battle was like none I'd ever heard before—worse than the worst thunderstorm—and growin' louder. We could barely hear Capt'n Rowan and the officers shoutin' orders over the roar. It was enough to make a man wanna duck every time a shell or ball would come close. Then L'tenant Davenport stepped forward with his sword in his hand.

"Form your ranks, boys," he shouted, and we began formin' our lines.

Fredrick and I, we had it all worked out and we knew just where to fall in when the regiment formed up in column of fours for marchin' so that we'd end up with Fredrick right in front of me when we changed formation into line of battle. We reckoned seein' as how he could shoot better than most any man in the company, and seein' as how I was no slouch at reloadin', it made for a good arrangement if the shootin' started gettin' hot. I'd fire the first few volleys with the whole regiment. Then, when the order came to fire at will, I could reload for Fredrick, and he'd do most of the shootin'.

Tommy and Arty ended up close together too, in the front rank just a few feet to my right, and Carlton Willis and Sean fell into line in the second rank just beyond the Johns brothers.

Then we heard the L'tenant holler out, "Front rank, lie down! Second rank, kneel!"

The "Stone Wall"

We tried to look across the valley to see what was goin' on, but it was impossible to see very far. The air was too thick with the smoke of a thousand guns, and we were too far behind the crest of the hill to see down into the valley. I thought my heart would explode from beatin' so hard as we knelt there on that hill for what seemed like forever, strainin' to see or glean some idea of how the battle was goin'. But one thing was sure from the sound of it: the fightin' was comin' our way.

Some of the artillery boys started limberin' up their guns and hitchin' 'em to the horses so they could be moved. My heart started beatin' even faster as I realized they were fallin' back from their positions along the ridge. I saw the familiar gray and red uniform of Capt'n Imboden, Gen'ral Bee's artillery commander, as he rode up to Gen'ral Jackson and shouted somethin' I couldn't quite make out. It was plain he wasn't happy. Ol' Jack motioned toward us and then pointed to the ground off to his left where he wanted the guns placed. This seemed to calm Imboden down a bit by the looks of it. He saluted, then rode off to meet the guns.

Out of the smoke on the hillside below, we saw soldiers—our soldiers—come streamin' back up the hill. Some were runnin'; some walkin' with heads down like they were too plum tuckered to care for their own well-bein'; and some wounded, limpin' along as best they could back up the hill.

Then Gen'ral Bee appeared on his horse, shoutin' as he rode up to Gen'ral Jackson. They were closer to us now, but I could still just barely make out the voices over the sounds of the battle.

"They're beating us back!" he shouted at Ol' Jack.

His voice sounded alarmed—kinda like a fox with his leg caught in the henhouse door and the farmer a-comin' with his gun. I reckoned that couldn't be a good sign. Lookin' around the battlefield, I could scarcely believe my eyes and ears. Our boys seemed to be fallin' back everywhere. It didn't seem possible. It was like bein' trapped in some kind of bad dream. I could feel the fear wellin' up inside me. Could we really be losin' the battle already?

But Ol' Jack just sat there in his saddle, cool as you please. What a sight he was, sittin' up there on Little Sorrel, all dressed for battle, with one gloved hand held up in the air! Then with a kick, he turned sideways so he could be heard by all, and shouted back.

"Then, sir, we will give them the bayonet!"

Then Gen'ral Bee turned on his horse and rode across the crest of the hill to our right, shoutin' to his men at the top of his voice and waivin' his hat wildly in the air as he rode.

"Look men!" he shouted, pointin' back at us. "There's Jackson, standing like a stone wall! Rally behind the Virginians!"

Then we heard Gen'ral Jackson shout, "First Brigade, forward! And keep low!" Capt'n Rowan stepped quickly forward, turned toward us, drew his sword, and shouted, "Second Virginia! Move up men! And stay low!" The boys in the first rank got up on their feet, and we began to crouch down and move forward. L'tenant Davenport was in front of us walkin' backward and facin' us. He held his sword level in front of him with the handle in one hand and the blade in the other to keep the lines straight as we moved up. The whole regiment moved forward with remarkable good order, and I noticed that the boys from the Fourth to our right and the Thirty-third to our left were movin' forward too. When we'd almost reached the crest of the hill where Imboden had placed the guns, the line stopped and the officers started shoutin' for us to lie down on the ground again, which we were only too happy to oblige.

The air was filled with thick smoke and dust, and the smell of powder burned my eyes and nose and left a gritty taste in my mouth as surely as if someone had scooped up a handful of it and thrown it in my face. And it was hot—real hot—and gettin' hotter by the minute. There wasn't a cloud to be seen in the sky, and now that we were out in the open, the hot Virginia sun beat down on us fiercely and showed no mercy. My shirt was drippin' wet, and I had to keep wipin' the sweat from my brow with my sleeve just so I could see. My hands were so sweaty from the heat and nerves that I could barely hold on to my rifle. A few of the boys had already gone down from the heat. I wanted a cool drink of water like nothin' else, but I couldn't move, and my eyes would only look in the direction of the fight.

The fed'ral shells were fallin' closer now and I felt my courage failin' again. All of a sudden I heard cheerin' and shoutin' off to my left. I turned to look and saw a man I'd never seen before ridin' in grand fashion with a whole host of color-bearers close behind. He had a thick mustache and one of those handsome dashing faces that made all the womenfolk swoon. Cheers went up from the men as he rode along the lines, smilin' and wavin' his gloved hand and lookin' like the noble Duke of York himself.

"It's Beauregard! The Hero of Fort Sumter!" Tommy shouted, grinnin' real big. "I remember him from his photograph!"

Then another voice yelled, "And look! There's General Johnston too!"

The cheers turned into a chorus of shouts that echoed off the hills and nearly drowned out the sound of the battle. I looked and saw Arty wavin' his hat and hollerin' at the top of his lungs, and I felt my strength begin to return.

"Hoorah! Hoorah! Hoorah!" Fredrick shouted, so I joined in the shoutin' too.

As the two gen'rals reached the end of our lines, I saw Bee's regiments reformin' on their colors just behind the Fifth Virginia boys to our right, not far from where the Twenty-seventh Virginia was lined up in the trees. Then Beauregard and Johnston turned and rode up to the summit of the hill, and there they stood, like a pair of oaks in a hail storm of Union shells, until all of our boys got back in line. They sure were a sight.

Here They Come, Boys!

But what happened next was even stranger. Bit by bit, a hush fell over the field like a thick fog rollin' in and swallowin' up all the sounds of the battle. The distant muskets fell silent, and even the fed'ral guns slowed their fire 'til they almost stopped entirely. For what must've been at least a full half hour we waited there in that meadow on our bellies just behind the top of the hill with the hot Virginia sun beatin' down on us, and the men started talkin' among themselves.

Finally Sean piped up hopefully, "Is that it? Is the battle over?"

"Maybe they ain't comin'," I heard another fella say.

"Oh, they're comin' alright," Carlton retorted matter-of-factly. "I'd bet my last penny on it."

Along about that time Pendleton's artillery finally arrived on the field, and started takin' up positions on the crest of the hill in front of us next to Imboden's guns. Between Imboden's guns and Pendleton's, our artillery line stretched a good ways across the hilltop now.

We reckoned if the Yanks finally did come they'd sure enough get a surprise.

The minutes went by and seemed to stretch into hours, but still we waited, watchin' for the enemy to come up that hill. Then we heard shouts from the Thirty-third on our left.

"Here they come, boys!"

Gen'ral Jackson just rode calmly back and forth behind the guns like we'd seen him do a hundred times before in the Shenandoah.

"Steady men! Steady! All's well."

His voice was clear and filled with conviction, and there was fire in his eyes. There was just somethin' about that man as he sat up there on that horse. Every time he went into battle, his eyes lit up so bright that the boys took to callin' him "Ol' Blue Light." To this very day I still can't explain it. It was like he possessed no fear. From the looks of him, we might just as well've been on that hillside back in Harpers Ferry listenin' to him address the Brigade—as if the enemy wasn't even there at all. Never have I seen such a man who could make an army feel so confident in battle like Ol' Jack—exceptin' Gen'ral Lee, of course, but we hadn't met him yet.

Then out of the smoke and dust we saw a line of dark uniforms comin' up the hill toward us. But were they friend or foe? They came closer, but still we couldn't tell. Then, through a gap in the risin' smoke, we caught a glimpse of the flags. One was mostly blue, but even with the wind as calm as it was there was no mistakin' the narrow red and white stripes on the other one.

The Sound of Fear

July 21, 1861

By 11:30 a.m., the First Battle of Manassas (or Bull Run, as it will come to be known in the North) is going badly for the South. After rushing their brigades forward to reinforce Evans on Matthews Hill, Bee and Bartow are now trying desperately to slow the federal advance. Their heroic efforts have bought precious time for Johnston and Beauregard, but even their combined forces are no match for the powerful column of Union troops arrayed against them on the field. Two federal divisions, led by Hunter and Heintzelman, push forward across Matthews Hill, and the southern lines soon falter, and then break in retreat. Panic begins to sweep the ranks of the southern army, and northern confidence runs high.

By noon, Jackson has arrived on the scene and has taken up a strong position just behind the crest of the neighboring Henry Hill. Mercifully for the Rebels, a lull begins to fall over the battlefield as the shattered brigades of Bee, Bartow, and Evans scramble up Henry Hill from the valley below and try to rally and reform behind Jackson's position. Pursuing Union forces are slowed as they cross the small creek that flows between the two hills, and then further slowed by inexperience as they try to reform for the pursuit. Artillery commanders from both armies now take advantage of the lull to reposition and resupply their guns.

By one o'clock, Hunter's lead regiments have reformed and are advancing up the slopes of Henry Hill, still partly obscured by the veil of smoke which hangs in the hot July air. The Federals are disorganized and uncoordinated, attacking as individual regiments instead of combining their strength. Still, they are confident that with one more big thrust they will sweep the enemy from the field.

But Jackson has been watching from atop his horse just beyond the hilltop, his sharp mind studying the approaching Federals for weaknesses. He has found what he hopes will be a fatal flaw in the enemy's tactics. During the lull, he has moved his entire brigade—over 2,200 men—forward. They now lie waiting just behind the crest of the hill for the Northerners to draw within a hundred yards of their position. As the first wave of Union troops nears the crest of the hill, Imboden's reinforced artillery, which is now placed in a long line just in front of Jackson's men, unleashes a withering fire that causes the Federals to fall back momentarily, but they quickly reform and press forward again, directly toward the strong center of Jackson's brigade.

On the Union right, a battery of federal artillery and a small force of supporting infantry has pushed too far forward, unaware that Jeb Stuart's cavalry troopers are placed perfectly to threaten their exposed right flank. The Union commanders on the field are also unaware that, during the morning's battle, Elzey's Fourth Virginia Infantry Brigade has arrived from the Shenandoah by train and is now rushing to the battlefield to reinforce the Confederate left, precisely where Stuart is poised to attack.

The tide of the battle is about to turn.

Jackson's position on Henry Hill, 11:30 a.m., July 21, 1862

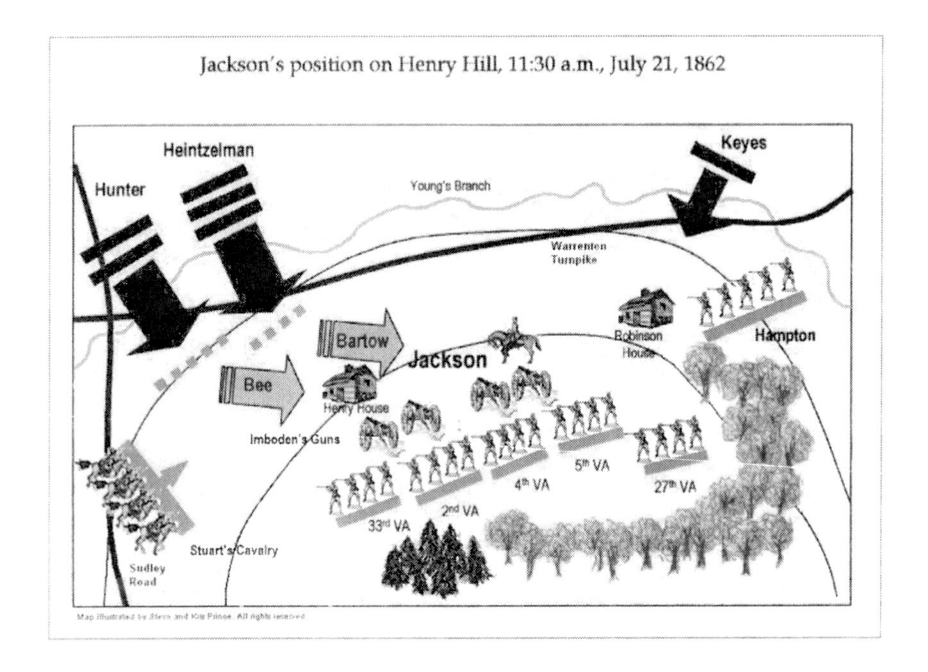

The Battle for Henry Hill

"FIRE!!"

Capt'n Imboden's voice boomed across the field so clearly that I half thought he was callin' out to the infantry, and very nearly aimed my rifle at the enemy lines. But then the cannons unleashed a barrage of such fierce intensity as to strike fear into the legions of Hell itself. The canister shot struck the Union lines with deadly effect, wipin' huge holes in the neatly formed ranks. Right about then I became convinced that war was an ugly business.

The gruesome image caused by the artillerymen applyin' their deadly craft defied my meager ability to describe. In an instant the air was filled with thousands of tiny bits of metal which didn't much care where they struck, but left in their wake piles of twisted and broken bodies. And blood everywhere—so much blood—enough to turn even the hardest man a tad pekid. I even felt sorry for those poor Yanks as the cries of pain and horror rose up from their lips, and those who were still standin' began to fall back. I wondered what I might've done had the shoe been found on the other foot and I'd been found on the receivin' end of such a terrible fate. Would I have the courage to reform like they were doin'? Or would I just up and run away? I hoped it'd be the former, but I feared it might be the latter, as it all started sinkin' in that perhaps I, too, might have to face such horror on the field of battle—maybe even this day. The very thought of it sent a wave of nausea washin' up from the pit of my stomach that left a foul taste in my mouth and made my whole body feel shaky and weak. It was lucky we were lyin' down, or my legs might've collapsed right out from under me.

We'd watched Ol' Jack givin' orders to the artillery only moments before they opened fire. Then we saw Imboden ridin' up and down the line of guns, stoppin' at each one as if to personally inspect every gun. I don't know exactly what it was he was doin', but it must've worked, seein' as how they sure did give the Yanks a mess of trouble.

Once the guns started firin', Capt'n Imboden rode back over to where Gen'ral Jackson and a few of the officers were watchin' the battle. He raised his field glasses briefly to check the damage, although at that range it hardly seemed necessary. Then the whole group of 'em wheeled their horses around and rode off to our right behind the line of guns 'til they disappeared into the smoke.

Of course there *was* one problem I hadn't figured on when it came to lyin' on the ground behind the artillery. When the Yankee guns started shootin' back, well, the perilous nature of our position became painfully evident real quick-like. Federal shot and shell were soon fallin' all around, and some of our boys were hit by stray Yankee rounds.

I didn't actually see what happened next on account of all the smoke hangin' in the air, but the word spread quickly back up through the lines like wildfire.

"Gen'ral Jackson's been hit!"

"The General's down!"

"Jackson's hit!"

There was genu-ine concern and a hint of panic in their voices, and my heart skipped a beat or two. My mind raced through the possibilities. *Is he dead? Wounded? Who's in charge?*

"What do we do now?" I heard the words come out of my mouth before I could catch 'em.

I wondered if maybe the boys would lose heart and run. And if they did, what would I do? Ol' Jack had no tolerance for deserters, but with him down, would we turn and run, or stand and make a fight of it?

"Steady, boys. Keep down, now."

Capt'n Rowan's harsh voice cut through the fog in my mind. What with all the Yankee bullets flyin' overhead, that was all the incentive I needed to stay put.

Fredrick was lyin' just in front of me and to my left with his feet next to my shoulder. He must've guessed I was feelin' a bit nervous because he turned his head and looked back over his shoulder at me to see if I was doin' alright. It must've been only a few minutes until the next word came, but it seemed like much longer.

"He's alright! The General's alright!" I heard a fella from the next company say. "It was just his hand! A Yank shot him in the hand!"

I saw the big grin spread across Fredrick's face, and I began to feel the panic loosen its grip on my heart. I looked around and saw the look of relief on the faces of the boys around me. Some smiled, some breathed a sigh of relief, and some even cheered, but this much you can be sure of: all were mighty glad.

Knowin' that Fredrick was right there in front of me made me feel a bit more courageous too. Capt'n Rowan had said he was gonna speak to Colonel Allen about maybe puttin' Fredrick in a company of sharpshooters when the chance came, but I for one was glad to have him in our Company. His skill with the rifle was nigh unto legend back home, and I reckoned I'd be alright as long as I stuck close to him.

Along about then we saw another line of men comin' up the hill toward us on our left past the small farm house. But were they friend or foe? We knew that Johnston and Beauregard would surely be sendin' more troops up to help us, but who were these fellas in the pale blue?

"Here they come!" Fredrick shouted.

"Them ain't Yanks! Them's our boys!" shouted another fella.

"No they ain't! Look! That's a fed'ral flag!" Fredrick shot back.

The Yankees formed up in a line only a few hundred yards from the Thirty-third Virginia and commenced to firin', but the Thirty-third was still lined up in the trees, which somewhat diminished the effect of the fed'ral fire. We waited for the boys from the Thirty-third to fire back, but they didn't.

Then I saw some horses pullin' cannons up next to the Yank infantry.

"What're they doin'?" I asked Fredrick, seein' as how he could see over the crest of the hill better.

"Movin' up some guns," he answered, soundin' just a bit concerned. "I count six. See 'em there?" he pointed.

I strained to see through the haze. "Yep. Sure looks like it," I agreed, from what I could see from where I lay, leastwise. But the thought that those guns might be aimed right at us made my heart beat a might faster than I'd care to admit, and I began to sweat even more, if that was possible.

Then we saw another regiment of infantry comin' up the hill behind the guns. They wore fancy foreign-lookin' uniforms with blue pantaloon trousers and bright red shirts, with white cloths wrapped around their heads instead of hats. They were quite a sight to behold.

I couldn't help but wonder how many more Yankees might still be comin' up that hill. It seemed like they'd just keep on comin' forever. What if there were too many of 'em?

I reckon it's true how a man's thoughts turn to matters of eternal significance when he's facin' his own mortality, seein' as how I found myself prayin' to the Good Lord for help right about then. I suspect there was many a man prayin' along with me too, in their own way, be they devout or heathen. Times like these a man was apt to find himself bein' tested as to what he truly believed. So I propped myself up on my elbows, folded my hands, and bowed my head.

"Be sure and put in a good word for me, son," I heard Capt'n Rowan say. I looked up to see who he was talkin' to, and sure enough, he was lookin' right at me.

"Uh . . . Yes, sir. Will do, sir," I answered back, soundin' somewhat bewildered. I wasn't rightly sure that was how it worked—this notion of 'puttin' in a good word'—but I didn't see any harm in it, so I did anyway.

> *"Hello Lord. It's me, Wil Harleck. I know this is a mighty strange time to be prayin' to you—layin' here on the field of battle with a rifle in my hand like this and all—but I'm a mite worried on account of I've never been in a battle like this before, and, well, I'd sure be obliged if you'd watch over me in this fight. But if this is the day you should come for me, then I pray you take my soul to Heaven with you . . . and comfort Mama so she won't mourn me too much. Oh, and please watch over Capt'n Rowan too, if it's not too much trouble. Thank you. Amen."*

About the time I'd finished prayin', we heard a chorus of shouts and cheers goin' up from the boys of the Thirty-third Virginia behind us on the left. As I looked over my shoulder, I saw that they were standin' up now at the edge of the pine grove on the left end of our line. I looked to see what they were cheerin' about but couldn't see what it was. Then the cheers started ripplin' down the line toward us, and we could finally begin to see what all the fuss was about.

It was Stuart's Black Horse cavalry! They were chargin' right at the flank of those fancy Union boys! I could feel the excitement risin' up inside at the sight of hundreds of horses chargin' at a full gallop right toward the enemy guns! Soon we could hear the sound of the hooves poundin' the hard ground and saw the great cloud of dust they were kickin' up behind 'em. So much that it was hard to tell who or what might be behind that front line of horses. They rode right into those poor boys with the fancy uniforms, slashin' and scatterin' the neat lines and causin' all nature of panic and disorder.

A Confused Affair

Almost at the same time, we saw some of the boys from the Thirty-third start to move forward as if to attack. As far as we could tell, no orders had come from Gen'ral Jackson yet, but those boys were clearly itchin' to get in the fight. At first it was only a couple of 'em that started to move ahead, then a few more, and a few more.

We could hear the officers yellin', "Hold the line, boys!" But it was too late.

More and more of the boys started off runnin' across the field until finally someone yelled, "CHARGE!" All of the sudden, the whole regiment let out a yell and commenced to chargin' across the field toward the Union guns!

The Union boys in the pale blue uniforms were still lined up behind the fed'ral guns, but they didn't fire. Neither did the cannons. They looked like they weren't sure what to do. Stuart's cavalry was almost on top of 'em from the right and behind, and our boys from the Thirty-third were closin' the distance quickly, but still the Yankees didn't fire.

Then we saw the boys from the Thirty-third stop and form their ranks, then they fired at close range right into the guns, and a good many of the Union gunners went down. Officers and horses too. The Union boys in the pale blue fired a volley of their own, but then they turned and ran back down the hill along with what was left of those boys in the fancy uniforms. A couple of the brave gun crews tried to limber up their guns to keep 'em from bein' taken, but the boys from the Thirty-third had reached the line of guns and the fightin' was hand-to-hand now. A moment later, all that was left of the Yankees were the dead and dyin', and only three of the guns had managed to escape. The remaining guns were soon turned around and pointed down the hill by the boys of the Thirty-third, but we could already see another Union regiment comin' up the hill toward the captured guns, with another one not far behind. The closest regiment stopped and fired a volley, then the boys from the Thirty-third reformed and fired back, and the fight was on.

The sun was high in the sky by now, and beatin' down on us somethin' awful, but there was no time for water. Our attention was rightly focused on the lines of Yankee troops comin' up the hill from every direction. Off to our right we could hear the fight heatin' up there too. We knew Hampton's Legion must be over there somewhere, along with the rest of the boys from Bee's and Bartow's brigades. It was plain to see the Yankees were fixin' to try and push us off that hill, and the fightin' was growin' fierce on both ends of our lines.

Stuart's cavalry was withdrawin' on the left, and fresh Union regiments were comin' up against the Thirty-third now. Our boys were pressed hard and began to fall back toward the tree line again, and two companies of the Second started movin' back to our left and turnin' to face the Yankees as they were comin' up the hill so as we wouldn't be flanked. Our line was bendin' back from the center toward the left into a dense thicket that covered the ground near the tree line where the boys from the Thirty-third were now reformin'. But some of our officers were yellin' that we should hold our positions. I heard one fella say it was Colonel Allen that ordered the line to be turned, but that only made for more confusion, what with the Colonel bein' wounded and all.

Before we could get that whole mess straightened out, some new Yank regiments appeared on the crest of the hill right in front of us. Our guns in the center of the line went back into action as soon as the Fed'rals appeared on the crest of the hill, but those boys in the blue and black uniforms, they just kept on comin' this time.

By now we'd had just about a belly-full of waitin' and watchin', and we were achin' to get up and fight too. It was hard to stay low what with all the action goin' on all around us.

But Ol' Blue Light just trotted down the line on that familiar horse holdin' his left hand up in the air and shoutin' out as he rode by. "Steady, boys! Let 'em get a bit closer!"

And get closer they did. I could make out their faces now, and still they came on.

The Gen'ral positioned himself just ahead of us and to our right, between the Second and Fourth regiments. If we looked closely, we could just make out the bandage he'd wrapped around his hand where the bullet had struck him. We figured he must really be "Ol' Tom Fool" to be sittin' up there with his hand in the air makin' such a splendid target for those northern boys. But he just sat there in the saddle, cool as you please. Then he wheeled around and shouted to us.

"First Brigade, UP!"

He looked like he was havin' the time of his life! That big smile flashed across his face and his blue eyes blazed like rays of sunlight as he sat up there on Little Sorrel surveyin' the brigade and watchin' while we stood up to form our lines. The soul of bravery, he was—the Good Lord as my witness.

The command was repeated by officers up and down the lines.

"Stand up, men! On your feet!"

We strained to hear Jackson shoutin' over the sound of the battle as we stood up.

"You must reserve your fire, men, 'til they come within fifty yards! Then fire and give them the bayonet! And when you charge, yell like furies!!"

Again Capt'n Rowan drew out his sword and held it high in the air.

"Second Virginia! FIX; BAYONETS!" The Capt'n shouted, his voice nearly breakin' with excitement.

"Fix Bayonets!" L'tenant Davenport repeated with sword in hand just in front of us.

The bayonet is a cruel weapon, and even more intimidatin' when there are hundreds of 'em all comin' at you on the ends of five-foot-long rifles. The bugle sounded clear and crisp across the field, and the clickin' sound of hundreds of bayonets could be heard all up and down the line as the boys all pulled the long blades out of their belts and attached 'em to the barrels of the rifles. I saw Tommy and Arty just a few feet off to my right, but I noticed Tommy's customary grin looked a mite more determined than usual, like he was steelin' himself for the charge he knew was comin'.

The next command came from Capt'n Rowan.

"Make ready!"

The front row stood in firin' position while the second rank stepped to the right so as we could fire in between the fellas in the front. From there we had a better view of the approachin' Yankees. They were very close now, and ready to fire. I lifted the rifle into the ready position and pulled back the hammer.

Then came their first volley. The loud cracks of a hundred rifles bein' discharged in our direction was followed immediately by the most terrifyin' sound any man ever had the displeasure of hearin': the sound of the Minie balls. The high-pitched whir of the balls that passed just overhead or just off to one side or the other was bad enough, to be sure, but it was the sound of the balls that didn't go by that made me wanna retch. If there'd been anything left in my stomach, the contents would've certainly been liberated from my body at the sound of a half dozen Minie balls strikin' flesh and bone all around me. Then I saw Tommy fall right where he'd been standin' just a moment before, as if I was watchin' it all happen in some horrible nightmare.

"Tommy!" I heard Arty yell. But his voice sounded like it was muffled and far off in the distance, and time seemed to slow down for a moment.

I knew I should be payin' mind to the enemy like we were trained, but I found myself starin' against my own will toward the place where Tommy fell. I couldn't tell how bad it was from where I was standin', but he was screamin' in pain, and I couldn't make my eyes look away.

Arty had already dropped his rifle and was stoopin' down to help Tommy, and I wanted to go and help too, but I couldn't.

"Take aim!" Capt'n Rowan's voice broke through the nightmare.

Two rows of rifles fixed with gleamin' bayonets leveled off toward the line of blue troops and blocked the way so as I couldn't get to Tommy.

I felt my legs grow weak. I could taste the bile in my mouth and felt it in the pit of my stomach, but somehow my eyes came back to the barrel of my rifle as I pointed it toward the enemy line, now only fifty yards away. May God in Heaven forgive me, but at that very moment I hated those people. I know they were just men and boys fightin' for a cause, just like me, but I couldn't stop thinkin' about Tommy. I kept hearin' that gawdawful sound and seein' him fall over and over in my mind. They'd made no bones about doin' their worst to kill us, and in that instant, I had no qualms about killin' them first.

"FIRE!"

I pulled the trigger and saw the flash and the smoke erupt from the barrel; felt the familiar kick of the rifle butt against my shoulder; smelled the gunpowder burnin' my nostrils; then looked to see if I'd hit my target.

I watched as dozens of Yanks fell from the effect of our volley. One of the Union boys fell right where I was aimin', but I couldn't tell if it was from my shot or someone else's. And it didn't matter. I felt like justice was done, and the wave of hatred inside me began to subside.

But the nightmare wasn't over yet. Only seconds later came a second volley from their lines, and I saw Sergeant Kline's head jerk back—struck square in the face by a Yank Minie ball. Sergeant Kline was no small man, but the deadly force of the ball threw his whole body backward like a rag doll into the fellas behind him. There could be no doubtin' he was dead.

I felt my knees weaken beneath me, my ears started ringin', the wave of nausea returned, and my head grew light. I thought I might pass out right then and there, but somehow I managed to stay on my feet.

Charge of the Furies

I heard Capt'n Rowan's voice again, clear and loud. It broke through the ringin' in my ears and cleared away the fog from my head.

"Charge, bayonet!"

All at once the whole regiment shouted out real loud, and in that shout I felt the courage wellin' up inside of me. We held our rifles at the ready and prepared ourselves for the charge. My heart was poundin' so hard in my ears that it nearly drowned out all the other noise of the battle. Then I heard the boys from the Fourth Virginia yell out the same way. I reckon they all felt like we did. All of us had had just about enough of that Yankee attack, and we were more than ready to put an end to it. The prospect of puttin' them on the frightful end of a bayonet charge seemed a far sight better than just standin' there and lettin' 'em shoot at us.

"CHARGE!!"

The bugle sounded, and all at once a shrill and piercin' yell that could never be described with any justice went up from our lines. The bone-chillin' scream seemed to take on a life of its own as we charged across that narrow space. I found myself yellin' like a madman too, and the yell got even louder as we crashed into the fed'ral lines.

The sounds of that battle still echo in my nightmares to this day: the screams of boys who've just learned the true nature of the bayonet attack first hand; the crack of wooden rifles against each other, or against bone; and the sound of wounded and dyin' men fallin' all around. These are sounds that no God-fearin' man oughta ever be forced to hear.

The fightin' didn't last long. The weight of nearly the whole brigade was too much for the Yankee lines, and they broke and started runnin'. But we kept advancin' after 'em.

I'd lost track of Capt'n Rowan in all the confusion, but then I spotted L'tenant Davenport with his sword drawn. He was pointin' toward the fed'ral guns that'd been placed part way down the hill. With the infantry on the run, they were nigh unprotected now.

"To the guns, boys! Turn the guns!" The L'tenant shouted.

As we ran toward the Union guns, a battery of Yankee artillery on the next hill opened fire upon us, and shells began explodin' all around me. Our lines weren't neat and soldierly anymore. Now they were more like a big herd of cattle all sorta runnin' in the same general direction and tramplin' anything dumb enough to get in their path. I stopped to reload my rifle for a few seconds, but Fredrick ran on ahead. His hat had come off during the fight, and it was easy to spot his golden hair wavin' in the wind as he ran.

I finished reloadin' and ran toward him, thinkin' that I should probably stay closer so we could fight together like we'd planned. He raised his rifle to fire, but then he was struck in the shoulder. I watched in horror as he went down just a few feet away from where I was.

NO!!

"Fredrick!" I shouted, bendin' down to see if he was hurt badly. His jacket had a big hole in it, and there was blood comin' out—a lot of blood—and his face looked pale. The blood stain on his jacket kept growin', and I found myself just starin' at it in disbelief.

This wasn't supposed to happen! He can't die! He and I, we're supposed to fight together!

"Just stay right here," I heard myself say desperately. "I'll go get help!"

What do I do now? I can't just leave him lyin' here!

"No!" he yelled weakly, pointin' at the Union guns with his good arm. "Go!"

I wasn't sure I could just leave him like that, but somethin' in his voice convinced me he was right. I fired my rifle at a group of Yankees who were tryin' to defend the guns, then I grabbed Fredrick's rifle from the ground and ran toward 'em.

I don't much recall what happened next.

It seemed like the whole world flashed bright white and red, and I felt the blast of the shell hit me like a railroad locomotive. Then all I could hear was the terrible ringin' in my head, and I saw my feet and legs flyin' through the air over my head. The world turned upside-down, and then it all went black.

When I opened my eyes again, I found myself lyin' face down on the ground with a searin' pain in the whole right half of my upper body. I couldn't tell how long I'd been lyin' there, or even where I was. The pain seemed to swallow up every thought until there was nothin' left but the pain.

I blinked hard and tried to get my bearings. When I finally managed to force my eyes to focus, I saw a group of Yankees chargin' in my direction, and it struck me that I was still in the middle of the battle. I tried to get up, but I couldn't make my body move.

Then I saw the unmistakable big form of Carlton Willis run past me, straight toward the Yankees. With his rifle turned sideways, I watched in amazement as he struck two Yankees at the same time, knockin' both of 'em off their feet. He let out an angry yell and sent a third Yank reelin' from a blow with the butt of the rifle, then drove the point of his bayonet into the chest of one of the two men he'd just knocked down. The terrible scream of the Yankee soldier filled my ears and blotted out the sounds of the battle all around. The second man tried to get up, but then I saw Carlton's rifle swing around again, the stock strikin' the man's head with deadly effect, and he crumpled to the ground like an ol' discarded coat.

The last two Yankees stopped dead in their tracks, then turned and ran the other way. With the Yanks in retreat, Carlton ran to the nearest cannon, lifted the carriage stock by himself, and started turnin' the gun around. Two more of our boys joined him, and they turned the gun on the fleein' Yanks and pulled the primer. The gun went off with a loud boom, and I began to feel numb. My eyesight got blurry, and I went out again.

The next thing I remember was bein' carried over someone's shoulder back up the hill toward our guns. But I couldn't tell who it was who was carryin' me, seein' as how all I could see was his back.

"What . . . ?" I fought through haze in my mind to try and make sense of what was happenin'.

"Save yer breath, preacher boy," answered the voice of Carlton Willis. "You can talk later." He sounded out of breath.

When we reached the hilltop, he laid me down.

"Fredrick—?" I tried again.

"—I'll git 'im," he interrupted. "You just stay here."

Then he stood and headed back down the hill to get Fredrick.

As I laid there lookin' down that hill, I could tell that the Yankees were in full retreat. I saw the flags of Elzey's Fourth Brigade comin' down the side of the bald hill across the valley against the Union right, and the fed'ral formations were beginnin' to come apart.

The Yankees tried to throw in a regiment of Regulars to stem the tide, but it was no use. They'd already broken in the center, and the Regulars couldn't stop Elzey's advance. I was in terrible pain, but I saw the last of the Yankees as they scrambled back across the small crick and fled to the north and east—with our boys hot on their tails like hounds after a 'coon. Then I started feelin' cold for the first time on that hot Sunday afternoon, and another wave of pain washed over me. My mind went fuzzy and the world looked like it was spinnin' around, and everything went dark again.

The Worst Place on Earth

July 22, 1861

Only one day after the first battle of Bull Run, panic begins to sweep the nation as news of McDowell's stunning defeat spreads rapidly. Telegraph wires from coast to coast are hot with news of the terrible loss, and newspapers from Boston to Saint Louis appear on newsstands bearing alarming headlines and staggering casualty lists. The shattered remains of McDowell's army slowly trickle back into the Union capitol, but so complete was the rout that many of the demoralized soldiers refuse to reform with their units. Some have even deserted and left for home. Worse yet, the three-month enlistment papers for many of these soldiers are about to expire. President Lincoln and his war cabinet are suddenly faced with the brutal gravity of their situation: Not only have they failed to bring the conflict to a swift end, but they have also left the country in a perilous and vulnerable position.

On the southern bank of the Potomac, the victorious Confederate Army needs only to press the routed Federals in order to occupy Washington D.C. and force the Union to sue for peace. But, alas, they are in no condition to do so. The green troops, both Union and Confederate, are too disorganized, inexperienced, and undisciplined to continue the fight.

Jackson, however, believes that new reinforcements should immediately be employed to occupy the Yankee capitol. While visiting with his surgeon after the battle to be treated for his wounded hand, Jackson is overheard to say,

"Give me 10,000 fresh troops and I would be in Washington tomorrow." Reinforcements have begun to arrive, yet, for reasons that remain unclear, no order to advance on Washington is forthcoming from Richmond.

The toll of the battle is high. Higher than many could have expected: Union losses total 460 killed, 1,124 wounded, and over 1,500 captured, along with twenty-five guns, thousands of rifles, and twenty-six wagons with all sorts of supplies. On the Confederate side, the losses are only slightly better: 387 killed, 1,582 wounded, and thirteen missing.

Citizens north and south alike are stunned by news of so many casualties, and struggle to come to grips with the carnage of war. But as horrific as the casualty list from Bull Run may be, it will pale in comparison to the bloodshed these two combatants will inflict upon each other in the days to come. In its young history, the American nation has never seen warfare such as will be witnessed for two days in April 1862, in southwestern Tennessee, near a small church called Shiloh; or on a single September day, near the Antietam Creek in western Maryland, that same year; or for three hot days in July 1863 in a small town in southern Pennsylvania called Gettysburg.

The once beautiful countryside near Manassas is now littered with the dead and dying, lying unburied where they fell the previous day. Farm houses and barns are pressed into service as makeshift hospitals, crowded with the wounded. The conditions are horrendous and worsening by the hour. Private citizens and army surgeons, many of whom have little or no formal medical training, struggle to provide care for the wounded and preserve some sense of dignity for the departed souls whose lifeless bodies now lie baking in the hot Virginia sun. There are not enough trained medical personnel and supplies, and many of the wounds which might otherwise have been less severe are now becoming critical. For many, the only prescription for a Minie ball in the arm or leg is amputation. As the day goes on, however, even amputation proves to be no guarantee of survival. Without the knowledge or means of providing for proper sanitation, infection now becomes the greatest threat to the wounded.

July 23, 1861

To: Private William Harleck
Second Virginia Infantry Regiment, First Brigade, C.S.A.
Army of the Shenandoah

My Dearest Wil,

We read in the paper yesterday of the great victory won by our glorious armies, and there is an air of great celebration throughout the whole of Jefferson County. I pray you are well. Since learning of the great many dead and wounded, I have been in dread of receiving news that you may have been among them, but pray that is not so, and I remain in earnest expectation that I may hear some word from you soon.

We are hopeful that this victory will quickly put an end to this awful war, and you will be able to return home soon. Amos and Vanessa miss you a great deal, and although she tries not to show it, your poor mother is sorely distressed that you and your brother Joseph, with whom you were once so close, have become so estranged over the matter of Virginia's secession from the Union. She misses you both so terribly.

While our brave legions have been away defending Richmond, we have been compelled to play host to the northern cavalry soldiers occupying Charles Town in your absence. They have set up their headquarters here in our home, and although their stay here has made many things more difficult, we have been treated well. Even so, I much preferred when I did not have to write to you secretly, and we remain hopeful that their stay will soon be shortened by General Jackson's return to the valley.

I think of you each day and remember fondly your visits before this war began. When I pray each night, I ask the Almighty to shelter you beneath His mighty wings and to keep *you safe, body and soul. I hope you do not think me too forward if I say that I earnestly hope you will be able to return to me soon. I have no intention of releasing you from your promise, and I long to see your face and gaze into your eyes again. I miss the sound of your voice and the warmth of my hand in yours, and I should very much like to see you again safely at home.*

Until then, I remain,
Your devoted Maribel

Laudanum and Grim Horrors

Most soldiers would rather just be shot through the head than to be found lyin' in an army hospital. Goin' to the hospital not only meant he was probably gonna die anyway, but also that it was highly likely that he'd suffer greatly before finally succumbin' to the grim reaper. Few places were as horrifyin' to the mind of a soldier as the hospital, and why on earth any man would go there on purpose is beyond me. The scene a fella was apt to find is one that no God-fearin' man should be caught describin' in mixed company. But so as to do justice to the poor souls who had to endure such things, I'll do my best to paint a portrait that's somewhat fit for the public to hear.

It bears notin', first of all, that hardly ever did battles occur near a hospital that was actually built for such a purpose. More often than not, the battlefield hospital was just a barn or house that had the misfortune of sittin' in close proximity to the battle, and which the local inhabitants had usually long abandoned. But since it conveniently offered shade and shelter and a place for the surgeons to work, it was pressed into service with the obligatory gratitude of the army, and usually not much else in the way of compensation.

The first thing you notice is that gawdawful stench. The pungent odor of blood and bile and death is enough to assault a man's senses at twenty-five paces. I reckon if a man wasn't already sick enough to require the services of the hospital, he would be by the time he got there. The addition of a plentiful supply of vomit, which was likely caused by the sheer smell of the place, only made the problem worse.

As putrid as I recollect that stench was, it isn't the smells of the hospital that still haunt my dreams—it's those horrible sounds. First, there's that eerie sound that seems to just hover low in the air all around like a mist in a graveyard. The low jumble of voices and whispers that float up to the ear from the lips of the wounded and dyin' might best be described as a strange and ghostly mixture of prayers softly whispered to Heaven and weakened pleas for help. It hangs suspended in the air like a deep bass note just beneath a chorus of painful moans and cries and the occasional callin' out of the name of some loved one or friend. This, of course, is punctuated every now and then by the bone-chillin' screams of some poor unfortunate soul undergoin' the application of the surgeon's saw. And it all mixes together like some ghoulish symphony of death and misery.

The man who's carried into the hospital unable to see because he's either unconscious or wounded by the head is truly blessed indeed. His eyes are not cursed to behold the sight of the men and boys layin' all around bleedin' and dyin'. Some with missin' arms or legs. Others mangled and twisted by the cannoneer or some other hideous battle wound. There are seldom enough sheets or blankets to cover all the bodies of the departed souls, which are usually just carried out behind the hospital and laid in rows to be identified and claimed by friends, comrades, or kin. And for the sake of common decency, I won't even begin to describe the sight of the surgeon's table, or all the cruel tools of his trade, or the baskets and piles of severed limbs lyin' everywhere. The rest, I'm compelled to leave to the imagination.

I don't recall bein' carried into the hospital after the battle, but it must've been Carlton Willis who got me to an ambulance and had me carried in, along with Fredrick and Tommy and some of the others who were wounded. What I do remember, though, I wish I could forget.

Laudanum has the effect of causin' a man to forget his pain by fillin' his mind with all kinds of strange and terrifyin' images the likes of which mortal men ought not to behold in the natural realm. Mostly what I can recollect are just vague images, really, as if they were dark and foggy memories: images of soldiers runnin' toward me, their shadowy forms hideously deformed, with fiendish faces against a blood red sky. They moved toward me in a ghostly fashion, as if their feet never touched the ground. Their voices were screams of the most ghastly kind. There were bodies, like phantoms, flyin' through the air as if thrown by some monstrous beast. I could see the faces of Tommy and Fredrick on those bodies, but their faces were ghastly and twisted, and then I saw the specter of Sergeant Kline's face, huge and contorted, as if it were hangin' there in the air just mere inches from my own. He was struck through the forehead with a Minie ball, and his eyes and mouth were wide open, and there was a deathly scream that seemed to hang in the air all around.

Somewhere behind me in the blackness just beneath the screams, I could faintly hear someone callin' my name as if from far away. Then the voice became clearer and stronger until it overpowered the screams of the phantoms.

"Harleck!"

The dark red sky turned to orange, and then lighter and lighter until it was completely white, and the images and screams faded away.

"Harleck! Wake up!"

The whole sky was lit up with a bright white and painful light, and I had to squint my eyes and try to focus. The face of Sergeant Kline appeared again, callin' my name, but it was different this time. Then the fog in my head began to clear, and I realized that it wasn't the Sergeant's face at all. It was someone else. Then I heard the voice again, much clearer this time.

"Wake up, boy!"

I knew that voice.

I blinked my eyes hard, and the face of Carlton Willis came into focus.

"You owe me one, boy," he said with a big grin on his face and, gave me a friendly punch in the arm that sent a wave of pain through my chest that brought me fully awake. That was when I realized that the pain wasn't only from Willis' punch in the arm. It was on the other side of my chest too, in my right shoulder. I looked down and saw that I was wrapped in a large bandage that covered my whole shoulder and the top of my arm and under my armpit.

The grin grew even bigger when he saw me wince in pain, and he couldn't keep from chucklin' in delight at the thought of givin' me a hard time on account of gettin' myself all shot up.

"Don't you go passin' out on me again, now," he went on. "You're lucky to be alive! Someone up there must be watchin' out fer you," he said, cockin' his head up toward the sky. "Three more steps and that there cannon shell would've took your head clean off, boy!"

Cannon shell? Is that what it was?

My thoughts went back to the battlefield again.

"The battle . . . ?"

"You done fine, boy. We whupped 'em but good."

Then I remembered . . .

"Tommy . . . ? Fredrick?"

"Don't you worry 'bout them. You rest now, boy." He looked around. "You need to git better and git yerself outta this here place."

The laudanum must've done quite a number on me. My ears were ringin' like church bells and my skull started to hurt like I'd been cow-kicked in the side of the head. Then the pain in my shoulder washed over me again, and that's all I remembered for awhile.

Remembering

For the next few days, I laid there in that God forsaken hospital just driftin' in and out of sleep. The laudanum was gone, and I was hurtin' just bad enough so as not to be able to sleep soundly, so I started lookin' for ways to forget the pain. The best way I could think of to do that was to think about somethin' else, so I found myself thinkin' of home, back before the war.

I thought about dinners around the table with Mama and Pa, Joseph, Amos, and Vanessa. We may not've had as much as some folk, but Mama had a garden where she grew the most succulent turnips and carrots, plus onions, sweet peas, string beans, beets, radishes, and a lot of other things that were good eatin'. With just a small amount of meat—usually chicken or whatever the good Lord provided from huntin' or trappin', or out of the kindness of Pa's parishioners—my Mama could make the best tastin' soups and stews in all of Jefferson County. A far sight better than any meal I ever had in the army, to be sure.

I remembered huntin' with Tommy, Arty, and Fredrick. The four of us liked to go out huntin' for duck, goose, turkey, or rabbit whenever we could find the time. Tommy and Arty had a good huntin' dog too. Sometimes we'd get lucky and bring home four or five birds. Fredrick and Arty taught Tommy and I how to shoot, them bein' older and all. But Fredrick was the best shot of us all. He'd been huntin' since he was knee high to a mule. I reckon that's how he got to be such a good shot with the rifle.

Sunday afternoons were always some of my favorite memories too. I remembered our family visits to Maribel's plantation after church with a great deal of fondness. The meals were always impressive and there was always plenty. Maribel's folks, they'd usually serve up the tastiest roast pork, or roast beef, or tender duck, or chicken, all surrounded by a feast of sweet jellies and fresh bread rolls, cobblers, and fruit pies—enough to make a simple preacher's boy consider becomin' a glutton! Funny thing about the Nellises though: they had money, but they were always happy to share what the good Lord had blessed 'em with.

After Sunday dinner, Maribel and I, we'd sit together on the porch sippin' lemonade and talkin' and laughin' about the strangest of things. My favorite memory was of the day I first knew I was in love with her. It was a clear and chilly Sunday afternoon in November, and the mountain sky was blue as blue could be, with white fluffy clouds that drifted by on the cool breeze.

"You see that cloud?" she asked, pointin' up at the sky.

"Uh-huh."

"Sometimes I like to pretend that clouds are something else," she said with a smile.

"Like what?"

"Well, I think that one looks like a turtle," she pointed again thoughtfully.

"A turtle?" I replied, pokin' fun at her with a smile.

"Sure, silly. See the head and the curve of the shell there?" she answered, tracin' a line in the sky with her finger. "And there are the feet."

"That's no turtle," I mocked. "That's the meringue on the top of one of my Mama's lemon pies!"

"Oh, you!" she laughed, smackin' me playfully on the shoulder. "Of course *you* would only see food!" she teased back.

"I can't help it if I appreciate good cookin'!" I smiled at her and found myself wonderin' if Maribel even knew how to cook. Come to think of it, I'd never seen her cook before. The Nellises always had Samuel and Sarah, the house help, do most of the cookin'.

"Alright, how about that one?" she asked, pointin' at a large round cloud. "What does *it* look like?"

"Aw, that's easy," I said proudly. "That's a big ol' pile of mashed potatoes!"

"Nope," she said with a grin and a mischevious sparkle in her eye.

"Alright, then, what is it?" I asked.

"That's your big fat belly if you keep eating every cloud you see!" she gloated gleefully with a big smile.

Yessirree. She was just about everything a simple boy like me could ever want: beautiful, charmin', clever, and willin' to sit on the porch with a boy who was beneath her class. And I was plum smitten.

I remembered the way she looked on the day I left home almost like it was a brightly colored dream. I could remember every detail, from the way her pretty green eyes sparkled with tears of pride, to her tear-streaked cheeks, all pink and blushin', to the way her long auburn curls fell down around her neck and shoulders, to the pretty blue dress with white lace trim, and it all seemed just perfect. I reckon maybe some folks might think I was foolish to think of her that way, but to me that's just how she was: absolutely perfect. And the thought of how close I'd come to not keepin' my promise made me wanna get better real quick-like. How I longed to hold her in my arms again, or just to feel her touch.

And whenever thinkin' about Maribel got me to missin' her too much, I'd think about those early days in the army, back in April. I remembered how Sergeant Robertson had lined all the boys up on Washington Street in front of the Market House on that first glorious day. All of the new recruits were given rifles, and he showed us all how to march with the rifle at the "shoulder arms," but I already knew all of that on account of Joseph teachin' me. The recruits all marched in the back of the Company. Tommy and I marched together, and Arty marched just in front of us, so as he could show us how to march like proper soldiers. Arty, he'd made the march to Harpers Ferry once before with Joseph back in '59, so he knew just what to do. By the time we got the whole Company ready for the march it was already well past mid-day. We marched to Halltown first, where we met up with some other companies, then on to Harpers Ferry later that same night. It really wasn't all that far—only about seven miles altogether—but it took us more than eight hours to get there, what with all the stoppin' to pick up new recruits or load more gear and supplies into the wagons and all.

When we finally arrived at Harpers Ferry on April the eighteenth, it was just about midnight, but we could tell we were already too late. As we marched into the town, we could see the smoke and smolderin' remains of the fed'ral arsenal. A company from Berkeley that called themselves the Berkeley Border Guards had already arrived, and there were some other men from Harpers Ferry there too, but the fed'ral garrison was nowhere to be found. The army regulars had done their worst to burn what they couldn't carry, and then skedaddled across the Potomac into Maryland just a few hours before we arrived. The boys from Berkeley and Harpers Ferry and some of the townsfolk had labored hard to put out the fires and save what they could, which included a couple thousand rifles and hundreds of boxes of ammunition, along with some other things we thought might be important if war was really comin'.

After settin' up a hasty camp, which consisted of a few bivouac fires and a couple of tents for the officers, we finally had the chance to rest. The new recruits had our first taste of army food that night—beans and bacon cooked on a fire—before we were allowed to sleep. Some of the older men set up their own tents, but most of us just tried to sleep on the ground close to one of the fires—when we weren't out on sentry post, that is. But sleep didn't come easy that night. It was a cold, clear night, and we were flushed with excitement from the day.

"Well, this sure ain't home cookin'," Tommy said grinnin' as he ate a bite.

"Sure beats eatin' nothin' at all, though," Arty finished, lookin' at Tommy in that way older brothers sometimes do.

"So what'll we do tomorrow?" I asked, hopin' Arty might know somethin' I didn't.

"Don't know," he answered. "Reckon we'll find out tomorrow."

But I could hardly wait until tomorrow. We hadn't even started our soldier trainin' yet, but I didn't care. I was ready to march right off to battle and win a glorious victory for Virginia. Oh what a young, innocent, naive fool I was.

The next day turned out to be not near as exciting as I'd hoped. Some of the other companies started to arrive, and we moved our camp to a better location. Every day the camp grew bigger, and it wasn't long before the whole regiment had arrived. On the third day, we were called to line up by company. Colonel Allen gave us all the latest news from Richmond, and reminded us all of our military duties.

The Second Regiment, Virginia Volunteers had been formed in June of '60. But that was before I joined up, of course, so this was the first time I'd ever seen the whole regiment together in one place. There were ten companies in the regiment: The Jefferson Guards—that was us—we were called Company A. Other companies from Jefferson County were Company B, the Hamtramck Guards; Company G, Botts' Grays; Company H, the Letcher Riflemen; and Company K, the Floyd Guards. The Berkeley Border Guards became Company D, and another company from Berkeley County, the Hedgesville Blues, were called Company E. There were also two companies from Clarke County: Company C, the Nelson Guards; and Company I, the Clarke Riflemen. The Winchester Rifles were the only company from Frederick County. They became known as Company F, which completed the regiment.

Our Colonel, Colonel James Walkinshaw Allen, was a fairly tall but not very handsome man with a long face and nose, and deep set eyes. He had a full head of dark hair, neatly parted to one side, and a large, full beard. He had no sight in his right eye, which some said was on account of some boyhood misadventure, and it caused him to cock his head to the right sometimes so that we were never quite sure who he was talkin' to. But he seemed a good officer, and the men liked him well enough.

For the next two weeks after we reached Harpers Ferry, more and more soldiers arrived—boys from all over Virginia and regiments from Kentucky, Tennessee, and even Georgia—until the soldiers soon outnumbered the townsfolk. But with so many soldiers all together in one place, and soldier's bein' what they are, trouble was always close at hand. Of all the soldiers there, the boys of the Second Virginia were, by the whole, the best behaved lot. Most of us did a mite less drinkin' and got into less trouble than the boys in the other regiments such that they all took to callin' us "The Innocent Second." Some mocked us for bein' more pious than the other outfits, but I reckon it was more likely because we figured we'd best keep our noses clean since most of us lived nearby and had friends and kinfolk all over the north end of the valley. If a boy from the Innocent Second was caught drunk and disorderly, well, there was a good chance his mama'd hear of it, and then there'd be the devil to pay!

A desperate scream pierced the air and reminded me that I was still lyin' there in that hospital. From the sound of it, some poor unfortunate soul was undergoin' the surgeon's trade, and likely losin' an arm or a leg. With all my soul I wanted to just up and walk out of that terrible place lickety-split, but the pain was too great and I didn't have the strength for it. I looked around for someone to help me, but the only other souls in the room were also lyin' on blankets on the floor like me. I wasn't quite in command of all my faculties yet, but I vaguely recollect seein' windows with the drapes all pulled shut so as to keep out the sun. There was a small table near the doorway with a lamp on it that burned softly in the dark room, and the pungent smell of blood assaulted my nostrils. I wondered how much of it might've been mine, but then concluded that it might be best not to think on that too much.

The screamin' continued from the other room, but it was more muffled this time, like someone was holdin' somethin' over the poor boy's mouth. I tried again to get up, but I was too weak and the pain in my shoulder convinced me to lie still. So, since I couldn't get up, and there was no one to help me, I tried my best to forget that horrible place by thinkin' back on those early days when the First Brigade was just formed.

It was April the twenty-seventh, as I recollect, and Colonel Allen had the whole regiment form up on the hillside just outside of town. Besides the Innocent Second, there were four other regiments there: the Fourth, Fifth, Twenty-fifth, and Thirty-third Virginia Infantry Regiments; and a battalion of artillery known as the Rockbridge Artillery. All together, I'm told there were 2,611 men assembled there, such that all of the men, formed as they were, fairly covered the whole hillside. That was the first day I ever saw Colonel Jackson. He stood down there at the bottom of that hillside where all the men could see, and he read his orders out loud and told us that from that day on we'd be known as the First Virginia Volunteer Brigade. Then he gave a speech about discipline and duty, and dismissed us all. But that was when all the drillin' and marchin' and drillin' and shootin' and more drillin' started.

For the next four weeks, we marched to and fro and hither and thither, all over the lower valley—that's the northern end, by the way—tryin' to keep the Fed'rals on the Maryland side of the Potomac. The cavalry scouts said there was a new Yankee army fixin' to cross over into Virginia, and its commander, Gen'ral Patterson, had intentions to drive us clean out of the Shenandoah Valley. In the seventeen days between June the fourteenth and July the first, we pitched our camp in seven different places. We nearly marched our feet clean off, marchin' up and down that valley from Winchester to Martinsburg and back 'til we thought we might wear ruts in the road from our boots.

Thinkin' about all that marchin', I got to rememberin' just how hard it was on the feet. I reckon those army brogans they gave us were either a blessing or a curse; I can't decide which. They were sturdy enough alright, and came up just above the ankle to help keep a fella from twistin' a foot on the rocky ground of the Shenandoah. But they were tougher than an old mule's hide and very cruel to the feet. Those of us who were unlucky enough to get 'em were both grateful for the small bit of protection they offered, and sorry that they were nigh as painful as havin' no shoes at all, leastwise for the first few weeks anyway. At least I had Mama's stockin's, which helped a little to protect my feet from bein' ground into a bloody pulp. Some of the old-timers took to savin' pee in a jar 'til it was ripe, then pourin' it into their boots to soften the leather. But others, like me, couldn't abide the smell, so we chose to take our chances with the hard boots. Some of the boys even gave away their army shoes altogether and just wore the shoes they'd brought from home.

But even with Mama's stockin's, I can safely say that after all that marchin', even our blisters had blisters, and every step was more painful than the last. Then, when the blisters broke open, our stockin's got all soaked with water and blood, and the inside of our boots stayed wet for days, which only made the matter worse. After a few days, the smell of the blood in our boots was enough to draw a steady swarm of flies which buzzed incessantly all around our feet every time we stopped. When we finally stopped for the night, we didn't dare leave our boots on for fear of the rot. On the other hand, any man foolish enough to take off his boots at night and not cover up his feet paid the price a day or two later when the maggots started crawlin' around in the open sores, which produced an agonizin' itch that was nigh intolerable. Mercifully, by the end of the third week, my feet were startin' to toughen up quite a bit, and the marchin' started to get a little easier.

Every now and then, the searin' pain in my shoulder would bring me back to that miserable hospital again. Once I found myself cryin' out in agony, and a young man in a blood-soaked apron came into the room and bent down to see if I was alright.

"Pain . . . " I muttered, tryin' to catch my breath.

"The laudnum's all gone, friend. All I got's whiskey." He held out a bottle for me to drink, but I waved it away with my good arm.

I'd heard my Pa preachin' about the evils of whiskey before, and I wasn't rightly sure if I should be takin' it for pain, so I resolved to try and do without it if I could. I thought real hard and tried to remember back to that first battle back in the Shenandoah. On the first of July, it was, the Yankees finally got up their courage and crossed the river at Williamsport. Colonel Stuart's cavalry reported the enemy movement, and the First Brigade marched back up the valley to Hainesville. We met the Fed'rals the next mornin' just north of that town near a small crick known as Hoke's Run. The Fifth Virginia was deployed across the turnpike, with the Fourth in support. The Second was placed in reserve on the right, not far from where we'd just camped the night before, and Stuart's cavalry was sent out on the left flank. When the Yankees appeared across the way, we were told to load our rifles but not to fire until the order came.

The Rockbridge Artillery commander for the First Brigade was an Episcopalian priest named Capt'n William Pendleton, who claimed he knew my Pa. He had four guns in the battery which the artillery boys affectionately named Matthew, Mark, Luke, and John, whereupon they pledged to do their best to spread the gospel everywhere they went. These they deployed across the turnpike behind the Fifth Virginia.

The Yankees came out in the open, formed up in line of battle, and then advanced straight at the center of our line. They fired a volley and the boys from the Fifth returned fire. Some of the fellas in the Second thought we oughta shoot too, seein' as how we were in a perfect position to hit 'em from the side, but the order to fire never came.

After returnin' fire, the boys of the Fifth were ordered to fall back, which allowed Pendleton's artillery to open fire with three of the guns. This had the effect of clearin' the Yankees off the turnpike and slowin' 'em down a bit, but then the order came for the whole brigade to fall back.

Some of the boys tried to persuade Colonel Allen to let us hit the Yankees while they were confused from the cannon fire, but the Colonel just smiled and said, "Easy, boys. Our orders aren't to attack; just to keep 'em in front of us and slow 'em down a bit." So we just fell back slowly without ever firin' a shot.

I heard tell that ol' "Jeb" Stuart single-handedly surprised and captured a whole company of Yankees from Pennsylvania all by himself! They say he just rode right into 'em and told 'em that they were surrounded and they had better lay down their arms and surrender, which they promptly obliged. Then he simply marched 'em all back to his troopers and took the whole lot as prisoners! What a character he was!

The battle of Falling Waters, or Hoke's Run, as some called it, wasn't much of a battle, really—more like just a skirmish. Turns out the Yankees had two brigades to our one, so Ol' Jack was wise to fight a delaying action, what with the rest of the army bein' all spread out as it was. The biggest loss for the Innocent Second that day was our tents and a little ruffled pride. The Twenty-seventh Virginia was assigned to guard the supply train that day, so they were supposed to pack up all the tents and gear from the campsites into the wagons. But before they could finish packin' up our campsite, they had to fall back on account of the Yankee army comin' right through our camp. And don't you know those danged Yankees tore up every single one of our tents! All 150 of 'em! And brand new tents they were too. We all thought there was no call for that kind of rude behavior, so we took it a mite personal.

By that evenin', the Yankees had occupied Martinsburg, and we were still fallin' back. But Colonel Stuart's cavalry sure was keepin' 'em on their toes. The Fed'rals advanced as far as Bunker Hill, but then they just stopped, almost within sight of Winchester. I reckon those cavalry boys were doin' such a great job of confusin' and confoundin' ol' Patterson that he figured us to be a much larger force, so he turned back to Charles Town, and then on to Harpers Ferry. And there he stayed 'til we got the order to march to Piedmont to join Gen'ral Beauregard at Manassas.

Another wave of searin' pain made me cry out again. It was gettin' worse, and my shoulder felt real hot all around the wound, like someone was stabbin' me with a red hot poker. I looked around but I didn't see the young man anymore.

"H-help me . . . " I tried to call out weakly, but I wasn't sure if anyone could hear.

After another minute or so, he came through the door from the other room with the whiskey bottle still in his hand. This time he didn't even ask. He just lifted up my head with one hand and poured the whiskey into my mouth with the other. But I was in no condition to object.

I tried to swallow, but coughed and gagged when the first gulp took my breath away. But he just smiled and gave me another drink. It burned as it went down, but it wasn't long before my head started feelin' like it was floatin' off my shoulders, and the pain didn't feel quite so bad. Then I drifted off to sleep.

Miracles and Mixed Blessings

When I awoke I found myself lyin' and shiverin' on a bed of straw on the ground outside that hospital, my clothes all soaked with sweat. I could tell the fever was settin' in, and I reckoned I'd probably been put out to die like an ol' broken down mule just waitin' for someone to come along and shoot me. I started wonderin' if I'd ever see home again, and the thought of never again seein' Maribel's sweet face or sittin' around Mama's table with the family got me started prayin' real hard.

The fever has a funny way of distortin' a man's thinkin' so he can't really be sure how much time has gone by. I'm not rightly sure if it was hours or days. I only know it seemed like a long time, layin' there sweatin' and shiverin' and fadin' in and out of sleep. My shoulder still felt red hot, and every time I tossed and turned I received a painful reminder not to do so much tossin' and turnin'. But layin' still hurt nigh as much.

I woke one evenin' with raindrops fallin' on my face and realized I was bein' carried on a litter somewhere. It was dark and gray and rainy, but I could tell it wasn't quite night yet. I still couldn't figure out where I was bein' taken, or why. But the pain in my shoulder was there to remind me that I was still alive—at least for the time bein'—although the pain did seem a bit more tolerable, now that I think on it. The men who were carryin' me climbed up a few steps, then set me down on the front porch of a house. Then they rolled me off the litter, stuffed somethin' under my head as a pillow, picked up the litter, and walked away without so much as a "how do you do?" Before long, a negro lady came out to check on me, gave me some water to drink, and covered me with a blanket. It was a warm night from what I could tell, but I still laid there shiverin' on the cold hard floor all that night.

The next day I awoke to a familiar voice.

"Here he is."

It was Arty Johns! I knew that voice right away.

"There ya are, Wil. We thought maybe ya done walked all the way back to Charles Town!"

I opened my eyes but had to squint because the sky was so bright, and I could barely make out the shapes of two people. Then the familiar lines of Arty's face started comin' into focus, and behind him stood Tommy! He had a crutch under his right arm which he leaned on a bit, and he was holdin' a package in his left hand. I was so glad to see my two best friends alive that I nearly forgot about the fever and the pain in my shoulder.

"You sure had us worried there, kid," Arty said. "You were in that hospital for over two weeks. Had a terrible fever too. Then when I couldn't find ya this mornin', we feared the worst."

Two weeks? Has it been that long?

"Lucky for you, one of the fellas at the hospital remembered ya and told me they moved you to one of the nearby farm houses to recover. We've been lookin' all over for ya."

"We got somethin' for ya." Tommy handed Arty the package with a big grin on his face. "It's a package from Maribel! Want us to open it for ya?"

I felt my heart poundin' a little faster. "Would you mind?"

Arty took the package from Tommy and sat down next to me on the porch. That's when I first noticed the bandage wrapped around Tommy's right leg where it came to an end a few inches below the knee as he struggled to sit down without the help of his right foot.

My heart sank. "Your foot—"

I didn't know what to say.

"Aw, it's alright. Don't hurt as much anymore." I could tell he was just tryin' to be brave about it, but his eyes couldn't hide the disappointment. I reckon maybe he was comin' to terms with it, but I couldn't help but wonder what it must've been like losin' a foot like that. I wasn't sure if I could've been so brave about it, but it was just like Tommy. As long as I'd known him, I couldn't recollect him ever lettin' anything get him down.

"Besides, could've been worse, ya know," he said with a grin.

"Ain't that the truth," Arty chimed in, matter-of-factly.

Then I remembered . . . "What about Fredrick?"

I knew right away on account of how both of 'em just looked down at the floor and couldn't make themselves look at me.

"I'm real sorry, Wil . . . " Arty said in a low voice, lookin' up from the floor. "Fredrick—well—he didn't make it. He was shot in the chest and died the next day."

The news hit me so hard I felt like the whole world was pressin' down on my chest 'til I could hardly breathe. Then Arty went on with the rest of the news. He knew I'd wanna know.

"He didn't die for nothin', though," he said with hope in his eyes. "We won the battle. Whooped them Yankees but good too."

Then Tommy chimed in happily, "I heard there was a bunch of big wigs came out from Washington to see the battle, and when the Yankees all ran, all those big wigs got all caught up with all the horses and soldiers and cannons and wagons, all tryin' to use the same road to get back to Washington! Caused quite a panic too. 'The Great Skedaddle,' that's what they're callin' it!"

But my mind was still back on the Henry Hill. "What about the other fellas from the Second?"

So Arty told me us much as he knew. He said that Colonel Allen's head wound was gonna be okay. Capt'n Rowan was wounded in the leg, but it looked like he'd survive too. Sergeant Kline was dead, of course. All together from the Second Virginia, fifteen died in the battle, six had died after the battle so far, and fifty-five more were wounded, but some of them weren't expected to make it either. He didn't say it, but by the way he looked at me, I wondered if I might be one of 'em.

Then I remembered how Carlton Willis had saved me from the battle. I reckon I had mixed feelin's about that. I was grateful for bein' saved, but I wasn't real fond of the idea of bein' beholden to Willis on account of his havin' done so. But I'd think on that later.

Arty went on to explain that we were still in Manassas. He said the First Brigade had been reassigned to the Army of the Potomac, at least for the time bein', along with a good portion of the Army of the Shenandoah, and that Gen'ral Johnston was now in overall command of the Confederate armies in Virginia. Most of the army had crossed the Bull Run and was camped up near Centreville now, about eight miles up the road, waitin' for orders from Richmond to cross the Potomac and seize the Yankee capital.

It was Tommy that finally brought us back to the moment.

"So do ya wanna open this package from Maribel, or don't ya?"

"My shoulder hurts like the devil," I answered. "Would you help me open it?"

And help me they did. And they were glad for it too, seein' as how inside the box was a baker's dozen of Maribel's famous macaroons, which we promptly ate right down. I hadn't realized how hungry I was on account of the pain 'til I took that first bite. Then I ate six more macaroons! And there was a letter too, which Arty read to me, seein' as how I couldn't use my right arm to hold it open.

"That girl loves you, Wil." Tommy chided after Arty finished readin'.

"You think so?"

"Heck yeah! And if you can't see it, yer a dang fool!"

I felt my heart warm, and it was like waves of warm water were washin' over my whole body. I knew I had to be blushin', but Arty just looked at me and smiled.

"Looks like you better get well quick and help us win this war, so's you can get back home and marry that girl before she gets away!"

I couldn't keep myself from smilin' at what Arty said. I was a mite embarrassed about it bein' that obvious, but also relieved that someone else thought it might be a good idea too. I'd thought about marryin' Maribel before, but I'd never said it to anyone. But now I had somethin' else to get well for.

A Long Road Home

November 1861

The fall of 1861 is marked by relatively little activity in the eastern theater as the Union scrambles to rebuild the shattered Army of Washington D.C. and restore confidence among the citizenry. The victorious Confederate Army, on the other hand, has also done little. Advancing to within sight of the spires and steeples of the Union Capitol, they wait day after day on the banks of the Potomac while perhaps the single greatest opportunity to bring a swift end to the war slips through their fingers and is lost forever.

Joseph E. Johnston has been placed in command of all Confederate military forces in the District of Northern Virginia, but Johnston is a cautious leader and not prone to aggression. To compound matters, he feuds with Confederate President Jefferson Davis over having been appointed to the rank of general behind three other officers whom he considers junior to himself—among them, a former U.S. Army Colonel named Robert E. Lee. Insisting on waging only a defensive war, Johnston sits behind fortifications near Centreville and prepares for the Union to make the next move.

Across the Potomac, Abraham Lincoln has appointed a new commander for his army in the person of Major General George B. McClellan. McClellan is a skilled organizer who works with zeal and charisma to shape the undisciplined northern troops into a formidable fighting force. But he is also choked by caution. Convinced that Johnston commands a still superior force, McClellan begins plans for an elaborate amphibious invasion around Johnston's flank, rather than risking a frontal assault.

In the western theater, an obscure Union soldier-turned-failed-businessman-turned-soldier named Ulysses S. Grant is gathering an army near the confluence of the Ohio and Mississippi Rivers to challenge Confederate possession of the Mississippi. His initial successes garnish little attention, but little could he know that he is soon to become the North's first battle-tested war hero—though embroiled in controversy—for his actions on two bloody days in April 1862 at a place called Shiloh.

Meanwhile, back in the east, the Confederacy has already found a new hero in Thomas J. "Stonewall" Jackson. The nickname being given, of course, in reference to General Bernard Bee's rallying cry citing the courage of Jackson's First Virginia Brigade in battle at Manassas. By October, Jackson is again promoted, rising to the rank of major general, and in November he is given command of the Army of the Shenandoah. With 8,000 men, Jackson detaches from Johnston's army and returns to the Shenandoah Valley to begin making preparations for its defense. Nestled between the Allegheny Mountains to the west and the Blue Ridge to the east, this vital expanse of land in northern Virginia is considered "the breadbasket of the Confederacy" for its rich and fertile farmland. But it also holds great strategic value. Screened by mountains on both sides, it forms a concealed highway through which an army might pass relatively unharrassed all the way from Maryland and Pennsylvania into the heart of Virginia—or, if used in reverse, as a flanking approach to threaten Washington D.C.

August 12, 1861

Army of the Potomac, near Manassas

Sweetest Maribel,

I received your letter on the Friday last, but was delayed in writing back as I have been down with the fever these last few weeks. By now you may have read in the newspaper that I was among those wounded in the battle, but I am recovering well now. For this, I owe a great deal of thanks to the Lord above for hearing my prayers and answering them, and as well to a kindly Negro lady named Margaret. I believe she is a house slave who lives with the family who have been generously caring for us this past week or so. She has tended my wound, changed my bandages, and brought me soup every day, along with a cup of strange tea which I cannot recall ever tasting before.

The army is camped here near Centreville, but I am still back in the rear near Manassas with the others who are too weak or ill to fight. I am hopeful that Mr. Lincoln will think twice about continuing down this bloody road to war after the thrashing we gave the Yankees, but I fear he will not, and this war will go on.

You may also have learned that my good friend Fredrick Ruyter was killed in the battle, and also that Tommy Johns has lost his right foot. Tommy somehow manages to move about with great agility on the crutch that was made for him, but it will no doubt be more difficult for him to find work now. I cannot imagine what it must be like to have but one foot, and I hope that I may never find out for myself, as I would not desire to live the rest of my life as a cripple.

Fredrick's loss has been especially hard for me. He was a good friend and a fine marksman, and very brave in battle. I will *greatly miss his presence should we have to face our enemy on the field again. He was well liked in the Jefferson Guards and he will doubtless be missed by many in the company. I shall always remember with fondness our hunting together and working together in Mr. Jennings' shop. I pray for Mr. Ruyter each day, and hope that you will too, as he has now lost both his wife and his oldest son.*

There are rumors that we may be recalled to the Shenandoah, and we are hopeful that we may be able to return to the Valley soon. With my whole heart I long to hold you in my arms and gaze upon the beauty of your face again. I pray you will wait for me until that day should come, by God's grace. Until then, may God keep you safe and well.

Your loving and devoted,
Wil

Reunions

I was never so glad as to be back on my feet again and to put that miserable hospital behind me as quick as I could. I'd spent the last nine days in the town of Manassas lyin' on the porch of a home that belonged to an older gentleman named Mr. Lewis. He was a lawyer there, and he and his wife had been gracious enough to take a few of us in while we recuperated. I didn't mind layin' on the porch so much. It provided some shelter from the sun and the rain, and it was a far sight better than lyin' in the blood-soaked straw in that converted barn that served as a God-forsaken excuse for a hospital. I'd've gladly traded everything I owned if it meant not havin' to see the inside of an army hospital ever again.

It was a hot August night when Arty came back for me. It struck me odd how the nights there weren't much cooler than the days, and the days were nigh intolerable. We weren't all that far from Jefferson County, maybe only three or four days' march, but at least up in the Valley the summer nights were cooler.

It took us the better part of two hours to get from the Lewis house to the place where the First Brigade was camped. Arty said they'd moved to the new camp in early August when conditions at Camp Jackson, near the battlefield, became unbearable. "Camp Maggot," he called it. He said the smell of the rottin' corpses and the foul-tastin' water were makin' a lot of the boys sick. Some even came down with a deadly fever they called Typhoid.

So Gen'ral Jackson ordered the brigade to be moved across the Bull Run to a new camp on the high ground about a mile or so from Centreville. There they'd built permanent quarters where the water was clear and they were far away from the stench of death that still hung over the battlefield. The new camp was called Camp Harmon, and it was a far sight better than any army camp we'd ever had before. Instead of our bivouac tents, or just sleepin' on the ground, we actually had wood huts for sleepin' in.

It was good and dark when Arty and I arrived at camp that evenin'. I reckon I should've expected some amount of teasin' and tauntin' when I first walked back into camp, but it still felt good to be back with the boys from home.

"Hey! Look who finally decided to come back to the land of the livin'!"

"'Bout time you got off yer back and got back ta work, Wil!"

"Next time be sure to duck, boy!"

And so on and the likes.

All this, of course, was followed by a round of chuckles and smiles all around.

Then I heard the voice of Carlton Willis out of the dark from just outside the fire's glow.

"Hey Harleck. Seein' as how you owe me one, boy, I guess you'll be takin' my sentry post fer the rest of the week—and doin' my cookin' too!"

Then he stepped into the light and I recognized that familiar crooked grin and the gleam in his eye right away. It was the same gleam he always got when he was gettin' his delights by pickin' on someone. But I'd long since resigned myself to it, seein' as how I was, in fact, in his debt after all. So I determined to just pay my debt and be done with it. Besides, I couldn't be sure, but I thought maybe I saw a hint of an honest smile in that mockin' grin for once.

"Don't you worry 'bout him, Wil. He's just glad to see ya," Arty said, not too loud, as he patted me on the good shoulder. "At least he ain't drunk this time."

A little while later, as we were sittin' around the fire havin' dinner, I realized I was actually enjoyin' an army meal! It must've been the first solid meal I'd had in weeks. Most of the Company was there that night, but I couldn't help but notice the missin' faces of Fredrick and Sergeant Kline. Capt'n Rowan was there, but he walked with a cane now and hobbled when he walked. Then I noticed that Tommy wasn't there.

"Where's Tommy?"

I searched Arty's face for some sorta sign to tell what'd happened to Tommy. But his easy smile reassured me that the news wasn't all bad.

"Mustered out. The army sent him home just last week. Can't march and fight with just one leg, ya know."

But the smile disappeared when the discussion got around to those departed souls who were no longer among us. I'd never figured on so many of us endin' up on the casualty lists in the newspapers. All in all, twenty-three men of the Innocent Second were killed; fifteen in the battle, and eight died later; and fifty-three were wounded, includin' Tommy, the Capt'n, and me.

After dinner, some of the fellas sat around the fire singin' and playin' on the fiddle and the squeezebox, but I went to collect my gear from the supply wagon, then Sergeant Robertson assigned me a bed in the same hut with Arty, Sean, Carlton, and a few other fellas from the company. I'd been thinkin' about what Willis had said.

I don't suppose it'd hurt me any to take his sentry for a night or two, seein' as how he did carry me off the battlefield, and he did come and check on me in the hospital and all.

So I went lookin' for him, and found him at the wash tub scrubbin' his shirt out. I don't seem to recall ever seein' Carlton Willis with his shirt off before. He had a chest like an ox, and pert nigh as hairy, and covered with scars such that I had to make myself look him in the eye so as not to stare.

"I've been thinkin' about what you said earlier," I started.

He stopped scrubbin' and looked up from the shirt for just a second to see if I was foolin' or serious, then he looked back down and went on scrubbin'. "Yeah? What about it?"

"Well, I reckon you're right. I do owe you one."

"Damn right you do," he went on scrubbin'. "Nearly got myself killed tryin' to save your hide." Then he paused and looked up with a skeptical look on his face. "So?"

"So I wanna pay my debt."

He went back to scrubbin'. "Ya do, huh?"

Before I could even get a word out, he went on. "Alright then. I got the second post tonight at ten."

"Consider it done," I blurted out, tryin' to sound confident.

"Alright then," he repeated. And that was all he said.

I passed a restless night after standin' Carlton's sentry post. Gettin' myself reacquainted with the tedious routines of camp life proved harder than expected. I'd only been gone for just over three weeks, but it might just as well've been three months. I felt like a new recruit all over again. Still, it was good to be back with friends and comrades. Heck, it was good to be anywhere besides that hospital or layin' around on that porch.

The next week stretched into a month of endless drillin', mornin', noon, and night, occasionally interrupted by sentry duty, latrine duty, which was called "johnny detail," cookin', or "mess duty," and then more drillin'. Since the First Brigade was camped behind the front lines, life in our camp was about as far from exciting as it could get.

There were days when we actually prayed that we'd get some orders to march somewhere—anywhere—just to have somethin' else to do.

There was a sizable collection of merchants and profiteers who'd set up a camp called "sutler's row" just at the edge of our camp where a fella could get just about anything he wanted for a price. I reckon they had just about everything from a shave and a haircut to tobacco and coffee to unsavory women and hard liquor, if a man was so inclined. I was only too happy to get a shave and a haircut for the first time in two months, and the coffee wasn't too bad, but I had no use for the liquor or the women.

Most of the boys from the Innocent Second pretty much stayed away from the drinkin' and the whorin', but liquor was Carlton's weakness and somehow he always managed to find some when the boredom got too much. One evenin' in early September, he and one other fella decided they were gonna go and have some fun, so they came by to see if they could get anyone else to go with 'em.

"Any of you fellas wanna go over to sutler's row tonight?" Carlton asked.

"Depends," Sergeant Robertson said, lookin' up from the skillet he was cookin' with. "What for?"

Now Carlton must've figured out right away that the Sergeant wasn't buyin' what he was sellin', because he didn't try very hard to talk him into it. "Aw, ain't nothin' but a little fun," he chided. "What ol' Tom Fool don't know won't hurt 'im."

Then he spotted me.

"How 'bout you, Harleck?" he grinned real big, showin' off his missin' tooth. He knew I wasn't a drinker, but he was bound and determined to corrupt my soul somehow.

"No, thanks," I said, lookin' away so as not to let him see how nervous I was.

"Aww, c'mon boy. I know a pretty girl over there who'll treat ya real good. Make a *real* man out of ya," he said hopefully. Then he slapped the other fella on the shoulder. "Ain't that right?" he added.

"Oh, yeah. She's real pretty alright. Take real good care of ya!" the other fella agreed. Then they both had a chuckle on me.

Now I'd never been with a woman before, but I remembered my Pa preachin' about harlots and adulteresses, and I wasn't about to go foolin' around with some strange woman I didn't know—especially not some harlot. Besides, I'd heard stories about some other fellas gettin' some sort of ailment from whorin' around, and I wanted no part of it.

"No, thanks," I said again, firmer this time.

"C'mon, boy. Can't stay a mama's boy forever," Willis taunted. "Gotta grow up and be a man sometime."

"Let the boy be, Willis," Sergeant Robertson shot back. But they were already walkin' away.

Carlton's visits to sutler's row were usually followed by Sergeant Robertson roundin' him up and gettin' him back to camp before he could get into some kinda trouble. After all, the Innocent Second had a reputation to uphold. What started back in April as a few of the boys from the Fifth Regiment pokin' fun at us had turned into a matter of pride for most of the fellas from the Second. The last thing we needed was to have our good name soiled and sullied in a fit of drunken tomfoolery.

Mid-September came but still no orders arrived to move on Washington, so we just sat by on our side of the Potomac and did nothin' while that danged Yankee army trained and drilled and grew larger every day. Ol' Tom was just about fit to be tied. So hot and bothered he was over the lack of orders from Richmond that he canceled his regular weekly speech to the brigade on account of how he could barely contain his contempt in front of the men.

Early in October we got word that he was to be promoted to Major Gen'ral and a new gen'ral was takin' command of the "Stonewall Brigade." It goes without sayin' that this news wasn't any too popular with most of the boys. In the days after the battle at Manassas, the man called Stonewall had quite outgrown all the jokes about his fatherly ways and his odd eccentricities. Oh, we may've still called him "Ol' Tom Fool" or "Ol' Jack" from time to time, but in truth he'd become a genu-ine hero and legend in the brigade. Whenever I'd see him sittin' atop Little Sorrel with that ol' yellow cap pulled down almost over his eyes always made me chuckle inside. But then I couldn't help but join in the multitude of cheers cascadin' down the length of the camp as he rode by. Say what you want about ol' Stonewall. He may've been a hard taskmaster, but he was *our* gen'ral and we didn't take too kindly to the idea of someone else takin' his place. Many a talk was had around the bivouac fires that week about just what was to become of the man and his brigade.

By that time it was plain to us that the Billy Yanks were all dug in behind their earthworks around Washington like ticks on a dog, and it sure didn't look like they were fixin' to come out. So we just sat there and waited. It was a cool and cloudy day on the fourth of October when the brigade was called to form up on the parade field. There was a light rain that was almost a mist that mornin', which, when combined with the chill in the air and the prospect that we were about to receive bad news, made us feel none too joyful. Four of the five regiments of the First Brigade were there that day. Only the Fifth Virginia was absent on account of picket duty. The Innocent Second was placed near the center of the brigade, and Company A was placed in the front row. And so it was, whether by some strange coincidence or by the hand of God Himself, that I found myself front and center of the brigade on that day.

After about a half hour or so, one of the colonels called the brigade to attention. There was no cheerin' for Ol' Jack this time as he rode up. I half expected the men to break ranks and try to crowd up around him, but they all held their place—and their tongues. When he reached the spot right in front of me, he wheeled the famous charger around and reared up, and for just an instant I saw the flash of that familiar smile. Then Little Sorrel lighted again on his front feet, and the smile was gone just as quick.

He stood up in his stirrups so as he could be seen and heard by the whole brigade. In his gloved hand he clutched a folded up piece of paper which I took to be his orders. He waived it in the air over his head briefly, then started to speak. I still recollect those words like it was yesterday, ringin' clear and true in my mind like a church bell on a Sunday mornin'.

"In the Army of the Shenandoah, you were the First Brigade . . . " he said loud and clear, then paused. "In the Army of the Potomac, you were the First Brigade . . . " He paused again like he was readin' poetry, then continued. "In the Second Corps of *this* army, you are the First Brigade . . . " Then he paused again and looked across the brigade like he was surveyin' a battlefield. "And you are the First Brigade . . . " he swallowed hard with pride, and his voice wavered, " . . . in the affection . . . of your general."

Then he took a deep breath and that familiar fire returned to his eyes, and his face hardened again just like it had on that hot day on the Henry Hill just before the attack. He cleared his throat, and his voice became loud and clear again.

"I hope, by your future deeds and bearing, you will be handed down as the First Brigade in this, our Second War of Independence! Farewell!"

And with that, he wheeled again, waived his hat in the air, and flashed that brilliant smile once again. Then he spurred the horse and rode off at a gallop, and the whole world broke out into cheers of, "Jackson! Jackson! Jackson!"

Home for Christmas

The October days were gettin' shorter and the nights cooler, and the leaves in the trees near Centreville turned bright as rooster feathers. I reckon the fall colors lasted a mite longer there than they did back home in the valley. Well, at least that much was good.

Colonel Allen, much recovered from his head wound, sent word to the commissary major that the Second Regiment needed new blankets, as the weather was turnin' cold. They were a welcomed comfort, to be sure, and made the nights a bit more tolerable. But the added warmth at night was small consolation for the conspicuous lack of fresh meat in our vittles. By the end of the second month of campin' in the same place, our huge army had all but used up the supply of livestock from the surroundin' countryside. Grain was still plentiful, it bein' harvest time and all, but most of our meat had to be brought in by train, which meant smaller meat rations. So our meals in camp mostly consisted of flour formed into hard cakes called "tack" and fried in a skillet with a little bacon grease for flavor. It was a far cry from home cookin', to be sure, but there wasn't much use bellyachin' about it.

Somethin' must've happened down in Richmond because, after three months of hearin' nothin' at all from our fair capital, all of a sudden the telegraph wires were alive with messages. It seemed like new orders were comin' in every day. On October the twenty-second, Gen'ral Johnston was promoted to overall command of the Confederate Army of the Potomac. Then Gen'ral Jackson was placed in charge of the Valley District back home.

Three weeks later, a new colonel named Richard B. Garnett was ordered to take command of the First Brigade, and the brigade was transferred to the Army of the Shenandoah under Gen'ral Jackson. This was welcome news to most of the fellas, seein' as how it meant that we'd still be marchin' with Ol' Jack. And it also meant we'd be goin' back home soon.

Our new brigade commander was also a Virginia man—from Essex County, I believe it was said. We didn't really know much about him, but he made a fair enough impression on the men. He was fairly young with a manly face and neatly trimmed mustache and beard, and he had a well-kempt appearance about him.

By mid-November, to our great relief, we found ourselves boardin' a train at Manassas Junction bound for Strasburg and home. When we arrived in Strasburg, it'd already been rainin' steadily in the valley for two days, and the ground was soft and muddy everywhere a man could put his foot. We retrieved our gear and piled out of the train into the cold rain. As I slung my pack up onto my back I was rudely reminded of my wound by the sharp pain surgin' through my shoulder and down through my chest and arm. Sean was standin' nearby and saw me wince in pain.

"That looked like it hurt a bit, Wil. You want me to carry that for ya?"

I was grateful for his offer, but I couldn't make myself take him up on it, even if it meant walkin' all the way to Winchester in pain.

"Nah. It's alright. Just a little tender, that's all."

"You sure? I can carry both yours and mine."

He sounded sure of himself, but I wasn't so sure. Sean was a farm boy and strong for his size, but not very big, and carryin' two packs was bound to slow him down on the march.

"Thanks, but I'm alright. I can manage it," I answered again, tryin' not to let the pain show.

"Alright then. Suit yerself." Then he just smiled and shrugged.

By the time we formed up for the march to Winchester, the rain had slowed to a light drizzle, but the roads were so rain soaked that the soft mud was already ankle deep and the water ran down through the wagon ruts like small streams. Funny thing about marchin' in the mud: the further back in the formation a man found himself, the worse the mud got. By the time a few hundred boots had stepped in the same place, the mud there was more like tar. It was slick and treacherous to tread on, and our boots picked up great accumulations of it with every step. Some of it was in turn deposited on the ground with the next step, only to be replaced by yet more mud as the foot again left the ground. After a few miles of this, a man's legs began to tire, so his marchin' started to bog down until it resembled more of a slow shuffle than a military march.

But we kept right on marchin' and sloggin' up that muddy road from Strasburg to Winchester. And even though my feet were gettin' heavier and the weight of the pack on my shoulder made it hurt more with each step, still every step closer to home seemed somehow easier than the last. Most of the trees in the valley were bare by then, but the fresh mountain air always made everything smell so fresh and green just after a rain. It'd only been four months since we left, but it seemed like a year, and the cool fresh air in our nostrils was like medicine for the soul.

By the time we arrived at Camp Stephenson, just north of Winchester, it was late evenin' and we were quite a sight to behold, all covered with mud from the waist down. One would've thought that our first order of business would've been to find some way to get our clothes—and ourselves—clean, but we were too exhausted from marchin' in that confounded mud. Some of the boys took the time to start a fire and cook a bit to eat before turnin' in for the night, but others just went straight off in search of a dry place on the ground to sleep. It was a cold night, and we were glad for our new blankets, but even they could only just take the edge off the chilly Shenandoah night air. So we piled up what little dry firewood we could find and I slept close to the fire, but not so close as to chance catchin' my oil cloth alight—with me on it.

The next day we set about cleanin' up and buildin' our winter camp. It was hard bein' so close to home and loved ones and all, and yet still not bein' able to see 'em, but that was life in the army. A few of the boys in other units got up the courage to slip away durin' the night, but most of us didn't dare try. We heard Gen'ral Jackson had three men shot for desertion. One thing about Ol' Jack: he wasn't one for toleratin' shirkers. He was a God-fearin' man, and in his book, laziness and dereliction of duty were sins of the most grievous kind.

So I contented myself with just knowin' that home was just up the road a bit, and I wrote letters to fill up what free time I had between buildin' and drillin' and cookin' and picketin'. Gettin' letters to and from home was quite a bit faster now that we were just one county away. So I wrote to Maribel, Mama, Amos, and Vanessa, and got letters in return from all of 'em.

One day in late November, L'tenant Colonel Botts stopped by to see Capt'n Rowan. Mr. Lawson Botts, Esquire, was a lawyer in Charles Town before the war. He was one of the fellas that was appointed to defend the Yankee abolitionist John Brown back in '59. When the war started, Botts formed his own company, Botts' Grays, which we now called Company G. Upon our return to the Valley, Ol' Jack had promoted him to Provost Marshall in Winchester, which post afforded him the privilege of travelin' around a bit.

Anyways, he and Capt'n Rowan bein' friends and all, he stopped by on his way up to Charles Town and offered to personally carry the Capt'n's mail back home for him. It was lucky for me that he was also a member of my Pa's congregation, so he'd sometimes stop by and check on me too, whenever he was around. And seein' as how he was goin' that way already, he asked if I had any letters or messages for Mama and Pa he could deliver, for which I was only too happy to be obliged.

We spent the rest of November and the first part of December there at Camp Stephenson waitin' for the Yankees to make their next move. We figured they'd pretty much lost the nerve to fight, so we set about makin' sure they stayed on their own side of the Potomac. On December the seventeenth, the regiment got orders to march up to the number five dam, just a few miles upriver from Williamsport. I reckon somebody thought that if we destroyed the dam, it might keep the Yankees from usin' the Chesapeake and Ohio Canal to ship coal to Washington D.C. Problem was, the Yankees didn't take too kindly to us tryin' to blow up that dam, so they placed a battery of artillery on the Maryland side to make life difficult for us. We tried workin' at night, but the fed'rals proved to be more clever and resourceful than we thought. To make matters worse, the water was so cold comin' down out of the mountains that we feared we might catch pneumonia. So, after five wet, cold, miserable nights of tryin' with no luck to destroy that dam, we finally gave up the idea and marched back to Winchester.

After we returned to Camp Stephenson on December the twenty-second, Colonel Allen obtained permission from Gen'ral Jackson to grant three days' furlough for some of the regiment for Christmas. Seein' as how we were so close to home, Arty, Sean, and I set out for Charles Town the very next mornin' along with several other fellas from the company. I reckon only the Almighty could've persuaded Ol' Jack to be so generous as to let so many of the men go home all at once, but we weren't about to question it. We were just plain "tickled pink," as my Mama would say, to avail ourselves of such a rare blessing.

By the time we arrived in Charles Town it was Christmas Eve and the weather was cool, damp, and cloudy, but the streets of home never looked better to my eyes. My tired feet carried me very quickly indeed down Washington Street past the court house all decorated with pine boughs and then around the corner and down Church Street toward home.

I was never so glad to see my Mama cry as I was that night when I came through the door of our old parish house. There were many hugs and tearful kisses to go around, and I can't recollect ever bein' so glad to see my little brother Amos and my sister Vanessa as I was that Christmas Eve. Even Pa had a smile on his face, and I could see the look of relief in his eyes as he stood nearby and watched our happy reunion.

I think it was about Mama's third hug when she squeezed me just wrong and made me wince just a bit in the face. She'd known I was wounded in the shoulder, but I didn't mention it much in my letters on account of not wantin' to make mountains out of mole hills. Well, judgin' by her reaction, she was so happy to see me home that she'd plumb forgot about it. I watched with some bewilderment as she let go and stepped back with a gasp and a confused look on her face.

"Wh—?!"

Then right away she remembered, and her whole face turned red with embarrassment.

"Oh, Wil . . . " she started to apologize, but then I thought I saw a flash of admonition in her brown eyes, like an ol' mother hen about to scold her chicks, as if I'd been dishonest with her about the whole affair.

"Now Wil Harleck, why didn't you tell me . . . " she started in, but then stopped again. Lucky for me, that also passed quickly, and a look of relief washed over her face. I reckon the fact that I was standin' there alive and well might've had somethin' to do with it. And it bein' Christmas Eve and all probably didn't hurt either.

"Well, never mind that," she said. "I'm just glad you're home." Then finally came the soft look of a mother's compassion, and her eyes welled up with tears again. She took me in her arms and buried her face in my good shoulder so as not to let anyone see her cry. Then, almost as quickly as it all started, she stepped back, wiped the tears from her cheeks with the corner of her apron, then smiled.

"Oh! You must be starved!" she exclaimed. "I'll fix you somethin' to eat." And just like that she was off to the kitchen and all was well again.

Dinner that night was like nothin' I've ever tasted before or since. It's remarkable how good chicken and dumplin's can taste to a man who's been livin' mostly on army rations. Heck, my best meal in six months had been that cup of rabbit stew before the battle.

Amos sat across the table from me at dinner and waited patiently while Pa said grace, but I could tell he was burstin' with excitement, just by the light in his eyes.

"What's it like, Wil?" he blurted out eagerly like a school boy who's just had his first kiss. He could hardly wait to talk about the war and what life in the army was like. It was no secret that he wanted to join the army like me, but I wasn't all that sure I wanted him followin' in my footsteps anymore.

"Worse than you could—" I started, thinkin' maybe I could discourage Amos, but then I caught the look of alarm that flashed in my Mama's eyes, and decided better of it. "Worse than . . . the stories Joseph used to tell us, that's for sure," I corrected quickly with a smile, "but it's not so bad, all things considered." I knew if I told Amos the truth of the matter, Mama would never sleep another night as long as I was gone, sure as I live. Worse yet, the look on Amos' face said he wasn't the slightest bit discouraged.

"How'd you get hurt?" he pressed. "I mean, what was it like in the battle?"

"Amos . . . " Pa warned with a stern look in his eye that made the smile on Amos' face fade just a bit. "That kind of talk is not for the dinner table," Pa scolded.

Amos looked down at the table for a moment, but it wasn't long before that excited look brightened his face again.

"I can't wait 'til I can join up too!" he announced proudly, but that only brought another disapprovin' look from Pa, and the look on Mama's face said she wasn't real fond of the idea, either. Well, at least the three of us agreed on that. I'd seen the horrors of war, and I didn't want Amos havin' any part of it.

"Not yet, Amos. Maybe next year," Pa said flatly—almost prayerfully. "Lord willing, the war will be over by then."

"Amen," I agreed, much to Amos' dismay. But I reckoned it was better he was disappointed in me—and safe and sound at home—than to have him fightin' in this war too.

"Won't it be nice to go to Christmas mass together tomorrow?" Mama asked, hopin' to change the subject.

"It sure will, Mama," I reassured her, glad to have somethin' else to talk about besides the army and the war.

We finished the rest of our dinner with pleasant conversation, and Amos and I even had seconds. Then Mama topped it all off with one of her famous sweet potato pies, and boy was it delicious. But if dinner was good, then takin' a warm bath and sleepin' in a real bed in clean clothes and linens for the first time since April was like heaven.

That Christmas was a day I won't soon forget either. Never before nor since can I recall a day of such momentous joy and such great distress all within the span of one sunrise to sunset. As happy as I was to be reunited with my family—all exceptin' Joseph, that is—I could hardly contain my excitement at the thought of seein' Maribel's lovely face again.

I rose early, got dressed in my Sunday clothes, which fit a mite more loosely than I remembered, and headed over to the church with Pa. I wanted to be sure and arrive early so as to surprise Maribel, and so as not to miss any chance of talkin' with her a little before church.

But Pa hadn't prepared me for what I'd see when I walked up to the front doors of the church. The once-beautiful doors that formed the entrance to the church now hung strangely on their hinges. And there were scratches in the paint and deep gouges in the wood that looked like they'd been made by the butts of rifles and the sharp ends of bayonets.

As we passed through the doors and into the vestry, the sanctuary, and the sacristy, I could scarcely believe my eyes and nose, and my blood boiled hot with fury. Didn't those danged Billy Yanks have an ounce of respect for the Lord's house? I knew my Pa'd done his best to clean up and repair the damage, but it was plain to see they'd used the church as their own personal bivouac and didn't even bother to have the decency to walk to the privy, but just used any corner they could find. I know because there was no hidin' that latrine smell. As many times as I'd done johnny detail, I'd know that smell anywhere.

I looked at Pa with disbelief and anger on my face, but his eyes just held my gaze, and he kept his peace.

"Yankees?"

He nodded.

"When?"

"Not three weeks ago. They left when Jackson returned to the Valley. I guess they figured they'd be safer on the other side of the Potomac for a while."

"They figured right." I couldn't look at Pa. I was too perturbed and distracted lookin' around to see what else might've been damaged.

Then I thought of Ol' Jack and how whenever he wasn't talkin' about military matters he was always talkin' about his faith in God. He'd've been most displeased with such behavior, whether it be done by Yankee hands or our own. He didn't take much of a likin' to blasphemers, no matter which side they were on.

"That's the nature of war, son," Pa said. "There've been atrocities committed on both sides, I can assure you. And now that you've seen with your own eyes, I'm sure no one needs to tell you that it's an ugly business."

But I was still mad as a wet hen.

"It's a good thing Gen'ral Jackson hasn't seen this," I said, gettin' myself all worked up, "or he'd have ol' Jeb Stuart cross over the Potomac and round 'em all up to be shot—every last one of 'em—sure as I'm standin' here!"

But then Pa got that far off look in his eyes that always told me he was about to say somethin' deep and wise.

"We're not guaranteed an easy life, son. War or no war, hard times come on us all, and life is full of disappointments. But God's love; now that's something you can always count on."

He paused to reflect for a moment, then his eyes brightened and the corners of his mouth turned upward ever so slightly, and I could tell he was ready to change the subject.

"No matter. It's Christmas. This is a time to be joyful. Let's be about the business of the day and leave the rest for another day."

Before long some of the folk started showin' up for the Christmas mass. A lone young boy of about twelve or thirteen arrived first, and Pa greeted him.

"Good morning, Thomas. Merry Christmas."

"Merry Christmas, Father Harleck."

"Would you light a few extra candles this morning, Thomas? I think it might help make the place smell a little more pleasant for Christmas mass," Pa said with a kind smile.

The boy went straight to the vestry and put on the familiar white robe I used to wear until about four years ago. But I was more accustomed to seein' Amos wear the acolyte robe in recent days. I looked at Pa, but he must've seen the question on my face. I didn't even get it out of my mouth before he gave the answer.

"Amos is seventeen now, son; practically a man. That old robe doesn't fit him anymore. Time to pass it to a younger boy, just as you did. Thomas, here, is the Eldridges' son. You know Mr. Eldridge, the apothecary?"

The young acolyte was dressed neatly enough beneath the robe, with a tussle of long brown hair on his head which had doubtless been neatly combed earlier that mornin'. And as he walked, it was plain to see he was accustomed to wearin' nice shoes. He went quickly about lightin' incense and candles for the mass, and in no time at all the church began to smell more like I'd always remembered it, and I could barely make out the foul odor the soldiers had left behind.

The Johns family was the next to arrive. Arty flashed me a smile and waved, and Tommy was grinnin' from ear to ear as he hobbled along on his crutch, though much quicker than the last time I'd seen him.

"Hey, Wil! Welcome home! Merry Christmas!"

"Merry Christmas, Tommy! Arty!" I went quickly to meet 'em and the three of us hugged and laughed in joyful reunion.

A small crowd of people was gatherin' at the church now, and there were many handshakes and warm greetings as folks began to make their way into the church.

"Welcome home, son. Folks 'round here are real proud of you boys."

"Welcome home, Wil. Merry Christmas. Good to see you well and back home."

Finally the carriage bearin' the Nellis family came up the street into view. It was the moment I'd been waitin' for all mornin', but now that it was upon me, I found my feet unable to move, my eyes unable to look around, and my mouth unable to speak. It's a cryin' shame the things a woman can do to a man without even sayin' a word or liftin' a finger.

Then I felt a friendly nudge in the shoulder to remind me that Tommy was still standin' beside me.

"There she is, Wil. The future Misses Wil Harleck!" he laughed in that friendly familiar way I'd heard so many times before. Thing about it was, I knew he was just foolin', but somethin' deep down inside of me desperately hoped it was true. So there I stood, watchin' that carriage draw up to the church and hopin' no one would notice how red my face was.

The carriage came to a stop and a young Negro driver dismounted and came around to open the door. Mr. Nellis was the first to step out, of course. And bein' a gentleman and all, he offered his hand to Mrs. Nellis, who looked up at me as she was steppin' down, and a look of pleasant surprise came across her face.

"Why, if it isn't Wil Harleck, home from the war! And aren't you a handsome sight?!"

I tried to say somethin' polite in response, but I couldn't make the words come out right. So I just blurted out, "Merry Christmas, Ma'am." Then my eyes caught sight of the most beautiful thing I'd ever seen. The wide brim of white lace and red ribbon on her hat blocked the sight of her lovely face as she looked down to find the carriage step. But my heart still skipped a beat or two at the sight of her long reddish brown curls which shone like gold in the Christmas mornin' sunlight.

She stepped down from the carriage with the grace of an angel; her light delicate hand still in her pa's. Her dress was dazzlin' white and all trimmed with red ribbon and pink lace. It had a wide neckline that spanned from the corner of one shoulder all the way across to the other and dipped down just low enough to reveal the smooth ivory skin of her neck and just a hint of her womanly attributes, while still bein' modest enough to keep the reputation of a proper young lady.

I thought my heart might just pound right out of my chest when she looked up and her eyes caught mine. Then that bright smile lit up her face and right near made my knees buckle.

"Wil!"

I was very glad my knees didn't actually buckle when she ran right up, leapt into my arms, threw her arms around my neck, and kissed me square on the lips! Good and long too! I reckon if it'd been any other occasion, folks might've thought her unladylike to be so forward and all, but the situation bein' what it was, I think most folk were inclined to let it pass. Besides, it was mostly our family and friends standin' around, and they were too busy smilin' to be offended.

My heart raced as I felt her warmth in my arms and her tender moist lips pressin' against mine. It was a kiss from heaven, and I never wanted it to end.

She took my head in her hands and kissed my face again as I set her back on her feet.

"You came back to me," she said with a big smile, her voice almost bubblin' with excitement.

I hesitated for just an instant, not wantin' to disappoint the girl.

"It's . . . only for a couple of days. I have to go back tomorrow."

The smile faded and her shoulders stiffened, and she got that look on her face that told me I was in trouble again. It was the same look she'd had when I'd left her standin' there on that April day eight months before, and I knew I was about to get a right proper scoldin'.

"Tomorrow? That isn't fair!"

Judgin' by the look on her face, I could tell she was wrastlin' with her inner feelings, and for a minute I thought she might slap me again, but she didn't.

"Eight months you've been gone now, Wil Harleck! Off to who-knows-where, fightin' this . . . detestable war!" she shouted, ballin' up her fists and raisin' her voice. "You were even—" she almost couldn't make herself say it, "—wounded in battle for pity's sake . . . and all the time the army can spare you to spend with your loved ones is *two days*?!"

I started to argue that it was really three days, but then I thought better of it.

"It's a good thing that general of yours isn't here right now, or I'd give him a piece of my mind!" I could hear her mama's voice echoin' in those words.

"Maribel," Mr. Nellis warned in a low voice that made her look over at him. He didn't say another word, but the look on his face reminded her that she was makin' a spectacle of herself. Maribel knew that from time to time her mama had a way of gettin' her dander up a mite more than a dignified lady ought. But then she was Grace-Anne Nellis, after all, and folks around Charles Town generally gave her a good deal of—well, grace—on account of who she was. But Maribel didn't want to take after her mama that way.

When she looked back at me the indignant look on her face had softened a bit.

"I thought you said the war would be over by now?" she scolded on, but her voice was lower and gentler now, and I could see the tears buildin' up in her eyes.

"I'm real sorry, Maribel," I said, tryin' to keep calm. She was right, but no one ever said war was fair. "We *all* thought this war would be over by now, but if they keep on fightin', well, we've gotta keep on fightin' too."

She was startin' to get ahold of herself now.

"Can't you stay a few days longer?" she pleaded.

"I wish I could, but we were lucky just to get these three days' furlough. If I don't go back tomorrow, I could get in real trouble."

She took a deep breath and let out a sigh, then looked up at me and her face softened again. Then I saw that sparkle in her eyes that said she was about to say somethin' precocious.

"Very well, then, Mr. Harleck. But you must promise me that you will do your best to end this war and come back to me again—" she pointed her finger in my face, "—for good this time."

"With all my heart, Miss Nellis," I smiled back.

"And—" she pointed her finger again, then smiled that playful smile and continued, "—you must join us for dinner after church?" She was half askin' and half tellin', but then she looked over at her pa to be sure it was alright with him too. "Please, Papa?"

"Why certainly," William Nellis replied with a courteous smile. "In fact, your whole family must join us. I insist."

"It would be our pleasure, sir," I was only too glad to accept. Truth be told, my Mama and Pa would never presume to invite ourselves, but it was becomin' a tradition for the Nellises to invite my whole family over for Christmas dinner every year, so Mama hadn't even made plans for our own family dinner, save the sweet potato pies she'd made to take to the Nellises if we were invited.

Talk of a New State

I s'pose the Christmas service was as nice as any I could recollect, but I hardly noticed. I could scarcely take my eyes off Maribel. The Nellises sat across the aisle from Mama, Amos, Vanessa, and me on the front row. I tried not to be too obvious, but I couldn't help it. I found myself stealin' glances at the vision in white sittin' just a few feet away. The long sleeves cuffed in lace gave her arms a slender angelic look, and the rest of the dress sure did show off the womanly shape the Good Lord gave her. I wasn't sure whether I should thank the Lord for His wondrous creation or repent for the lustful feelings in my heart. So I did both.

After church, we journeyed the short distance to the Nellis home for Christmas dinner. It was a fine feast, just like I remembered, with roast pork and green beans and bread puddin' and another of Mama's sweet potato pies. The table was set very nicely with candles and fine silver and the most beautiful dishes I'd ever laid eyes on, all spread over a fine white table cloth with a lace fringe. The dining room of the Nellis plantation was always an impressive place, but I reckon they outdid even themselves that day.

Over dinner, Mama and Mrs. Nellis talked about dresses and fabrics and how the price of clothes and the other essentials of livin' had gone up so much on the Confederate dollar. Then it was Mr. Nellis' turn to talk.

"Have you heard the talk about forming a new state—a *northern* state—Wil?"

"Not much, sir. Just rumors, really."

I remembered hearin' talk at Camp Harmon before we'd returned to the Valley, but didn't know much about it. I gathered it was mostly just talk, and I wasn't much for talkin' politics anyway.

"I'm afraid it's somewhat more than just a rumor now," Mr. Nellis' voice brought me back. "They actually took a vote back in October, but the soldiers kept over half of the county under house arrest for sympathizing with the Confederacy."

"Can you believe the nerve of those people?" Grace-Anne added.

"They really took a vote?" I asked.

"They most certainly did," she replied with all the feigned indignance she could muster. "Why the whole town's abuzz with the talk. Most of the counties west and north of the Shenandoah voted to break off from Virginia and form a new state loyal to the Union. Of course there are some folks who say Virginia should not have seceded from the Union in the first place."

To my shock and surprise, it was Pa who spoke next. "That may be true, but I very much doubt that they are the majority here in Jefferson County." When my Pa wasn't preachin' he was a man of few words, but he could read a person like a book and knew how to use his words to influence folks. Then he chuckled and added, "Of course I suppose it *would* be quite a bit easier to speak of loyalty to the Union with the boots of federal soldiers at your doorstep."

Mr. Nellis smiled and sat back in his chair. "That is true, Reverend," he replied. "I suppose that's why some folks decided it might be wiser to vote themselves back into the Union rather than risk being forcibly dragged back into it."

Pa nodded in agreement and then added, "And with the Federals occupying most of the counties west of the valley, it's no wonder so many folks have stayed loyal to the Union up that way."

Right about then, Mrs. Nellis got that look on her face—that look that only a southern woman can get—the one that lets everyone in the room know that she's downright shocked and appalled about somethin' you just said. "Well, most of *Jefferson* County still remains loyal to Virginia, I can assure you," she added, soundin' incredulous.

Pa leaned forward with a polite smile and raised his glass in Mrs. Nellis' direction. "My dear Grace-Anne, I believe Jefferson County owes much of its loyalty to Virginia and the Confederacy to the deep ties of your esteemed family," he said. "And let us hope it remains so."

My Pa could talk a bear down from a tree. He just had a way with words. I s'pose it worked too, 'cause Mrs. Nellis just blushed and raised her glass without sayin' a word.

"Hear, hear," added Mr. Nellis, with his glass also raised.

Pa wasn't talkin' about the Nellis family though. Grace-Anne Nellis was a distant cousin of George Washington himself—and proud of it she was too. In fact, it was a point of pride that Jefferson County was home to more members of the Washington family than any other county in Virginia. Why Charles Town itself was even named for George's brother, Charles, who founded the town back in 1787. Heck, even the streets were named after members of the family.

Now I don't think my Pa was foolish enough to believe that all of the Washington family was loyal to the Confederacy, but I reckon he was hopin' Grace-Anne might put some of her considerable influence to work to that end.

Mrs. Nellis gathered herself with poise and grace, like her name, and accepted Pa's toast with a polite reply. "Yes. Let us hope it remains so indeed, Reverend." She sipped from her glass and went on talkin'. "But I'm sure you are aware, as I am, that many of my family are federalists, and although they love Virginia, they would be just as likely to cast their lots on the side of the Union should the state be divided."

"Well then, we shall pray for them, Madam," Pa smiled back.

We all couldn't help but laugh. Then Mrs. Nellis spoke again.

"I wasn't aware you had such strong feelings for the South, Reverend. Isn't your own son Joseph also a Union sympathizer?"

This time it was Mama who spoke up. "Well, I'm not so sure if it's really sympathy for the Union or just opposition to the war itself . . . " She trailed off, soundin' a little unsure of just how much she should be sayin'. Then she brightened up and went on. "He's just completed his first term on scholarship at Pennsylvania College. All high marks!" She was beamin' with pride now. "He says he may try to find work as an intern between terms this summer—if there's any work to be found, that is."

"Oh, well . . . how proud you must be," Mrs. Nellis replied, doin' her best to sound polite. But she wasn't very good at hidin' her feelings.

Pa cleared his throat so as to get Mama's attention, then looked back at Mrs. Nellis to answer her question, but his voice sounded a mite unsteady, like he wasn't quite sure he meant what he was sayin'. "Yes, well, I'm ashamed to admit, Grace-Anne, that my own feelings about this whole secession business may have been tainted a bit of late by the ill behavior of some uniformed 'representatives' of the United States toward the citizens and respected establishments of this community. One would think they might have a greater respect for the rights and property of peaceful civilians, not to mention houses of God."

Then he let out a deep sigh and looked up at the ceiling like he was lookin' up there for some help with what he was about to say next. "As for Joseph," his eyes fell back on Grace-Anne, "he's a man of deep convictions. He may be against this war, that is true, but that doesn't mean that he doesn't love Virginia, our home. These are trying times for all of us. I suppose Joseph is just doing his best to do what he believes is right, and for that, I'm proud of him."

I can't recall ever hearin' my Pa talk about his feelings for Joseph before. Nor me, either. I wasn't sure if I should be glad he was proud of Joseph or jealous that he didn't say anything about bein' proud of me. He was a deeply private man in many ways. He once said his faith in God was better shown than spoken. Maybe he felt the same way about his family. Still, a boy needs to hear it from his pa at least once or twice.

"Well then, let us also pray for Joseph" added Mr. Nellis.

"Pa says I can join up next year when I'm eighteen!" Amos blurted out. He'd been dyin' to get into the conversation, and all this talk about the war was just too much to resist.

Mr. Nellis looked at Pa with surprise on his face. I reckon he hadn't expected Pa to give his blessing to Amos joinin' the army. But Pa just looked at Amos with that gentle patient look he got when any of us boys spoke without thinkin'.

"I said 'maybe', son," he said with just a hint of a smile, "if the war isn't over before then."

"Aww," Amos conceded, lookin' disappointed. So I reached over and patted him on the shoulder and gave him a big smile to cheer him up. I knew this was important to him, and even though I didn't want him fightin' in the war, I understood how he felt. It was the same way I'd felt about Joseph before the war.

"Indeed," Mr. Nellis replied. Then he sat up and motioned to Samuel, the old Negro house slave, to bring more of the Christmas wine, then continued. "And let us refill our glasses and drink a toast to our very own hero of Manassas, Wil Harleck."

I didn't wanna seem ungrateful for Mr. Nellis' kind gesture and all, but I didn't much feel like a hero, and bein' called one made me feel a mite uncomfortable. Heroes rode on horses and led armies. Stonewall Jackson was a hero; I was just a plain ol' lowly soldier boy. But all around the table there were glasses raised and nods of agreement with a chorus of "Hear, hear." So I just did my best to be humble about it.

"That's mighty kind of y'all, but I really didn't do all that much, except get myself blown up by a cannonball, that is. It was really Gen'ral Jackson and the whole Brigade that deserve all the credit."

Every eye around the table was on me, and I felt like they were hangin' on every word I said as if they'd never really heard how it all happened. Then it struck me: they probably hadn't. So I went on.

"Of course the Innocent Second was a part of it too, but I was just one of many. Though I did witness some of the most incredible bravery I'd ever seen that day. Matter of fact, I owe my life to Fredrick Ruyter and Carlton Willis and some of the boys from the Jefferson Guards. I s'pose they're the real heroes, leastwise as I see it anyway."

It was Mr. Nellis who spoke next, glass still raised.

"Indeed. To the Jefferson Guards then. To their valor and patriotism. May God protect them."

Then Mama added with reverence in her voice, "To Fredrick, God rest his soul."

There was another chorus of, "Hear, hear," and we all drank the wine, exceptin' the children, of course.

New Hopes and Old Wounds

As we passed that Christmas afternoon together, the memories of so many lazy Sundays spent at the Nellis homestead in my childhood all seemed so far away, as if I was lookin' back through an early mornin' fog. But I can still recollect every moment of that Christmas day. It was almost like time itself was standin' still. We sat around and talked for awhile, and I found myself gettin' lost in the moment. Next thing I knew, Maribel was givin' me a mighty strange look and fiddlin' with her hair.

"Is there something wrong with my hair?" she finally asked. That's when I first realized I must've been starin' at her just wrong.

"Oh . . . No . . . nothin's wrong with your hair," I tried to sound apologetic. "I was just thinkin', that's all."

"Thinking? *You* were thinking?" she teased with a gleam in her eye. "Pray, do tell us what about, Mr. Harleck." She said with a giggle, knowin' she'd got the best of me again, all of which I suspect made me a mite red in the face.

"Well, if you must know, Miss Nellis," I saw my opportunity, "it was you I was thinkin' of—how much I've missed you these past eight months."

Now it was her turn to blush. But I wasn't done yet.

"I guess seein' the true nature of war up close like I have, and havin' a brush with death, has a way of makin' a man reevaluate his priorities . . . you know . . . makes him realize how short life is . . . makes him appreciate the time he has with the folks he loves a bit more . . . treasure each memory."

"I suppose that's true," Mr. Nellis said, puttin' his hand on my shoulder and startlin' me a bit. Guess I hadn't realized he'd stood up while I was busy waxin' poetic, and now he was standin' right behind me. "Perhaps we should make a few new memories to treasure. What we need now is music. Maribel, would you be so kind as to regale us?" he asked, lookin' at her proudly.

"Oh, Papa, you know I can't play that well," Maribel blushed again.

"Nonsense," he smiled. "You're a fine piano player, and you have a very pleasant voice," he insisted.

"Yes, please, Maribel," Mama injected eagerly. "Please play for us!"

"Yes, Maribel, you must play for us," Grace-Anne added.

She looked at me like she was half afraid I wouldn't approve of her musical talents, so I just smiled hopefully and said, "It sure would be a welcome change from the fife and drum."

"Oh, very well, since you all insist so nicely," Maribel conceded with a shy smile.

She played "Jeannette Isabelle," her mama's favorite. Then she played "The First Noel," and we all sang along. But as I stood there watchin' her play and listenin' to her sing, I thought about leavin' her again, and I knew what I had to do.

William Nellis had given me his blessing to court Maribel the year before. I remember how nervous I'd been to go and ask him, seein' as how I didn't have much to offer in the way of worldly things. But he was a wise man and not so self-important as some other men of means.

I remembered how he'd leaned over to me and said, almost in a whisper, "I'll tell you a secret, lad. Men with money are easy enough to find, but men with character and honor are not. Should Maribel choose to marry a man of character and honor, as I hope she does, she will never have to worry about money. I'll see to that. You're an honest young man, William—polite and well mannered—and you've got a good heart. Any man would be honored to have you as a son."

Up until that day, I'd never really thought I had a cat's chance in Hell of marryin' the daughter of William Nellis. But I knew he was no idle flatterer, and I took it to heart as a great and prodigious trust not to be taken lightly. If he thought I was an honorable man, well, I had no intention of lettin' him down. It was true there was nothin' I wouldn't do for Maribel, and I reckon he figured she'd be happier with someone like me than with some rich young man who was only lookin' for a wealthy socialite bride so as he could increase his own standin' in society.

So I waited until we were finished singin' and everyone was in a joyful mood, then I took Maribel's hand as she stood up from the piano bench.

"Maribel, I do believe you must be an angel," I told her.

She blushed.

"You sure do play nicely," I went on, "and you sing like an angel too."

She smiled and curtsied and batted her eyes playfully just for show. Then with the same playfulness in her voice, she replied, "Why, thank you kindly, Mr. Harleck. Why, if I didn't know better, I'd say you were tryin' to flatter a lady."

"Perhaps I am," I admitted, "but it's the truth nonetheless."

There were a few chuckles around the room.

"Which is why . . . " I knelt down on one knee, "I'm compelled to ask for your hand in marriage—if you'll have me, that is?—before some other man more worthy than I finds out about all this angelic talent and sweeps you off your feet?"

I could hear my Mama draw in her breath and hold it. I didn't even have to look. I could tell she was holdin' her hands over her mouth with that surprised look on her face she always got when somethin' good happened. But I couldn't take my eyes off the vision that stood before me with her hand in mine. Her beautiful green eyes grew wide in amazement, and I was quite a bit relieved to see the look of delight there as I'd hoped I'd see. She glanced at her mama and papa to see their reactions, then her gaze met mine again and a hopeful smile appeared on her delicate lips.

"Oh, Wil, do you mean it?"

"With all my heart." I put on my best gentleman face and cleared my throat. "Maribel Catherine Nellis, will you marry me?"

There was a pause for just a moment while she let the gravity of the whole situation sink in, then the smile widened across her whole face and her eyes watered up.

"Yes! Yes, I *will* marry you, Wil Harleck!"

I stood up and she threw her arms around my neck and kissed me again. Then she turned and looked around the room with excitement on her face.

"Well, then," Mr. Nellis said confidently. "It appears we have another reason to celebrate! Grace-Anne, is that wassail ready? We're in need of some refreshment."

"It sure is! Samuel!"

There were hugs and handshakes and congratulations all around, and Maribel stayed very close to me for the rest of the evenin'. Neither she nor I were willin' to waste a single moment together. Just havin' her beside me, hand in arm, made me feel whole again.

Along about eight o'clock that evenin' there was a knock at the door, and we all looked to see who it might be. Then Samuel opened the door and in walked a familiar figure.

"Joseph!" Mama exclaimed.

"Welcome home, Joseph," Mr. Nellis added. "Samuel, his coat and hat, please."

"I hope you'll pardon me for just walkin' in like this," Joseph started. "I just arrived from Williamsport, and when I didn't find anyone at home, I hoped I might find y'all here."

"Please, won't you come in?" Mrs. Nellis asked.

I wasn't altogether sure just exactly how I felt about seein' Joseph at that precise moment. At first, I was real glad to see him, but then the memory of that day back in April when we'd had harsh words came floodin' back, and I felt that same sinkin' feeling in the pit of my stomach. It was like that feeling you get when you just ate somethin' that disagrees with you and you're not sure if it's gonna stay down or come back up.

I couldn't help but wonder if his feelings about the war had changed any since we'd last parted, and I was sure he was wonderin' the same about me. My mind flashed back to that day on the battlefield when my heart burned with anger toward the Yankees. I remembered how I'd seen Tommy go down, and I thought about Fredrick, and how I'd watched him fall after bein' struck by the Yankee Minie ball. Then I thought about the church and how I'd felt when I learned what the

Yankees had done there. I felt changed alright, but it was a fair bet it wasn't the change Joseph was hopin' for.

So there we stood, lookin' across the room at each other, neither of us able to say a word to the other one. I could feel the eyes of everyone in the room starin' at me—waitin' for me to say somethin'—but no matter how much my mind willed it to open and speak, my mouth just wouldn't do it.

It was Joseph who finally broke the silence.

"Hello, Wil. Good to see you're well."

"Hel—" my voice cracked and broke, so I cleared my throat and tried again. "Hello, Joseph."

The words still weren't comin' easy, but at least they were comin'.

It was Pa who spoke next. He stepped over to where Joseph was standin', put his arm around his shoulder, and said, "Welcome home, son. It's good to have you home."

Then he turned toward the rest of us and said, "You're just in time for the celebration."

The corners of his mouth turned up just so, like they always did when he was about to deliver good news to someone.

"I believe your brother has some news you might find interesting."

He paused just long enough for that familiar quizzical look to appear on Joseph's face—the look that said he was interested, but wasn't about to ask—then he continued.

"Wil, here, has just proposed to Maribel."

Pa watched the look on Joseph's face change from quizzical to surprised, then his own face broke out in a smile that we hadn't seen in a while.

"Your brother's getting married."

Now it was Joseph's turn to smile, and our differences were forgotten just in that moment.

"Well, whataya know! Congratulations, Wil!"

He came straight toward me and hugged me, and I could feel the uneasiness drainin' out of me like it was runnin' right out through the bottom of my shoes and onto the floor. He was still a good three inches taller than me, and even though I was a man now, I still felt like a teenage boy when I stood next to him.

I nearly forgot that Maribel was still standin' next to me until I heard her clear her throat.

"Uh-um."

Joseph smiled sheepishly at her, embarrassed that he'd forgotten his manners, then stepped back and turned to her.

"Forgive me, miss." He bowed with a flourish of his hand, looked up at her, and put on his most charming voice. "My most humble apologies, and congratulations, of course."

She held out her hand and he took it in his own and kissed it.

"Why thank you, kind sir," she said, returnin' his feigned charm with another playful curtsy of her own. Her whole face was a smile, and her voice could barely contain the giggle of delight.

Joseph held his bow and continued, still holdin' her hand in front of his face, and glancin' in my direction with a gleam in his eye that said he was about to say somethin' at my expense.

"Though I'm not quite sure whether I should be apologizin' for my own rude conduct or for the fact that you are about to marry my little brother."

Joseph straightened up and smiled, and I couldn't help but smile back.

Maribel hesitated but for a moment, glanced at both of our faces, then back at me with a mischievous sparkle in her eyes.

"Your apology is accepted in either case." Her voice turned downright giddy at the chance to poke fun at me, but then the warm smile spread across her whole face again. "Welcome home, Joseph." She stepped up and hugged him and kissed him on the cheek.

For one brief moment on that blessed Christmas afternoon, everything was just as it had been before the war. We talked and laughed just like those lazy Sunday afternoons at the Nellis plantation with Joseph, me, Maribel, Amos, and Vanessa. What good times we'd had. And for just that one moment, Joseph and I forgot about the war and there was peace on earth.

Funny thing about those moments: they never seem to last. Joseph and I could only dance around the matter until the small talk ran out.

"So, you must tell us all about college," Maribel asked eagerly. "It must be so exciting!"

"Not much to tell, really," Joseph replied. "Lots of books and writin'. Mostly English and arithmetic so far. But the folks up Gettysburg way seem nice enough. It's a pretty little town."

"I've never heard of Gettysburg before. Is that anywhere near Harrisburg?" she continued.

"Not far. Maybe just a day's hard ride south of there. It's only about three days' ride from here on a good horse." Then he got a thoughtful look on his face. "Did you know the college was founded in 1832 by the Reverend Samuel Simon Schmucker? Ever hear of him?"

"I'm afraid not," Maribel answered politely. "Is he famous?"

"He's a well-known abolitionist up in those parts."

There it is. He just couldn't resist bringin' up the war, could he?

"I see," she replied.

The war seemed to hang in the air over our heads like a thick smoke that couldn't be ignored. It was only a matter of time until the conversation was bound to come back around to it before the evenin' was over, sure as daylight was a-comin'.

"So, you goin' back?" he asked finally, lookin' at me.

It seemed like a simple enough question, but it felt more like a stab in the heart. I knew how Joseph felt about the rebellion. I couldn't look him in the eye because I knew what was comin' next, so I found myself lookin' around the room nervously like a school boy who was in trouble with the teacher.

"I reckon so. We only have three days furlough. Arty, Sean, and me, we leave for camp in the mornin'."

"Just Arty? What about Tommy?"

I knew I was losin' control of the conversation, and I could feel the knot formin' in my belly.

"Tommy . . . was mustered out. Lost his right foot at Manassas."

I could see the look of admonition in Joseph's eyes, and his mouth turned into a frown.

"You didn't mention Fredrick. Isn't he goin' back too?"

My heart was beatin' faster now, and I could feel the anger risin' up inside my chest like a cannon set to go off, but I couldn't make myself speak.

"Joseph . . . " It was Mama's voice. " . . . Fredrick was killed."

The look in Joseph's eyes turned to anger as well, and I braced myself for what I knew was comin' next.

"Haven't you had enough of this cursed secession business yet, Wil? Dear God, little brother!" he shouted. "For the life of me, I don't know why you have to be so blasted eager to pick up the rifle against your own countrymen!"

It was plain he was gettin' his dander up, and so was I. I opened my mouth to argue back, but he cut me off.

"Don't you see it?" he blustered on. "This war is a curse from God upon our land. It's His righteous judgment and punishment for toleratin' the blight of slavery on this continent for over two hundred years!"

He stopped when he remembered that William Nellis—a slave owner—was standin' right there in the room next to him.

"Beggin' your pardon, sir, ma'am," he said, bowin' his shoulders slightly in the direction of Mr. and Mrs. Nellis. "I don't mean any disrespect to you kind folks, but the only peaceful way out of this whole mess, as I see it, is to free the slaves, repent of this cursed institution, and ask God in His mercy to heal our nation."

Then he looked back at me with daggers in his eyes. "But all you 'Seceshes', you'd rather fight and spill innocent blood than to free the slaves and keep the country together!"

My heart was poundin' in my throat. Joseph had never gotten all wrapped around the axe handle about the slaves before. It had always been about preservin' the Union up until now. My mind raced to find the words to say.

Does he really think this war is a punishment from God on account of a handful of rich gentlemen who own slaves? I don't believe that! There are lots of good folks like the Nellises who own slaves, but they're more like family than property. What about them? And what about all the good southern folk like us who don't own slaves at all? Does he think God is punishin' us too?

Then my mind went back to that hilltop near Manassas. In a flood my thoughts filled with the images I'd witnessed. I remembered the lines upon lines of soldiers—federal soldiers—on Virginia soil. I could see the smoke and flame from the Yankee guns; smell the air thick with powder; hear the cries of agony echoin' again in my mind. *Could all of that really be on account of the Darkies? Somethin' just didn't add up about it all. Where did Joseph get that idea from? What're they teachin' him up there at that college?*

The more I thought about it, the more I got my dander up. Finally, I couldn't hold my tongue any longer. I heard myself blurtin' out things I wouldn't ordinarily say to my own kin, but the soldier inside me had got the better of me, and he was not about to be denied the chance to be heard.

"It ain't about the danged Darkies, Joseph! Not for me! And it wasn't my 'countrymen' who shot Fredrick and Tommy and me on the battlefield, either! It wasn't my 'countrymen' who defiled the church! *My* 'countrymen' would never take up arms and invade the sovereign territory of another state without good cause! No sir! They might be *your* countrymen, but they are most certainly not *mine*! We have a right to defend our homes against *any* army that invades our land and threatens our freedom! And that, my dear brother, is *exactly* what the Yankees have done! May I remind you that the battle of Manassas was fought on Virginia soil?!"

"That's enough!" It was Pa's voice that broke through the blood poundin' in my ears. My Pa made a point of not preachin' when he wasn't in the pulpit, but on rare occasion he broke his own rule. It was undeniably his preachin' voice he was usin' now.

"You are brothers, and this is neither the time nor the place for this sort of contemptible display of hostility. It's Christmas, for God's sake! Can we not be civil enough toward each other to set aside our differences and be a family for just a few short hours?!"

A long pause hung in the room as Joseph and I both glared at one another, neither one of us willin' to admit we were wrong. Then Joseph's face softened just a bit.

"You're right of course, Father. Forgive me," Joseph said. Then he turned and walked toward the door to retrieve his coat and hat.

"I should not've come here tonight. Mr. Nellis. Mrs. Nellis. Please forgive me. Thank you for your hospitality." he nodded in courtesy to them.

"Joseph . . . " Mama's voice pleaded with him to stay, but he'd made up his mind. Then, quick as you please, he was his usual calm and well-mannered self again. Puttin' on his coat, he turned to Amos and Vanessa.

"Amos, Vanessa, Merry Christmas."

"Merry Christmas, Joseph" they replied together, no doubt a mite stunned at all they'd just witnessed.

"Mother, Father, Maribel, please forgive me. Merry Christmas. God bless you all."

And without another word, he turned around, placed his hat on his head, and walked out the door into the cold night.

The Good Hard Winter

January 1862

The winter of 1862 is, for many soldiers, North and South, like none they have ever experienced. Not since the days of the Revolutionary War have such large armies bivouacked on American soil in harsh winter conditions such as these. But the brutal conditions faced by the soldiers of the Civil War are even worse than those faced by their Revolutionary ancestors. The great armies now assembled are vastly larger than those of the Revolution, and the sheer magnitude of tens of thousands of men encamped in close proximity presents many challenges and dangers to health and welfare, even for experienced soldiers under the most ideal of weather conditions. But most of these soldiers are green, and they suffer greatly from their lack of experience in the bitter winter weather.

Disease is rampant in the camps, and death is not uncommon. In fact, disease and unhealthy living conditions will claim nearly twice as many lives as battlefield casualties during the course of this war. For many, frostbite is a daily reality. The life of the average soldier is filled with misery and boredom, and desertion is becoming an increasing concern. As each day goes by, the muster for morning drill grows smaller, and the hospitals and infirmaries become engorged with the ranks of the sick and lame.

In many of the units, morale begins to plummet and good order and discipline begin to break down. It is becoming increasingly difficult for the officers to enforce even the most ordinary regulations, and marshal discipline becomes the order of the day. Indeed, the punishment for desertion and other major offenses, should the offender be found guilty by competent authority, is often death by firing squad. Other punishments might include flogging with the whip, restraint or confinement in a public place with a humiliating sign hung around the neck, forfeiture of pay, confinement with only bread and water for up to sixty days, or, if the offense is minor enough, extra duty for up to sixty days.

For most soldiers, the only bright spot in their otherwise miserable lives is the occasional letter or package from home. But many of the soldiers are illiterate, or have only a rudimentary education, and they must rely on friends and comrades to read and write for them. Still others may wait in vain for letters or packages which will never come, whether by virtue of the substandard postal service provided for the army, or because, for various reasons, none are sent from home.

Yet for the Confederate soldier, brutal as it may be, the winter of 1862 will prove to be the best of the war when compared to those yet to come. At least for now he has adequate food, clothing, and supplies to make life tolerable. By the following winter, however, this will change dramatically. Even now, Abraham Lincoln and his war cabinet are planning a grand strategy for victory which includes the blockade of every southern seaport by Union Navy warships and control of the Mississippi River in the west. The goal of this aptly named "Anaconda" strategy is simple: to cut off the life-giving trade and supply lines of the Confederacy, and strangle the rebellion into submission.

January 24, 1862

Prvt. W. A. Harleck
Army of the Shenandoah
Camp Stephenson, Winchester

Dear Mama,

I thought I might take a moment to prevail upon you and Pa and all of the good folks back home to pray for my friend Sean McAlistair, who is in dire need of the Good Lord's grace at this moment. He fell ill with pneumonia a week ago, and I fear he is not doing well. The surgeon says that he has done all he can do and the rest is in God's hands now.

I received with a grateful heart the extra blankets you sent in response to my last letter. Although these wooden huts we have constructed for our winter camp here provide better shelter than sleeping in tents, they are still considerably cold and drafty. The extra blankets will do us good on the cold nights, and the new stockings you gave me for Christmas have been divine.

Life here in camp is difficult, but I am well and in general good health. I would much prefer the comfort of our warm hearth and your home cooking to this hut and the army food they give us, but I am willing to endure this hardship for the sake of our cause. We have not seen any action in over a month now, though we did march out to Berkeley Springs for awhile where we came near to the Federals there, but they did not come out and give battle. I believe I would greatly have preferred that over just sitting around waiting for Mr. Lincoln to make his next move. This miserable weather is more hazardous than the shells and musket balls of the enemy, and I fear it is to blame for Sean's illness.

I pray for the safety of all our family and loved ones with Charles Town being so close to the border and the Yankee troops so nearby. I long to see you all again, and hope it shall be soon. God willing, perhaps this war will be over soon, but I fear it may go on for some time yet to come. Pray for me often, and tell Pa that I am alright. Hug Amos and kiss Vanessa for me.

Your loving son,
Wil

A Soldier's Friends

I would not wish it upon my worst enemy to be found in an encampment of the Army of the Shenandoah during winter. I don't rightly know which was worse; the sheer boredom, the rampant disease, or the mind-numbin' cold. Ever since the danged Yankees destroyed our brand new tents at Falling Waters, all we had was the spare tents we'd been usin' since July, and they were old and leaked like an ol' rusty bucket. When the winter wind and snow blew down off the mountains into the valley, they were almost like havin' no shelter at all. We tried to find solace by sittin' near the fire singin' and makin' music, but even that was little comfort after a while. A fella can only abide singin' "Home Sweet Home," "Willie Has Gone to the War," and "Do They Miss Me at Home" just so many times before he starts to wonderin' if maybe he oughta be at home with his kin instead of sufferin' out in the bitter cold.

Early in January, the regiment was sent out to reconnoiter the fed'ral movements near Berkeley Springs, which was home for the boys in Company D, the Berkeley Border Guards. We came near to the Yankees there, but the weather was too miserable for fightin', what with all the ice and snow and sleet. I would've preferred it if the Yankees had come out to fight that day. Anything to take our minds off the cold. I hadn't felt my fingers in days, and my toes had gone and turned purple and numb from the constant cold wet weather. One mornin' when we woke, we found ourselves covered in snow half a foot deep. On the day the Bath hotel caught fire, that glorious blaze was a welcome sight, as it provided us with some much needed warmth and heat. Some of us tried to help fight the fire. Others, they just stood around nearby so as their clothes could get dry.

I don't need to tell you that we were glad to return to Winchester where we set about buildin' our winter quarters at Camp Zollicoffer just northeast of the town. It was quite the welcome relief to be livin' in a dry building and sleepin' on a bunk for the first time since we'd left Manassas. Our hut wasn't much. There were no windows at all, and until a fireplace and chimney could be built, the only heat came from a can of charcoals in the middle of the room. It smelled of sweat and there were eight of us crowded into one small hut, but it was shelter from the wind, rain, and snow, and it sure beat sleepin' in tents or on the ground. The worst part of havin' so many men in one hut was when one became ill and all the rest had to wonder who'd be next. And someone *always* seemed to be ill.

On January the twentieth, Arty, Carlton, and I finished our supper—beef gravy on potato cakes—under a gray and cloudy sky. After supper the cold north wind chased the clouds away, the stars came out, and the night got bitter cold. We stoked the fire up high to keep us warm, but the problem with stokin' the fire up high was that one side got too hot while the other side stayed cold such that a man had to keep turnin' himself around like a hog on a spit just to stay warm.

"Where's Sean?" I asked Arty, lookin' around to see if I'd missed him somewhere nearby.

"In the hut," Arty replied. "Said he wasn't feelin' well."

"You think maybe we should go inside too?" I asked, tryin' not to shiver too much.

"Heh!" Carlton scoffed from behind me. "You can go in there if ya want, Harleck, but I ain't stayin' in that hell-hole any longer than I have to. We done lost one man from the fever last week; Munroe, he's already among the walkin' dead; and now McAlistair's comin' down with it too."

I didn't know Munroe very well, but I knew he was a drinker—though not as much as Carlton, I reckon—and I knew he'd been sick for a few days. *But no one said anything about Sean havin' the fever. He just said he wasn't feelin' well, right?*

"I'm sure Sean'll be alright," I said, tryin' to sound confident. But Carlton wasn't buyin' it.

"Look, boy, I can tell when a man's sick, and he sure as hell looks sick to me. He's pale, he's got the shakes, and now he's startin' to cough too. And I ain't gonna be next."

"I ain't sure which is worse," Arty chimed in, half jokin' and half serious, "goin' in there and gettin' sick or stayin' out here and freezin' to death."

Carlton pulled another log off the firewood pile and threw it on the fire, then shot back in that cynical voice we'd all come to expect whenever he was out of booze. "Didn't you hear? Gen'ral Jackson's orders: The only friends a soldier's allowed to have in this here army are death, disease, boredom, and misery." He wrapped his blanket tight around him and sat down on a log near the fire. "I'll take my chances with the cold."

I stayed out by the fire for a while that night thinkin' about what Carlton said. I thought about writin' to my sweet Maribel, but my fingers were so cold they could barely hold the pen. I hadn't written home as much as I would've liked, but I sure did miss Maribel and thought of her all the time. Just knowin' that my lovely bride-to-be was so nearby—only a couple hours' ride away—but not bein' able to be with her, was like torture to the soul.

I'd received letters from Maribel and Mama and Amos, which I'd read over and over to make the cold nights a mite more tolerable, but on this particular cold night I couldn't make my hands hold the paper still enough to read. Mama'd sent a bundle with two blankets that she and some of the ladies from the church had made to keep me warm, so I contented myself to wrap up in my blankets and hunker down near the fire—but not so near as to catch my new blankets afire—until I was so cold and tired that I couldn't stand it anymore. Then I finally gave up and went inside to sleep.

When I awoke on the mornin' of January the twenty-first, I heard Sean shiverin' and coughin' in his bed, and I knew it was worse than he'd led us to believe. He usually had a youthful roundish face with full cheeks spotted with freckles, and bright green eyes under a head of thick wavy hair the color of pumpkin pie. But that mornin' his cheeks and forehead were flushed red, which made his hair look even more reddish than usual, and his eyes seemed hollow and dark.

"Sean, you don't look too good," I told him, "and you don't sound any too good, either. You oughta go and see the doc about that cough."

But he wouldn't have it. He just smiled and waved his hand and said, "Aw, it ain't nothin' but just a little cold," then went back to coughin'.

By the third day, we knew it was more than just a little cold. He couldn't make himself stop shakin' and coughin', and the coughin' was gettin' worse. The Sergeant had me take him over to the infirmary, seein' as how I was his closest friend in our hut. When we got to the infirmary, the surgeon's aide took one look at him and ordered him right back to bed.

"Son, you've got pneumonia. You shouldn't oughta be walkin' around. You need rest."

When I asked if there was anything he could do, he just shook his head and said, "Nope. Rest is what he needs." Then he looked at Sean and said, "Sorry, son. There's nothin' we can do for ya here. Now off to bed with you."

For the next couple of days, I tried to help take care of Sean. I took him food and water, but he wouldn't eat much and only drank a little. He just kept gettin' weaker and weaker. By the fifth day, the fever was so bad that his blanket was soakin' wet with sweat and he couldn't stop shakin' from the chills, so I shared one of the new blankets Mama had sent to help keep him warm. His cough was growin' so bad that when the coughin' spells came he could scarcely catch a breath. He was so weak by then that he couldn't walk to the infirmary without help, so we carried him over. This time, the surgeon kept him there.

I knew it was bad, and I spent all my spare time that day prayin', and even wrote to Mama to ask her to have Pa and the folks back home to pray too. A few of the fellas liked to poke fun at me from time to time when I was prayin'. They'd say things like, "Hey, Harleck, while yer talkin' to the Man upstairs, why don't you ask him why he don't just help us win this war so's we can go home?" or, "Be sure and thank him for all this lovely weather we been havin'." But no one said a word that day. They just passed on by real quiet-like. Maybe that was just their own way of prayin' too.

When it comes to matters of the eternal, most soldiers are a bit of a contradiction of nature; sorta like a bird that can't fly. On the one hand, they aren't real religious, seein' as how when you boil it all down to the bones their trade is to commit murder and keep on doin' it 'til someone's finally had enough and gives up. So they believe they're pretty much goin' straight to Hell when they die anyways. But then on the other hand, they have their own strange kind of faith. They know there's somethin' out there that's bigger than they are, but they just can't figure it bein' like the God they learned about when they were young'uns. I reckon maybe that's just because they never took the time to get to know Him and all. Whatever the reason, prayin' just doesn't seem to come natural to some soldiers—most of the time, that is. But for some strange reason, the more I prayed, the closer I felt to God, even when I wasn't sure what His answer would be.

Only the Good Lord knows why He chooses to answer some prayers but not others. Some boys say it doesn't do any good to pray, seein' as how God isn't listenin' up there anyway, but I know that can't be true. Like my Pa used to say, "God always answers prayer.

Sometimes the answer is just 'no'." The way I figure it, when He doesn't answer our prayers the way we think He should, it's just on account of His plan bein' different from ours—and a mite better, I should think. Whatever makes a man think he should be able to figure out the ways of The Almighty is beyond me. What kind of God would He be if His plans always made sense to the likes of us?

Anyway, the next mornin' I rose early and went over to the infirmary before breakfast to check on Sean, but he wasn't where we'd laid him the day before. I knew in my heart that the Good Lord had taken him home. It felt like a knife in the belly, but I needed to see for myself. After a few minutes, I located a surgeon's aide and asked him.

"Excuse me. Sean McAlistair?"

For a few seconds he didn't say a word. He just looked at me with dread in his eye, clinched his lips together and shook his head.

"Sorry, son. We did all we could. He's gone."

"Take me to him?"

"Can't. No one's s'posed to be back there," he said. But then he stopped and looked at me again like he was lookin' at his own son. " . . . Alright, c'mon."

He took me out onto the cold back porch where there were several bodies lyin' around all covered up with blankets. When he pulled the blanket down that covered Sean's face, I could see his lips were blue and his skin was as pale as the snow against his light auburn hair. A familiar sickening feelin' welled up from down in my gut—like the one I'd felt on the battlefield at Manassas when I'd watched Sergeant Kline die right there in front of me. But I just had to look at Sean's face once more. I took a deep breath and the wave of nausea subsided, and my eyes fell upon his young and frail face one final time. He looked like he was restin' peacefully for the first time in a week.

A Night to Remember

The skies turned dark gray that day, as if Heaven itself was in mournin'. Another snow storm settled in over the valley but I don't recollect much about it. My soul was as numb as my fingers and toes, and I couldn't get the image of Sean's face out of my head.

By lunchtime, the snow was pilin' up deeper and higher so as to make even the simple act of walkin' from one place to the other difficult and miserable. At every step, my boots filled with more snow, formin' a frozen ring of ice around each ankle between boot and stockin' which melted just enough so as to soak the stockin', but not so much as to warm up the foot. It occurred to me that I might just be the next unfortunate soul to catch pneumonia.

The snow kept fallin' all that day, and just after lunchtime, L'tenant Colonel Botts came by to talk to the Company officers. He said that afternoon drill was canceled and Gen'ral Jackson had authorized a week's furlough for any soldier who wanted it, seein' as how the weather was sure to keep the Yankees from stirrin' up any trouble. Some of the fellas weren't all that happy about havin' the offer of furlough and not bein' able to take advantage of it, seein' as how their homes were too far to travel in the deep snow. But most of the boys from the Innocent Second lived nearby and were sure glad of it.

Botts had just returned from fifteen days furlough in Charles Town himself, so he asked Capt'n Rowan if he'd personally see that Sean's body was returned home to his gramma and grampa and offered to pay for the grave marker since they didn't have much money. Capt'n Rowan asked Arty and me if we'd like to take our furlough to go home and help him take Sean home on the way, which we happily obliged.

The next mornin', I packed up my haversack and met Capt'n Rowan at the infirmary. He had a wagon with two horses there to take Sean's body home. Arty met us there too, and a few others from Company A, includin' Sergeant Robertson, Carlton Willis, and two older fellas whose names I can't recall. There were eight of us altogether, countin' Sean. The Capt'n drove while the rest of us rode in the wagon with Sean. The journey took almost twice as long as it should've on account of the heavy snow, but we managed to arrive in Charles Town while it was still early in the afternoon. Our arrival was greeted with mixed emotion, as you might well guess. We stopped first at the McAlistair farm on the edge of town. Carlton took me by surprise when he volunteered to stay around and help Sean's Gramma and Grampa prepare the grave. When I thanked him for doin' such an honorable thing, he tightened up his mouth and gave me a scornful look.

"Don't get used to it, boy. I aim to go get drunk first chance I get, but there ain't no harm in showin' a little respect for the dead first."

Mrs. McAlistair hugged Arty and me, and thanked us for bringin' Sean home, but she couldn't hide the tears in her eyes. Mr. McAlistair was quiet, but we could tell he was deeply sorrowful too. After we took Sean's body from the wagon and carried him gently into the house, Capt'n Rowan handed Mr. McAlistair a letter from Colonel Allen and the envelope from Colonel Botts. He spoke in a hushed tone, but we knew it was the money for the tombstone, and probably more, since they were gettin' on in years and barely able to put food on their own table. There were tears runnin' down Mr. McAlistair's face as he gripped Capt'n Rowan's hand and thanked him for his kindness.

From there, Sergeant Robertson and the other older fellas left directly to their homes, while Capt'n Rowan took Arty and me into town. He left us at the courthouse with instructions to meet him there on Sunday, five days hence. From there, each of us went his own way to our homes where I can safely say we each received a somewhat more joyful welcome.

There was a memorial service for Sean at my Pa's church on Thursday and most of us were there. Pa preached a fitting eulogy and little else was said. Maribel was there and sat with me during the service instead of sittin' with her own family. It was a hard day and the thought of Sean's young age bein' so close to my own was not light upon my heart.

In the afternoon, we laid Sean to his final rest in the grave Carlton had dug next to his mama's and daddy's at the McAlistair farm. We said our good-byes and there were hugs and tears all around, but then we were all relieved to put such unpleasant business behind us and return to merrier company. As we were preparin' to leave, Maribel turned to me with a gleam in her eye and said, "Papa's got something he'd like to ask you, Wil." Then she took me by the hand and led me to where Mr. and Mrs. Nellis were standin'.

"It's good to see you well, son," Mr. Nellis said cordially.

"Thank you, sir," I replied.

"I realize this may not be the best timing," he started, "but since you're home for a few days, and since we have no way of knowing when this war might be over, or when you might be able to come home again . . . "

"For goodness sake, William, don't keep the boy in suspense. Just ask him," Grace-Anne prodded.

"I'm getting to the matter, darling," he answered with a grin and a sideways glance. "Grace-Anne and I thought perhaps you and Maribel might like to be married this weekend."

Out of the corner of my eye, I saw Maribel's face break into a bright smile, and she couldn't keep herself from bouncin' up on her toes. "Papa says we can have the ceremony at home!" It made my heart beat faster just seein' how excited she was.

"If it suits your fancy, that is," Mr. Nellis added.

I must admit that I too was thrilled at the prospect of gettin' married so quickly to the beautiful young lady standin' next to me. I felt myself blush at losin' my own self control when I heard myself blurt out, "Yes, sir!" Then I saw the smile broaden across his face and realized there was nothin' to be embarrassed about.

"It's done then," he said, lookin' as if he was the King of America. "Well, let's get to it. There's much to be done."

The next day was a blur, and before I could blink twice, it was Saturday—my wedding day. Mama had washed and mended my uniform and had it lookin' as if it was brand new, just like the first day of the war. Pa took me down to the barber shop for a shave and a haircut. Then it was off to the Nellis plantation.

I asked Arty and Tommy to stand up with me, and Amos to be my best man, which, of course, they were delighted to do. Vanessa was quite excited to accept Maribel's invitation to be her maid of honor, and Maribel even asked her to carry the beautiful ring which Grace-Anne graciously provided from her mother's wedding.

Even Tommy, with only one foot, could hardly stand still with excitement when Maribel appeared with her pa at the back of the room. She was a vision too heavenly to behold standin' there in her mama's wedding dress. It was the most breathtakin' white dress I'd ever seen: all trimmed with ribbon and lace, narrow at the waist, with lots of lace petticoats down to the floor, and the top was curvy in all the right places. Her hair was all done up in long curls with bows of white and blue. Her face beamed and her eyes seemed to sparkle brighter than the stars in the night sky, and her smile lit up the whole room.

"See," Tommy whispered, leanin' over behind Amos and nudgin' me in the ribs. "Look at her."

But I didn't need Tommy to tell me. My eyes were already fixed on her as she walked down the aisle between the small gathering of guests.

"I told you that girl loves you," he chided, still whisperin'. "You can see it all over her face!"

But I was rendered completely speechless by the overwhelmin' beauty of the woman I beheld across the room.

What happened next I can scarcely remember, exceptin' a vague recollection of sayin' "I do," followed presently by the most glorious kiss a small town boy from the Valley could ever imagine.

William and Grace-Anne Nellis were classy folks, and they knew how to put on a wedding banquet fit for—well, fit for far better than the likes of me. Even still, I didn't much notice what was on the table. I was too captivated by the appearance of my new bride. Between the exquisite lines of her small nose and high cheekbones, the deep pools of joy found in her green eyes, and the curve of her ruby lips which seemed to invite me to sample again the wonder of that wedding kiss, I reckon I was just about as hopeless as a lost pup.

As the afternoon twilight waned and the meal came to a close, and after all of the customary toasts and well wishes were said, Mrs. Nellis stood up and loudly announced, "Thank you all for honoring us with your presence today. And now, we should all excuse ourselves so our darlings may have our leave to retire upstairs for the evening. The day is wasting and I want grandchildren before I'm too old to enjoy them!"

This, of course, brought an uproar of laughter, table poundin', and cheers of "Hear, hear!" from around the room. I looked at Maribel only to find that she was just as embarrassed as I, but in her eyes I saw only the love and desire in her heart. So I took her hand in mine and we stood up, thanked everyone for the wonderful afternoon, and politely excused ourselves.

The events of the day may have been a blur, but time just seemed to stand still that evenin'. I can still remember every detail of that night like it was yesterday. I'd never seen the inside of her bed chambers before, with its fine draperies and rugs and well-crafted furniture. It was quite a sight for a boy like me. But the room itself paled in the wondrous light of my lovely bride in all her surpassin' natural beauty by the candlelight, and the taste of her lips again like sweet honey.

So swept away in that moment was I that I completely forgot about my wounded shoulder until Maribel delicately lifted my shirt off over my head and her eyes found the scar for the first time. She was taken aback for a moment and I felt my heart skip a beat, but then the look of concern in her eyes was replaced by tenderness as she reached out to touch the patch of rough skin that was left where the shrapnel had gone in.

"Does it still hurt?" she asked softly, studyin' the wound with her fingertips and eyes with incredible tenderness.

"Nah. Only a little when I shoot or when it gets real cold."

Without another word, she leaned in and kissed the scar ever so gently, and when she looked up and her eyes met mine, there was longing there the likes of which I'd never seen before. She laid back on the bed with her head on the plush pillow and gently pulled me down toward her with her slender arms around my neck. Then she kissed me again, her lips burnin' with desire, and I thought my heart might pound right outa my bare chest as I lay down upon her bossom and was swept away in her sweet embrace.

Surely this is how God in Heaven intended the love between a man and wife oughta be. Aren't you glad you kept from defilin' yourself with those women of the night, Wil Harleck?

I reckon no twenty-year-old preacher's boy from the mountains of Virginia ever dreamt of how deep was the love I felt in my heart for her in that moment. In the deep rapture of our union, it was like our souls became entwined as one, and I knew in that moment that I would never share my bed with another woman as long as I lived. I don't believe all the demons in Hell could ever remove from me the memory of that blessed night.

Trying Times

If I could've willed that night to go on forever—well, but that's just not the way of things. Anyway, Sunday mornin' came around all too soon, and may the Good Lord forgive us for missin' church, but I surely didn't wanna get out of bed and leave Maribel that mornin'. I reckoned the Lord could overlook a man and wife missin' church on the mornin' after they were wed, even if it was for purposes most folk don't speak about. After all, we had no way of knowin' when we'd be together again, and the Good Book did say we were to be fruitful and multiply, didn't it?

When we finally emerged from her bedroom, I was famished. I may never understand why on earth womenfolk feel like they have to spend such an excessive amount of time so as to make themselves presentable, when it seems to me to be entirely unnecessary. But after Maribel was finally satisfied that she was suitably attractive as a newlywed bride oughta be, she finally came out and asked Samuel to whip us up some lunch, which he did with great dispatch: fresh cornbread and jam with bacon, and we even had a glass of the wine left over from the wedding banquet.

Afternoon came and put me in remembrance that my time together with my lovely new bride was fleetin'. I didn't wanna be late meetin' Capt'n Rowan, so we packed up my things, includin' a new pair of stockin's Maribel had made for me and some cookies Samuel had baked the day before, and we took Mr. Nellis' carriage and headed into town. After a brief stop at home to say good-bye to Mama, Pa, Amos, and Vanessa, we headed down Church Street to Washington. When we arrived, Capt'n Rowan wasn't there yet, but Arty and Tommy were there, and so was Sergeant Robertson. The small gathering burst into cheers and whistles as our carriage pulled up in front of the courthouse.

"There's the happy couple," I heard Arty say.

Tommy was a mite more candid, as was his usual style. "Glad you two could come up for air long enough to be troubled to meet us!"

Maribel blushed and smiled, leanin' one slender arm out the carriage window. "When are you going to find yourself a good woman and settle down, Tommy Johns?" she teased.

"Who, me? Nah! You know how the ladies love war heroes. Turns out I'm the most popular one-legged man in town!"

Then Arty chimed in good-naturedly, " . . . And he ain't ashamed to use it, either, whenever it suits him."

Sergeant Robertson stepped up to the carriage and opened the door. "Congratulations, Wil," he said with a nod, then nodded again to Maribel, "Mrs. Harleck."

"Thank you kindly, sir," Maribel replied courteously. "I'm afraid you have me at a disadvantage."

"My apologies, ma'am. Richard Robertson."

"Pleased to meet you," she held out a gloved hand for him to take as she stepped down from the carriage into the snow.

That's when I realized I was fallin' down on the job. I followed her out of the carriage as quickly as I could without makin' a fool of myself, and did my best to sound civilized.

"I'm sorry. Sergeant Robertson, may I introduce Mrs. Maribel Nel—uh— Harleck."

"The pleasure is all mine, ma'am," he said with a dashing smile, and kissed her gloved hand in his.

Before anything more could be said, Capt'n Rowan arrived with the wagon, which, of course, was followed by another round of introductions and congratulations. Capt'n Rowan was polite and cordial enough, but I could tell he was gettin' anxious to get on the road back to Winchester. "We're picking up the other men on the way out of town. Anyone seen Private Willis?"

"I'm sure he'll be along shortly, sir," Sergeant Robertson replied.

"Drunk, no doubt," the Capt'n responded with a note of disdain in his voice. "Well, he'd better be—along shortly, that is—or he'll have to find his own ride back to camp."

Half an hour went by and still no sign of Willis. Capt'n Rowan took out his pocket watch, checked it, looked around anxiously, then finally broke the silence.

"Well, it doesn't look like he's coming. We'd best be on our way. It'll be dark soon, and we still have hours to travel, and the snow will no doubt slow our progress."

The other fellas tossed their packs up into the wagon and climbed on while Maribel and I said our good-byes.

"I'm still holding you to your promise, Mr. Harleck," she said playfully. "You still have to come back to me."

"You can count on it, Mrs. Harleck—I do like the sound of that," I admitted with a smile.

I wrapped my arms around her delicate waist and she put hers around my neck. I could feel the passion in her kiss as I lifted her off the ground and held her there, and for one brief final moment, the whole world faded away and the memories of the night before came floodin' back.

To his credit, Capt'n Rowan didn't say a word, but just waited quietly as I set her gently down, gave her one final kiss, and climbed up into the wagon. I watched her standin' there and wavin' in her pretty red cloak with the white-furred hood covered in a light layer of snow as we drove away out of sight.

The rest of the trip back to Winchester was quiet enough, but I thought of Maribel the whole way, save when we stopped on the outskirts of town to pick up the two older fellas. Neither of them had seen Willis either, which prompted Capt'n Rowan to remark, "Well, he'd better be at muster in the morning, or there'll be hell to pay."

The next mornin' was pretty much a normal mornin' in camp. We got up at reveille, ate breakfast, and fell in by company for mornin' muster. I was more than just a mite surprised to see Carlton standin' in formation just one row behind me to the left. He was a big man, and not easy to miss, but I caught myself starin' at him anyway when he noticed I was lookin' in his direction.

"What's the matter, boy? Didn't expect to see me, did ya?"

Bad enough that I was both embarrassed and intimidated, but I could scarce believe what I heard myself say next.

"N-no—I mean, yeah. Uh—I knew you'd be back." *Idiot! Why do you let him intimidate you like that?*

"Heh. Yeah, I'll bet you did," he shot back with a glare.

I was only too happy to hear Capt'n Rowan yell, "COMPANY! ATTENTION!"

I turned my eyes back to the front and came to attention. I knew he was still lookin' at me, but I didn't look back. Better to be drillin' than crossin' words with Carlton Willis.

The weather turned from cold to worse the next week, and conditions in camp were so bad that some boys up and decided they were quittin' the army. But most of us were more afraid of Ol' Jack's wrath than we were of the weather. It'd been made perfectly clear to us that anyone caught desertin' would be shot. Still, there were a few that figured it was worth the risk.

A few of us took to sittin' around the fire in the evenin' and singin' to keep the cold away. Michael Chathaway, one of the older fellas in the regiment, had a fiddle which he played with some great skill, and which had the effect of makin' us feel a bit warmer, on the inside, leastwise. On some particularly cold nights, we'd stoke the fire up high and sit around singin' songs like "Goober Peas," "Mary of the Glen," "Home Sweet Home," and at least a dozen other songs we'd either learned in camp or remembered from home. There was always some fella who wanted to sing "The Bonnie Blue Flag" or the ever-popular "Dixie," and I even taught Michael "The Sabbath Bell," one of my favorite hymns from church. Many a night we wiled away the time by the fireplace in one of our log huts, singin' and playin' and sometimes even dancin' our cares away until the night was far gone. Then finally we'd all make our way back to our own huts and try to get a few hours' sleep.

On the sixth of February, I drew the late guard. It was a night not fit for man nor beast: dark and cold and windy, and the snow was blowin' like the devil himself. At about half past midnight on the seventh, I was patrollin' near the company mess when I heard a scuffle, and some of the fellas started to shoutin'. I ran around the corner to find three men in an all-out brawl, and a fourth one lyin' on the ground bleedin' by the head. One of the fellas still standin' was Carlton Willis, but I didn't recognize the other fellas. Willis held a log in his hands, which he was usin' as a weapon. They were fightin' and cussin' up a storm. I figured they must've been drunk, and no amount of my yellin' "STOP!" seemed to have any effect. So I did the only thing I could think of. I fired my rifle into the air.

This, of course, immediately brought men and boys runnin' from every direction with guns in hand, includin' Sergeant Robertson. It also had the effect of breakin' up the fight.

"What's goin' on, here?" the Sergeant demanded, lookin' right at me.

"I heard these men fightin', Sergeant, and they wouldn't stop."

A small crowd was startin' to gather now.

"Which men were fightin', exactly?"

I pointed out Willis and the other two fellas.

"What happened to him?" he pointed at the man lyin' on the ground.

"I don't know. I found him like that."

By then, Capt'n Rowan and L'tenant Davenport had arrived.

"Sergeant, what's this all about?" Capt'n Rowan demanded.

The Sergeant came to attention and saluted the Capt'n. "Private Harleck witnessed these men fightin', sir."

The Capt'n returned the Sergeant's salute, then looked at the men, who were still collectin' themselves. Willis was standin' near the fire, breathin' heavily. He'd dropped the log, and was moppin' the blood from his busted lip with the back of his hand, but the other two could barely stand upright, and their fallen comrade looked like he might be hurt bad.

"Somebody get this man to the surgeon," the Capt'n pointed at the man on the ground. The other two men started movin' to pick up their friend, but the Capt'n stopped 'em. "Not you two! Someone else." He looked around and pointed to two other fellas who were lookin' on. "You men, help this man."

They quickly picked up the man and carried him away, then the Capt'n looked back at the other two men who'd been fightin'.

"What outfit are you men with?"

One of 'em stood up in a manner that somewhat resembled attention, made a poor attempt to salute, and answered.

"Company B, Fifth Virginia, Cap'n. We didn't mean no harm," he slurred. "We was just lookin' for a little somethin' ta eat."

"You men get on back to your own camp. I'll talk to your company officer in the morning."

The men obliged as quickly as they could, what with the condition they were in, but it was plain they were glad to be leavin'. Then the Capt'n turned his attention to Carlton.

"Well, Private Willis, what do you have to say for yourself?"

I didn't know if Willis was drunk or not, but it was plain to see he was madder than a wet hen—so mad he could barely see straight, let alone talk calmly.

"Don't look at me!" he shouted, still breathin' hard. "It was them sons-a-bitches that started it! What'd you let 'em go for?!"

I was gettin' used to hearin' soldiers cussin' all the time, but I still didn't much care for it and tried not to do it myself. But bein' around the likes of Carlton Willis, a man was bound to hear it, and usually a mite worse. Maybe that was partly why he didn't care too much for me. I reckon he figured any man who didn't cuss and drink wasn't a real man. The way I see it though, a man's gotta do what he knows is right, and it doesn't much matter what other folks think.

Carlton went on rantin'. "They come a-stumblin' in here drunk and tried to take our cakes and bacon," he said, spittin' blood on the ground from his busted lip. "It's a damn good thing I was watchin' too, or they'd'a got away with it!"

But Willis' reply only made the Capt'n mad, no doubt partly on account of how he'd had to get his coat and boots on and come out in the cold and snow, and partly on account of Willis' disrespectful tone and choice of language. It was no secret that Carlton didn't like takin' orders, and had little respect for officers in general. But when he was mad or drunk, it really showed.

"Sergeant, clap this man in irons! He's drunk, and I'll have him charged with disorderly conduct, assault, and insubordination!"

"I ain't drunk! I swear I ain't had a drop!" Carlton protested loudly, but the deed was done.

The Sergeant looked at me and another private who was standin' nearby with his gun.

"Privates, put this man in the stocks."

The other fella tried to take Carlton by the arm, but Willis shrugged him off and jerked his arm back.

"Git yer hands off me!" Then he shot a nasty look at the Capt'n and protested again, "I didn't do nuthin' wrong." But the Capt'n stood his ground.

Sergeant Robertson motioned again for the other sentry and me to take Carlton into custody, so I pointed my rifle in Willis' general direction. He knew I'd already fired it, so it wasn't loaded, but it still had the bayonet fixed on the end, which was required for every picket or sentry. That was all the persuasion Willis needed, and I was very glad of it too. I'd seen Willis in action. He was a man accustomed to fightin', and I knew he could easily whoop the two of us if he was so inclined. But he went along peacefully while the other private and I put him in the stocks like we were ordered.

The cold was brutal that night, and there was no fire close enough to the stocks to provide any heat. As my sentry watch wore on, and the night got colder, it was all I could do to stay warm, even though I was able to walk around and occasionally pass near the heat of a fire. I started wonderin' how Carlton must've felt, tired and alone in those cold stocks, away from the fire, and not able to move his head or hands. It made me wonder if maybe the punishment wasn't a bit more severe than the crime, and I found myself actually feelin' sorry for him.

I waited 'til my watch was over, then I went back to my hut and got the thickest blanket I had and took it to the stocks. I knew I might get in trouble for helpin' a condemned man, but I couldn't abide lettin' the man freeze to death over such a trivial thing. As I walked up to him, I could see him shakin' and shiverin' severely. The thick black hair on his head was dusted with snow and blew in the wind with no hat to protect his head. His bearded and scarred face was pale and his lips were blue with cold. I reckon he'd reached the point where he was too cold to be mad anymore, and all he could think about was tryin' to survive the cold. I put the blanket over his jacket across his back and shoulders and tied it around his waist with a piece of rope to keep him as warm as I could.

For a long time, he never said a word. He just stood there shiverin' and lookin' at me like he was both confused and thankful. I could tell he was tryin' to figure out why I'd risk gettin' myself in trouble on his account, so I said the only thing I could that made any sense.

"No man oughta freeze to death over a little fight."

Then, as I turned to walk away, he got up the strength to speak.

"Harleck," he said in a weak voice. He was shiverin' so bad he could hardly talk.

I looked back at him.

"Thanks."

It was all he could say, but it was all that needed to be said.

The next day, we got the news in the papers that some Yankee gen'ral named Grant had captured one of our forts out west somewhere. Fort Henry, I think it was. But I didn't have time to dwell on that too much. By mid-mornin', all of us that witnessed the event of the night before received orders to report to the Provost Marshal's office on the Monday three days hence to give accounts of what we'd seen. I was greatly relieved that Carlton had survived the cold night, and no one had mentioned the blanket at all—leastwise not yet, anyway.

I'll tell you true: the trip to the Provost Marshal's office was a mite unnervin' for me. I knew L'tenant Colonel Botts, sure enough, and he knew me too, but I also knew he was a lawyer and he'd do his job, even if it meant doin' it at my expense. I'd never been involved in anything like this before, and I had no earthly idea what to expect.

I cleaned up my uniform as best I could and marched on over, which was a good little hike from our camp. It was a cold, clear day, and most of the snow on the road between Camp Zollicoffer and Winchester had been trampled into half-frozen mud, which made it hard for a man to keep his shoes clean. I found the Provost Marshal's office in the Winchester and Potomac railroad office, where the telegraph office next door would be of the most benefit. I stacked my rifle and knocked on the door. The chill air didn't keep me from sweatin' like a schoolboy, but there was nothin' to be done about it.

Sergeant Robertson opened the door.

"Come on in, Private."

I stepped inside and saw two privates with rifles standin' guard on both sides of the door just behind me as I walked in. Colonel Botts was seated behind a desk in the center of the room. Behind him stood Colonel Allen and another colonel who I reckoned was probably Colonel Baylor, from the Fifth Virginia. Sergeant Robertson walked over to stand next to Capt'n Rowan and Carlton Willis on the right side of the room, and the three other fellas from the Fifth stood to my left with a Sergeant I'd never seen before. One of the fellas had a bandage on his head. The familiar flag with the three wide stripes and the blue star field in the corner stood behind Colonel Allen, and there was a small table with a lamp on it behind Sergeant Robertson, but there was no other furniture in the room.

"Private Harleck?" Colonel Botts opened.

"Yes, sir." I stood at attention and saluted.

"Stand at ease. Do you understand why you're here, son?"

"I think so, sir."

"This is an inquiry into the events that occurred on the night of Thursday last, the sixth of February. Did you witness the events in question?"

"Not exactly, sir. I mean, not entirely, sir."

"Can you explain just exactly what you *did* witness?"

"Well, sir, I was on guard near the company mess just after midnight the morning of the seventh when I heard some men shoutin'. It sounded like there was a fight goin' on, so I ran around the corner and that's when I saw the fight, sir."

"And did you see *who* was fighting?"

"Yes, sir. I saw three men fightin', and one man lyin' on the ground. He was bleedin' from his head."

"*Which* three men did you see fighting, Private?"

"I saw two men from the Fifth, and . . . " I glanced at Carlton, not sure what he might do if I gave his name to the Colonel, but there was no anger in his eyes. Just a blank stare.

"And . . . ?"

" . . . a-and Private Willis, sir."

"The two men from the Fifth Regiment, were they the same men you see standing here?" He pointed to the fellas from the Fifth Virginia.

"Yes, sir. I believe they were."

"Could you tell what they were fighting about?"

"No, sir."

"And what did you do?"

"I tried to stop 'em, sir. I yelled for 'em to stop."

"And did they stop when you yelled to them?"

"No, sir."

"What did you do then?"

I dreaded what might be comin' next. I knew that firin' my rifle might get me in a mess of trouble, but there was no sense denyin' it, since half the camp heard it and came runnin'.

"I . . . fired my rifle, into the air, sir."

"You discharged your weapon?"

"Yes, sir."

"Why?"

"I didn't know what else to do. They wouldn't stop fightin'."

"Are you aware that discharging your weapon without proper authorization is a punishable offense, son?" His voice was stern and fatherly-like, but his eyes said somethin' entirely different.

"Y-yes, sir. I'm real sorry."

"Private, were these men drunk when you found them fighting?"

His question made me pause for a moment, seein' as how I couldn't really be sure. I reckoned at least the boys from the Fifth were, but

I was havin' my doubts as to whether Willis was actually drunk, or just mad.

"I don't rightly know for sure, sir."

"Did they appear to be drunk to you?"

"Yes, sir. At least one of 'em did, sir."

"Only one of them?"

"I can't be sure of the others, sir."

"*Which* one was drunk, Private?"

I pointed my finger in the general direction of the man who had tried to stand up at attention and answer Capt'n Rowan's question on that night.

"I believe he was, sir."

"And what made you think he was drunk?"

"He sounded drunk when he talked, and he could barely stand up straight."

"And was Private Willis drunk that night?"

I had to stop again and think back on what Willis had said that night, and how he'd acted when we took him to the stocks. I'd seen Carlton drunk many times before, and I could tell when he was drunk.

"Now that I think of it, sir, no, sir, I don't think he was."

Colonel Botts leaned forward and pointed to the man with the bandage on his head.

"Private Harleck, did you see Private Willis strike Private Murphy on the head with a log?"

"No sir." I was relieved that I could truthfully say I hadn't seen that part of the fracas. "He was already lyin' on the ground when I found him."

"Thank you, Private. That'll be all. You're dismissed."

"Thank you, sir," I said, salutin' and breathin' a big sigh of relief.

I could hardly wait to get out of that office, and nearly tripped tryin' to turn around to leave, but finally managed to get out the door again. I was greatly relieved to march back to camp in the cold, but I couldn't stop thinkin' about Carlton, and what might become of him. I even found myself talkin' to the Good Lord on the way.

Dear Lord, I know the Good Book says to pray for our enemies and forgive those who hurt us. Well, if you could help Carlton out of this jam he's in, I'd be real grateful. I think maybe he's not such a bad guy deep down inside, once you get to know him. In Thy Holy name I pray. Amen.

I saw Carlton the next day. It was his turn to cook supper for the mess, so he was stokin' up the cookin' fire and gettin' a pot of beans ready to cook. I wasn't rightly sure if I should ask, but I was dyin' to know what the Colonel had decided.

"You alright?" I asked carefully.

"Yep," he answered without lookin' up from pourin' the beans into the pot. "Why?"

"I was just wonderin' . . . "

"Wonderin' what? Wonderin' why the Colonel ain't had me shot yet?" he fired back, lookin' up at me with a helpin' of hostility in his voice, then went back to pourin' beans out of the bag.

"No!" I defended. "I was hopin' the charges'd be dropped."

He stopped pourin' the beans, and then looked up at me again with just a smidgen of surprise on his face. Then that hard look came back into his eyes again.

"Yeah," he smirked. "Sure you were."

"It's the truth," I protested. "The way I see it, you didn't do anything wrong."

The hard look softened again just a mite.

"That's because I didn't," he said calmly. "Them other boys was the ones that come a-lookin' fer trouble."

"I know."

"Well, then, why'd ya have to go and shoot off yer gun and git me in trouble like that?" he asked, pickin' up the pot and hangin' it over the fire.

"I don't know . . . " I confessed. "I didn't know what else to do . . . I thought maybe you might've been drinkin' or somethin'."

"Well I wasn't," he objected, turnin' back to look at me again.

"I know," I admitted, "and I'm sorry."

I can't be sure, but I thought maybe I even saw a kind look in his eye right then. "Well, no harm done I reckon," he said, pickin' up a wooden spoon and turnin' to stir the beans.

I didn't know what else to say, so I breathed a sigh of relief, and turned to walk away while he was still in a forgivin' mood.

"And Harleck . . . " he called after me.

I stopped and turned back to look at him again, half afraid of what he might say next.

"Thanks fer puttin' in a good word fer me with the Colonel," he said in a low voice, so as not to be heard bein' nice to me.

"You're welcome," I smiled back. "See you at supper." Then I turned again and walked back to our hut to get warm until suppertime.

The next couple of weeks passed without much incident, exceptin' more bad news from out west. It wasn't but a week after Fort Henry that we heard the Yanks had captured another fort and our boys were on the retreat in the west. This second bit of bad news started me to thinkin' about the war.

Maybe we've bit off more than we can chew. What'll happen to Maribel and my folks if we lose this war?

It wasn't a pleasant prospect to consider, so I didn't think on it for too long.

One mornin' in late February, we woke to the news that they were formin' a firing squad, and the whole regiment was to form up as witnesses.

"Seems a cryin' shame to waste good bullets on our own men when we oughta be shootin' at the Yankees," I told Arty as we were finishin' up breakfast.

But that was the way it was. And not just once, either. This time it was a cavalryman from Jefferson County—one of our own local boys, though I didn't know him myself—who'd gone deserter and got caught.

Sure enough, about 11:30 that mornin', bugle calls started goin' off all over the camp to form up our regiments, and the Innocent Second formed up in the snow like we'd done a hundred times before. But this time was different. Watchin' an execution isn't like listenin' to a speech, or musterin' for drill.

There's somethin' just not right about watchin' another man die on purpose.

I reckon there were plenty of men thinkin' that it might've been them if they'd only been a mite more desperate to get out of this army and this war and go home. It got me to thinkin' and wonderin' what I'd do if Maribel needed me at home, or maybe somethin' would happen to Mama or Pa.

It was L'tenant Colonel Botts who had to give the order for the execution, with Gen'ral Jackson, Gen'ral Garnett, and Colonel Ashby lookin' on.

How ironic that the same man who defended a Yankee abolitionist like John Brown, who'd committed an act of violence against Virginia, should have to give the order to shoot one of our own boys just because he wanted to go home.

But this was war.

The provost guards brought the man out and tied him to the post, and then blindfolded him. He was a young man, not much older than me, and he was cryin' and beggin' the guards not to shoot him.

The guards formed a line, marched off about ten paces, and then turned and stood at attention. Then Colonel Botts read the charge and the verdict and pronounced the sentence, and the Capt'n of the Guard gave the order.

"Make ready!"

Five guards unshouldered their rifles.

"Please! Please don't shoot me! Please!" The young man cried out desperately.

"Take aim!"

Five rifles were aimed.

I wanted to close my eyes, but I couldn't make myself look away. As I stood there and watched, I started to thinkin' and wonderin' whether or not this war was really worth all this death and destruction. It sure did give a man pause.

"FIRE!"

Five muskets sounded as one.

A Taste of Defeat

March, 1862

Although there is relatively little combat during the winter months of 1862, the absence of major engagements belies the true state of the war. In fact, there is much activity on both sides of the line dividing North from South. Confronted now with the prospect of a prolonged and costly war, both Union and Confederacy alike begin searching for a plan which will bring the war to a rapid end in their favor with the lowest possible cost in human life. Thus begins a grand chess game of sorts, with each side seeking to outmaneuver and outwit the other.

In Richmond, Confederate President Jefferson Davis and his new government are keenly aware that their fledgling nation cannot possibly compete with the industrial, economic, and military might of the Union. They must now pin their hopes on the cunning of their own military leaders, and the winds of political favor. Their only chance to win this war is to achieve key victories on the battlefield and hope that new alliances can be formed with Europe, thus making the war unpleasant and unpopular among Union citizens and forcing Lincoln to accept the separation.

In Washington, the grand "Anaconda" plan is slow to develop as Lincoln finds himself mired in a war of politics and popularity with his own newly appointed commander of the Union Army of the Potomac, Major General George B. McClellan. Lincoln tries in vain to accelerate McClellan's meticulous plans, but the charismatic and self-important McClellan refuses to heed the urging of his Commander in Chief. Having been fooled by the clever designs of Confederates, McClellan is persuaded that the rebel force near Washington is much larger than it actually is, and opts instead for a massive amphibious invasion of the Virginia peninsula. Assembling an army of nearly 100,000 men, the largest to set foot on American soil to date, he intends to bypass the Confederate defenses in northern Virginia and drive northward from Norfolk toward Richmond with an irresistible force.

In the west, Brigadier General Ulysses S. Grant is suddenly propelled to notoriety by his success against two key Confederate forts which form the hingepin of the Confederate defensive line in the western theater: Fort Henry, on the Tennessee River, and Fort Donelson, on the Cumberland River. When the garrison commander at Fort Donelson asks his terms for surrender, Grant's famed response earns him the immortal nickname, "Unconditional Surrender" Grant. The success of his campaign has opened a gateway into the deep South through Kentucky and Tennessee, and also helps to tip the delicate balance of Kentucky's neutrality in favor of the Union.

Meanwhile, in the mountains of Virginia, "Stonewall" Jackson's Confederate Army of the Shenandoah, consisting of 8,000 fighting men, is encamped near Winchester. Winter in the Valley is finally beginning to break, and Jackson vigorously renews his efforts to defend this vital stretch of land. He knows that even now two separate Union forces are forming to oppose him. To the north, Major General Nathaniel P. Banks commands a federal army more than twice the size of Jackson's own force, with orders to occupy the Shenandoah Valley and deprive the Confederacy of its primary food source. To the west, a smaller garrison force occupying most of western Virginia is being reorganized under the veteran Major General John C. Fremont, nicknamed, "The Pathfinder," to close in on Jackson and force him out of the valley.

Jackson's strategy is simple, but bold: "Always mystify, mislead, and surprise the enemy," he tells his men. "Once you get them running, you stay right on top of them, and that way a small force can defeat a large one every time . . . Only thus can a weaker country cope with a stronger; it must make up in activity what it lacks in strength."

As March arrives, McClellan orders Banks to cross the Potomac at Harpers Ferry. Two weeks later, Jackson, waiting for the right opportunity to strike, abandons his headquarters near Winchester and withdraws up the valley to the outskirts of Mount Jackson, where he waits for Banks to make his first mistake.

Jackson in the Shenandoah Valley—March 1862

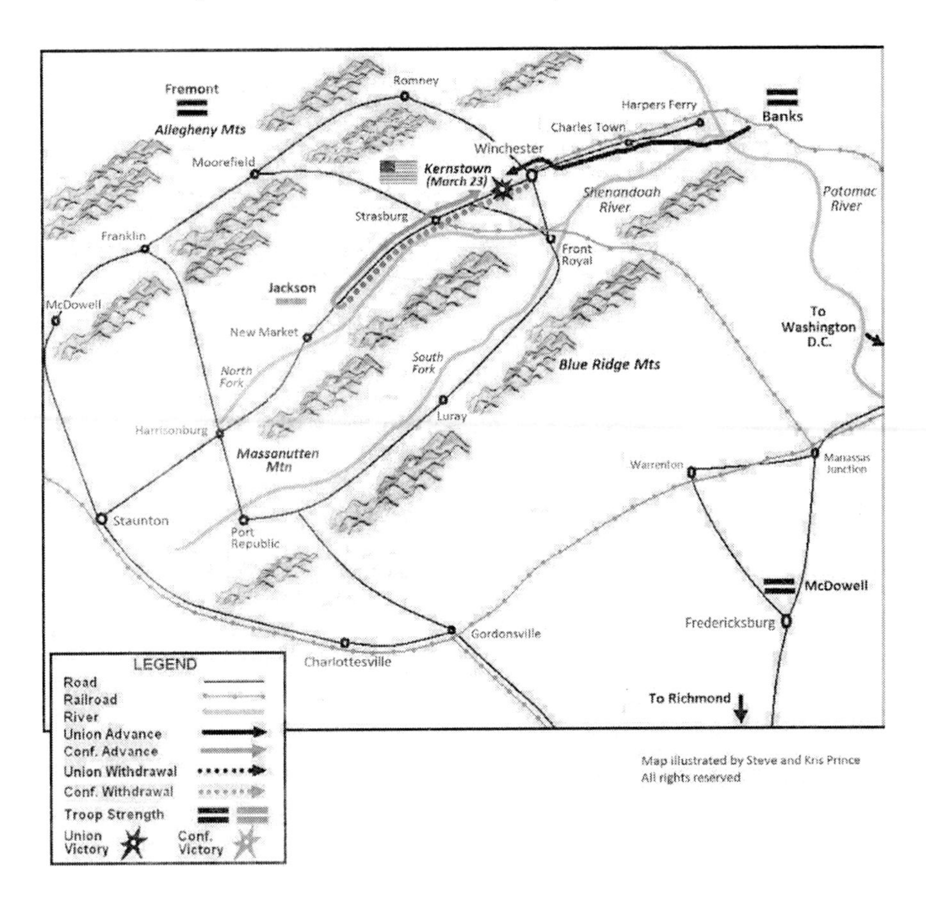

The Valley Campaign Begins

By early March the snow started meltin' off a bit and the days grew a little warmer, which was only a small blessing. All we really did was trade the cold snow for cold mud. And the more the snow melted, the more mud there was. Mud, mud, mud everywhere. There seemed to be no escapin' it. Every day we had to scrub the mud off the floor of our hut so as not to get it into our beds, but then as soon as we stepped foot outside the door, we'd be covered in it again in no time at all.

By the end of the first week, Colonel Ashby's cavalry reported that a new Yankee gen'ral, Gen'ral Banks, was movin' across the Potomac with a new army. The report said that Banks had orders from ol' Abe Lincoln to throw us out of the Shenandoah Valley. I was a mite worried for Maribel and my family, knowin' that Charles Town stood right in his path, and I wondered why Ol' Jack didn't just march us right out and attack the invaders as they came across the river. I reckoned we were likely outnumbered, but Jackson didn't seem the type to concern himself much with that. I knew we were makin' preparations to move out soon, seein' as how there were wagons and horses everywhere, and we were issued new rations, ammunition, and supplies for takin' on the march. But until the order came to march, all I could do was pray that maybe somehow, by God's grace, the Yankees would just march on through Charles Town and not cause any fuss.

One bright Monday mornin', March the tenth it was, as I recall, L'tenant Davenport came back to the company with the telegraph news from Richmond. After the officers read it, the L'tenant brought it out to the mess for anyone who wanted to read it.

"Good news, boys," he said, layin' the paper on the table.

Arty jumped up and grabbed it and began readin'.

"Look at this, fellas," he said. "'Great Naval Battle!' it says here."

"Naval battle? I thought the Yankees had all the ships," I said.

"Me too," Arty said lookin' up. I reckon news of a great battle was quite a surprise to both of us.

"What else does it say?" I asked, gettin' up and walkin' over to where he was standin' to see for myself.

He read on. "Says here, 'The Iron Marine Battery *Virginia* Engages the Federal War Ships --- Sinking of a Fry-gate!' whatever that means."

"That's a 'frigate'," the L'tenant corrected. "It's a warship."

"Hmph," Carlton gru'nted. "Iron ship, huh? Ain't that the damnedest thing you ever heard?"

Arty kept on readin'.

The Battle Still Raging

Norfolk, March 8. A grand naval battle was fought this afternoon off Newport News. A glorious victory was gained by the great marine iron battery *Virginia*, formerly the *Merrimac*. She left the Navy-Yard at half past 11 o'clock this morning, accompanied by three gunboats, and proceeded to Newport News. At a quarter of 2 o'clock, the federal frigates, supposed to be the *Congress* and the *Cumberland*, commenced to fire upon the Virginia. The latter, when at close quarters, opened her powerful rifled guns upon the frigates.

At a quarter past two the battle raged with terrific violence, and at a quarter to three one of the frigates careened and sunk, it is supposed with great loss of life. The other blockading vessel, being badly disabled, set her sails and ran well ashore in Newport News, and is at present sinking. Two larger frigates, supposed to be the *Minnesota* and *Colorado*, went up from Old Point to Newport News . . . The *Minnesota* stopped at a respectful distance below Newport News and fired

> almost incessantly upon the *Merrimac* until night. The frigate is supposed to be aground.

At 9:15 o'clock P.M. the engagement was renewed. A huge fire has been seen in the direction of Newport News. It is supposed that the *Congress* had been set on fire by the Confederates.

"Can ya believe that?!" Arty exclaimed.

I must tell you, there was a great deal of hollerin' and shoutin' all around as news of the great victory spread through the company.

"Wait! There's more!" Arty shouted, and everyone got quiet and gathered 'round while he continued readin'.

> "**Norfolk, March 9.** The Erricson iron battery appeared in the Roads this morning, and had a fierce engagement with the *Virginia* which lasted four hours. The latter ran into the Erricson, damaging her considerably. The *Virginia* fired a shot through her. A large tug boat, in attempting to get the *Minnesota* off, blew up. It is supposed that the *Minnesota* is so much damaged that she cannot float, and will be a total loss. A large portion of her stern works have been shot away."

It sure was nice to get a bit of good news for once after that long miserable winter. I'd hoped it might put a kink in ol' Lincoln's plans to blockade our ports, but the fortunes of war come and go, and the hope was short-lived. Some weeks later we learned that our glorious *Virginia* had to be burned to keep her from fallin' into Yankee hands. Well, I reckon a short-lived victory was better than no victory at all. At least we had a reason to feel better, even if it was just for a short while.

On Tuesday, the eleventh of March, orders came to pack our gear and fall in. News had come that Gen'ral Banks was marchin' south toward Winchester with 15,000 men or more—nearly twice our number. The bugles sounded assembly, and the Army of the Shenandoah marched out of camp like a great snake, turned south through Winchester, and on up the valley toward Mount Jackson. The next day, Banks occupied Winchester. A smaller Union force under Gen'ral Shields was sent to pursue us, but we'd marched so far and so fast, and so great was Colonel Ashby's skill at hidin' our movements from the Fed'rals that they were convinced we'd left the valley and headed for Richmond, so they withdrew back northward again.

On March the twenty-first, Colonel Ashby received a report that Banks was withdrawin' northward, and had left a small rear guard force of only 3,000 men in the little town of Kernstown, just south of Winchester. That was all Ol' Blue Light needed to hear.

Confused Orders

Most of the boys from the Innocent Second didn't take too kindly to the idea of givin' Charles Town and Winchester back to the Yankees while we were marchin' the other direction, so we were glad when we heard that they were withdrawin' northward again. By the middle of the afternoon of March the twenty-second, we were marchin' back down the valley toward Winchester again. It didn't make horse sense to us, first marchin' this way, then that way, but we kept on marchin' anyway.

"Keep on pressin', boys. Ol' Jack knows what he's doin'," Sergeant Robertson said. "We'll give them Billy Yanks hell soon enough."

Colonel Fulkerson's Third Brigade was first in line that day, and the Stonewall Brigade was right behind them. We'd seen couriers ridin' back and forth all day bringin' news to Gen'ral Jackson which we took to be of some importance, seein' as how they always rode by at a gallop. But it wasn't 'til later that afternoon that we got word that Colonel Ashby's cavalry had engaged the Yankees near Kernstown. So we marched on.

When we finally stopped for the night near Cedar Creek, we were all so whooped that we didn't much care that there wasn't time to set up tents on account of the supply train bein' too far behind. We had neither the energy nor the gumption to set up tents anyway, so we just pitched our oilcloths on the ground and slept as best we could, keepin' as close to the fires as possible to stay warm. Late that night I drew sentry duty again. While I was marchin' back and forth along the ridge above, I could look down into the camp and see the lamps still burnin' plain as day in Gen'ral Jackson's headquarters. I reckoned we were in for a tussle the next day, sure as the sun was gonna rise.

The bugles sounded early the next mornin', and we ate a hasty breakfast, put out our bivouac fires, and fell into column of fours for the march to Kernstown. It was a Sunday again, just like Manassas. It struck me as a mite ironic that we were about to be drawn into battle once again on the one day of the week that Ol' Jack preferred never to fight.

We marched 'til mid-day, then the regiment stopped to rest for a short while. There was no time for cookin' so we just ate whatever we could. Most of the boys just had marchin' rations of hard tack and salt pork. It surely wasn't anything to write home to Mama about, but it was pretty much the standard fare for an army on the march.

Before we finished up with lunch, Capt'n Rowan stopped by lookin' like he was in a hurry. "Wil, do you have your prayer book with you?"

The question caught me off my guard. Not only was it mighty peculiar and improper for an officer to address a private by his first name in front of the men, but it also wasn't the usual kind of question I'd come to expect from Capt'n Rowan. I s'pose it stood to reason that I might have a prayer book, but what did the Capt'n want with it?

"My—? Uh. Yes, sir."

"Good. It's Sunday, as you know, and since there wasn't time for a proper church service this morning, how would you like to lead a prayer for the Company?"

"Sure. Yes, sir. I guess, so." I didn't rightly know what to say. I'd never led a prayer in public before, but how could I say no to the Capt'n?

"Good. It's settled, then. I'm appointing you as Lay Reader for Company A. I'll call the men together while you get ready." Then he turned and hobbled off. (He still had trouble walkin' on account of his wound from Manassas.)

Lay Reader? My mind was still wrestlin' with the suddenness of it all, but somehow I managed to get the right words out.

"Yes, sir. Thank you, sir," I hollered so as he could hear even though he was already walkin' away.

I don't rightly recall much about that prayer, but the Good Lord must've gotten me through it somehow. I know it was just a simple thing, readin' a prayer out of a book, but I've never been much for any kind of speakin' in public. My Pa had all the talent for preachin' in the family. But there I was, standin' in the middle of fifty men leadin' a prayer. It was a good thing too, 'cause it turns out we surely did need the Good Lord's help on that particular day.

It wasn't long before we were back on the Valley Turnpike headed north for Kernstown. By around one o'clock we could begin to hear the poppin' of musket fire from skirmishers and the deeper booms from what sounded like it might be a light artillery battery—probably Ashby's horse artillery. So we picked up the pace and marched on.

It was a cool, crisp afternoon, and the early spring breeze was quickly chasin' away what few clouds there were in the sky 'til they blew over the mountains to the east and disappeared altogether. By two o'clock, we were comin' down the hill into the town. We could hear the battle goin' on just off to our right up ahead, but then, all of a sudden, we got orders to turn left off the turnpike. What followed next was a whole mess of confusion the likes of which confounded even the old graybeard vet'rans in the regiment.

We started off through the woods toward a small church and across a crick they called Hogg Run, which ran around the base of a hill that overlooked the town. The boys from Fulkerson's Brigade were in front of us, and as we came out of the woods near the church, we could see at least three Yankee regiments up on that hill. Fulkerson's boys lined up and started advancin' up the hill. But just when we thought we might follow 'em up the hill and drive the Yankees away, orders came to move down the road to the left, quick as we could.

So down the road we went at the double quick, and shortly came to a bridge where the road crossed another crick. Beyond the crick, the road led across a wide open meadow sprinkled with wildflowers among the light golden grass. The meadow ended before a low ridge that was partly covered with trees. When we reached the bridge, Colonel Allen was sittin' there on his horse. Gen'ral Garnett was there with him too, along with several l'tenants and another colonel, whose face I recognized, but whose name I couldn't recall.

I was close enough to see Gen'ral Garnett boost himself up in the stirrups and point his ridin' crop in the general direction of the low ridge as he shouted.

"Quickly, boys! If we hurry, we can flank 'em!"

He was a fairly young man with dark hair and a well-trimmed beard and mustache, and fiery eyes that flashed out from under the large brim of his hat. His uniform was plain enough, though, for a gen'ral, that is. If not for a small bit of gold embroidery on his coat sleeves and the stars on his lapel, he might easily have passed for just any ordinary officer.

The sound of the battle was growin' louder now, but it wasn't just behind us anymore. It seemed like it was behind us and in front of us and all around us, all at once, and there were cannon firin' and shells flyin' back and forth over our heads. My heart started poundin' like I remembered at Manassas. I looked down and I could see my feet movin' and my hands clutchin' the rifle, but I couldn't feel a thing except the poundin' in my ears from the beatin' of my heart. My feet and toes were already numb anyway from all that marchin', but it was the strangest thing that I couldn't seem to feel the rest of my body either.

Almost as soon as we'd crossed the bridge, we were startled by the sound of hundreds of muskets all goin' off at once. I looked to the right to see where the volley was comin' from, and saw Fulkerson's two regiments advancin' toward the left across the big hill.

Then I could see the fed'ral troops formin' all across the big field, and it suddenly occurred to me why we were runnin' to get to the ridge first. If the Yankees got up there on that ridge before we did, we'd have to pay the devil to get 'em down off of it.

We moved down the road through the big field at the double quick 'til we passed the house there and came to a crossing in the road. Then, instead of turnin' right and headin' up the ridge, like any fool would've thought we should do, we turned left, away from the Yankees! Danged if I know why! Up the road behind us a ways we could hear Fulkerson's regiments still hotly engaged. They were tryin' to turn the fed'ral flank, but they were fast becomin' outnumbered. There sure did seem to be a lot of Yankees comin' across that field in our direction—a far sight more than we were expectin', to be sure.

Before long we came to a stop at the base of the ridge. From our position there, we could just see Fulkerson's boys fallin' back toward us with at least three Yankee regiments hot on their heels. Then we got orders to move again, this time toward the Yankees, to our great relief. The fight was growin' fast and we were itchin' to get in it. We ran up to the crest of the ridge, then we turned and ran quickly along the top of the ridge toward Fulkerson's boys as they were fallin' back. The Thirty-third Virginia was just ahead of us, and the Fourth Virginia fell in behind and followed us up the ridge, but the Fifth Virginia was left in reserve, and we hadn't seen the Twenty-seventh in quite awhile. It didn't seem like somethin' Ol' Jack would do, sendin' in only part of the brigade to fight, but then I was just a simple soldier boy. What did I know about such things?

We came to a low stone wall that ran crossways across the top of the ridge and through a grove of trees down the back slope. Gen'ral Garnett placed the Thirty-third to our left just behind the wall, and we took up a position on the right end of the line and prepared for the Yankee counterattack. I thought the Fourth Virginia would fall in to our right, but when I looked back to see if they were comin', they were nowhere to be seen. So the Innocent Second was the end of the line that day.

By the time we got in place, several Yankee regiments were already comin' across the field and startin' up the ridge toward us. We barely had time to load our rifles and kneel down behind the wall before the first Yankee volley was fired.

Gen'ral Garnett was ridin' back and forth behind the line yellin' out orders.

"Stand your ground here, boys!" Then he wheeled around and galloped away quick as you please.

The Trap

Formin' up in line of battle that day without Fredrick felt somethin' like I reckon David must've felt fightin' Goliath with only a sling and stone and no armor. Fightin' with Fredrick had always made me feel a bit safer somehow, and I sure was wishin' he was there with me right about then. But I'd prayed for God to be with me, and that seemed to help some. Well, the Good Lord sure must have a sense of humor, seein' as how I found myself right behind Carlton Willis in line of battle that day. So I set about tryin' to calm my nerves so I could hold the rifle still enough to hit what I was aimin' at. I didn't want Carlton thinkin' I couldn't shoot straight.

Up until that time, the artillery had been occupied over yonder toward the town, for the most part. But now a battery of our guns opened up behind us somewhere, and the shells started fallin' near the approachin' Yankees, which had the effect of slowin' 'em down a bit. We were placed at the end of the stone wall where it curved back to offer us just a small amount of cover. The Yankees came up close enough that we could read their battle flag as it fluttered in the breeze—the Eighth Ohio, it said. They came to a stop just a couple hundred yards away and fired a volley. The rocks and the dirt in front of me and the air overhead came alive with the sounds of the Yankee Minie balls. I heard someone cry out in pain somewhere off to my right, but I didn't have time to look to see who it was or how bad he was hit.

"Ready, boys!" It was Colonel Allen's voice, no doubt about it.

"Take aim . . . FIRE!"

The sound of hundreds of muskets all goin' off at the same time filled my ears, and that unmistakable smell of smoke from the powder burned my nose as I tried to breathe. I felt the painful kick of the rifle in my wounded shoulder, and saw the smoke from my own powder risin' up from the hammer and the muzzle as it kicked up in the air. For an instant I nearly forgot I was aimin' at another man, and thought maybe I was back in the practice field at camp. But then the sound of Carlton's voice brought my attention back to the Yankee line just in time to watch four or five of 'em fall.

"Aha! I got me one!"

Then he yelled even louder, so the Yankees could hear.

"C'mon closer, ya lousy bastards! I got another one for ya!"

I'll say this for those Billy Yanks: they sure seemed a mite braver and more determined than they had at Manassas. They just kept a-comin' and a-comin' up that hill. We fired again and again to drive 'em back, but there were just too many. Those boys from Ohio, they just wouldn't give up. They came right up to that wall, and we had to fall back to the tree line behind us. Then we reformed, fired a couple more volleys into 'em, and charged back to the wall. I reckon they weren't expectin' us to hit 'em back so quickly like that, 'cause they started fallin' back even before we reached the wall.

Twice we battled back and forth over that wall. Both times, the Yankees drove us back, and both times we reformed and then drove 'em back down the hill. But it sure didn't look like they were plannin' to run away. No sooner did we drive back one regiment then another would form up to take its place.

"Banks must have turned around," I heard Capt'n Rowan say. He was just to my right about twenty feet, lookin' out over the big field through his lookin' glasses. "That's at least division strength."

There was a touch of alarm in his voice, and it occurred to me that we just might've stumbled into a trap. I figure there must've been only about three thousand of us on the field that day—not even three whole brigades—but there were two or three times that many Billy Yanks.

Along about four o'clock in the afternoon, we were all startin' to get mighty tired, and we were runnin' low on ammunition. An Irish battalion that was part of Burks' Brigade appeared presently and took up position on our right to extend our lines so as to prevent the Yankees from flankin' us around to the side and behind. The Irish didn't have the wall in front of 'em like we did, but they sure were stubborn, and they fought like a mama bear defendin' her cubs that day.

By five o'clock, the sun was gettin' low in the sky, and it's a good thing too, seein' as how we were clean out of ammunition. We sent word over to the the Thirty-third to our left, but they had no help to send us. The word spread up and down the lines. With no ammunition, we'd have no choice but to fall back. Colonel Allen said to collect all we could from the dead and wounded, then use the bayonet if we had to. I reckon that last order scared me the most. I'd seen what a bayonet charge looked like, and I wanted no part of another one.

We'd barely had enough time to scavenge up a couple of extra cartridges for each man when we saw another Yankee regiment comin' up out of the trees just down the hill to our left a short ways. More boys from Ohio, from what I could tell. They got quickly lined up and fired a volley, and again came that terrible symphony of sounds and cries of pain that made a man shudder down to the bone.

"Make ready!" Colonel Allen's voice broke through the haze in my mind.

"Get ready, boys! Load 'em if ya got 'em!" Capt'n Rowan's low smooth voice wasn't always the easiest to hear over the sound of a battle, but it was enough to remind me to focus on soldierin'. I only had two rounds left in my box, so I pulled out the first cartridge and began loadin'. Almost before I could finish, the second volley came: more Minie balls strikin' earth and stone and flesh. One of 'em passed by so close I could feel it rip through the air right next to my ear and it sounded like a banshee as it shrieked by. Two more balls tore holes in our regimental flag.

"Take aim!" the Colonel shouted.

"FIRE!"

I squeezed the trigger, and my rifle sounded off in the chorus of rifles, but the volley wasn't as loud as before.

"Reload, men! Fire at will!" The Colonel was tryin' to keep us fightin', but there was no denyin' that we were about to be in a mess of trouble. I could see the looks on the faces of the boys and heard the worry in their voices.

"With what?" Carlton called out loud enough for the Colonel to hear. "We ain't got nothin' left ta shoot with. How can we fight with no ammunition?"

I wondered what the Colonel might do, seein' as how he didn't usually take too kindly to that kinda talk from the men. But truth be told, Carlton was just sayin' out loud what most of us were thinkin'.

"Here they come!" Sergeant Robertson hollered, pointin' toward the Ohio boys.

I reached into my pouch and tried to grab my last round, but my fingers fumbled around and I couldn't get hold of it. I looked up at the Ohio boys, and my heart started racin' as I saw the line movin' quickly up toward our position. I must've froze for just a moment, except for my fingers, which were still searchin' around furiously in that box for the last cartridge. Finally, I felt it way down in the corner and made a grab for it.

Just about then the Thirty-third fired a volley at the Ohio boys. A few of 'em fell, but the volley hardly slowed 'em down at all.

"Charge!" I heard a Yankee officer yell out. Then a bugle sounded and they all started runnin' right toward us.

"Stand your ground, boys! Give 'em the cold steel!" I expected the voice of Colonel Allen, but it was actually Gen'ral Garnett, still mounted on his horse not twenty yards behind our line.

The next voice I heard was Carlton's, and he was in the process of workin' up a good temper. There was anger in his voice as he shouted and cursed at the approachin' Yankees, and his face was turnin' red.

"C'mon, boys! Let's get 'em!" He looked back at me and hollered, then he stood up and waved his arm, lept over the stone wall, and started runnin' and yellin' toward the Ohio boys. Some of the men jumped up to follow, but I was still tryin' to make my hands reload my rifle, and it was pert near all I could manage at the moment. A few of the men who still had ammunition fired into the oncomin' Fed'rals, then more and more of the fellas started off after Carlton.

"Hold the line, men!" Gen'ral Garnett was shoutin', but it was no use. The Yankees were too close, and our boys all had their dander up. They weren't about to just stand there and let the Yankees run us over again.

By the time Carlton reached the Yankee line, he was swingin' his rifle and screamin' like a madman. I saw his rifle come down hard on the side of one man's head, and it struck him so hard it sent him flyin' into the fella next to him, and they both crumpled to the ground. Some of the other boys had reached the line by then too, and the lines broke down into a mass of blue and gray all swingin' and stabbin' and brawlin'. It was a gawdawful mess.

Stick with Carlton, ya fool! Just like Fredrick!

I looked for Carlton and found him right in the middle of the fracas. He was wrestlin' with another Yankee, and both of 'em were fightin' over the same rifle, but they'd gone and got all turned around so as the Yankee had his back to me, and Carlton had his back to the Yankees. That's when I noticed the Billy Yank with the shaggy beard runnin' toward Carlton, and I knew he was fixin' to run Carlton through with the bayonet.

I stood up, leveled my rifle, and fired, and I was greatly relieved to see the bearded man drop to the ground right there in his tracks. The next thing I knew, I was runnin' toward Carlton, yellin' like a fury, almost against my own will. I knew the fight was becomin' desperate, and I was more scared than I'd ever been in my whole life, but I just couldn't stay behind that wall anymore. I had to help our boys. And my heart was strengthened to see Artie and a good many of the other boys runnin' with me.

When we reached the melee, I tried to stay close to Carlton, but not so close as to get clobbered by him swingin' the rifle around. One of the Ohio boys came chargin' right at me, and I was astonished to see myself block his thrust with my rifle stock, then strike him in the face with the butt, and then run him through with the bayonet as he fell, just like we were taught back at Harpers Ferry. Strange, I'd never considered myself a killin' man before, but there was a wave of guilt that washed over me at the sight of my bayonet piercin' a man's chest, and a part of me was changed in that moment. I was no longer just an innocent boy. The question of kill or be killed was answered. But there was no time to dwell on the matter.

I don't much recollect what happened next. It was all just a blur of arms and bodies and rifles, all movin' as if to some strange deadly sort of dance. But then—only the Good Lord knows why—those Ohio boys started fallin' back down the hill, and just that quick, it was over.

I felt shaky and numb from hunger and fright and exhaustion, but somehow I kept myself movin'. I helped a few of the other fellas get our wounded back to the wall, and then I just collapsed right there on the ground. When I looked up, Carlton was standin' there lookin' down at me. There was sweat and blood all over his face, and his hat and jacket were all crooked and splattered with blood, but the look on his face was almost like a proud father lookin' at his son.

"Ya done good, boy," he said with a grin as he reached down his hand to help me up. It was all he could make himself say, but it was good enough.

For a few short minutes we were able to catch a rest, but we all knew they were fixin' to come at us again. More and more Yankee regiments were linin' up in that field down below, and they were spreadin' out around our flank so that the Irish boys had to curve the line back to the right just to keep 'em from gettin' around behind us as they came up the hill.

We were very glad that most of the Yankees were in front of the Irish boys this time, instead of comin' our way. But it didn't matter how stubborn those Irish boys were, or how fiercely they fought. It was only a matter of time before the Yankees had enough men comin' up that hill to break our lines. And we had no ammunition left to help 'em.

Fateful Decisions

I don't rightly know how decisions are made by gen'rals and all, but we thought the decision to withdraw didn't come a minute too soon. What we didn't know then was that Gen'ral Garnett was makin' a decision he'd regret for the rest of his life.

Just as the new Yankee regiments on the right started comin' up the hill toward the Irish battalion, we saw another regiment comin' up through the woods toward the wall where the Second Virginia met the Thirty-third. Every man and boy in the regiment, and in the Thirty-third too, knew we couldn't hold against another attack. And the Yankees sure did seem hell-bent on attackin'.

That's when I heard the bugler sound the retreat.

"Fall back, men!" Colonel Allen shouted.

What happened next was a messy and embarrassin' affair. There was a lot of shoutin' by the officers, and a lot of confusion on our part. We didn't know whether we should fall back or stay and fight. It didn't much feel right pullin' out. We knew that if we did, we'd leave a big gap in the line, and the Irish boys and Fulkerson's regiments couldn't possibly hold against the Yankee attack without us. But with no ammunition left, it sure didn't make much sense for us to try and stick around and fight either.

It didn't much matter, anyhow. The Billy Yanks were determined to take the ground, and there sure were enough of 'em to do it. Colonel Ashby'd obviously been wrong about their strength. It seemed like the whole Yank army was there in front of us and comin' up that hill.

It was startin' to get late, and we'd had just about a bellyful of fightin' that day. We were all exhausted from marchin' and fightin', and we weren't about to just stand there and let the Yankees shoot us down like a gobble of turkeys just waitin' to be shot on account of the Good Lord not givin' 'em enough sense to run away. No man among us wanted to be called a coward, but what else could we do?

It was the most disorganized I'd ever seen the army. Men and boys everywhere; some walkin' this way, some runnin' that way, and some standin' still, not sure what to do. Red-faced officers shoutin' orders and then countermandin' each other; horses runnin' here and there, some with riders and some without; guns goin' off all around, but we couldn't be sure who was shootin' at who. What a miserable, messy affair it was.

What few of us as managed to stay together weren't even out of sight of the Irish boys when the final Yankee attack came. Our boys were hopelessly outnumbered, and it wasn't long before they were fallin' back too. Then the whole line broke and men scattered everywhere.

What with all the confusion, I made sure to stay close to Arty and Carlton. I reckoned at least we'd be safer that way—less chance of bein' shot as deserters and cowards—but it still just didn't feel right leavin' the battlefield.

"We should reform and go back," I said, lookin' to Carlton and Arty to see if they felt the same way.

"It's no use, boy," Carlton said, matter-of-factly. "This fight's over." His face was grave and steeled. "Besides, who're we gonna reform with? Everyone else is runnin' too, and we ain't got nothin' left to fight with."

I knew he was right, but I didn't much care for leavin' the field to the enemy, and I knew ol' Tom Fool was gonna be fit to be tied. The word "retreat" wasn't in his vocabulary. I looked at Arty, and he didn't say a word, but the look on his face said it all.

He's right, Wil. This fight's over.

"I'll say this for ya though, Harleck," Carlton spoke up again. "You got guts."

I was speechless. Carlton Willis had never paid me a compliment before.

"I never figured you for a fighter . . . " he started, but then changed his mind, and just kept walkin' without sayin' another word.

Arty didn't talk either. He just patted me on the shoulder and we walked on in silence. As we came down off the back side of that ridge, we saw the flags of the Fifth Virginia deployin' across the road in the meadow just below us. We went around to the right so as to get out of the line of fire, and quickly found ourselves in a long ragged line of men and boys stragglin' down the road back toward camp.

We heard rumors among the boys that the Yankees were comin' after us, but by sunset it became apparent that the rumors weren't true—at least not that night, anyway. I reckon the Billy Yanks must've been slowed by the boys from the Fifth Virginia, then, likely as not, they had to give up the pursuit on account of it bein' too dark.

All night long the men straggled back into camp, but we had no earthly idea what to do next. We'd never been whooped like that before. The next mornin' when the sun rose and the bugle sounded for assembly, those of us that were still left fell into ranks, whereupon we were promptly reminded that we were soldiers and we had better do our duty. What was to become of the men who didn't come back wasn't said, but we knew at least five or six of our boys, or maybe more, would never see their homes again, and dozens of others had been taken prisoner by the Yankees during the worst of the fightin'.

The rains came the followin' day, and the roads and fields all turned to mud again. All but a handful of the men had returned to camp, but it was clear the fightin' wasn't over yet. Ashby's cavalry was skirmishin' with the Yankee vanguard just a few miles back, so we had orders to form up and march back to Mount Jackson.

The march back up the Valley Pike was as damp and gray as our spirits. Even the drummers didn't play, and there was nary a man who could make himself look up as we trudged along in silence in the mud and the cold spring rain. If the Good Lord was tryin' to keep us from gettin' too proud, He was doin' a good job.

By the time we arrived at Mount Jackson and began settin' up camp, the whole regiment was buzzin' over the rumors.

"Did you hear, Wil?" Arty asked.

"Hear what?"

"Ol' Jack went and had Gen'ral Garnett arrested for givin' the order to withdraw the brigade at Kernstown!"

"What?! How do you know that?" I asked. But it wasn't all that hard to believe.

"It's true! I overheard the officers talkin' about it this mornin'."

"I know how he can't abide cowards and all," I said, "but there was nothin' else we could've done. We were outnumbered and out of ammunition, and they were about to run us clean over."

"That may be true, but Ol' Tom Fool's steamin' mad over it! Called Gen'ral Garnett a coward, I heard, and blamed him for losin' the battle. Even went and drew up Court Martial papers!"

We knew Gen'ral Jackson was a mite eccentric—even downright strange from time to time—but this time we thought he'd gone completely mad.

"I heard Colonel Allen talkin' to the rest of the officers at breakfast this mornin'. He said we're gettin' another new brigade commander. Winder, he said was the name."

"Never heard of him," I remarked, shruggin' my shoulders. "You?"

"Nope, but one of the officers called him a 'Maryland bastard'. Said he was real strict."

"That's *Gen'ral* Winder to you, Private Johns," the voice of Sergeant Robertson interrupted. "Brigadier Gen'ral *Charles Sidney* Winder, to be precise. And he arrived just today to take command," he warned in a hushed voice, "so you best not let anyone hear you repeatin' that 'Maryland bastard' remark either, if ya know what's good for ya."

"Yeah?" Carlton piped up loudly. "Well, I don't take too kindly to no . . . Yankee from Maryland . . . comin' in here and actin' all high and mighty like he was God er somethin'. Who the hell does he think he is, anyways?"

"I reckon he thinks he's in charge," the Sergeant shot back dryly, "and he'd be right. Besides, he's no Yankee. He commanded the Sixth South Carolina at Fort Sumter. He's been in the service of the Confederacy longer than we have."

Carlton glared at the Sergeant, but Sergeant Robertson wasn't backin' down. Finally Carlton just looked down and spit on the ground.

"I still don't like him," he said, turnin' and walkin' away while he talked.

"We hardly even got to know Gen'ral Garnett," I remarked.

"Haven't you heard, Wil?" Arty said with a grin. "The lifespan of a brigade commander in this here army is only about six months. If the Yankees don't kill 'em, Gen'ral Jackson will!"

We all had a laugh, but somehow it didn't make us feel much better.

We camped there at Rude's Hill for three weeks. While we were there, the company officers took to scoutin' around for new recruits to replace our losses. It was there we got news from Richmond about the Conscription Act. L'tenant Colonel Botts informed the regiment of the new law at muster one mornin' in late April.

"The Congress of the Confederate States of America has passed a new Conscription Act," he announced. "Every able-bodied man or boy between the ages of eighteen and thirty-five will be required to serve in the army or naval forces of the Confederacy for a period of three years, or until the war ends, whichever is sooner."

Maybe he thought it might make the boys feel a mite better if we knew we'd be gettin' some "fresh fish"—that's what some called new recruits—comin' into the regiment, but it didn't work.

"Any man who does not wish to serve," he went on, "may, in his stead, hire a substitute to serve on his behalf." But that only brought a new wave of grumblin' and whisperin' in the ranks.

"Sounds like a rich man's war, but a poor man's fight to me," Carlton said in a low voice.

"What was that, Private?" Colonel Botts shot back.

Carlton stiffened up and said it again, louder this time.

"Sounds like a rich man's war, but a poor man's fight to me."

That brought a chorus of voices all talkin' at once.

"Yeah, that's right!" one man shouted out loudly. "That don't seem hardly fair. What chance does a poor man have of gettin' outa the war?"

"Fair or unfair, it's the law," Colonel Botts shot back in a stern voice like a father chastisin' a child. "The matter is not open for debate so hold your tongue. I'm not finished yet."

There's more? If it's more bad news, I think I'd prefer not to hear it.

"The law also says that any man over the age of thirty-five who has already served in the war may receive a discharge, and may go home, if he desires."

There were several sighs and looks of relief in the ranks, mostly from the graybeards.

Well, I reckon that makes it more like a poor young *man's fight, now, doesn't it?*

I was surprised that Carlton didn't just up and quit right there on the spot, what with him bein' over thirty-five and all, but he just acted like nothin' ever happened.

"You're not quittin'?" I asked him that night at supper.

"And do what?" he asked, stabbin' a piece of meat with his knife. "Go home and let you young'uns lose the war for us? I ain't *that* stupid!" Then he just grinned and put the bite in his mouth and went back to eatin'.

"Don't you have any kinfolk back home?"

"Just my good-fer-nothin' brother and his good-fer-nothin' wife and boy," he answered, still chewin' his meat.

"When was the last time you saw 'em?" I asked, curious to find out why he called his brother 'good-fer-nothin'.

He swallowed, but didn't look up. "We don't talk much . . . "

I thought about askin' why, but the look on his face told me to just leave it be. Maybe he was right where the Good Lord wanted him to be.

Altogether, 270 new men joined the regiment that month, some through enlistment and some because of the draft, but the new recruits didn't do much to raise our spirits. What with the defeat at Kernstown, plus Gen'ral Winder takin' command, and the Conscription Act, the morale of the regiment was never lower. Then came the dreadful news of another defeat somewhere out west at a place they called "Shiloh." I was beginnin' to wonder if things could get any worse. Several of the boys just up and deserted. I reckon they'd had just about all they could take.

As for me, the only thing left to do was to pray for somethin' good to happen. As I said, the Good Lord has a strange sense of humor.

Jackson's Foot Cavalry

April 1862

The rout at Kernstown is recorded as Jackson's only defeat, but it still accomplishes much for the Confederacy. Most notably, Jackson still has a viable force in the Shenandoah Valley, which makes him a threat to the Union Capitol. This, in turn, prompts Lincoln to divert strength away from George McClellan's grand invasion of the Virginia Peninsula.

By late winter of 1862, the overcautious McClellan has convinced himself that the Confederate defenses and fortifications between Washington and Richmond are too formidable to attempt a direct approach to Richmond. Instead, he opts for an amphibious invasion from the southeast up the Virginia Peninsula. On March 17, his Union Army of the Potomac, some 100,000 strong, boards more than 400 ships and sails down the Chesapeake Bay to Fortress Monroe. Though located in Virginia, the federal stronghold has remained in Union hands and guards the entrance to Hampton Roads Harbor near Norfolk. This same fortress, which only a week before had witnessed the decimation of the Union naval squadron by the Confederate ironclad Virginia *(formerly* U.S.S. Merrimac*), and the ensuing epic battle between* Monitor *and* Virginia*, is now choked with federal troop ships. But the mighty* Virginia *is helpless to prevent the landing. Even with her legendary iron plating, she is no match for the monstrous shore batteries mounted by Fortress Monroe, and the Confederate Navy can scarcely afford to risk losing their prize flagship.*

Despite the relative ease of the landing, the long journey up the peninsula between the York and James Rivers toward Richmond is slowed by rains and flooding, and slowed even more by McClellan himself. Though he possesses nearly ten times as many troops as the Southern defenders, McClellan now becomes his own worst enemy. Falling prey to the clever ruses of the rebels, he has convinced himself that the Confederates have assembled a massive force to oppose him. Exasperated, Lincoln strongly urges McClellan to advance toward Richmond, but McClellan refuses, demanding more troops instead. Meanwhile, in Richmond, Confederate General Joseph E. Johnston can't believe his luck. Taking full advantage of the delay, he redeploys nearly 50,000 additional troops to the peninsula to defend the Southern Capitol.

In April, Robert E. Lee, military advisor to President Jefferson Davis, sends a letter to Jackson asking him to attack Banks in the Shenandoah Valley in order to reduce the pressure on Richmond. Jackson immediately begins to formulate plans, commissions a set of highly detailed maps of the valley, and sets his strategy in motion to "mystify, mislead, and surprise the enemy."

Lincoln begins to realize that before he can take Richmond he must first eliminate Jackson in the Valley. Only then can he move on Richmond with all of his combined strength. To this end, Lincoln orders his armies in western Virginia to converge on Jackson and destroy him. Both Banks and Fremont possess forces larger than Jackson's, but Lincoln is leaving nothing to chance. He also orders Irwin McDowell, who has now pushed southward to Fredericksburg, to cease his advance on Richmond and send reinforcements to the valley to trap Jackson and defeat him. Reinforced by Ewell's division, Jackson's 17,000 men are now skillfully keeping more than 50,000 federal soldiers occupied in the Shenandoah Valley, thus depriving McClellan of the overwhelming force he so desperately seeks.

March 28, 1862

Pvt. W. A. Harleck
Army the Shenandoah, near Mount Jackson

My Dearest Maribel,

Perhaps you may have heard news of our defeat at Kernstown this Sunday last, but my darling wife, you must not believe everything you hear. I am well and unharmed, and though our army may be bruised, we are far from beaten. Lieutenant Davenport informs us that among the losses suffered by our company from Charles Town were Privates Crist and Campbell, who were mortally wounded, and ten others missing and presumed captured. Others received minor injuries, but, by some miracle of Heaven, I and all of my closest friends are unharmed.

Do not be concerned, my love, at the loss of but one battle. General Jackson is a good and God-fearing man and a cunning leader, and I believe we will yet see victory and independence for our beloved Virginia if we but trust in God and do not lose hope. I must confess to you that I would trade a thousand days of life in this army just to hold you in my arms for one more night. But you would no doubt think me a less honorable man were I to forsake our noble cause for such a selfish reason as to come home to you now in the face of all that has been sacrificed. So I will content myself to pray to Almighty God that this war may be brought to a swift and just end, and I will bide my time until that sweet day when I may once again hold you in my arms and gaze upon your lovely face.

I have heard that the Yankee army has again occupied Charles Town, and I pray that you remain safe and that my parents and family are also well. I know you will do all within your power to remain so until our army returns to drive the invaders from our home land. Our regiment has been sorely reduced by the long hard winter, and even more so from the recent affair at Kernstown, but we are told we may receive new recruits soon to replenish our ranks. I earnestly hope we shall then turn northward again and show the enemy the strength of our resolve until he has had all he can stand of this war and gives up this foolish notion of forcing us to return to the Union.

I look forward every day to your next letter, and I pray for you each day that Almighty God may keep you in His grace until my return.

Until then, I remain steadfastly,
Your loving husband,
Wil

Jackson in the Shenandoah Valley—May 1862

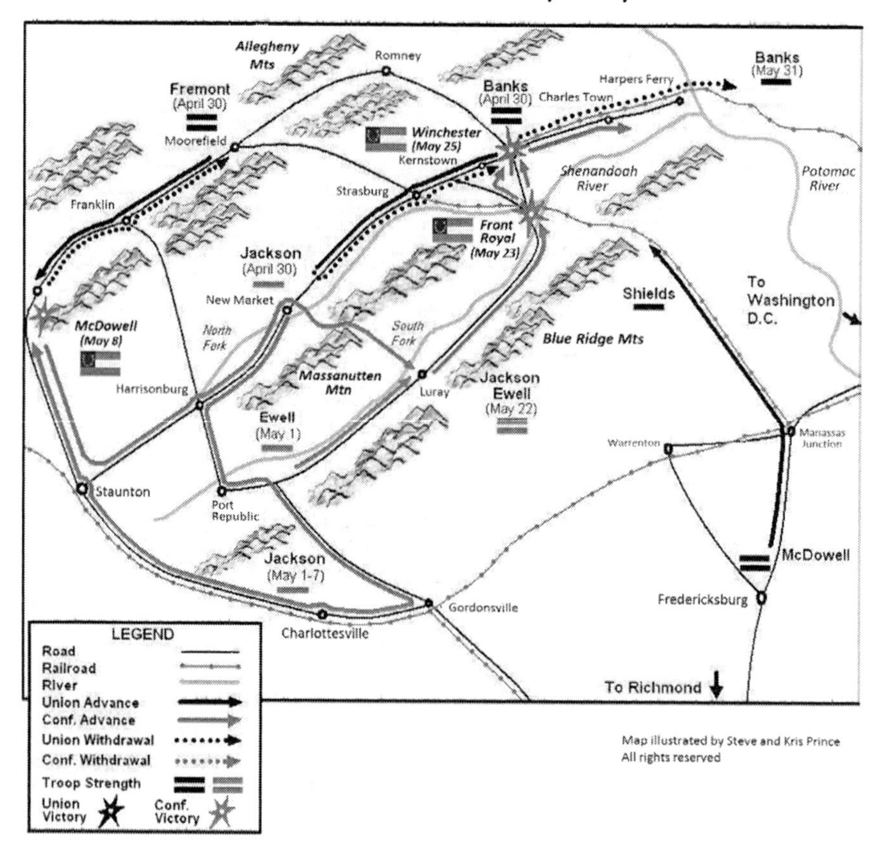

"Old Blue Light"

For the Army of the Valley, May of '62 was a far sight better than the previous two months. We were surely glad to see Gen'ral Ewell's division arrive on April the thirtieth, which more than doubled the size of our army. And when we received orders that we'd be movin' out soon, well, that didn't hurt things either. In just a couple of days' time, the morale of the army went from the valley of despair to the top of the mountain. We'd had just about enough of lickin' our wounds, and we were itchin' to go and express to ol' Gen'ral Banks our extreme displeasure at his unwelcomed presence in the valley.

Early on the mornin' of May the first, we left Ewell's boys at Swift Run Gap and headed back up into the valley, then turned southward to Port Republic. Even the drivin' rain wasn't enough to dampen our spirits at the thought of gettin' back into the fight. But it sure seemed strange that we'd be headin' south up the valley when ol' Banks was to the north near New Market when last we heard tell.

Then somethin' even stranger happened. Ol' Tom Fool turned us east again and marched us clean out of the valley toward Gordonsville, there to board another train. I was surprised when Capt'n Rowan and L'tenant Davenport climbed up into the rail car with the rest of the boys from Company A instead of ridin' with the officers like before.

"Good afternoon, Private," Capt'n Rowan said.

" . . . Afternoon, sir." I tried to stand up, but he held out his hand to stop me.

"Don't get up, son," he said. Then he gestured toward the floor next to where I was sittin'. "May I sit?"

I wasn't rightly sure what to say, so I just nodded, but he was already sittin' down anyways.

"Much obliged." He sat and leaned back against the wall of the rail car and let out a sigh like he was powerful tired.

"That was quite some march, eh?" he asked, takin' off his hat and moppin' his brow.

"Yes, sir. Some march."

I reckon marchin' was a mite tougher on the Capt'n since his injury at Manassas. He mostly rode his horse when we marched, but horses need rest too, so sometimes he'd dismount and limp along with the horse.

"Mighty glad to have this train. Much better than marching, wouldn't you agree?"

"Yes, sir. I reckon so."

"Amazing things, trains. You can travel three days' march in just a few hours."

"That they are, sir. A little hard on the backside, though."

"Ha!" he chuckled. "Well, I suppose you're right. Riding in these here livestock cars could be a little uncomfortable. Normally I'd prefer not to ride back here—no offense to you fine men—but since there are no coaches for the officers, well, I guess you're stuck with us."

"I don't mind, Capt'n."

Likely as not, some of the boys didn't take too kindly to havin' the officers ridin' with us, but there was nothin' to be done about it so I just kept my peace. Besides, at least with the officers there Carlton was more apt to keep himself out of trouble.

The train started rollin' and my curiosity started to get the best of me. "I don't s'pose you might know where we're goin', would ya, sir?"

"No, I'm afraid I wouldn't. But I do know we're headed west."

"West?" I couldn't hide my surprise. "Are you sure?"

"Sure as the afternoon sun," he pointed up at the sun through one of the windows of the railcar, "which is how I know we're headed west."

Why didn't you think of that, Wil? Ya fool!

"Hmph. Then why'd we have to march all the way east out here to Gordonsville?" I asked. "If we're tryin' to get west, wouldn't it've been easier just to march west?"

"That's our General," he chuckled. "He sure likes to keep us guessin'—and the Yankees too." He smiled and shifted around to look at me while he was talkin', bein' sure to keep his bad leg stretched out. "They say he only has two rules."

I looked up, curious to hear about these rules.

"The first is, always mystify, mislead, and surprise the enemy, if possible . . . "

This time it was my turn to chuckle.

He smiled and went on. " . . . and then never let up in the pursuit' as long as you have the strength to follow. You see, he believes that once we get the enemy running, if we pursue them hotly, they'll begin to panic, then they can be destroyed by half their number."

"Is that the second rule?" I asked.

"No. The second rule is this: Never fight against heavy odds if you can maneuver your own force to attack only the weakest part of your enemy and crush it," he said thoughtfully. "He believes that if we do that we'll win every time, and even a small army can destroy a larger one in detail. And repeated victory will make us invincible."

I reckon Ol' Jack was a true military genius if ever there was one.

By May the fifth, we began to see the brilliance of Gen'ral Jackson's plan. By marchin' us out of the valley, he'd managed to fool ol' Banks into thinkin' we were headed to reinforce Richmond. So Banks withdrew his army back down the valley toward Winchester, which left only Fremont's Fed'rals to hold the upper valley by themselves. And they were all spread out on account of they weren't expectin' us to turn around. It wasn't long before we caught up with part of the Yankee force near the town of McDowell.

On the afternoon of May the eighth, the Billy Yanks came out to give battle against three of our brigades on a part of Bullpasture Mountain called Sittlington Hill, but the Innocent Second was not engaged there. The sound of cannon fire and muskets came down off that hill and bounced around the valley late into the night, and the flashes lit up the sky like lightnin' on a warm summer's eve. But we were too far to the rear to get into the fight.

Sometime about ten in the evenin', things started to quiet down. We got word that the Blue-bellies were fallin' back. By midnight, the Yankees'd had enough. They withdrew to the north and left us in command of the field, which delighted Ol' Blue Light no end. Seein' him ridin' high on that horse with his eyes all gleamin' bright like they did in battle made a fella wanna stand up and shout. Someone once told me that they heard Ol' Jack say the reason he was so brave in battle was on account of his belief in God. I reckon he figured the Good Lord would come for him whenever He was good and ready, and the matter of when and where was just sauce for the goose after all. Whatever it was that made him so cool and calm in battle, it sure was a sight to behold.

We thought maybe he might wanna go after the Billy Yanks, seein' as how he was so riled up and all, but the moon was settin' behind the mountains and it wouldn't be long before it'd be too dark for a fella to even see his own hand in front of his face, to say nothin' of mountin' a pursuit. We didn't much care anyway. We were just glad it was the Yankees that were givin' up the ground this time. If they were runnin', well then, all the better, but if not, there'd be plenty of daylight tomorrow to teach 'em another lesson.

We slept that night under a cold and cloudless sky. There was no time to set up camp, so we just slept on the ground. Thing about marchin' with Ol' Jack was the army had to travel light so as we could move quickly. So most of the boys either left everything they didn't absolutely need back with the supply train or dropped their extra items along the way when they got too heavy. There were times when we didn't see the supply train for days, so how each man decided what to carry with him was carefully calculated accordin' to what the other fellas in his company were already carryin'. One man might drop his skillet because it was too much for the march. Another fella, further back in the line, would pick up the skillet because his company had none, and lay down his axe. Then a third man may pick up the axe, and lay down somethin' else he didn't need as much. And so it went all down the line. It was the darnedest thing.

But on that particular night, many a man and boy passed a cold and hungry night wishin' he'd not left his extra blanket behind. Those who'd carried their axes along were very glad of it and were quickly befriended by others who needed firewood to stay warm. The night sky was strewn with countless stars which shone even more brightly than usual without the moon and the clouds to hide 'em. What a sight it was to see so many stars above and so many fires on the earth below, as if some of the stars had fallen from the sky.

As it turns out, pursuin' Fremont wasn't Ol' Blue Light's plan anyway. He'd already set his mind on drivin' Banks and Shields out of the valley first. After another couple days' march, we found ourselves back at New Market and bivouacked there at Camp Jackson for a few days. The Billy Yanks had been there, sure enough, but when Ewell's Division advanced down the eastern valley to Luray, ol' Gen'ral Banks had to fall back down the western valley to Strasburg so as not to let Ewell get behind him.

We finally saw the supply wagons there and were very glad not to have to forage for food for a few days. The mail arrived too, and there was a letter from Joseph. I hadn't heard from him since that cold Christmas night in Charles Town. I was surprised to find that the letter began with an apology.

"My dear brother, Wil,
I feel compelled to write you to apologize for my behavior this Christmas night last. I've been giving this matter much thought of late, and it was impolite of me to allow my feelings about the war to eclipse the night of your engagement. William and Grace-Anne Nellis must think me outspoken and ill-tempered, for which I am sorry."

This, of course, got me to thinkin' about my own behavior on that night. I reckon neither of us had been a shinin' example of Christian charity, to be sure.

Anyways, he went on to explain how he understood why I'd made my choice to side with 'the rebellion', as he put it—truth be told, that's what it really was anyway—but he was compelled to stay with the Union on account of the slavery issue.

"I believe our nation is being judged for its sins against God and humanity, brother," he wrote, "and we are paying the price in blood."

I must admit, I'd been givin' a lot of thought to the matter of slavery since that night. I couldn't deny that both sides were indeed payin' a heavy price in blood, and I wondered just how much more blood would have to be spilt before this war was brought to a resolution. But was it really some kind of judgment from God? Or was it just the pride and foolishness of men? That was the question, and I didn't have the slightest idea how to answer it.

He went on to say:

"The Bible tells us, in Hebrews, the ninth chapter and 22nd verse, that 'without shedding of blood is no remission.' I believe this war is a necessary part of God's will to purge the blight of slavery from our land once and for all time. But I fear, little brother, that you may have allied yourself with those who oppose God's will."

His words wounded my heart just as sure as if someone had stabbed it with a knife. I'd long wrestled with the issues of war and bloodshed and God's will, and believed myself to be a man of faith. Was he callin' me a heathen? Was he sayin' that the whole Confederacy was a brood of sinners who opposed God's will? All of these thoughts raced through my mind, and I felt my heart racin' too, at the insult—whether or not it was intended—and I suspected it was, knowin' Joseph.

His letter continued:

"And if this war is indeed God's judgment against the sin of slavery, then I believe repentance must accordingly be the order of the day. For this reason, I am prepared to devote myself to the cause of aiding in the freedom of the Negro man to whatever extent I am able."

Could this be the same brother I'd once looked up to and idolized? The same brother who used to tell me stories about marchin' to Harper's Ferry with the Jefferson Guards to put down the abolitionist rebellion of John Brown and his followers? I'd always imagined the two of us—Joseph and me—servin' in the army together. Was he now sayin' we were to be enemies? Was he now sayin' that crazy ol' John Brown was an instrument of God? I swallowed hard, not wantin' to believe what my eyes told me.

"Wil, you are my brother," he appealed, "and I do not wish to become your enemy." I felt the faintest hope of redemption in my heart at the words that might come next. "I hold no ill will toward you, and I have no wish to see any harm come to you. I urge you, therefore, to please reconsider, lay down your arms, and forswear this foolish rebellion."

But my heart sank as I read his final words. "The choice is yours, brother. But know that I will do what I must, as God wills it."

And you should also know, dear Joseph, that I, too, will do what I must . . .

"Private Harleck? A word, if you don't mind." L'tenant Colonel Botts' clear voice broke through the haze in my mind. He'd obviously been standin' nearby as I read the letter.

"Y-yes, sir." I tripped over my tongue and my feet both, tryin' to stand up and salute.

"At ease, son. Walk with me a moment, if you please." We walked a little ways from the company.

"Was that letter from your brother, Joseph?"

" . . . Yes, sir. How did you know?"

"I'm the Provost Marshall, remember? All of the mail comes through my office, and the threat of spies has compelled us to keep a closer eye on any personal letters that come from across the Potomac. Wil, I allowed that letter to be delivered to you because I know your Pa, and I've known you and Joseph since you were young lads. But I do still have my job to do, and I wouldn't want to have to accuse you of conspiring with the enemy, now would I, son?"

"No, sir. I s'pose not."

"Of course not. So would you mind letting me see that letter?"

"Yes, sir—I mean no, sir. I wouldn't mind."

I held out the letter and watched him take it. He opened it and read it for a moment, then looked up at me with a familiar concerned look in his eyes.

Colonel Botts was not an overly tall man, and a mite on the thin side too, but he had an honest and sincere face. He had brown hair and a well-trimmed beard that came to a short point under his chin. His eyes were set deep under his stern brow so that when he looked at a man it always gave the impression that he was lookin' right through into your soul.

"So Joseph thinks you should quit and go home, huh?"

"Yes, sir."

"He thinks it's against God's will for you to fight on the side of the Confederacy?"

"Yes, sir. I reckon so."

We came to a stop under a nearby tree and he leaned back thoughtfully against it.

"And what do you think?"

"Well, that's just it, sir. I'm not really sure what to think anymore."

His look of concern turned into somethin' more like perplexed.

"Do go on . . . "

"Well, I used to be sure of the righteousness of our cause, but now I'm not so sure. What if Joseph's right? I mean, with all the killin' and death, and this war goin' on the way it is, well, I can't help but wonder, whose side is God on anyway?"

The quizzical look turned into a gentle smile and I could see him relax a bit.

"Well, that's the real question, now isn't it?"

He produced a pipe and a small pouch of tobacco from his jacket pocket, tapped the pipe against the tree, and started fillin' the bowl with tobacco.

"I suppose there are some pretty godly men who share your brother's opinion," he continued. "John Brown sure did. He may've been convicted for breaking the laws of men, but he went to the gallows convinced that he was a soldier of God, and nothing I could've said would've convinced him otherwise."

I remembered that it'd been Colonel Botts who'd served as John Brown's lawyer, which leastwise gave him some insight into the matter.

"Then there's General Jackson," he went on. "I don't know that I've ever met a more devout Christian man, except perhaps your father, of course. And yet he seems pretty convinced that God would not ally himself with any nation or state which invaded the sovereign territory of another."

He took a match from his pocket, struck it, and lit the pipe.

"Truth be told," he went on with the pipe clenched in his teeth, "I wasz againsht sheshession, myshelf."

I was dumbfounded by his candid revelation. "Sir . . . ?"

His voice became serious. "That'sh right, but I don't share my pershonal political viewsz with jusht anyone, and I'd be obliged if you wouldn't either."

He took a puff on the pipe and looked thoughtfully up at the sky. Then he took the pipe in his hand and went on in a more pleasant tone of voice.

"I love the Constitution, and the United States, but my higher duty has always been to Virginia, and I will do my duty above all." He paused to take another puff and continued. "Wil, I don't rightly know if God really takes sides in the affairs of men, but I suspect that there'll be both northerners and southerners in Heaven. I think what really matters is that each man fears the Lord and does what he believes is right in God's sight."

"I think I see what you mean, sir."

He took another puff, and then held the pipe in his hand again. "I hope this means you've decided to stay and do your duty? Desertion is a serious offense, you know."

"Yes, sir. You can count on me."

"Good. Then let us put this matter to rest."

"Yes, sir." I came to attention and saluted, and he stood up straight and returned my salute.

As I turned to walk back to the company, I heard him call out again.

" . . . And, Private,"

"Sir?"

"Don't let anyone else see that letter. We don't want anyone getting the wrong idea." He smiled and put the pipe back in his mouth.

"Yes, sir."

Praying Men

Early the next week, Capt'n Rowan came by with one of the new fellas. He was a mite older than me. I reckoned he must've been goin' on thirty-five, with a full head of brown hair and a full beard. He wore a farmer's hat and shoes, and although he had a soldier's pants and braces, his shirt wasn't uniform issue. He had a jacket too, but he was carryin' it instead of wearin' it. I figured he must've been one of the new conscripts.

"Private Harleck, I'd like you to meet Private James Lancroft." Then he turned to the man who was with him. "Private Lancroft, this here's Private Wil Harleck. He's the Lay Reader for Company A."

I stuck out my hand and Private Lancroft shook it.

"Call me Jim," he said.

"Wil," I replied. "Nice to meet ya."

"Private Lancroft here," the Capt'n said, lookin' at me again, "is a praying man like yourself. I thought maybe you two boys might like to get to know each other."

"Thanks kindly, Captain," Jim said, saluting as the Capt'n turned to walk away. I reckon the Capt'n didn't even see Jim's salute, seein' as how he just left him standin' there with his hand up to his head. But I could tell by the look on the private's face that he felt himself slighted.

"Have a seat if you want," I said, gesturin' to a fat log that was sittin' up on its end.

"Don't mind if I do," Jim Lancroft replied, lookin' grateful.

"So, where ya from?" I asked, sittin' down across from him.

"Culpeper. You?"

"Charles Town."

"Not very friendly, folks around here, huh?"

"Aw, don't think too much on it. Capt'n Rowan's a good man. I'm sure he just didn't see you salutin'."

But the look on his face said he still wasn't convinced.

"It ain't just him," he said, lookin' around the camp with a nervous smile on his face. "It's everyone."

I'd noticed it'd been quieter around camp of late, but didn't really put it all together in my mind until just that moment. There was a mite less music and merriment to be heard, and the men all huddled around in their own little broods, vet'rans with vet'rans, and conscripts with conscripts. What few new volunteers could be found were usually found with the new conscripts—not on account of them not wantin' to be there, but just on account of them bein' new.

"Well maybe we just don't want no freeloadin', yella-bellied, no-account conscripts 'round here," Carlton fired at Jim with a glare from where he'd been sittin' just a few feet away.

Jim looked down at the ground for just an instant, but then he looked up at Carlton again with a determined look in his eye. "I may not be here on my own accord, but seein' as how I'm here anyway, I intend to pull my own weight," he said with conviction in his voice.

"Ha!" Carlton smirked and went back to what he was doin'.

Jim thought about it for a minute, then his eyes flamed as he looked over at Carlton again. "Alright. I'll prove it."

But Carlton just rolled his eyes and smirked again. "What're you gonna do? Promise not to run away?"

"Well for starters, I know my way around a rifle. I could clean yours for ya."

"Touch my rifle and I'll kill ya," Carlton said, deadpan. "I don't trust nobody else to clean my rifle, least of all the likes of you."

"Alright then. What *will* you trust me to do?" Jim asked, undaunted.

"Nothin'! Except maybe my johnny detail!" Carlton laughed smugly.

"Done," Jim answered flatly.

Carlton glared at Jim for a moment, then finally his eyes softened a mite.

"You ain't serious . . . "

"Serious as a preacher on Sunday."

And he was too. He took Carlton's johnny detail that very night—not that it changed the way Carlton felt about him all that much, but at least it shut him up. There was hardly a chore in the army worse than johnny detail. It was the filthiest, smelliest, and most disgusting chore a soldier could do—except for burial detail, that is. And Carlton was just like the rest of us. He hated johnny detail.

On May the twenty-first, we got orders to march again, and we were glad of it. We'd been itchin' to head north down the valley and throw ol' Banks out of Strasburg. But only Ashby's cavalry was sent northward toward Strasburg—most likely to keep Banks from guessin' what we were up to. I reckon he must've had a devil of a time figurin' out what Ol' Blue Light was plannin', seein' as how even we didn't know.

Anyways, the rest of the army turned east from New Market, followin' the narrow windin' road across Massanutten Mountain to Luray. There, we joined up with Ewell's division, then on the twenty-second, we turned north down the Luray Valley between Massanutten and the Blue Ridge toward the town of Front Royal. Rumor had it there was a small Yankee force there, and we were hopin' Ol' Jack was intendin' to give 'em a nice hot welcome, southern style.

Our march down the Luray Valley was quick as our feet would carry us. We were becomin' quite accustomed to marchin' that way. The marchin' made us dog tired, for sure, but our feet were gettin' a mite tougher and our boots were well broken in by the many miles we'd already marched. Some of the fellas from the other units weren't so lucky though. Most of the Stonewall Brigade had been given new boots with our new uniforms when the war broke out, but we couldn't help but notice that some of the other boys were wearin' older shoes, and they were startin' to fall apart.

At least it was a blessing that the weather wasn't too bad. May in the Valley brought warm days and cool nights that made even the long marches more tolerable. In the early mornin' and late in the afternoon, the shadows from the mountains on either side grew longer, which kept us much cooler and made for nice marchin' weather, and the cool nights were perfect for sleepin' by the fire under the starry night sky.

Early Friday mornin', May the twenty-third, we were awakened and ordered to eat quickly and form up to march, but after we ate we mostly just stood around waitin' for the order to march. Ewell's men marched out first, along with the cavalry, headed north toward Front Royal.

We never saw any action that day, but we learned afterward that the battle of Front Royal was fought mostly by Marylanders on both sides—both usin' the same regimental designation. The First Maryland, C.S.A. moved into the town and forced the First Maryland, U.S.A. to withdraw in retreat. By day's end, the town of Front Royal and the river crossings over both the North and South forks of the Shenandoah River were all in Confederate hands. And almost 700 Yankee prisoners to boot.

I reckon the victory at Front Royal got Ol' Blue Light foamin' at the mouth! He marched the army through the town and across the Shenandoah River, even though the Billy Yanks had tried to burn the bridge over the North Fork in their flight. By nightfall, the camp was ripe with rumors about what the next day would bring. Some said we were gonna march west to throw the Yankees out of Strasburg; others said Banks would have to withdraw back to Winchester; and still others said they were already skedaddlin' out of the valley altogether. I wasn't sure who to believe, but any way it came out seemed like good news to us, so it didn't much matter. Besides, we'd find out for sure in a day or two.

On Saturday, we rose early and started preparin' to march again.

"Get yourselves ready for a long march today, boys," L'tenant Davenport told the company.

"Capt'n says our scouts have reported that Banks is withdrawin' up the valley Turnpike toward Winchester, and unless I miss my guess, Gen'ral Jackson will wanna try and catch him before he gets there."

"I thought Banks was dug in at Strasburg, L'tenant," one of the older fellas said.

"When we took Front Royal yesterday, we turned his flank," the L'tenant answered. "He can't hold Strasburg anymore without us gettin' in behind him and cuttin' him off from home."

I reckon the L'tenant must've been right, seein' as how Ol' Jack divided the army that day so as to keep Banks from slippin' around behind us. The Stonewall Brigade, marched north, followin' behind Ashby's cavalry, and the rest of the Division fell in behind us. When we reached Cedarville, we turned west across the valley and caught the end of the Yankee column as they were fallin' back to Winchester.

Most of the fightin' that day was done by the cavalry and the skirmishers, but it was clear as mountain air that we were right on ol' Banks' heels like a hound on a hare. All day that day we pressed on through a shower of Yankee ambushes and skirmishes thick as fallin' leaves in October. But Ol' Jack hardly missed a beat. After each skirmish, he'd get us right back into column of fours for the march and right back on the road again. Darkness began to fall, but we just kept right after those Yanks, just like Ol' Jack said.

So quick was the marchin' and so dark was the night that Carlton tripped over a stone in the road and fell down hard on the side where the bayonet was tucked through his belt, jabbin' the tip of the bayonet right into the back of his own leg. This, of course, made him cry out in pain and brought a stream of obscenities flowin' from his mouth that would've made a harlot blush. He got back up, mad as a hornet and embarrassed at bein' so clumsy, but he hobbled on without even stoppin' to bandage up the wound. And no one dared speak a word to him about it.

We kept on goin' into the night, and didn't stop 'til we saw the lights of Winchester. Finally, at about one o'clock Sunday mornin', Colonel Allen sent word to the company officers that we could bed down for a few hours. We were so tired from marchin' and fightin' all day, we didn't even bother to make a fire. We just dropped right where we were and went right to sleep. Arty drew the first picket that night, but before he even finished his watch, orders came to get the men up, so he got no sleep at all that night.

It was still dark when we rose, and a spring fog was comin' down off the mountains. While the rest of us were tryin' to make a hasty fire for breakfast, the Colonel had the officers assemble for officers' call. Within twenty minutes, word came that we were retakin' Winchester and the Stonewall Brigade was leadin' the attack. Cheers and shouts echoed through the camp, and we were so overjoyed at the news that we plum forgot we'd only had two hours sleep!

"I thought Ol' Jack didn't like to fight on Sunday," I heard one fella say, "but we sure do seem to do a lot of fightin' on Sunday!"

"Any day's a good day to whup them Yankee bastards," Carlton added, still soundin' a mite hot under the collar.

"Yeah. I reckon that Sunday rule only applies when the Yankees ain't tryin' to get away!" Arty chimed in, and the other fellas all laughed.

Then it was Capt'n Rowan's voice I heard next.

"Speaking of Sunday; Private Harleck, would you lead us in a prayer, since there'll be no time for church this morning?"

"Pleased to, sir," I said, a smile breakin' the corners of my mouth just a tad, "if I can find my prayer book in all this darkness and fog."

The Capt'n retrieved a lantern from his tent and the company gathered around. I opened up my prayer book and found the Morning Prayer. The men all took off their hats and bowed their heads, and I started readin'.

> "The Lord is in His holy temple; let all the earth keep silence before Him." Habakkuk 2:20.

"When the wicked man turneth away from his wickedness that he hath committed, and doeth that which is lawful and right, He shall save his soul alive." Ezekiel 28:27.

"If we say that we have no sin, we deceive ourselves, and the truth is not in us, but if we confess our sins, God is faithful and just to forgive us our sins, and to cleanse us from all unrighteousness." 1 John 1:8-9.

Almighty and most merciful Father, We have erred and strayed from Thy ways like lost sheep. We have followed too much the devices and desires of our own hearts. We have offended against Thy holy laws. We have left undone those things which we ought to have done; and we have done those things which we ought not to have done; and there is no health in us.

But Thou, O Lord, have mercy upon us, miserable offenders. Spare Thou those, O God, who confess their faults. Restore Thou those who are penitent; according to Thy promises declared unto mankind in Christ Jesus our Lord. And grant, O most merciful Father, for His sake, that we may hereafter live a godly, righteous, and sober life.

To the glory of Thy holy name. Amen."

"Amen," the men echoed. Then they put their hats back on and got about their business preparin' for the battle that was comin'. All except one, that is.

"Harleck?" It was Carlton, still standin' a few feet behind me, with his hat still in his hand and a scowl on his bearded face.

"Yeah?" I answered, wonderin' just what the scowl was for and what he wanted with me.

"You really believe all that religious hogwash you just said?"

"I s'pose so. Why?"

"Well, it just don't make no sense to me," he said, and the look on his face made me think again about my answer.

I could hear Pa's voice in my mind: "*Sometimes God's ways are a mystery to us. That's why it's called faith.*" But then I got to thinkin': *Maybe Carlton's right, Wil. Do* you *really believe what you said, or is that just your Pa talkin'?*

"Truth is, I reckon it doesn't always make sense to me either," I was ashamed to admit. I thought maybe tellin' the truth might help, but the doubt on his face was still there. "Maybe it doesn't have to make sense. My Pa says that's what faith is—believin' when it makes no sense." But somewhere deep down inside, a seed of doubt still echoed in my mind.

"Bah," he scoffed, wavin' his hand in the air like he was pushin' the idea away. It was plain to see Carlton wasn't buyin' it.

"Well, what doesn't make sense, exactly?" I asked.

"You know, all that stuff you said about God bein' good and us bein' bad and all," he said, "well, I just can't figure it."

I took a breath to build up the courage to ask "Why not?" Maybe it was because a part of me was askin' myself the same question.

"I know I ain't really lived a very good life, but I just can't . . . " His voice broke off and he looked away like he didn't wanna say what he was thinkin'.

" . . . can't what?" I pried.

"Nuthin'." He turned like he was gonna walk away, but then he winced in pain and reached down to grab the back of his left leg just below the knee, and the angry scowl returned to his face. "Damned stupid bayonet! Marchin' around in the damned dark! It's like a bad omen or somethin'!"

When he straightened up there was blood on his hand. I looked down and was surprised to see a flow of fresh blood runnin' down his pant leg. His face and eyes looked powerful tired, and the look of anger had turned to pain and frustration.

"Look here," he argued loudly. "I don't know if this God of yours is real, but if he's s'posed to be so good, like you say, then why would he take a boy's mama away and let his daddy drink himself to death?" I reckon he was gettin' his dander up a mite more than he'd planned on, judgin' by the red of his face.

I was surprised by the revelation about his folks, and I didn't rightly know what to say. I s'pose that'd be enough to turn any man hard—and away from God too.

"I'm sorry—"

"Just forget about it! It ain't important no how." He growled.

"I didn't know—"

"I said just forget about it!"

I tried to think of what my Pa would say, but all I could hear was, "*the Lord giveth and the Lord taketh away.*" But deep down I knew there had to be a better answer than that.

I reckon that was the first time I'd ever had to face the question, *how could a good God let bad things happen?* In that moment I knew in my heart that there must be a deeper truth, and I felt the conviction risin' up inside of me.

"I don't believe God took your mama and daddy . . . " but the rest of the words just weren't comin', and the doubt on Carlton's face wasn't goin' away.

"But He let it happen, didn't he?" he shot back.

"I can't explain it," I admitted, "I just know there must be a good reason." But my words just didn't seem to be helpin' any, and I had to wonder why we were even havin' this talk in the wee hours of the mornin' before a battle. Then I heard Carlton's words again: *It's like a bad omen or somethin'!*

"What did you mean when you said it's like a bad omen?" I chanced.

He heaved a sigh and shrugged his shoulders, lookin' down at the ground. "It's just . . . I got a funny feelin'," he confessed. "I can't explain it, neither."

I waited, not sayin' a word. I reckoned if he was gonna talk, I needed to keep out of the way and let him talk.

"How's a man s'pose ta know when it's his time ta go?"

Well, Wil Harleck, what're you gonna say now?

The way I figured it, the best thing was just to be honest.

"Well . . . I don't rightly know," I confessed. "Only the Good Lord knows when it's a man's time."

He looked off thoughtfully into the distance for a moment, then looked back at me.

"Do you think maybe He warns some people when their time's a-comin'?"

"Is this because of the bayonet?" I asked, pointin' to his leg.

"It ain't just that." The frustrated look reappeared and he wrinkled up his brow. "I just got a bad feelin', that's all." He sighed again, then shook his head like he was tryin' to clear it all out of his mind. "Would ya . . . would ya just put in a good word fer me with the Man up there," he asked, waggin' his finger toward heaven.

I didn't mean to look surprised, but I reckon it was plain to see on my face.

"Just forget it," he said, turnin' to walk away.

I had to think fast.

"Sure," I replied quickly.

He stopped and turned back, lookin' at me suspiciously like he was eyein' a counterfeit greenback.

"I'd be glad to," I added.

The suspicious look softened just a mite, but didn't go away altogether.

"Thanks," he managed with a half-hearted look of gratitude.

Before I could think of anything else to say, he just turned again to walk away.

I wasn't sure when I'd have the next chance to pray, what with the battle comin' up and all, so I just got down on my knees, closed my eyes, and started prayin' right then and there.

"Dear Lord, please watch over Carlton in the comin' fight and spare his life if it be your will. Nevertheless, if it should be your will to take him home this day, then I pray you prepare his soul, that he might receive eternal life with you in Heaven. In the name of your Son, Jesus, I pray. Amen."

Before I could open my eyes, Carlton's voice surprised me.

"Amen," he echoed. Then he turned again and hobbled off.

"Commissary Banks"

Just before dawn, the fog got even thicker, and we marched the last mile or so down the Valley Turnpike without bein' able to see where we were actually goin'. There were no drums or music for that part of the march, seein' as how we didn't wanna let the Yankees know we were comin'. It was quite the sight. The spectral forms of the men were like somethin' from a Washington Irving story: an army of ghosts in the foggy twilight with only the sounds of our shufflin' feet on the road. If the Yankees could've seen us, they'd likely just up and run away in terror.

We reached a Quaker cemetery along the side of the road at the base of a hill just as the eastern sky begun to turn light. When orders came to form the brigade in line of battle, the Fifth Virginia was placed in front as skirmishers, then the Second and the Fourth Virginia regiments formed in the center of the brigade, with the Thirty-third Virginia to our left and the Twenty-seventh Virginia to our right.

The fog was beginnin' to lift and we advanced up the hill, whereupon we were promptly met by tremendous fire from the fed'ral guns on a second hill, which could just be seen a half mile or so to the north. This compelled us to halt our advance and take cover 'til our own guns could be brought up. When our guns finally arrived, they commenced to duelin' with the Yankee batteries. This went on for about two hours and made our lives unpleasant for awhile. Meanwhile, a group of Yankee sharpshooters opened fire on our guns from behind a small stone wall on our left, which did not make our gunners very happy at all. They got their dander up and turned two of the guns on the stone wall with solid shot to drive the sharpshooters away, then we moved up close and they scurried down the other side of the hill toward the town.

The sounds of the guns were deafenin', and we never knew just where the next shell would fall. More than a few of the boys were killed or wounded there. One shell exploded close in front of Carlton and me—so close that it knocked me down and tossed Carlton through the air like a rag doll 'til he landed behind me all crumpled in a heap.

I got back up on my feet and ran back to see if he was still alive, but couldn't find any serious wounds, exceptin' a few powder burns and some nicks and scratches. He was knocked out but still breathin', so I called for help to see if a couple of the fellas would help me carry him back from the lines.

I felt a hand on my shoulder and Jim's voice said "Get his other arm."

We lifted Carlton by the arms and dragged him back a ways down the hill and laid him under a tree.

"You stay here and rest," I told him. "We'll be back for you." I didn't know if he could hear me or not, but I couldn't just walk away. I had to say somethin'.

I looked at Jim and knew we needed to get back with the rest of the boys, but I must admit I felt worse scared goin' into battle without Carlton. For all his faults, he was a good soldier in battle, and I'd hoped we might become a good fightin' team.

Jim and I rejoined the regiment again at the top of the hill just as the sun was comin' up over the mountains to the east. The fog was mostly gone, so we could see the battlefield a far sight better. The Yankees were dug in on a broad hill just across the way, where their guns were keepin' us busy. Off to our left stood another ridge which ran along the Yankees' right flank, and we could see the flags of our boys goin' up that ridge. In just minutes they'd be up over the fed'ral flank!

Gen'ral Winder must've seen it too, because he suddenly appeared on his horse, yellin' and shoutin'.

"Forward, men! We're flankin' the bastards!"

"C'mon, boys! Let's go!" yelled another officer, but I couldn't tell who it was.

Before I knew it, we were on our feet and chargin' down the hill. We crossed a small crick at the bottom and broke out in the rebel yell as we ran toward the Yankee positions at the top of the wide hill. By the time we reached the top, the Billy Yanks were already fallin' back into the town below.

"They're breakin', boys! Let's push 'em back across the Potomac!" It was Colonel Allen, standin' at the crest of the hill with sword drawn toward the enemy, and wavin' us on into the town with his other hand.

When we reached the town, the Yankees were reformin' to make a stand on the main street. So we formed up lines and fired a volley, and when we went at 'em again, they broke and ran down through the town.

By lunchtime, the Yankees had abandoned the town and were fleein' in a panic the likes of which we hadn't seen since Manassas, leavin' guns and wagons and horses and all manner of supplies and equipment behind as they ran. We chased 'em nearly five miles up the road toward Charles Town before the courier finally caught up with orders from Gen'ral Winder to stop and reform the regiment.

I thought about goin' back to keep my promise to Carlton, but we'd plum chased those Yankees nigh off the edge of the world, and there was no way to get back to that hill before sundown. We were all tired as dogs from the day's work, anyways, so I resolved to try and find him in the mornin'.

I rose early the next day, rolled my oilcloth, and set off back down the road toward Winchester to find Carlton. I reached the town in less than two hours, and was directed to a hospital where I was told some of the boys from the Stonewall Brigade were bein' treated. After another hour, I located the hospital and found Carlton sittin' on the grass outside with his head all bandaged up.

"You alright?" I asked.

"Yeah, I'll be fine. Just a bump on the head," he said with a touch of embarrassment in his voice. But before I could think of anything else to say, he looked up and spoke again. "They said you pulled me back from the lines."

"Jim and me. It was nothin'."

"Jim, huh?" he asked, lookin' a mite unhappy. Then he just smirked. "Ain't that somethin'," he said, shakin' his head.

Carlton still didn't take much of a likin' to any of the new conscripts—even Jim. But I wondered if just maybe the Good Lord thought it might be funny to fix it up for Jim to be part of the answer to my prayer for Carlton. It just figured to be like somethin' He'd do.

"You feel like walkin'?" I asked.

"I told ya, I'm fine."

"Wanna get outa this place?"

"Does a bear sh—" he started, then stopped himself right in the middle of the word, "*live* in the woods?"

I helped him get to his feet, and we set off to find the rest of the regiment.

The Innocent Second was assigned provost duty in Winchester for the next three days, where we had the pleasure of roundin' up all the the guns and ammunition, uniforms and boots, and food and supplies the Yankees had left behind. Not to mention the Yankee prisoners—thousands of 'em. So great was the amount of arms and provisions left behind that the boys awarded Gen'ral Banks a new nickname: "Commissary Banks."

The morale of the army was never as high as it was in those two or three days followin' the battle of Winchester. It was a welcome relief to have all the food and provisions we wanted. And good food it was too. Ham and beef and bacon, beans and potatoes, and even some early radishes and cucumbers and carrots. Some of the boys got new socks and shoes too. Best of all, a couple of the regiments from Georgia and South Carolina even got new Yankee Enfield rifles, and there were several captured Yankee cannons and wagons full of ammunition.

On that first night there was music and merriment in the camp the likes of which we hadn't seen in over a month. It was one of my fondest memories of the army. The Jefferson Guards had roasted beef with potatoes and carrots almost as good as Mama made, and we ate hearty after three days of almost continuous marchin' and fightin'. The Yankees had even left us some plates and silverware to eat with, which a couple of the fellas were more than happy to confiscate for the company mess. There were now only about twenty-five of us left in the company, even countin' the new recruits, which made it easier to get enough things such as plates and the like for the whole company whenever the supply trains were nearby.

Jim came over and sat down next to me during supper. It was the first time we'd really had a chance to talk much since the day we met.

"So, you got family, Wil?"

"Sure do. Just married, not four months ago." I was smilin' from ear to ear just from talkin' about my beautiful Maribel.

"Well, bully!" He put out his hand with a big smile.

"Thank you." I put out my own hand and he shook it firmly.

"She pretty?" he asked, pretendin' like he couldn't tell already just from the smile on my face.

"Is she pretty?! She's the prettiest little thing you ever did see! Why she's the prettiest thing in the whole great state of Virginia!"

Jim laughed and went on. "What's her name?"

"Maribel."

"Maribel," he repeated with a smile. "Beautiful name for a beautiful girl."

"So how about you? You have any family?"

He looked down at his feet. "Wife and two daughters. Had ta leave 'em to take care of the farm by themselves when the draft law was passed. Reckon that's why I didn't enlist when this whole thing first started."

"How old . . . ? Your daughters, I mean. How old are they?" I asked.

"Adaline is seven and Dorothy's four."

"Still pretty young. No hired hands or anyone else to help 'em?"

"Nah. Nothin' left but women and old men back home. Not since the draft, anyways. Besides, we couldn't afford a hired hand if'n there was one to be had. Barely make enough ta keep us alive as it is. There's an older couple lives nearby, but they can't hardly be of much help. It's all they can do just ta keep food on their own table."

"You must worry about 'em."

He looked up from the ground and looked me right in the eye. "Every day," he said. Then he heaved a deep sigh and sat back, and his gaze shifted off toward the fire. "But I reckon it don't do much good to worry. All's a man can do is pray and hope that the Good Lord will watch over his kinfolk while he's away."

"Amen to that." I found myself lookin' at the fire too, as thoughts of Maribel came floodin' back.

"You got other kinfolk back home in Charles Town too—besides Maribel, that is?"

"Yep. Mama and Pa and my younger brother Amos and sister Vanessa." I was about to mention Joseph too, but then I remembered what Colonel Botts said and thought better of it. I didn't rightly know if I could trust Jim with that bit just yet.

"Must be hard, what with the Yankees occupyin' the town, and it bein' just up the road and all."

"Sure is, but I reckon we're shortly about to take care of that problem."

"Sure hope so," he said.

"We oughta be in Charles Town by now, instead of sittin' here in Winchester," I protested.

"Ain't that the truth," said a voice from behind us.

It was Carlton. He turned a log with his foot and sat down on the end of it while he balanced a plate in his left hand and clutched his knife in his right. I was stunned. I never figured Carlton to be one to sit with the likes of Jim and me. He usually seemed to prefer spendin' time with the few fellas who'd rather be drinkin' than soldierin'.

I looked up but couldn't make myself say a word.

"How you feelin'?" Jim asked.

"I'm alright," Carlton answered curtly, lookin' at Jim. Then he turned to me.

"'Bout time we got somethin' good to eat around here, huh?" he asked, stabbin' a piece of beef and shovin' it into his mouth with the knife.

"Sure is," Jim tried again. Then he put out his hand by way of introduction. "Jim Lancroft."

Carlton didn't shake the hand, but raised his knife and plate toward Jim with a nod.

"Yeah, I know who ya are," he said, still chewin' his meat.

"Glad yer alright," Jim continued.

Carlton looked a mite irritated. "I shuppose you want me to shay thanksh for shavin' my life?" he grumbled, still chewin'.

"No need to thank me," Jim replied with genu-ine humility. "From where I stood, looked to me like it was the Good Lord had His hand on you."

Carlton swallowed his food and looked at me, and I knew he was thinkin' the same thing I was thinkin': *That prayer! I reckon we plum forgot!* But he didn't say a word. He just set his plate and knife aside and turned to stare into the fire for a moment like he was miles away. It goes without sayin' that only a matter of great importance could make Carlton Willis let a good meal like that go to waste, but it was plain he'd lost his interest in supper. Then, just like that, Carlton got up and turned back to look at Jim and me again.

"Well, thanks anyway," he said in a low tone. Then he just turned and walked away.

Jim and I just sat there for a minute watchin' him walk away, then Jim turned back to me. "What's his story, anyway?" he asked noddin' his head in Carlton's direction.

"Don't rightly know for sure. He used to be real mean. Still is when he's drunk, I reckon."

"Has he got a family?"

I shrugged. "Brother, I think, but I get the feelin' they don't talk much. Said God took his mama when he was a boy and his daddy drank himself to death."

"Hmm," Jim said, strokin' his beard. "You s'pose maybe the army's the closest thing to a family he's got?"

"Could be," I answered.

Strange thing about soldierin': havin' a real enemy out there tryin' to kill you has a way of makin' a man think twice about who his friends are. I wasn't rightly sure if I could call Carlton a friend just yet, but he sure didn't seem quite the enemy anymore, either.

Jackson in the Shenandoah Valley—June 1862

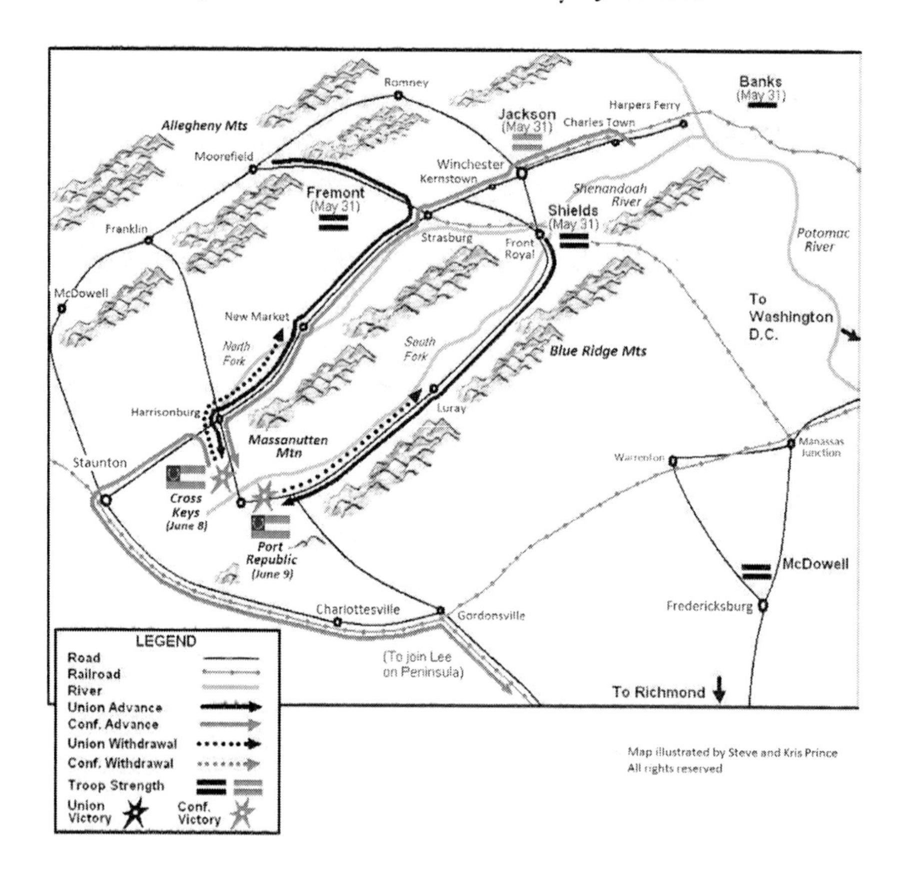

The Long March South

On the mornin' of the twenty-eighth, Ol' Jack ordered the Stonewall Brigade to advance to Charles Town but left the Second Virginia in Winchester, much to our great dismay. But the next day, orders came to march to Charles Town and rejoin the brigade. When we arrived in Charles Town, we found that Gen'ral Winder and the rest of the brigade had fought a short battle the day before. They'd caught the Billy Yanks just west of the town near the Cooke house, not far from the Nellis plantation, whereupon they promptly ran 'em out of town.

The First Brigade then marched to Loudon Heights on the Potomac, just across the Shenandoah River from Harpers Ferry. There we were ordered to demonstrate against the Yankees in case they had any thoughts about crossin' back over into Virginia. This we did until the thirty-first, when we received orders early in the mornin' to march with all dispatch to rejoin the rest of the army. We had no idea why, but the urgency of the matter was such that we had no time for breakfast, and didn't even stop for lunch, but marched straight on through that day.

The rains started again that mornin', and when we reached the Shenandoah at Keys Ferry to cross back over to Charles Town, we found the river risin' quickly and already too deep to cross on foot. Fortunately for us, some of the boys from the Second Virginia Cavalry Regiment were there. Turns out a good many of 'em had once served in the infantry in the First Brigade, and they were kind enough to help us across the river on horseback. The cavalry scouts also told us that two fed'ral columns were marchin' on the upper valley to try and cut us off from Richmond. I reckoned that was why we were marchin' south in such a hurry. We'd already whooped one Yankee army, but that wasn't good enough for Ol' Jack. He wanted the other two as well.

We marched straight on through that day, through rain and mud, through Charles Town and Winchester, and then on south to Newtown, on the Valley Turnpike between Winchester and Strasburg. By the time we reached Newtown, it was ten o'clock at night, we were soaked to the bone and starvin' half to death, and we thought our feet were about to fall clean off. We'd marched thirty-six miles—the furthest the Innocent Second ever marched in a single day—in the rain with no food, and we were none too happy for it. I heard rumors that night that the regiment had left behind more than a dozen stragglers, and more had deserted on the march, includin' two from Company A.

I must admit, bein' so close to Charles Town and all, the thought had crossed my mind that I could just fall back behind the regiment and straggle along for a while, and then just slip away when no one was lookin'. That'd sure make Joseph happy. It didn't sit right with me that we'd done all that fightin' and dyin' to retake Winchester and the whole lower valley, and now we were just givin' it back to the Yankees. But I'd come to trust that Gen'ral Jackson knew what he was doin'. So I just kept on marchin'.

On June the first, we passed through Strasburg and caught up with the rest of the army shortly after noon. We had no idea where the fed'rals were—whether they were ahead of us or behind us—but we kept on marchin' through the heavy rains and mud, on southward through New Market, 'til we reached Harrisonburg in the upper valley and bivouacked there on June the sixth.

It was there we finally got word of what was goin' on. After the officers' call that mornin', Capt'n Rowan called the company together and gave us the latest news. We learned that in the Shenandoah Valley we were keepin' two Union armies busy. To the east, Shields was comin' up the Luray Valley. To the north, Fremont had come over the mountains and was followin' us up the Shenandoah Valley. The Capt'n said the two Yankee forces were fixin' to try and catch us in an old-fashioned bear trap. But Colonel Ashby's cavalry had been screenin' our movement, burnin' bridges, and keepin' the Yankee cavalry busy, so as they couldn't catch us. And he'd been doin' it so well that Gen'ral Jackson went and promoted him to Brigadier Gen'ral.

Capt'n Rowan also told us the news from Richmond. Gen'ral Johnston had engaged Gen'ral McClellan's Union army and was badly wounded at a place called Seven Pines. The Capt'n said there was a new gen'ral in charge of all Confederate forces in Virginia now. His name was Lee. I'd never heard of him before, but it I reckoned it was an easy enough name to remember.

On June the seventh, we marched from Harrisonburg to Port Republic where we seized the bridges across the North and South Rivers where they flow together into the South Fork of the Shenandoah. By doin' this, Ol' Blue Light had managed to keep Shields and Fremont from joinin' forces. Then he sent Ewell's division northwest to the town of Cross Keys to wait for Fremont while we waited for Shields at Port Republic.

The next day, Sunday, the Innocent Second camped outside Port Republic. Company I was assigned to guard the supply train that day, and we were hopin' to have a day of rest on the Sabbath. We even had church services for the brigade at nine o'clock. The brigade Chaplain led the service, and even Gen'ral Jackson himself attended. The Chaplain was an Episcopalian priest too, like my pa, only he was from Shepherdstown.

Just after church, about ten o'clock in the mornin', we started hearin' the echoes of artillery off to the north. We knew Gen'ral Ewell was up that way just a few miles, so we figured he must be engaged with Fremont's boys. We thought maybe we might be called up to join the fight, but the orders never came. Then, in the afternoon, some audacious Yankee cavalrymen decided they'd try and take one of the bridges across the North River, nearly catchin' Ol' Jack by surprise, but he managed to escape across the bridge. When Colonel Allen saw what was goin' on, he called up the regiment to beat the Yankees back. One volley from us was all it took to persuade the Blue-bellies to ride back across that bridge and skedaddle up the road.

That night we got word that Ewell had held against the Yankees at Cross Keys and Fremont was retreatin' back northward. But our scouts reported that Shields was comin' down the east bank of the Shenandoah and would be in Port Republic by mornin', which meant there was another fight comin'. Funny thing about an army camp the night before a battle: the senior officers were up most of the night anyways, talkin' and plannin' for the comin' battle, but the rest of the camp was buzzin' with excitement too. We wanted to get some sleep so we'd be well rested, but most of the boys couldn't sleep worth a darn. We were either too anxious or too nervous to sleep. Maybe both. So we did our best to get some rest but didn't sleep much that night.

Reveille came early the next mornin', before four o'clock, and we were glad of it. Better to be up and movin' than just layin' there wishin' we could sleep. We got up, ate a hasty breakfast, and prepared for battle, leavin' most of our things in camp. Since we'd just had church the day before, Capt'n Rowan didn't ask me to lead prayer for the company, but some of the fellas asked me if we could pray before the battle. Jim and Arty were there, and we were all surprised to see Carlton there too.

While I was diggin' through my pack for the prayer book, Jim put a hand on my shoulder.

"Don't worry 'bout that, Wil," he said. "I think I'd kinda like to pray for us this mornin'—if you don't mind, that is."

> Merciful God, our Father, I confess that I'm a sinful man in your holy sight, and I reckon I don't deserve your love. But I sure am glad of it. Be with us in battle today, give us courage, and grant us your protection. And if there's any man here today who hasn't confessed his sins to you and asked for your great mercy, Lord, let him do it now, so that if we should meet our death in battle this day we can come to you with clean hearts.

A couple of other fellas prayed too, but I don't rightly recall what they said. I was still marvelin' over Jim's prayer. But then somethin' truly unexpected happened: Carlton spoke up and started to pray.

> God . . . well . . . you know I ain't never been much of a religious man . . . and I ain't never prayed before, but I think maybe there's a reckonin' a-comin', and if'n it's my time to die, well, I reckon what Jim said was right . . . and I wanna die knowin' that I done what's right, and . . . well . . . I guess that's all.

Seems to me it took a lot of courage for Carlton just to say that much.

Victory in the Valley

By seven in the mornin', a thick fog covered the valley. Gen'ral Jackson ordered Gen'ral Winder to march the Stonewall Brigade into Port Republic and across the South River to the east bank. Once across the river, Gen'ral Winder deployed the Fifth and Twenty-seventh Virginia Regiments to our left and the Fourth Virginia to our right. The Thirty-third Virginia was kept in reserve to guard the bridge across the river into Port Republic.

The fog started thinnin' out as we moved forward, and we deployed two companies out ahead of us as skirmishers. It didn't take long before we ran into the fed'ral pickets, and the sound and smell of musket fire began to fill the air. We were about to push back the Yankee pickets when their artillery opened fire on us with shot and shell. We saw Gen'ral Winder ride over to Colonel Allen, pointin' and shoutin' somethin' we couldn't hear over the sounds of bursting shells. Colonel Allen turned to us, drew out his sword, and pointed toward the trees to our right, and we followed him into the thicket. At least there we were a mite safer from the fed'ral guns.

We moved through the woods toward the Yankee guns, which were sittin' on a small hill near the treeline, but we were slowed up by the thick underbrush. When we finally came out of the brush near the hill, we found three regiments of Yankee infantry protectin' the guns. Colonel Allen ordered us to target the gunners, but that just made 'em mad. They responded by turnin' their guns on us with a terrible barrage of canister shot that wounded two of the boys in our company and knocked Carlton's hat clean off his head, causin' us to fall back in a hurry. To our right, the Fourth Virginia didn't seem to be farin' any better, and out in the clearing to our left, we could hear the sounds of battle growin' louder as more muskets and cannon joined in the fightin'.

From where we were, we could see Gen'ral Winder tryin' his best to reform the men at the bottom of the hill, but the boys didn't look on Gen'ral Winder like they did Gen'ral Jackson, and they were losin' heart quickly. It was along about then we saw Ol' Blue Light himself ride up, and the boys started cheerin'. He sat uneasy in the saddle and turned his horse to and fro so he could eye the brigade. Then the familiar smile flashed across his face, and he drew out his sword and held it in the air.

"The Stonewall Brigade never retreats!" he shouted. "Follow me!"

Then he spurred the horse forward and, with Gen'ral Winder right behind him, headed back up the hill toward the Yankees. I swallowed hard with pride, and a small amount of shame too, as I watched him ridin' up that hill toward the Yankees, lookin' so fearless like that. Shouts and cheers broke out all around, and we reformed and followed our gen'rals.

It was a little after nine o'clock then, and presently we saw the Sixth Louisiana and Wheat's Louisiana Tigers from Taylor's Brigade comin' up behind us. They were movin' to the right through the thicket to flank the fed'ral guns, and we were glad to see them. The sounds of the battle seemed to be everywhere around us now, but we stayed close to the Fourth and advanced toward the Yankee guns again. The boys from Louisiana took up positions on our right and started their attack. It took three attempts by the Stonewall Brigade and the Louisiana boys to finally break the Yankee lines. Each time our boys would take the ground where the enemy guns stood, the Yankees would counterattack with a fresh regiment. But, finally, the Blue-bellies fell back in retreat, and our own artillery shelled 'em as they retreated.

By half past ten, the battle was all but over, and the Fed'rals were withdrawin' back down the valley toward Luray. Ol' Blue Light had done it! Somehow, by God's grace, we'd marched over 350 miles in just two months and whooped three Yankee armies! So quick and so tasking was all that marchin' that we started callin' ourselves "Ol' Jack's Foot Horse," or "Jackson's Foot Cavalry," and only partly was it said in jest.

No End in Sight

June 1862

With the Shenandoah Valley secured, at least for a time, Stonewall Jackson rushes to aid in the defense of Richmond, but the Valley campaign has taken a toll on Jackson's victorious army. The many days of long marches and frequent battle have left both the men and their commander exhausted. Although they will arrive on the Virginia Peninsula barely in time to participate in the coming battles, they will prove unable to live up to their reputation for lightning movement and brilliance in battle.

Jackson's astounding success has effectively deprived McClellan of nearly 60,000 additional federal troops which he desperately desires for his campaign to capture Richmond, but President Jefferson Davis still has great cause for concern. McClellan still possesses nearly 106,000 troops, and his vanguard is now camped less than twenty miles from the Confederate capital. To oppose the massive Union force, Joseph Johnston commands only half the number of McClellan's army, a mere 55,000 Confederates. But now, in an ironic turn of events, Johnston is seriously wounded at the battle of Seven Pines (also called Fair Oaks) on May 31, and President Davis appoints General Robert E. Lee to overall command of the Confederate Army. This appointment will prove to be perhaps the single greatest decision ever made by Davis, and it will have profound effects on the war.

In an attempt to find a weakness in McClellan's plan, Lee orders his cavalry commander, Jeb Stuart, to reconnoiter the strength and position of the federal right flank. Taking his orders to the extreme, on June 12, Stuart embarks on a 150-mile ride completely around McClellan's army and returns to Richmond with a veritable gold mine in supplies, prisoners, and intelligence. The boldness of his actions makes Stuart an instant hero in the South, and a source of embarrassment for McClellan. But perhaps more importantly, Stuart has the vital information Lee needs: McClellan's huge army is divided by the rain-swollen Chickahominy River, leaving Fitz John Porter's Union V Corps trapped on the north bank apart from the rest of the army—a perfect target for Lee.

Lee wastes no time seizing the initiative with a bold plan to strike at McClellan's most vulnerable points. In just seven days, Lee strikes savagely and repeatedly at McClellan; first repelling a Union feint at Oak Grove, then striking Porter's isolated V Corps at Mechanicsville (also called Beaver Dam Creek) and Gaines' Mill, then pressing the retreating Federals at Savage's Station and Glendale (or Frazier's Farm), and finally assaulting a strong Union position atop Malvern Hill.

Though nearly all of the Seven Days Battles prove to be tactical victories for the Union and produce heavy casualties for the Confederates, the cautious McClellan continues to retreat further from the rebel capital with each successive strike. Finally, hopelessly outgeneraled, and convinced that Lee possesses more than twice the number of his own troops (possibly further influenced by Stuart's ride), McClellan abandons his plan and withdraws down the James River to Harrison's Landing. Richmond, for now at least, is saved.

May 7, 1862

To: Private William Harleck
Second Virginia Infantry Regiment, First Brigade, C.S.A.
Army of the Shenandoah

My darling husband Wil,

I pray this letter finds its way to you and that you are in good health and spirits. It has been some time now since I received your last letter. I live in fear and apprehension for your well-being, and in hope of hearing some word from you which would greatly diminish my fear. It is a cruel trick of war indeed that we must so often be separated without word from one another for long periods of time. I imagine that it is not always possible for you to write when you are on the march so often. Or perhaps you may have already written, but, alas, our mail service is not as reliable as it once was, and even less so now that the northern soldiers have again occupied Charles Town and Winchester.

I write with news that I hope may cheer you if by chance you should need cheering. This feeble pen can scarcely express my joy as I write to tell you that I am carrying your child, and I hope to make you a father by October, if the Lord is willing. I had so hoped to see you and deliver this news to you in person so I might see the look on your face myself, but it seems General Jackson has other plans for the army, so I will content myself with writing instead.

I do so long to hear some news from you as soon as you are able to write, and I pray every day that the Lord, in His divine wisdom, will bring this dreadful war swiftly to an end and return you to my loving arms. Dare I even hope that He may do so in time for you to see your first child come into this *world? Oh, would that it be possible, but I fear that peace may not come so easily or swiftly as we would like. So I will bide my time in prayer, and wish you all of my love until you return.*

With all my heart,
Your Maribel

A Sobering Realization

If ever there was a time in the whole ugly war when my heart was most thankful, it must be the week followin' the battle at Port Republic. We were more tired than a pack of dogs after a hunt, and just as glad for the victory, and sleep came easy that week. On June the twelfth, Gen'ral Jackson ordered the brigade to cross back over the South River with the rest of the army, and we made camp near a place called

Weyer's Cave. There we rested for three more days. On the mornin' of Sunday the fourteenth, we had church to thank the Good Lord for givin' us such a great victory. But I had an even better reason to be thankful that day.

It was unusual for us to get parcels on a Sunday, but the postal wagon arrived in camp the night before, and there hadn't been time to pass it out, so we got it that afternoon. It was always a strange thing to watch when the mail came. The boys would sorta gather around so they could hear if their name was called, but they'd try not to look too interested, just in case it wasn't. But you could see it in their eyes. Some of the fellas got letters from home more often, but most didn't get many letters, and some got none at all. Carlton Willis was one of 'em.

"Harleck," the private called out.

"Here!"

I got to my feet, still sore from all the marchin' and fightin', and trotted over to receive the letter. It was from Maribel! So precious were her letters to me that I kept 'em tucked inside my shirt so I could read 'em over and over again. They were sweeter to me than Mama's blackberry jam (which was the next sweetest thing I could think of). And not just because they were from Maribel either. A fella just never knew when might be the next time he'd get any news at all from home, what with the postal service bein' so unreliable on account of the Billy Yanks always snoopin' about in the lower valley whenever we weren't around to chase 'em away. I wondered how many of my letters might've just up and disappeared instead of reachin' my loved ones back home, and how many of theirs might've actually been written that I'd never received.

I was so happy to get that letter from Maribel I couldn't make myself sit down. When I opened it and read it, I thought my heart might jump clean out of my chest!

"She's carryin' my child! I'M GONNA BE A FATHER!"

I reckon I didn't realize how loud I was shoutin' 'til I heard all the voices callin' back.

"That's great, Wil!" Arty couldn't hide his own excitement and came runnin' over, threw his arms around me, and lifted me off the ground with a big ol' bear hug. "I swear you are so lucky!"

"Congratulations, Wil!" Jim chimed in, shakin' my hand. Then some of the other fellas came over to congratulate me too. Even Carlton strolled over and slugged me in the shoulder.

"Bully for you, Harleck, you ol' dog! Wasn't sure ya had it in ya!"

"Congratulations, son. Well done," Capt'n Rowan offered. "This calls for celebration." Then he disappeared into his tent and returned a moment later with a bottle of wine, which he presently popped the cork and opened.

"I've been saving this for our victory over the Yankees and the end of this war, but since it looks like that's not too likely to happen any time soon, will you join me?" I felt the blood all rush to my face. I didn't know what to say. I'd mostly only had wine at Christmas dinner and for Holy Communion—and of course on my wedding day.

"Well . . . I reckon this *is* a special occasion!" I answered.

"Good. A toast then!" He poured some of the wine into my dipper and took his own cup out and poured himself a small drink. Then he held up the bottle so as to offer a drink to the fellas that were gathered around, who were happy to oblige.

After all the drinks had been poured, he held up his cup in front of his face with a gesture that made all of the other fellas raise their cups too.

"The health of your wife and child," he offered, raisin' the cup in a toast.

"The health of your wife and child," the others repeated in chorus.

"Hear, hear!" L'tenant Davenport chimed in.

I didn't know what to say, so I just smiled and drank the toast.

"What we need now is some music!" L'tenant Davenport added. A couple of minutes later, he reappeared with another fella I didn't recognize—a private from one of the other companies, I think—and they sat down and started playin'. The L'tenant played his gui-tar, and the private had somethin' I'd never seen before. It had a wooden sound box shaped like an hourglass, and a fret with three strings on the top. He played it on his lap—sometimes with a bow, and sometimes just pluckin' or strummin' with his fingers while he slid a small stick up and down the strings. I'd never heard anything quite like it before, but it sure did make a nice sound.

"What in blazes is that?" Carlton asked the boy.

"It's a 'hog fiddle'. Made it myself." He stopped playin'.

"You made that yerself?"

"Yep. My daddy taught me how a few years back."

Then he started playin' again and the L'tenant joined in. There was music and merriment in the camp that night the likes of which I'd never seen before nor since. I reckon we did have some pretty good reasons to celebrate.

In between the singin' and the dancin', we ate a good dinner, with roasted boar and early carrots, which was a rare treat in the army. Then we settled in for more singin' and makin' merry. Capt'n Rowan didn't usually sit with the men—somethin' about it bein' unbecomin' of an officer—but that night was a special occasion, and all the company officers joined in the celebration too.

I sat down next to the Capt'n. "I've been thinkin' about what you said, sir—you know—about the war not bein' over anytime soon?"

"Yeah?"

"Well, did you mean that, sir?"

"Doesn't look like Lincoln plans to give up yet."

I heaved a deep sigh, lookin' up into the heavens. "I was hopin' maybe the Yankees would head for home after the whoopin' we gave 'em."

"We may have beaten Banks and Shields and Fremont here, but the newspapers say McClellan is at Richmond's door."

After all we'd accomplished, the thought of our capital bein' captured by the Yankees made my heart sink.

"What do you think'll happen if . . . ?" I couldn't make myself finish sayin' what my mind was thinkin'.

"Hard to say for sure," he answered thoughtfully, "but rumor has it we may be ordered to Richmond to help General Lee defend the city." He shuffled his feet a little, then went on. "One thing's for sure: ol' Abe Lincoln'll think twice before moving more troops down to help McClellan. With the Valley in our control, there'd be nothing to keep us from just marching right into Washington." He paused, tilted his head thoughtfully, and stared off into the distance, then continued in a voice that sounded far away. "Who knows? Maybe McClellan won't want to try to take Richmond without more troops. Or maybe Lincoln'll order him back to Washington, Lord willing. Ol' Jeff Davis would like that very much." He looked back at me again, then stood up and straightened up his uniform. "Well, nothing to be done about it tonight. Best get some rest. All of us are pretty tired."

I stood up and saluted, "Thank you, sir."

I went off to find a quiet place to sleep if I could. I thought briefly about my talk with Capt'n Rowan, but then my thoughts turned again to Maribel and my unborn child.

What will it be like, bein' a father? Will it be a boy or a girl? I hope it's a boy! Will he, or she, be born healthy? What if the war isn't over by then? Will I even get to see my child? What will Maribel do if she has to raise our child by herself?

And somehow in all those thoughts, I drifted off to sleep.

The next day, the word came down that we'd be movin' out in the mornin', and by the mornin' of the sixteenth, we were on the march again. We marched for two days, arrivin' in Staunton late on the seventeenth, where we cooked dinner but were told not to bivouac. Shortly after midnight, on May the eighteenth, we started boardin' trains. I reckon there was one question on most of our minds: *Where are we headin' now?* I remembered how we'd boarded trains once before, thinkin' we were headin' for Richmond, only to find out we were goin' the opposite way. And Ol' Jack wasn't in the habit of tellin' us where we were goin' 'till after we got there. But somewhere deep down inside, I knew we must be headed east to help Gen'ral Lee defend Richmond, and I realized that my hopes for a quick end to this war were fadin' fast.

For the next week, we took turns ridin' and marchin' from one town to the next. It was the strangest thing. The railroad didn't have enough rolling stock to move the whole army, so one brigade would march to the next town while another rode the train. Then the brigade on the train would get off and start marchin', and, when they arrived, the other brigade would board the train and ride to the next town. It wasn't pretty, but it worked. Usin' this method, one train could move two brigades faster than either brigade could march the whole way. This kept the army from gettin' too spread out, and it was a far sight better than marchin' all the way to Richmond.

This went on day and night, stoppin' only long enough to rest the men for awhile, then pressin' on toward Richmond again. Sometimes Ol' Jack would ride by with his aides as we were marchin' down the road, and when he reached the front of the column, he'd stop the whole column to rest awhile. We were mighty glad for it, but it never lasted for long. After half an hour or so, we'd be back on the march again.

We finally arrived in the town of Ashland, about twelve miles north-east of Richmond, on the evenin' of the twenty-fifth, and camped near there. We'd heard rumors of a battle somewhere south of there earlier that day, but we were too plum tuckered from all that marchin' to be much good to anyone.

The Seven Days Battles

We saw Gen'ral Jackson again on the mornin' of the twenty-sixth. He looked old and tired and ragged like we'd never seen him before. His uniform was rumpled, and the fire was gone from his eyes, and he didn't sit quite so high in the saddle as before. I reckon he must've felt like an ol' coon dog who'd hunted one too many times.

He talked with Gen'ral Winder for a few minutes, then rode off at a trot instead of his usual gallop. Not long afterward, we got orders to fall in to march again. We marched on through the day, stoppin' only long enough to rest for a short while, then marchin' on a little ways further. It was hot as the devil that day, and the goin' was slow. So hot it was that the drummers just stopped playin' after the first mile or so. No sense in playin' when the men are too hot and tired to even stay in step. By the middle of the afternoon, we could begin to hear the unmistakable sound of cannon firin' in the distance. There was a battle goin' on not far away, sure enough, but we'd already marched fifteen miles that day, and most of the boys were out of water. Some had even gone down from the heat. We didn't wanna miss a chance to whoop the Yankees, but we were in no condition to be marchin' into a fight. That much was certain.

We reached the town of Hundley's Corner a short while later, and Gen'ral Winder ordered the brigade to stop and make camp for the night. Some of the boys were so hot and tired they refused to even so much as lift a finger to help set up the camp. That is 'til Gen'ral Winder came along and lit a fire under their britches. He was a stickler for discipline, the Gen'ral was, and not given to toleratin' any shenanigans from the boys.

"Captain, I ordered the brigade to make camp, but I do not see many tents set up. Why aren't these men working?"

We felt especially sorry for Capt'n Rowan. He'd had to make most of the march that day with one lame leg and no horse, seein' as how his had been needed with the supply train, which was still miles behind. We thought he might simply collapse from exhaustion, but somehow he kept his head and managed to muster a salute.

"Yes, sir. Right away, Gen'ral."

"That is not an answer, Captain. When I come back around the next time, I had better see this camp set up properly or there'll be no supper rations for the entire regiment. Is that understood?"

"Yes, sir. We'll get it done, sir!"

The Gen'ral returned his salute and rode away, and the Capt'n nearly stumbled as he turned around. His face was pale and his eyes looked sunken in.

"You heard him, boys. Get to it if you wanta eat tonight!"

Carlton got to his feet with a scowl on his face.

"If'n the Yankees don't shoot that man, I surely will," he muttered, barely loud enough to be heard. It was no secret he held no love for the Gen'ral in his heart.

We managed to get the camp all set up, but somethin' just didn't seem right about settin' up camp with the sound of battle goin' on in the distance. We got the fires goin' and sent some of the boys off to find the supply train and bring back some meat for cookin'. The rest of us just sort of sat around uneasy-like, listenin' to the sound of the battle.

There was no music or singin' that night, even after the sky turned dark and the sounds of the battle died out. For the most part, we just ate in silence and then turned in for the night. But as tired as we were, we didn't get much sleep. A bad storm came through that night, blowin' the branches out of trees, knockin' down some of our tents, and gen'rally soakin' everything we owned. It was just bad enough to make everyone miserable, but not enough to bring any relief from the summer heat. All it did was make everything wetter and more humid, so much that a fella could actually see the steam comin' up from the ground. So I mostly just laid awake wonderin' if there'd likely be another battle in the mornin' and thinkin' about Maribel and home.

The next day was June the twenty-seventh—the Battle of Gaines' Mill—and it would be a day long remembered by the men of the Innocent Second. It started out pretty much like a hundred other days before: clear and bright and warm—and wet. We rose early and started makin' ready to march again. A couple of the boys had managed to keep enough firewood dry so as to cook a hot breakfast, and it wasn't long before the hot Virginia sun began to dry up the ground and most of the outer clothes we were wearin'. But all that moisture just seemed to hang in the air, and the humidity just made my underclothes cling to my skin all the more.

Before long, Colonel Allen came by with orders to move out. "The Blue-bellies are on the move, and we're goin' after 'em," he said.

We marched toward the town of Old Cold Harbor, but got lost somehow along the way and had to countermarch to get back to the road we were supposed to be on. Then, when we finally reached the town, we stopped again. There we were placed in reserve in a field just outside the town.

The sound of the battle started just after lunch and kept growin' all through the afternoon. We were close enough to hear the musket fire, and even smell the smoke, but still no orders came. We'd just about made up our minds that we'd be sittin' this one out too, when Gen'ral Winder rode by and ordered us to form up.

Around five o'clock in the afternoon, Gen'ral Winder ordered the Second and Fifth Regiments to provide support for a battery of guns in a field not far from where the fightin' was goin' on. But almost before we could get ourselves placed, we were ordered to rejoin the rest of the brigade. Then, while we were tryin' to get back across that open field, some Yankee artillery opened up on us with long range solid shot, which, I don't have to tell you, made life a mite less tolerable for awhile.

It was nigh on seven o'clock in the evenin' when we finally came to where the action was. The ground where the Yankees chose to stand and make a fight of it was more wrinkled than an old hog's snout—full of gulleys, cricks, ridges, and hills. And what with the dense Virginia underbrush almost everywhere a man could see, every step was a tiresome chore.

We finally came out of the tree line near where the Fed'rals had formed up at the top of a ridge with a deep gulley before it. We formed up in line of battle with the Thirty-third and Twenty-seventh on our right, the Fifth on our left, and the Fourth in reserve behind us. We started advancin' down into the gulley, and then up the hill toward the Yankee positions on the top. The fed'ral fire was gettin' mighty hot by then. There were Minie balls whistlin' overhead and shells explodin' all around, and it was enough to remind me how much I hated fightin' in battles. Right about then, it struck me that this was nothin' like the stories Joseph used to tell sittin' around the fireplace back home.

The sound of the rebel yell risin' up through the trees somewhere off to our right was enough to bring my mind back to the present business at hand, and we knew the Billy Yanks must be gettin' close to breakin'. Then, along about eight o'clock, a courier rode out of the trees and handed a dispatch to Colonel Allen. The Colonel took the dispatch, but before he could even read it the courier was gone, lickety-split.

The sky was startin' to grow darker, and the shadows of the trees grew long as the sun fell toward the horizon. We knew if we didn't break the Yankees soon it'd be nightfall, and the thought of a night battle scared me even worse than the ones in daylight.

"Forward, men!" Colonel Allen's voice sounded urgent. "Press forward!"

We marched forward as best we could, tryin' to keep somewhat in a line, but it was difficult, what with the uneven ground and the Yankee artillery shells fallin' all around. Still, somehow we'd managed to get out ahead of the boys from the Twenty-seventh and the Fifth on either side of us and found ourselves face to face with a line of bluecoats near the top of the hill.

The Yankees fired, and the trees and brush and the air all around me came alive with the sounds of musket balls, but I didn't see anyone hit. Then we took careful aim and fired back. I was gettin' quite a bit faster at reloadin' by then, even with my hands shakin' like they were. Then came that deadly order.

"Fix bayonets!"

A second volley from the Yankees blanketed them in smoke and us in the sounds of more Minie balls. Just a few feet away, Jim cried out in pain and dropped his rifle, then dropped to one knee and clutched his right hand with his left. I wanted to go and see if he was alright, but I remembered how I'd gotten separated from Fredrick at Manassas, and how Carlton and I had fought well together at Kernstown. I knew if I stayed close to Carlton we'd both have a better chance of survivin' the battle. So I made myself stay in line and fixed my attention on the enemy. It was kill or be killed, and I had no desire to die that day. Especially seein' as how I was gonna be a father now.

I must survive this day! I have a family now.

We aimed and fired our second volley and advanced up the hill close to the Yankee line. Three times we moved up close, and three times the Yankees stood their ground. But each time their line got thinner, and we could tell they were about to break.

The Colonel drew out his sword and raised it up high. "C'mon, boys! They're breaking! To the top!" Then he turned, aimed his sword at the Yankees, and started runnin' up that hill. So we followed.

The Yankees fired just as the Colonel reached the crest of the hill only a few yards ahead of us. To our horror, a Yankee Minie ball hit him clean in the forehead, spinnin' him around and tossin' him to the ground like he was an empty burlap sack. I knew right away he was dead. My feet froze, and I couldn't look away from our poor Colonel as he lay there all twisted on the ground. His face wore a look of utter shock, and his mouth and eyes were both wide open, like he was lookin' right at me, and I felt the contents of my stomach, what little there was left, tryin' to come back up.

Carlton stopped and grabbed my shoulder with his free hand, and his voice broke through the fog in my mind. "Get ahold of yerself, Harleck! No time fer stoppin' now! C'mon! We gotta break 'em!"

"He's dead, Wil!" Arty shouted over the noise of the battle. "There's nothin' can be done. C'mon, let's go!"

I don't rightly know how, but, by some miracle, we kept on pressin' forward up that ridge. I followed Carlton to the top, and then, when we were but scarce feet away from the fed'ral line, he shouted, "For the Colonel!" Then he gave the rebel yell, and the other boys joined in. We all charged, yellin' and screamin' at the tops of our lungs like madmen, and the Yankees finally broke and fell back in retreat.

I was relieved to see Jim back with the regiment later that night, his hand all wrapped up in a bandage.

"Just my little finger," he said with a weak grin. "Coulda been much worse." But I could tell he was hurtin'.

"Looks painful," Arty said just what I was thinkin'. "How bad?"

"Shot clean off," Jim remarked, matter-of-factly.

"Well," Carlton chimed in, "at least they didn't have to amputate!" he chuckled at his own joke.

Jim smiled again, but I reckon he knew Carlton was right. Better to get it all over with at once.

Still, I was mighty glad it wasn't worse, like Jim said. The thought of losin' another friend in this war was almost enough to make me want to quit fightin' and just go home.

I couldn't sleep at all for most of that night. I couldn't eat. I couldn't even pray. I was too haunted by the image of the Colonel's face, and my mind wouldn't let go of the ever-risin' price of this ungodly war. I kept thinkin', "*What if that had been me?*"

It suddenly occurred to me that bein' a high-rankin' officer in this army was a hazardous occupation, and I wondered, "*How many other colonels and gen'rals have already been killed? And how many more might be killed before this war comes to an end?*"

I'd heard tell that Gen'ral Jackson once said somethin' about feelin' just as safe on the battlefield as in bed on account of his faith in God. It got me to thinkin' about my own fear in battle, and how inspired I'd been by his bravery. He sure was a brave man.

But doesn't he have a family too? How does he do it?

I thought about Maribel and our child, and how much I wanted to stay alive so as I could go home and be with them. But I also wanted them to be proud of me, knowin' that I fought with honor and courage, knowin' that the Good Lord was gonna come for me whenever He was good and ready. And did I really have much say in the matter after all?

But how can both be possible? How can I love my life and yet not be afraid of death at the same time?

I wasn't rightly sure how to balance the two, but I reckoned if Gen'ral Jackson could do it, it had to be possible.

That was when I finally fell asleep.

The next few days were like a strange long and morbid dream to me. First, we were assigned to remove the dead and wounded at McGehee's Hill where we'd fought the day before. From our location there, we could hear cannon firin' somewhere off to the south.

"Sounds like another battle," I said, lookin' up from my shovel.

"Yep, and here we are in the rear doin' burial detail," Arty said, droppin' the body he'd dragged over to where I was diggin'.

"I ain't rightly sure which is worse, battle or burial detail," Jim added as he was walkin' back to retrieve another of the slain who were lyin' about thirty feet away.

"Hell, I'll take fightin' any day," Carlton replied. "I *hate* burial detail."

"I reckon I do too," I had to admit.

"I reckon we all do," Arty added.

"If there's a Hell, this must be it," Carlton threw down his shovel and tiraded on. "Ain't *nothin'* worse than this: standin' out here in the hot damned sun all day . . . " he motioned toward the sky, "diggin' and sweatin'; dead and maimed bodies lyin' around everywhere, rottin' in the damned heat!" he said loudly, wavin' his hand at all the bodies lyin' around on the ground. He was buildin up a good head of steam now. "This here's work fer niggers, not men like us!"

I never much cared for that word. It reeked of arrogance and insult, and left a foul taste in my mouth, like the stench of an animal three days dead. Somethin' just didn't feel right about treatin' others like they were less than men on account of their skin color. I remembered my Pa preachin' once about how masters should treat their slaves with kindness, and how they were God's children too, and I started to say somethin', but before I could even open my mouth there came a shout from a little ways yonder.

"Here's one that's still alive!" Jim hollered.

I dropped my shovel and we all walked quickly over to where Jim was standin'. Sure enough, there was a Reb boy there, not much older than me. He was hurt bad—shot in the belly—and barely alive, and he made a low moan that almost couldn't be heard from more than a few feet away.

"Must've got separated from his outfit," Jim said. "Why else would they just leave 'im here to die?"

"C'mon, let's help him to a hospital," I said, bendin' down to help the man.

"It ain't no use," Carlton said. "He's done for."

Arty shot Carlton a look that said he shouldn't oughta say things like that in the presence of a poor soul who was soon to be leavin' this world, but Carlton wasn't convinced.

"Well, it's the truth. He might as well hear it," he argued.

"Isn't there anything we can do for him?" I asked.

"Sure." Carlton walked over to where our rifles were stacked and picked his up, then walked back toward us, diggin' in his cartridge box for a cartridge to load.

"What're you doin'?!" Arty objected. "You ain't shootin' him!"

"The hell I ain't!" Carlton fired back hotly, pullin' out the ramrod, and rammin' the load home.

It was a strange irony that a dyin' horse on a battlefield could be shot for mercy's sake, but a dyin' man had to just lie there and suffer 'til he died. After all, these were men—somebody's sons or brothers or husbands or fathers. It just didn't feel right shootin' a man like that.

"NO!" Arty shouted, standin' up in front of Carlton so as to protect the boy with his body. "Tell 'im, Jim! We ain't shootin' that boy!"

"Carlton, wait," Jim said calmly as he stepped toward Carlton, and took hold of the rifle.

"The boy's dyin' and in pain!" Carlton objected, jerkin' the rifle out of Jim's hand. "If I was layin' there bleedin' to death from bein' shot in the gut, I'd want someone to shoot me and git it over with quick-like, 'stead of makin' me lay there and suffer for God knows how long!"

I wanted to do somethin' or say somethin', but I wasn't rightly sure he was altogether wrong.

Is there really a difference between shootin' a man in anger and shootin' a man for pity's sake? And does it really matter after all if he's friend or foe?

I looked down at the boy again, and there was fear in his eyes, and a lot of pain. I reckon he knew he was dyin', but he wasn't ready to die just yet.

"Isn't there anything else we can do for him?" I asked, lookin' up at Carlton.

For a while, he just stood there lookin' at me with a mad look on his face like a wet cat. But then he must've figured arguin' wasn't gonna change my mind—or Arty's either—and the look changed to a smirk and he just shook his head.

"Fine then. Suit yerself," he huffed.

He started to walk away, but then he stopped and put down the rifle, then finally turned around and reached into his jacket and pulled out a small bottle of liquor.

"Here," he said, still smirkin'.

He took the cap off, took a gulp, and then handed me the bottle.

"He needs it more than me," he said, then he took a deep breath and let it out through his nose, sorta like a half-huff and a half-sigh. "Besides, I was tryin' to quit anyways."

I wasn't rightly sure what to say. Carlton givin' up his booze was no small matter, but I didn't have time to think on it much. I lifted the boy's head up a little and gave him a drink. He tried to swallow but it made him cough and choke. But then he looked up at me with pain in his eyes and pursed his lips for another drink, so I gave him another sip which he swallowed this time. His eyes closed and he let his head fall back on my hand. He had a blanket rolled up on his back which I put under his neck and head for a pillow.

His eyes opened again, and he looked up at me and said in a weak voice, "Thank you."

"Can you tell me your name?" I asked the boy.

"P-Peter . . . S-St . . . Stough . . . baugh," he managed with some great effort.

"Where're you from, Peter?"

"Ch-Charlottesville . . . " he coughed.

I gave the boy another drink from the bottle to ease his pain, and he swallowed it hard, then let his eyes go closed again and his head fell back on my hand.

"Peter? Just hang on, now Peter. We're gonna get you home now," I lied. I knew I shouldn't be lyin' to a dyin' boy, but I reckoned if ever there was a proper time for lyin', this was it. Besides, I didn't rightly know what else to say.

His eyes opened once again while I cradled his head in my hand, but he was too weak to hold his head up or even keep his eyes open any longer. And as he lay there breathin' his last, my thoughts turned to Maribel and my unborn child.

What if this boy was me? My child would've been born without ever knowin' his father; I'd have to break my promise to Maribel. And Mama—I'd break her heart.

Then it struck me that this boy probably had a mama too. Maybe even a pa and brothers and sisters, and a sweetheart back home who'd never see him again. And the only thing I could do was to try and make his last moments on earth more comfortable, and offer up a prayer for his soul and his loved ones. So that's just what I did.

"Dear Lord, into Thy hands we commend Peter's spirit, and we ask your tender loving presence with his loved ones. In Thy Holy name we pray. Amen."

"Amen," Jim and Arty echoed. That's when I looked up and saw the three of 'em standin' there lookin' down on me and Peter.

He wasn't breathin' anymore, and the look of pain was finally gone from his face, now pale and peaceful.

I handed the bottle back to Carlton.

He took it and looked at it long and hard, then put the cap on and handed it back. "In case there's someone else who needs it," he said.

We finished up with the burial detail, and were glad of it. I could scarce eat a thing all day that day, so I was powerful hungry by nightfall.

I was relieved when Capt'n Rowan said that L'tenant Colonel Botts had been given command of the regiment that day after Colonel Allen's untimely death. I knew Colonel Botts was a good man and worth his own salt as an officer. His first act after the battle was to have Colonel Allen's body sent back home to his family. This was a fairly common practice for colonels (though rarely ever for privates), but we were still glad to hear that our beloved Colonel would get a decent and respectable burial among the company of loved ones. Especially seein' as how many a young soldier that day had just been tossed into a shallow grave, mostly unmarked.

On the night of June the twenty-ninth, after two days of buryin' the dead and tendin' to the wounded, we got orders to cross over the Chickahominy, and we marched south toward where we'd heard the sounds of battle the day before. But we didn't know the land, so the march was mighty confusin' and we got lost several times, especially after dark. All night that night we made our way down the narrow windin' roads through the dense forests of the peninsula. About noon the next day, we finally arrived at a damp and dismal place called White Oak Swamp. It was there we were told to bivouac for the rest of the day.

The heat was swelterin' that afternoon. We could hear the sounds of battle just a couple of miles away, but the only action we saw that day was an artillery duel with a Yankee battery just across the crick there. The ground was still soaked from the recent rains, and everywhere we walked our shoes made a squishin' sound. It wasn't long before our feet and stockin's were all soaked again. To make matters worse, a swarm of mosquitoes descended upon us to torture us incessantly. The only relief we could find from those miserable despicable creatures was to stoke up the bivouac fires and stand near the intense heat and smoke of the fire, which made the hot summer sun even more intolerable, if that was possible.

"I reckon Carlton was right," Arty remarked, swattin' a mosquito on his neck. "This here place *is* hell on earth."

"Nope," I argued. "I've heard my Pa preach about Hell before, and this here isn't Hell. It's worse!"

"Ha! Ain't that the truth!" Carlton chuckled, takin' off his shoes to dry out his stockin's by the fire. "The devil himself wouldn't wanna stay in this place very long."

"What I wouldn't give for a nice cool bath back home right now," Jim said.

That got me to thinkin' about home and Maribel again. I wanted to write her but I was plum out of dry paper.

"I got some paper you can have," Carlton offered. "I ain't usin' it anyway."

"Thanks," I replied.

Jim saw his chance. "Don't you have any kinfolk back home to write to?"

"Naw. Just my no-account brother and that bit—witch . . . he's married to."

"They got any young'uns?"

"One—my nephew—but he hates me," he admitted. Then the tone of his voice changed a mite. "I reckon I deserve that," he said more sullen-like.

"How old is he?" Jim pried.

"I don't know," Carlton's voice was startin' to sound agitated. "Maybe ten or twelve, or maybe fourteen. I ain't seen 'im in awhile."

"Then how do you know he hates you?"

"Look, I don't wanna talk about it!"

"Sorry. Just askin'. Didn't mean to offend," Jim said with his hands up in the air.

The next day was July the first, and we were held in reserve near a small church where there'd been a bit of action just the day before. There we waited most of the day 'til orders finally came around supper time. Since supper was just marchin' rations, it was no trouble to eat quickly and get ready to march. By the time we finally got formed up to march it was gettin' dark. We marched down the church road a ways, along with the boys from the Fifth Virginia, but we got lost again as darkness set in. We tried to find the rest of the brigade, but when we finally got out of the woods into a field where we could see, we were promptly shelled by Yankee artillery. So we spent most of that night takin' shelter in a ravine not far from the battle.

It wasn't until sunrise the next mornin' that we finally found the other regiments of the Stonewall Brigade. But by then, the Yankees were already withdrawin'. We made camp again that night, but it wasn't until July the third that we finally figured out what had really happened. L'tenant Davenport bought a Richmond newspaper from a passin' cavalry officer. It said that the Army of Northern Virginia—that's what they were callin' our army now—had gloriously routed the invaders and they were in full retreat back down the peninsula. They were callin' it the Seven Days Battles, but that's not what most of the men were callin' it. It felt more like a right proper taste of Hell to the likes of us.

We stayed in camp there for another week, just to make sure the Blue-bellies weren't changin' their minds, then we finally marched back to Richmond for some much needed rest and relaxation. Once in camp near Richmond, the army seemed quite a bit more refreshed. Music returned to the camp each night, and I finally had time to write letters to Maribel and my family back home. We even got paid and had time to go into the city and spend a little of the money we'd earned, though I'm pretty sure when you consider all we'd been through, the small amount of money we were paid was a war crime all by itself. Nevertheless, the gen'ral feelin' was one of celebration. McClellan had withdrawn southward down the peninsula, and Richmond was saved—at least for the time bein'.

A House Divided

July 1862

In April 1861, Virginia's Ordinance of Secession passes by a landslide, but the vote is not unanimous. There are still areas of the state where separation from the Union is not a popular idea. In fact, a large portion of northwestern Virginia remains loyal to the Union, and the northern panhandle counties closest to Ohio and Pennsylvania are particularly ardent in their opposition to secession. One month later, almost immediately after secession is ratified in Richmond, a convention is called in Wheeling declaring that the secession vote was illegal and is therefore invalid, and establishing a new state government loyal to the United States. Thus Virginia now has two state governments: one pro-Union and the other Confederate.

In October 1861, an election is held by the pro-Union government on the question of forming a new state loyal to the Union, but the results are highly suspicious, and rapidly become the subject of hot debate. Although the measure passes by an overwhelming margin, the vote occurs almost exclusively in the western counties, mostly because the Confederate election officials in the eastern counties refuse to honor the election. But there are also widespread allegations that Union soldiers in some western counties have interfered with the vote by placing Confederate loyalists under house arrest to prevent them from casting their ballots, especially in the counties nearest the border of the proposed new state.

So it is in Jefferson County, the easternmost of the disputed counties. The residents of Charles Town, the county seat, are hotly divided over the subject of loyalty. Claims of election tampering and fraud are rampant, and many feel that the county should not be included in the new state. A majority of the citizens are sympathetic to the southern cause, and many have lost sons and brothers in the service of the Confederacy or have loved ones still fighting for southern independence. Indeed, many of the voters are absent during the election due to their service in the Confederate Army, and therefore cannot vote since absentee ballots will not be used until 1864. Still others remain loyal to the United States and see an eventual Union victory as inevitable. The town itself has already changed hands more than a dozen times in the first year of the war. Nevertheless, on April 11, 1862, when a petition is sent to the federal government to admit West Virginia to the Union, Jefferson County is included within the political borders of the proposed new state.

Further to the east, the war seems to be going well for the fledgling Confederacy. Robert E. Lee has driven George McClellan's huge army back from the doorstep of Richmond, and the war begins to shift again to northern Virginia. Abraham Lincoln places Major General John Pope in command of the new Union Army of Virginia, and Pope deploys his forces in a large arc across the northern part of the state. Wishing to catch Pope unprepared, Lee dispatches two divisions of Stonewall Jackson's Second Corps, Army of Northern Virginia, to Culpeper County in early July. Two weeks later, Lee sends a third division, under Major General A. P. Hill, to reinforce Jackson. Now with 24,000 men at his disposal, Jackson plans to strike Pope at the center of the arc, cut the Union army into two halves, and destroy each of the separate halves in detail.

Early in August, Jackson crosses the Rapidan River to strike the center of Pope's line near the small town of Culpeper at a place called Cedar Mountain, or Slaughter's Mountain, as it is known by the locals. It is the first in a series of brilliant maneuvers by Jackson which will completely confound and humiliate Pope, and keep the mighty Union war machine off balance.

July 6th, 1862

Dearest Son,

I was so very relieved to get your letter today. It does my heart good to know that you are well and unharmed. Yesterday we received the dreadful news of the death of Colonel Allen in battle and were greatly concerned for your welfare.

I am delighted that Maribel is expecting to make you a proper father with my first grandchild in just a few short months. She checks in on us frequently. I can assure you that she is in fine health, and the child also, it would appear.

Life here in Charles Town has been difficult of late, but you mustn't worry about us. The Lord has been faithful to watch over our family. Vanessa took ill with a fever last month, but, thanks be to God, she is much better now. She is growing into a fine strong young lady. Your brother Amos is nearly a man now, and in a few months he will be eligible for the draft. I have prayed that he would be spared the evils of war, but he seems intent to follow in your footsteps. This does not make Joseph or your father very happy. We received a letter from Joseph a few weeks ago informing us that he has moved to Williamsport, in Maryland, to serve as an intern for the summer with a priest there.

By now, I'm sure you've read in the papers that the western counties have broken away to form a new northern state. It seems that our own Jefferson County is to be included within its borders. It seems clear that this reprehensible imposition is nothing more than a transparent ploy by those who would seek to drag our country back into the Union. Your father says it is because of our strategic location on the Chesapeake and Ohio canal and the Potomac and Shenandoah Rivers. Wil, you *must know that most of the citizens of Charles Town remain loyal to Virginia and the Confederacy, despite the frequent yoke of Union occupation which has been thrust upon us.*

I pray you will remain safe and well, and that our triumphant forces may soon put an end to this dreadful war and finally settle the question of our independence once and for all.

You remain always in our hearts, minds, and prayers,

Your Loving Mother

Slaughter's Mountain

It was mid July before we left Richmond and headed north. And hot it was too. The hottest summer I can recollect. The goin' was slow, and lots of fellas took ill from the heat, but Ol' Jack was not about to let the Yankees get a moment's rest.

Word came that Lincoln was puttin' together another army up in northern Virginia with a new commander—Pope, I heard his name was—it was so hard to keep track of 'em all. Anyway, we reckoned he was fixin' to move on Richmond. Well, seein' as how McClellan didn't appear to be goin' anywhere, we thought perhaps we oughta go welcome Pope to Virginia, properly. On July the thirteenth, we got orders to cook extra rations and prepare to march, and we left Richmond early the next mornin'.

It took us five days of marchin' in the scorchin' heat just to get to Gordonsville. Then, when we finally arrived, we just sat there like bumps on logs for three more weeks, doin' nothin'—except sufferin' that is. The unusually hot summer brought on two pestilences that made life in camp there nigh intolerable. First, the heat caused all the meat to go bad real quick-like, the unfortunate result of which was often a case of the "Virginia quick step," or, as we called it back home, "the runs." But the worst was the lice, which some of the boys took to callin' 'freeloaders' since they were content to gorge themselves heartily upon our scalps but did no work in return. These despicable creatures were the scourge of every man and boy in the army—sent as tormentors, no doubt, from the devil himself. And they seemed to spread like wildfire in the heat, such that the soldier who wasn't afflicted by 'em was as scarce as hen's teeth.

There was one bright spot in that miserable month: I was very much pleased to get a letter from Mama with news from home. The letter said that Maribel was doin' fine and that my family was well, for which I was more than just a mite grateful. Not a day went by that I didn't think of Maribel and my unborn child, and Mama, Pa, Amos, and Vanessa. I knew the war was makin' life difficult for them back home too, but even just thinkin' of bein' a father and raisin' a family with Maribel was enough to get me through the hardest days. It reminded me to pray for them every day.

But Mama's letter also said it was true what I'd heard: that Jefferson County was to be included in the proposed new state—a northern state—even though most of the good folks back home were loyal to Virginia. I'd heard the rumors about how the Yankees had fixed it so as only Union sympathizers could vote in Charles Town, and most folks in the county were none too happy about it. Hearin' Mama talk of how the whole state was comin' apart made me mad as a hornet. Didn't those danged fools know what the Yankees had done to our homes? Our farms? Our towns? Didn't they know how much blood had already been spilt?

Bad enough Mama was livin' in a divided nation, a divided state, and a divided county, but the worst was knowin' that her own family was divided north and south too. I knew it must've been hard on her, but I reckon there was nothin' to be done about it, leastwise not until the war was ended anyway. So I prayed for that too. There was a day when it might've struck me as odd that I was the soldier gone off to war, and yet I was the one prayin' for the folks back home, instead of the other way around. But that day was long past. My own prayer time was just about the only time I found any peace to speak of, so I took to prayin' a lot that summer. After a while, prayin' for Maribel and our child just sorta seemed the natural thing to do. But it was no small comfort knowin' that she and the folks back home were prayin' for me too.

By early August, A. P. Hill's division arrived from Richmond, and we got ready to march again. On August the seventh, we moved north toward Culpeper Court House but had to stop again on account of the terrible heat after marchin' only eight miles. The heat was so bad that every piece of clothing I had was drenched in sweat and a fella could hardly get enough water to drink. More than a few of the boys went down from the heat that day.

Then, on the eighth, our cavalry took the river crossings over the Rapidan, and we made ready to cross the next day. We knew the Yankees were nearby and there was probably another fight comin' soon.

"Hey boys, guess what?" It was one of the fellas from the Fifth Virginia with a big smile on his face. He was so excited he couldn't wait 'til someone answered.

"Colonel Ronald says the Yankee commander is none other than ol' "Commisary" Banks, himself! Guess he ain't had enough yet—come back for another whippin'!" Then he was off, lickety-split, to spread the news.

"Who's Colonel Ronald?" I asked, not really talkin' to anyone in particular.

It was Arty who looked up from fryin' his biscuit and answered up. "He's got the brigade now, Wil, what with Gen'ral Winder bein' promoted to division commander and all."

Then it was Carlton's turn to speak up. "Yeah. Seems this here brigade goes through commanders faster than we go through stockin's."

That was sayin' somethin' when you considered how far we'd marched in the last six months. A decent pair of stockin's was becomin' a valuable commodity in the Stonewall Brigade. Not to mention shoes.

By nine o'clock the next mornin', we were crossin' the Rapidan and marchin' toward Culpeper, but by eleven o'clock, the column had halted again. By midday, we could hear the guns goin' into action up the Orange Turnpike ahead of us somewhere, and we got movin' again presently, not wantin' to give the Yankees any upper hand in the comin' fracas.

When we finally reached the scene of the battle, it was mostly just an artillery duel. Our guns were deployed across the turnpike and firin' at the Yankee guns on the high bank of the crick to the northeast. Off to our right was a large hill that stood high above the trees and fields all around. The brigade deployed behind the guns, with the Second Virginia on the left end of the brigade, but we didn't advance. I reckoned we were waitin' for Hill's division to arrive before tanglin' with the Blue-bellies.

Around about five o'clock in the afternoon, there was a ruckus up ahead on our left, and the sound of musket fire grew heavy. Before long, we saw the flags of one of our brigades, and all the boys with 'em, come streamin' back in our direction with the Yankees in hot pursuit.

"They're tryin' to flank us! They've turned our left! The Yankees are flankin' us!" one fella shouted at the top of his lungs as he ran past.

"Steady, boys! Hold your ground!" It was Colonel Botts ridin' in front of the regiment on his horse.

The Yankees came into view and tried to get back into line when they saw us, but they didn't have much success.

It was just about that time when Ol' Blue Light appeared ridin' Little Sorrel, with a gleam in his eye and a grin on his face. He tried to draw out his sword but it was stuck, so he just took it off his belt, scabbard and all, and waved it up over his head.

"Stonewall Brigade!" he called out loudly. "Forward, men! And give them the bayonet!" Then he spurred the horse and rode back and forth in front of the brigade, still shoutin' to rally the men.

"Make ready, men!" Colonel Botts shouted. Then he and the gen'ral rode around behind the regiment so as not to be in the way when the volley was fired.

"Take Aim . . . FIRE!"

We fired into the Yankees at about 400 yards, and it slowed 'em down a bit.

"CHARGE!"

We charged across the field and hardly a single Yankee fired at us. They all just turned and started runnin'. We chased 'em all the way back to the crick, but then they got up reinforcements and reformed.

"Fall back, boys!" someone shouted.

I didn't really know who it was, but we saw the boys from the Fourth Virginia fallin' back to our right, then the boys from the Second started fallin' back too, so I fell back with 'em.

Around seven o'clock, a fresh brigade from Hill's division arrived and deployed to our left, and then another brigade. They formed up, fired, and advanced toward the Yankee lines, and it wasn't long before the Yankees finally broke and gave up the field.

By ten o'clock that night it was all but over. The next day, we camped there on the battlefield while both sides collected the dead and dyin'. It was another hot day. The sun baked the bodies where they lay 'til that familiar stench began to rise up through the air. A plague of flies descended over the field, buzzin' all around the poor mortified souls. Someone said that the name of the hill there was called Slaughter's Mountain. I thought that was a fittin' name, considerin'. Most of the dead were from Garnett's brigade, which the Yankees had shattered on our left with their flankin' attack. But we gave 'em a quick burial so as to get rid of the flies and the smell as quick as we could.

That was when we learned that Gen'ral Winder had been hit by a shell during the battle. One of the boys comin' back from the hospital told us that he was hit bad and the wound was mortal. Some of the boys were even glad when they heard the news. It was no secret that the Gen'ral wasn't too well liked by the men, but I just couldn't find it in my heart to be glad of any man's demise.

By August the eleventh, Ol' Jack had Hill's and Ewell's divisions diggin' in to prepare for a Yankee counterattack, but he sent what was left of our division to the rear. The Second marched back to Orange Court House where we stayed for another week while Ol' Jack was tryin' to figure out what Gen'ral Pope was up to. We'd whooped the Yankees again, but this time they weren't runnin' away like before.

Back To Manassas

The bivouac at Orange Court House was particularly miserable, and the "blue line" for the infirmary got longer every day. It seemed if a fella wasn't sick from the heat, it was either the quick step, or lice, or some other miserable malady. There was hardly a man in the camp who didn't at least have somethin' to complain about.

Some of the boys from the Thirty-third took to makin' their own remedies out of tree bark and whatever they could find cooked into their own homemade liquor. They called it "bark juice", "O be joyful", or "John Barleycorn", but whatever the name, it was bad news. Gen'ral Winder would've never tolerated it, but with him gone, morale and discipline in the camp wasn't what it had been before. Every day there were more drunks, more bummers and deserters, more sick and lame, and fewer likely men to do the work, and the regimental muster was shorter than it'd ever been before—only about 135 able-bodied men were left of the whole regiment—quite a difference from over 800 just the year before.

The wind whipped up and the clouds rolled in on the twenty-fourth of August, and Capt'n Rowan came back from the officers' call that mornin' with orders for us to cook three days' rations and get ready to march again. That usually meant we'd be marchin' where the supply train couldn't go—somewhere close to the Yankees, no doubt—and likely into a fight. It was the kind of news we always took with mixed feelings. On the one hand, at least it meant we'd be movin' out, instead of just sittin' around in camp all miserable-like. But then on the other hand, we weren't exactly whistlin' with joy about the prospect of marchin' into battle in the state we were in. Marchin' into battle always meant there was a good chance some of us wouldn't be comin' back, even when we were at our best.

The sun was still scorchin' that mornin', but we had to build small cookin' fires anyway for the rations. By then, our army rations mostly consisted of flour and a little bacon grease, which was made into hard tack or sloosh. On the march, sloosh was easier than hard tack, seein' as how it didn't have to be fried in a skillet. We just mixed the bacon grease right into the dough, rolled it up 'til it looked like a small snake, wrapped it around the ramrod or bayonet, and cooked it over hot coals. Every now and then we might have real bacon or some other meat, but most of the time it was just salt pork, which could be cooked until it was tough and dry and carried on the march for days without havin' to cook it again. It was enough to keep a man alive, but it sure enough wasn't Mama's home cookin'.

The storms rolled through later that day, which provided only a short spell from the heat, but then they were gone just as quick as they came, and the heat came back with a vengeance. Only now everything was wetter and even more uncomfortable than before.

I learned to keep my paper and pen in my cartridge box when it rained, it bein' just about the only dry place I had to put 'em. I reckoned I'd better write home that night, seein' as how I had no earthly idea when the next time to write might come. Somehow writin' to Maribel seemed to help make the time go by faster and took my mind off the miseries of camp life for a while.

The next day we marched north toward Culpeper again. We started out early but had to stop every hour to rest from the heat. The march was so long and the heat so bad that day that Colonel Botts detailed his old company, Company G, Botts' Grays, just to march behind the regiment with bayonets so as to keep the bummers and no-accounts from stragglin' too far behind. Twenty-six miles we marched that day, and by the time we finally stopped for the night, we were dead on our feet.

The Second was assigned to picket duty that night, and I drew the midnight watch. I'd only been able to get a couple of hours' sleep before my sentry post, but at least the weather was pleasant. There was a refreshin' breeze, and the night was much cooler, so I rather enjoyed my watch—at least for a while.

Somewhere just before two o'clock in the mornin', I heard a ruckus not far off in the darkness. Then a voice shouted, "HALT!" From the direction of the voice, I knew it had to be the next sentry. I ran toward it and came to a small clump of trees at the end of my post. I knew the voice had come from the other side, but just before I got there, a man came a-runnin' out of the trees and right at me like an angry mama bear. I couldn't see his face in the darkness, but he was wearin' only a shirt, britches, and boots—no jacket or hat—and he wasn't carryin' a rifle either.

A deserter? Or maybe a spy!

"HALT!" I shouted, and braced myself. But he didn't stop. He just ran right at me so fast I didn't even have time to raise my rifle. He lowered his shoulder, and—WHAM!—hit me hard right square in the chest, knockin' us both to the ground. I tried to grab at him, but he just rolled off and scrambled to get back on his feet. I got hold of one boot and tripped him up to keep him from gettin' away.

"Let GO!" he hollered, and the other boot came back hard into my left cheek and eye.

I cried out on account of the pain in my face, and let go, but there was somethin' familiar about that voice. Then he was back on his feet lickety-split and off like a hare bein' chased by a coon dog. But before he could even take three steps, I saw the other sentry come a-runnin' out of the clump of trees toward us. He stopped, leveled his rifle, and pulled back the hammer.

"Halt or I'll shoot!" he shouted.

I didn't rightly know if he'd shoot the man in the back or not, but every soldier knew there was no worse fate than gettin' shot in the back. Even if a fella did somehow survive the gunshot, he'd be branded a deserter or a coward—or both—and then probably shot or hanged anyways. Whatever the outcome, it didn't figure to be good.

I was a mite relieved to see the man stop runnin' and put his hands up in the air. But then, in the pale light of the quarter moon, I could just make out that his right hand was missin' a finger—the little one. As I got to my feet, he turned around and I could see his bearded face for the first time.

"Jim?" I could scarce believe my eyes.

"Wil Harleck? Is that you?" He looked just as surprised as me.

"What're you doin'?" I asked angrily, still nursin' my tender cheek with one hand.

"You know this man?" the other sentry asked.

"Yeah. I reckon I do," I said, tryin' to hide the betrayal in my voice.

I never figured Jim for a deserter.

"We gotta take 'im in," he warned, just in case I was havin' any thoughts about lettin' him go.

I looked at Jim, then checked my hand to see that my face was bleedin'. He saw the blood and I could tell he felt bad for kickin' me.

"Yeah, I know. I can handle this one," I said, pointin' the bayonet end of my rifle at Jim.

"You sure?" he asked, lookin' like he wasn't so sure he should trust me to do my duty.

"Yeah," I answered. "He's on my post. I'll take 'im to the Sergeant." I reckon he could tell I was still a mite perturbed about that kick in the head, which was startin' to hurt like the dickens right about then.

"Suit yerself," the private replied, then turned to walk back to his post.

I could just make out the look on Jim's face. I knew he was both upset that he was caught and sorry that he'd hurt his friend whilst he was tryin' to get away, but the pain in my face was a brutal reminder of what he'd just done.

"Well, let's go," I said coldly, so as to let him know I was still mad.

We turned and started walkin' back to camp, Jim in front of me with his hands up, and me with the rifle at his back. But before we got too far, he stopped again.

"What're you stoppin' for?" I demanded.

"Wil," Jim turned around with tears in his eyes, "I know you gotta do your duty . . . " He paused and took a deep breath, like he was gatherin' his courage to say somethin' more. "But before ya take me in, there's somethin' I gotta show ya."

I was a mite confused, but I reckoned Jim must've had a real good reason to be desertin' like this. I nodded my head and he reached into his shirt pocket and pulled out a folded and crumpled piece of paper.

I took the paper from his hand and opened it. It was a letter. It was too dark to read what it said, but Jim's face said it all.

"Please, Wil. Ya gotta let me go," he begged, and I saw a tear run down from the corner of his eye into his beard.

"What is this?" I asked, tryin' to settle my disposition. My hands were still shakin' from the fracas, and the side of my face was achin' somethin' awful.

"It's my Dorothy." He could barely get the words out. I could see his face more clearly now, and he was fightin' just to keep from weepin' openly. "My sweet child . . . "

He didn't have to finish. I knew his little girl was gone. My heart sank. I couldn't let him go without furlough, even though we were only just a few miles from his home. God in Heaven knows what'd happen if I did. But how could I make him stay?

"Please, Wil!" he begged. "For the love of God, my family *needs* me! You gotta let me go!"

What if it was your own daughter, Wil Harleck? What would you *do?*

Truth be told, I didn't rightly know what I would've done. I'd never been a father before, and just knowin' that I'd soon as likely become one wasn't helpin' much.

What'll happen if I do *let him go?*

Maybe it was selfish of me to be thinkin' only of myself, but the thought did occur to me that if I let him go, not only would they likely shoot Jim if they caught him, they'd just as likely shoot me too, for lettin' him go.

"You know what they do to deserters, Jim!" I argued. "You'll be shot—or hanged!"

"I don't . . . They ain't . . . " he started again, but the words still wouldn't come out. I reckon maybe it was because he was finally thinkin' it through.

"They *will* catch you, Jim. It's not like they won't know where you went, for Pete's sake! Your farm can't be more than a few miles from this here spot! They're gonna know where you are! And *then* what? You want your wife to lose her daughter *and* her husband both?"

He just stared at me with tears runnin' down both cheeks, and in his eyes I saw a broken man—a man who'd give his own life for his family, but was feelin' as powerless to help them as a tiny ant tryin' to stop a flood from washin' away the whole anthill.

"For pity's sake, Jim, they already know you tried to escape. The other sentry saw you."

"He doesn't know who I am! He's from D Company!" Jim argued, still holdin' out the faintest spark of hope in his eyes. "Besides, they ain't shot anyone for desertion in months, Wil. Not since the Valley."

Come to think of it, he did have a point. There'd been dozens of deserters in just the last few weeks, but even the ones that were caught were only flogged and assigned extra Johnny detail. Maybe the army was finally realizin' that they couldn't afford to keep shootin' good fightin' men, even for desertion. But that didn't keep 'em from punishin' the bummers, shirkers, and deserters in other ways. And there was always the chance . . .

"It doesn't matter, Jim! He has to report the incident, and then they'll figure out that it was *me* that let you go! Then we'll *both* be in trouble."

But even as those words came out of my mouth, I was feelin' guilty for bein' more concerned about myself than I was my friend who'd just lost his child.

If I could only be sure they'd only punish me, and not him too, I'd let him go.

I s'pose Jim must've been feelin' the same way about not gettin' me in trouble. The hope faded from his face and he heaved a deep sigh. Then somethin' strange happened: I saw an unexplainable peace settle over his face.

"You're right . . . " he said, lookin' down at the ground then back up at me. "I reckon I *have* been a bit overwraught about all this," he went on, straightenin' up his back and blinkin' to try and dry his eyes. "I'm sorry, Wil . . . I never meant to get you involved in this."

"A man has a right to get emotional over the death of his child," I said, tryin' to reassure him. "Let's see if we can't work somethin' out with the Capt'n."

"Already tried. Capt'n says we're movin' out tomorrow, and there's nothin' he can do about it." Then he sighed again and wiped his eye with the back of his hand. "Well, I reckon you oughta turn me in now."

I didn't want to report my friend for attemptin' to desert, but I knew some kinda report would have to be made.

"Yeah . . . I reckon so," I said, lookin' down at the ground and tryin' hard to think of some other way to avoid gettin' Jim in a mess of trouble. But nothin' was comin' to mind. Then it struck me. "But maybe we oughta do somethin' else first," I said lookin' up at him. "My Pa used to say, 'When there's nothing a man can do, the best thing a man can do is pray.'"

So we sat down on a fallen tree and I prayed.

> Lord, I'm not really sure how to pray about this, but my friend Jim could really use your help right about now. I don't rightly know how it feels to lose a child, but I know *You* know how it feels. If You could see fit to help Jim get back home, I'm sure his wife and daughter would be much obliged, and Jim would be real grateful too. Oh . . . and if You could fix it so neither of us was to get into any trouble over this here incident tonight, we'd be mighty thankful. We ask these things in the name of Your Son, Jesus. Amen.

Then we walked back to the camp, and I found the Sergeant of the Guard. I made my report and turned Jim over to him. I told the Sergeant that Jim was just sorely distressed at the news of his daughter's death, and wasn't thinkin' straight. Then I handed him the letter. It occurred to me as I stood there watchin' him read the letter that I hadn't even read it myself yet! But I knew Jim would never lie about somethin' like this. The Sergeant finished the letter, folded it up, and tucked it into his jacket. Then he looked at Jim and said, "I'm real sorry, but I have to take ya to the Captain."

Then he turned to me and said, "Thank you Private. I'll take care of 'im from here."

I finished the rest of my post, but I couldn't stop thinkin' about Jim, and how I might've been tempted to do the same thing if I was to find myself in his shoes. Thoughts of Maribel and my unborn child came floodin' in, and I started to wonderin' if I'd done the right thing. But there was no changin' it now. The deed was done.

I was still a mite shaky in the knee and tender in the face for awhile, but eventually I felt my strength return again. It was a good thing too, seein' as how the next day brought little rest.

August the twenty-sixth saw cooler weather. The sky was cloudy and hid the hot Virginia sun, and the wind blew through the trees to cool the land, and us with it. Early that mornin', before breakfast, I was called in to report to the Capt'n of the Guard. I made my report as before, then the tent flaps parted and the sergeant outside shouted, "Attention!"

Colonel Botts came into the tent lookin' a little pekid from the heat. But he stood up as straight as he could in the tent and called out. "Bring in the accused."

The tent flaps parted again, and Jim came in, followed by another private with a rifle. The private stood behind Jim but wore a look that was none too serious. I still don't know how we fit all five of us in the Capt'n's tent. As it was, the Capt'n and I had to stand all bent over so as to stay out of the Colonel's way.

"Captain, your report, if you please?" the Colonel said calmly.

The Capt'n stepped forward, stood up straight, and saluted, and the Colonel returned his salute.

"Sir, Private Lancroft here, was caught attempting to slip through the picket line last night. Private Harleck here, apprehended him. He was carrying this."

The Capt'n took the letter out of his jacket and handed it to the Colonel. Colonel Botts' face softened a mite as he read the letter. He looked up at me and then at Jim, and I could tell he knew that Jim and I were friends.

"My sympathies, Private," he said simply.

"Thank you, sir," Jim replied meekly.

"I have only one question for you," the Colonel said with a quizzical look on his face.

"Sir?"

"Why didn't you bring this matter to the chain of command?"

"Would you've approved my request, Colonel?" Jim asked boldly, lookin' him in the eye. "With the regiment on the march, and bein' well below half strength like we are, and seein' as how we're likely headed for a scrap with the Yankees? I don't mean any disrespect now, sir, but I went to Cap'n Rowan. He said he was sorry, but we needed every man, and there was nothin' else he could do."

"I see," the Colonel answered thoughtfully. "So you decided to take matters into your own hands."

"Tell me, Colonel, would you've granted me the furlough?" Jim pressed.

Colonel Botts paused for a moment. "Perhaps not," he admitted, "but that is why we have a chain of command, is it not?"

Jim hesitated. "Yes, sir. I reckon so," he answered, lookin' down.

The Colonel stepped back, sat down at the Capt'n's table, and commenced to writin'. After a minute or two, he looked up.

"Regrettably, this case deserves more time than we have today. We're moving out soon, and that includes you. Understood?" He looked sternly at Jim.

"Yes, sir," Jim answered.

"Good. I'll speak to Captain Rowan and give it some more thought. I'll render my decision at the next opportune moment. You will return to duty immediately, and I'll expect you to do your duty without question until such time as this case can be properly adjudicated. And Private Lancroft, if you make any further attempts to desert, I *will* have you shot. Is that understood?"

"Yes, sir."

"Very well. Dismissed."

Jim glanced up at me like he was sayin', *I forgive you*, but I knew his heart was still breakin', and doubtless he was wishin' I hadn't caught him in the first place. At least then he'd've been home with his wife and daughter. And what with the army marchin' so quickly and all, it wasn't likely anyone would be comin' for him any time soon, leastwise not until after the battle was decided, anyway.

He straightened up, looked at the Colonel and saluted. Colonel Botts stood up and returned his salute. Then Jim turned and walked out of the tent without sayin' a word. And that was that.

All day that day it felt like it was gonna rain, but the rain never came. It was a welcome relief from the heat, though. We marched through the Thoroughfare Gap, a low gap in the Bull Run Mountains, which were really just a line of high foothills just west of Manassas town. There we found Yankee cavalry near Bristoe Station on the Orange and Alexandria Railroad. Colonel Botts deployed the regiment across a small stream, and we attacked the Fed'rals there, but they didn't have much of a stomach for fightin'. After a short skirmish, they skedaddled and left the ground to us. So we marched on, stoppin' along the way just long enough to destroy anything valuable to the Yankees.

When we finally stopped for the night, I found Jim again.

"Did you get your letter back?"

"Nah. The Colonel still has it. Probably so he can prove I'm guilty."

"You think he'll call you in tonight?"

"Don't know. Maybe."

"What did the letter say . . . if ya don't mind my askin'?"

Jim paused for a moment before answering. "It was from my wife, Sarah. She said Dorothy took ill of fever a few weeks back," he said, his voice gettin' all choked up again. "She passed in the night . . . I reckon it was five days ago now."

"I'm real sorry, Jim," I said softly. I wasn't sure what else to say.

"She begged me to come home," he went on with pain in his voice. "Said Yankee soldiers took the hog . . . " He broke off and looked at me with his eyes full of tears again. "They're starvin', Wil. Sarah and Adaline, they've got nothin' left to eat. I sent every penny I could when we got paid in Richmond, but, what with the doctor and all, that's all gone now. They need my help to bring in the crop. They did their best to work the field, but when Dorothy took ill, they had to tend to her and couldn't keep up with the crop. That's why I had to go—or try, leastwise."

I felt ashamed for only thinkin' of how we might get punished, when he was just tryin' to go and help his wife and daughter.

"I'm real sorry," I admitted.

"I know. You did nothin' wrong. You did your job." He patted me on the knee, almost like my Pa would've done, and somehow managed the slightest reassuring smile as he stood up and walked away.

I prayed for Jim and his family again that night like I'd never prayed before. And I repented of my own selfishness too. Everything just seemed to be fallin' apart, and there was nothin' I could do to fix it. All I could do was pray and hope the Good Lord was doin' His part.

By afternoon of the next day, we'd captured the Yankee supply depot at Manassas Junction. In just three days, we'd marched clean around the end of Pope's army, got between him and Washington D.C., looted his supply base, and left a trail of destruction behind us that even a blind man could follow. It was for sure they'd be comin' for us now.

Gen'ral Jackson ordered the Yankee supplies to be distributed to the army right away, which we were mighty glad to get after that long march. There was food and ammunition in plentiful supply, plus rifles and all sorts of equipment, and even some shoes and socks, though not as many as we needed. My shoes were becomin' a mite worn, but some of the boys who'd been with Ol' Jack since the Shenandoah had marched their shoes clean off!

We camped and rested that night at the base of a hill called Sudley's Mountain, not far from where we'd fought the Battle of Manassas just a year before. There we partook of some of the Yankee hospitality we'd just liberated. There were wagons of beef and bacon, beans and peas, goobers, and some early corn and squash, plus apples and cherries by the barrel full. All of which made for quite a feast for men who'd been eatin' nothin' but hard tack and "salt horse" for three days. They told us it was salt pork, but I reckon the boys took to callin' it salt horse on account of there was no tellin' just what kind of meat it really was.

In camp that night the men were mostly quiet and reserved, partly because we had full bellies for a change, partly because we knew the Yankee army wouldn't be far behind, and partly because the boys were just too tuckered for celebratin' much. There was quiet music playin' nearby, but for the most part, the boys just sat around the bivouac fires and talked or found a place to sleep for the night. We had no tents, seein' as how we'd out-marched our own supply train again, and what few Yankee tents could be found in the Manassas depot were allotted to the big bugs—that's what we called the politicians and important officers: gen'rals and colonels and such—so the rest of us just made do with what we had.

Along about bedtime, when most of the other fellas were sackin' out for the night, Arty and Jim and I said our evenin' prayers—mostly prayin' for Jim and his family, and that Jim would be spared any harsh punishment for the crime of tryin' to go home to take care of his wife and daughter. While we were prayin', Carlton came by and sat on a log and waited 'til we finished our prayers. Then he spoke up.

"Heard you tried ta make a run fer it," he jabbed at Jim.

My mind froze. I was sure Carlton was fixin' to pick a fight with Jim, and I wasn't altogether sure that Jim wasn't just in a frame of mind to give him one. But Jim didn't seem any too bothered.

"Yep," he answered, like it was nothin' important.

"Lucky you got caught," Carlton grinned.

"I s'pose." But Jim wasn't convinced.

And then somethin' truly incredible happened.

"Well . . . real sorry 'bout yer little girl, anyhow," Carlton added.

I nearly fell off my log in shock, and had to catch myself and act like nothin' happened.

"Yeah, I know," Carlton shot a patronizin' look at me. "But there ain't no sense in kickin' a man when he's down."

Oh really? Is this the same Carlton Willis who kicked me in the back when I was sittin' down on the train just last year?

"I didn't say a thing . . . " I argued, lookin' as innocent as I could. But I couldn't help but smile.

"No, but you was thinkin' it!" he pointed his finger at me with a grin.

Does he even remember kickin' me on that train? Somehow I doubt it. Well, I'm just glad to see that he's not always a drunken agitator. I much prefer this Carlton to that other fella.

"Anyhow, it don't matter," he said, changin' the subject. "I heard a report from a cavalry scout a while back. Said the Yankees are camped less than a day's march down the Warrenton Turnpike. Should be here tomorrow. Looks like we're gonna have another fight on our hands, sure enough."

"Reckon so," Jim replied.

"You think this one'll be 'the big dance'?" I asked. All of us were hopin' for one big final battle that would put an end to all the fightin', once and for all.

"Depends on the Yankees," Arty said. "Think they've got the belly for it?"

"Hmph!" Carlton smirked. "Can't say for sure, but they oughta be good and riled up by now, what with all the damage we've been doin', and us sittin' here between them and Washington. I can just see Lincoln now, all red-faced and got his dander up good, I bet! Yeah. They'll be ready for a fight."

"Well, let's hope so," Jim agreed.

"Sure would like to whup 'em once and for all, so's we can put an end to this here war," Carlton confessed.

"Yep," Jim nodded in agreement, "and the sooner the better too."

"Hear, hear," Arty added.

"Me too," I heard myself say.

"Yep," Jim repeated.

There was silence for several minutes while each man was lost in his own thoughts. Then Carlton cleared his throat, stared at the ground, and started to talk again.

"You remember that night you prayed for me before Winchester?" he asked. Then he looked up at me with just his eyes.

"Yeah."

"You s'pose it was God that saved me from gettin' killed that day?"

"I reckon maybe so, yeah."

He looked down at his feet and paused again, like he wasn't really sure he wanted to say what was comin' next. Then he got up his courage and looked back up at me.

"You reckon maybe y'all could pray for me again? I just got that funny feelin' again, like I ain't too sure but that this here battle might be my last. Y'know what I mean?"

"Sure," I heard myself say. But to be honest, I couldn't recollect ever feelin' that way myself. My head was swimmin' with thoughts, and I wasn't sure just what to do. Carlton had a way of makin' a boy say whatever you thought he wanted to hear. I knew what he needed was a far sight more than just a prayer, but a prayer was a good start. My eyes glanced quickly over at Jim and found him lookin' back at me. He caught my glance and figured out what I was thinkin'.

"I will," he chimed in, lookin' to see if Carlton approved.

"I reckon that'd be alright," Carlton nodded.

Arty and I had just finished prayin' for Jim, so maybe he figured it was time to return the favor. So I closed my eyes and bowed my head, and Jim prayed. It went somethin' like this:

> Lord, we beseech Thee to keep us safe in the comin' battle, and shelter us all from harm under Your mighty wings. Give us the courage and strength to fight with honor, and forgive us if we should take a life against Your will. We ask Thy blessing upon our cause, that it may be found just in Your sight, and be with us, both now and always . . .

He paused for a moment, and I looked up at Jim again to see if he was alright. He glanced back at me and went on:

> Lord, I also pray for my friend, Carlton, tonight—not just that You would keep him safe in the battle, but also that You would save his eternal soul and forgive him of his sins, so that if he should fall in the comin' fight, or at the time of Thy choosin', he might have eternal life with You in Heaven. In the blessed name of Thy Son, Jesus Christ, I pray. Amen.

"Amen," Arty and I echoed.

Carlton hesitated, and then finally blurted out, "Amen."

It occurred to me that he probably just said 'Amen' because it's what a fella's s'posed to say after someone prays, but I was just glad he said it at all. He didn't say another word the rest of the night, but just sat there on that log for the longest time, lost in thought.

Bloodbath at Brawner's Farm

The camp was buzzin' like a beehive the next mornin'. All mornin' long our cavalry scouts brought a steady stream of reports of a column of Fed'rals approachin' up the Warrenton Turnpike. We were all busy cookin' breakfast and preparin' our cartridge boxes and rifles for the comin' fight, but then nothin' happened. Lunchtime came and went, and still we sat waitin' for word to move out.

It wasn't 'til the mid-afternoon that we finally lit out quick-like across the unfinished railroad bed and through the woods toward the turnpike. The division moved quietly through the woods and formed up in the edge of the trees next to a large field that looked down on the road. The Stonewall Brigade formed at the right end of the division, with the Innocent Second on the left of the brigade, and the Thirty-third next to us on our right. The Fifth Virginia formed the center that day, with the Twenty-seventh and Fourth Virginia on the right of the brigade near a small farmhouse. There we waited for the right moment to catch the Yankees by surprise.

A Yankee regiment came into view, but they paid no mind to us and just marched on by down the road without even noticin' we were there. Then another did likewise. We thought for sure Ol' Jack would give the order to attack, but none came. We let a couple more regiments go by, 'til it was nearly five o'clock in the afternoon. Then, finally, the signal gun went off, and the artillery opened fire from the hill just behind us to our left. Then we stepped out onto the field and started advancin' across the field.

At the sound of the openin' guns, the Billy Yanks on the road below started scatterin' and took to the cover by the side of the road in a hurry. But it wasn't long before we saw a Yankee regiment wearin' handsome tall black hats movin' across the field toward us. There were about twice as many of us as them, so we kept on movin' forward, right at 'em. The Yankees came to a stop at a distance of only about 100 yards and fired the first volley. It was terrible and deadly, and I saw several of our boys go down, but then we fired right back and gave 'em a dose of their own medicine. What followed next was by far the most dreadful and awful thing I ever lived through in all my days of soldierin'.

We poured volley after volley of deadly fire into the Yankee lines, but those boys with the black hats, they just wouldn't budge. They just stood their ground with courage the likes of which we'd never seen before from any Yankee regiment. And they fired back with terrible effect too. After a short while, the boys of the Fourth Virginia on the right end of the brigade started to curve around the Yankee left, and we thought maybe we'd finally push 'em back. But just then they got up another regiment to reinforce their lines. The boys from the Fourth poured hot lead into the new regiment, but they refused to give up the ground.

In the heat of the battle, Colonel Botts was ridin' his horse back and forth just behind our lines and shoutin' for us to stand firm and keep firin'. I can't rightly be sure exactly when it happened, on account of bein' focused on the enemy, but one minute he was there, and the next he was gone—shot clean off his horse—struck in the face by a Yank Minie ball, one fella said. It felt like a stab in the heart. The Colonel was popular with the men, and I was especially fond of him. Hearin' that he was shot fairly made us wanna charge the Yankees and make 'em pay for what they'd done, but we had no idea who was in charge of the regiment now, so we just stood our ground and kept on shootin'.

The fightin' went on for quite some time, with both sides addin' new regiments to the fray, and the terrible stand-off kept on growin' across that big field. On our left, Gen'ral Jackson brought up some new regiments from Georgia, but they were met by another new Yankee regiment, and their attack stalled out. Then, a while later, we saw what looked like it might be Gen'ral Trimble's brigade formin' up across the field to the left of the Georgians and marchin' toward the Yankee lines. But every time more of our boys arrived to press the attack, the Yankees would bring up another fresh regiment, and neither side could whoop the other. We just stood there in that field, toe to toe, killin' each other.

I reckon we never met a group of Yankees as stubborn and brave as those boys in the black hats. Whenever the Stonewall Brigade had fought together as one, we'd never lost a battle. But those black hats, they just stood their ground like stubborn ol' army mules that day, and wouldn't budge an inch, even when we pressed the attack.

It was a terrible affair, and it went on for hours, back and forth across that dreadful field, attackin' and then fallin' back, only to reform and attack again. At times the smoke was so thick we could scarcely see the Yankees only fifty yards in front of us in the gatherin' darkness. We just had to aim for the flashes of their muzzles. The stench of gunpowder filled my nostrils 'til I could hardly breathe, and I thought I'd likely go mad from the ghoulish sound of the Minie balls buzzin' by like angry hornets, or strikin' the earth at my feet with a thud that could be felt in my bones. But when they struck some poor soul and the cries and screams of the wounded rose up through the thick smoky air, it reminded me of the nightmares I'd had in the hospital after Manassas, and made me wanna retch. That was the reason I'd learned never to eat just before a battle.

Once, when the fightin' was hot and heavy, a bullet struck me on the shoulder, and there was a pain in my arm that nearly made me drop my rifle. Turns out the ball just tore through my shirt and jacket, leavin' only a deep scratch on my arm which bled a little, but wasn't serious. Sergeant Robertson was struck in the arm, Arty had a hole in the leg of his pants too, and Jim's left ear was bleedin' steadily from a near miss by a Yankee Minie ball. Only Carlton came out of the battle without a scratch. But by some miracle of God, we all survived.

Just before dark, we saw a battery of horse artillery go into action off to our right just beyond the farmhouse. Then three more regiments arrived on the field in that same area. I don't rightly know whether it was the horse artillery, the new regiments, or the arrival of nightfall, or maybe they just plain ran out of cartridges, but the Yankee fire finally dwindled out, and they fell back to the road under cover of darkness. We—those of us that were left standin', that is—were too tuckered out to follow after 'em, and we had no cartridges left to shoot anyway, so we just collapsed right where we'd stood.

That battle would later come to be known as "the Nightmare at Brawner's Farm," and it was the worst fight I was ever in. I don't know about the other boys, but I'd shot two boxes of cartridges in just the first hour, then had to take more off the dead and wounded to keep up my firin'. The field lay covered with the slain and wounded, and the eerie sound of their moans and cries seemed to just hover there in the thick smoke and darkness.

The cost to the Stonewall Brigade was terrible. Colonel Baylor, who was in temporary command the after Gen'ral Winder's death at Cedar Mountain, was killed whilst tryin' to rally the brigade on the field. In our own regiment, Colonel Botts was shot and mortally wounded. Eight other men from the Innocent Second were killed, six more were mortally wounded, and twenty-four others were wounded. Capt'n Nadenbousch, from Company D, was shot in the groin and had to be carried from the field that terrible day.

After dark, we went out onto the field to collect our dead and wounded. Then what was left of the brigade limped back through the forest to our camp behind the unfinished railroad bed at the foot of the Sudley's Mountain. A good many of the boys were too tired and spent to even eat, but sleep did not come easy that night.

The next mornin' was August the twenty-ninth, and we learned that Capt'n Colston, of Company E, was ordered to take command of what remained of the Innocent Second. There were less than 100 of us still able to fight. Our own Capt'n Rowan was the senior company officer after Capt'n Nadenbousch was wounded, but he refused to take command on account of his bad foot from the first battle we'd fought there at Manassas just the year before.

One thing was for sure: nary a man in the regiment was unaffected by the loss of Colonel Botts. He was a soldier's colonel, and well-liked and respected by every man and boy. It seemed ironic that Arty, Jim, and I had prayed for the Lord to spare Jim from any harsh punishment, and the colonel had been shot before he'd even decided what that punishment oughta be. Was it possible that maybe it was just the Colonel's time, and it was just a coincidence that it came as answered prayer for Jim? My mind searched for answers, but there were none to be found. I reckon the Good Lord truly does work in mysterious ways, like some folks say.

By breakfast, we were starvin'. We did whatever we could to find somethin' to eat, then we set about tryin' to get some more ammunition. But there wasn't much to be had. Even with all the captured Yankee ammunition, the brigade quartermaster only had enough to issue one box of "forty dead men" for each man. And from what the scouts were tellin' us, it looked like we were gonna need every round we had. The Yankees didn't appear to be leavin', so it seemed they were plannin' to fight.

The attack started later that afternoon. We could hear the battle down the hollar to our left a ways, but we were placed all the way at the right end of the line. Aside from a few stray Yankee artillery shells, it didn't come near us at all. All afternoon, we could hear the Yankee attacks, but they were driven back, and when nightfall came on the second night, we still held our ground at the base of that mountain.

On the third day, August the thirtieth, along about four o'clock in the afternoon, a long line of Blue-bellies came out of the trees just across from us, and we were ordered forward to the railroad bed to stop their advance. Capt'n Colston ordered the regiment to form up in line of battle, and we advanced to the railroad bed under heavy fire and at some great cost.

By the time we reached the railroad bed, we'd lost more than thirty more of our numbers, and our ammunition was all but spent. For those of us who were left, all we could do was to dig in as best we could and pile the rocks up high as possible. Some of the boys even took to throwin' rocks at the Yankees when they ran out of cartridges.

By late afternoon, most of us had come to realize that this might just be our last dance. We were tired, shot up, and out of ammunition, and the Yankees were still comin'. I just hunkered down behind that railroad bed and commenced to prayin'. Now I don't claim that my prayers were the cause of our victory, but just about then somethin' truly miraculous happened. The sound of battle had been steadily growin' off to our right toward the town of Groveton for the last hour or so, but all the sudden we saw a long line of troops clad in gray and butternut comin' out of the forest to our right, almost behind the enemy's exposed flank!

"It's Longstreet!" Capt'n Colston shouted. "The day is saved, boys!" And a great chorus of cheers rose up from our ranks.

Gen'ral Longstreet had come up with his First Corps from Richmond and caught the Yankees flat-footed on the flank, and he was sweepin' the field! In almost no time at all, the Yankee lines melted away and fled back into the woods, and that was the last we saw of 'em that day. The second battle of Manassas was over, and by God's grace, we'd held the ground. But the price of victory was almost too terrible to mention. In just over forty-eight hours, the Innocent Second had lost eighty-two of 130 fightin' men. There were less than fifty of us left.

After the battle, Capt'n Colston persuaded the new acting brigade commander, Colonel Grigsby, to give Jim a week's furlough to go home and bury his daughter and help his wife bring in the crop so they would have somethin' to eat for the fall.

On To Maryland

News that we were headed north after the battle was almost expected, but the men still took it with a mixture of relief and dread. The canard had been flyin' around camp for weeks that Gen'ral Lee was achin' for a chance to get the war out of Virginia and take the fight to the Yankees for a change—maybe even give 'em a reason to talk peace. Of course every soldier knew better than to just take such things as the gospel. There always seemed to be an abundance of false rumors circulatin' around—most of 'em made up by fellas who'd had a mite too much O be joyful or pop skull, and were just lookin' for a story to tell—but in this case the canard just happened to be true. The victory at Second Manassas gave "Ol' Granny" Lee, as some of the boys called him, just the perfect opportunity, and he was gonna take it.

Most of Pope's army was stragglin' back into Washington, so Gen'ral Lee saw his chance to slip away. The whole Army of Northern Virginia marched north to the Potomac River, and on September the fifth, we slipped across into Maryland by way of White's Ford. Gen'ral Lee passed along orders for the men to sing "Maryland, My Maryland" once we'd crossed the river. I reckon he thought it might be popular with the folk there and maybe even persuade a few of 'em to join us. I s'pose they were friendly enough folks, but it sure didn't seem like many of 'em cared much for joinin' the Confederacy. More likely they were just tryin' to keep us from takin' all their crops and livestock to feed the army. And they didn't care much for our Confederate money either, even when the commissary officers tried to pay for what we needed. So when our own supplies started runnin' low, we pretty much had to just take what we needed anyway.

We marched north to the town of Fredrick and camped just north of there along the Emmitsburg Road. But then Gen'ral Lee divided up the army, which he was known to do from time to time, even though some considered it unwise, especially in enemy territory. Still, we were ordered to march with Gen'ral Jackson west to Boonsboro, then on to Williamsport on the Potomac. There, Gen'ral Jackson was to recross the Potomac and advance toward Harpers Ferry while the rest of the army remained in Maryland.

On September the tenth, we crossed South Mountain at Turner's Gap and bivouacked near Boonsboro. The next day, we marched to Williamsport, but we'd much rather have gone to Hagerstown where it was rumored there was a supply of shoes which we badly needed. Some of the boys in the Stonewall Brigade had plum wore out their shoes and had to march with nothin' on their feet at all.

But shoes weren't the only thing in short supply. Once again, we'd outmarched our own supply train, so we had to forage for food and fresh water everywhere we went. When I learned we were marchin' to Williamsport, I remembered what Mama wrote in her letter. She said that Joseph was studyin' as an intern for a Presbyterian minister there during the summer, and I was mighty tempted to look him up if he was still there. Bein' as it was September already, it occurred to me that he might be back in school up in Pennsylvania by then.

I rightly knew that if I did find him I'd likely have to swallow my pride, seein' as how our last meeting hadn't gone so well. And his letter had left little doubt as to how he really felt about me servin' in the "Reb army", as the Yankees called it. But my empty belly compelled me to try and find him and beg his hospitality—or leastwise appeal to his humanity not to let a brother starve to death. I reckoned maybe brothers could forgive each other more quickly than other folk—especially when the necessities of nature motivated at least one of 'em to start by apologizin'.

I found the church just around noon and went to the parish door and knocked. The face of an old woman appeared through the small crack of the door. She wore a look that made me suspect I was makin' her mighty uncomfortable just bein' there. I suspect it was on account of me showin' up on her doorstep in the gray uniform lookin' all bedraggled and all.

"Good afternoon, ma'am." I tried to straighten myself up and look more presentable, but it was no use. I reckon I must've been quite a sight standin' there on that porch all covered with dust and dirt from all that marchin'. My shoes were full of large holes, I had no serviceable stockin's left, my face was covered with whiskers, my hair was long and straggled, and I hadn't eaten more than just a few vittles of hard tack in three days.

"Yes? What may I do for you?" she said softly and slowly in that familiar Shenandoah Valley drawl. Even with my appearance bein' what it was, she struck me as too much of a proper lady not to at least try and be friendly.

"My name's Wil Harleck, ma'am. I'm lookin' for my brother, Joseph. I was hopin' that maybe—"

"One moment, if you please."

The door closed for a minute, but finally it opened wide, and the woman appeared again. She wore an old black and white dress that looked like it'd probably been mended more than once, but it was clean and well pressed. Her silvery hair and wrinkled face gave away her years, but there was still a youthful fire in her eyes that lit up her whole face and told me that she was likely a woman of deep conviction.

"Do come in, won't you?" She opened the door and led me inside, took my old dirty soldier hat, then turned and called up the stairway. "Joseph? Joseph! There's someone here to see you."

A moment later, the familiar tall and slender form of my brother appeared on the steps. He stopped halfway down the stairs when he caught sight of me, and just stood there with a stunned look on his face for a moment like he'd just seen a ghost or somethin'. When he finally got himself together enough to talk, his voice was scarcely more than a whisper.

"Wil? What're you doin' here?" His eyes glanced nervously toward the old woman, then darted around the room and back to me. "You can't be here . . . " His voice was hushed and strained, like he was tryin' to whisper loud enough to be heard but not overheard.

I didn't rightly know what to say, so I just stood there like a fool lookin' up at him like I was still that little kid brother from years ago. I reckon part of me'll likely always feel that way. Somethin' about older brothers: they just have a way of makin' younger brothers feel even younger and more foolish than they already are.

"Joseph . . . I, uh . . . " I could scarcely find the words.

"Well now, there's no need to be rude, Joseph," the woman interrupted, soundin' a mite motherly. "There's no harm in helping a young man in need."

"Good God in Heaven, little brother," Joseph said, a little louder this time as he came down the steps. "You look like . . . well, you look terrible. What're you doin' here?"

I got up my courage and put my shoulders back. "The regiment's here in town. Marched in from Boonsboro this mornin'."

"The Reb army? Here? Why?"

"I didn't come to talk about the army, Joseph."

"Uh-um . . . " the woman cleared her throat to remind Joseph of his manners, but he wasn't gettin' the hint. "Well," she said a little louder, "aren't you going to introduce me?"

"I'm very sorry. Please forgive me." Joseph's face went red with embarrassment. "Mrs. McDavitt, meet my brother, Wil," he said, noddin' his head toward me. Then he nodded toward the woman. "Wil, this is Mrs. Dorothy McDavitt, Father McDavitt's wife."

"Pleased to meet you ma'am," I said in my best cordial voice.

"Indeed, the pleasure is all mine," she returned with a smile and a slight curtsy. "It's so nice to finally meet you, Wil. Joseph speaks of you often."

I couldn't rightly be sure what she meant by that, but I gathered it wasn't all in a bad light, so I took it as a good sign anyway.

"Oh, Father McDavitt will be so pleased to meet you when he comes home. I do hope you can stay for a while. I'm sorry he isn't here right now. He's over in the church preparing his sermon for Sunday mornin', but he'll be home for dinner later."

"That's alright, ma'am," I did my best to sound gracious.

"We were just about to sit down to lunch," she said with a smile. "Won't you please join us?"

"Why, thank you, kindly, ma'am," I accepted eagerly.

I was powerful hungry, and I could scarcely contain my excitement at the prospect of a real home-cooked meal. I followed her into the dining room, and Joseph came in behind me. Mrs. McDavitt motioned for us to sit at the table, which I happily obliged. She left the room to fetch lunch, but Joseph still stood there with a strange worried look on his face.

"I read in the paper this mornin' that Lee'd invaded Maryland, but I thought y'all were up near Frederick," he said. "What ungodly secesh business brings you all the way down here?"

"I'm hungry, Joseph. I haven't had a good meal in three days."

"Well, I reckon that makes sense," he smirked. "It's probably a mite difficult for the army to feed y'all, seein' as how your Confederate money is only fit for usin' as toilet paper here in Maryland—and not even *good* toilet paper at tha—"

"Joseph!" Mrs. McDavitt scolded as she reentered the room with a tray of soup bowls. "I'll thank you to mind your manners in this house, young man!"

"My apologies, again, Mrs. McDavitt." Joseph looked embarrassed at havin' been scolded twice. "I didn't mean to offend. I just got a little carried away."

She gave him a stern look and said, "Sit," which Joseph obediently did. Then she set the bowls of soup on the table and returned to the kitchen. I picked up my spoon, hopin' we could start eatin', but Joseph just sat there. He took a deep breath to calm down, and lowered his voice.

"I s'pose y'all've just been stealin' everything you need, is that right?"

"If I'd been stealin' to eat, why would I need to come here askin' you for help?" I answered, doin' my best to keep calm.

"Well maybe *you* haven't, but I bet a lot of others have," he shot back.

"It's war, Joseph. We do what we have to do."

"At what cost, little brother?" His voice was gettin' louder again. "How many of our friends have been killed or wounded on account of this little rebellion of yours?!"

Mrs. McDavitt walked back into the room with some bread and a kettle of tea, which she served to us. Then she sat down at the table and said grace. I wasted no time diggin' right into my soup—peas, green beans, carrots and potato in a beef broth—which tasted like pure heaven to my empty stomach, but Joseph hadn't even picked up his spoon yet. He cleared his throat and then spoke to her in his best polite voice.

"I was just remarkin' to Wil about what an unnecessary tragedy this war is, and how many husbands and fathers and sons and brothers, North *and* South, may never be comin' home to their loved ones again." It was plain to see he'd been givin' this matter a good deal of thought since our last meeting and had it all worked out in his head.

"So I heard," she replied politely, slicin' the bread with a knife.

I didn't wanna seem ungrateful, so I decided it might be best to remember my manners first. I swallowed another spoonful of the soup and smiled at our hostess. "Thanks for the soup, Mrs. McDavitt. It's delicious."

"You're certainly welcome, Wil," she replied, returnin' my smile.

But Joseph's jab was still echoin' in my mind, and I couldn't just sit there and let him put all the blame for the war on the South. So I smiled at her again and spoke politely. "I was just about to remind Joseph here," I started, dippin' my spoon into the bowl for another bite, "that perhaps, if Mr. Lincoln hadn't tried to invade our homes and impose his will on us . . . " I glanced at Joseph, "perhaps, it may not've come to war at all."

"And who was it that fired on Fort Sumter, little brother?" Joseph shot back, raisin' his voice. "I s'pose now you're gonna try and blame Lincoln for that too?"

I could tell he was gettin' his dander up, but so was I.

"South Carolina has the right to take possession of any foreign military outpost on its own native soil," I protested. "If Lincoln hadn't forced us into it, we wouldn't be fightin' this war! And all for what? To free the darkies? Why can't they just let us be?"

That was all Joseph could take. He stood up and started shoutin' louder. "They ain't 'darkies', Wil. They're people! And no person oughta have the right to own another! You know that! Heck, you don't even believe in slavery yourself!"

His eyes flashed again in the direction of Mrs. McDavitt, and a blind man could've seen that she was mighty uncomfortable with the direction this whole argument was goin'.

But I was gettin' all riled up too, and I wasn't about to back down now. "That ain't why I'm fightin' this war!" I stood up and shouted back.

"Then why *are* you fightin' this war?!" he shouted, glarin' at me and pointin' his finger in my face. "And don't tell me it's just because Abe Lincoln invaded Virginia either, because now here you are in Maryland invadin' other people's homes!"

My mouth was waterin' from the smell of the soup, and I could still taste it in my mouth, but I couldn't make myself sit back down.

"To end the war!" I argued.

"It could've been ended long ago, Wil!" he shot back hotly. "All you had to do was lay down arms and go home!"

"That ain't how it works, Joseph, and you know it! If I lay down arms and go home now, I'll be branded as a deserter and a traitor—or worse yet, shot or hanged! A man needs his honor above all!"

"Well then I reckon you've made your choice, little brother," he said, leanin' in and lookin' me in the eye with a low ominous tone in his voice. "I hope you're willin' to die for your precious honor, 'cause it'd be a real shame if you were to widow that pretty little bride of yours already, what with her carryin' your unborn child and all."

How dare you bring Maribel and our child into this!?

My heart was poundin' so hard in my throat I could scarce say a word. I couldn't see my own face, but I knew it had to be red with rage. I couldn't do anything else, so I just stood there glarin' at him like a schoolboy who'd just been whooped by the schoolyard bully. But he stood his ground and stared back at me with his jaw set hard. I'd seen that look before, many times. It was the look he always got when he knew he was winnin' the argument. I recognized that miserable feelin' in my gut. It was like that awful moment in a battle—like at Kernstown—when you knew the line was breakin' and you were about to lose the fight, but there was nothin' you could do to stop it.

"Please sit down and eat, boys. Your soup will get cold," Mrs. McDavitt pleaded, tryin' her best to calm us both down.

I heard my breath escape in a big sigh and couldn't stop my eyes from lookin' down at the steamin' bowl of soup on the table, then back up at him. The smell of the soup and the hunger pain in my empty stomach was beginnin' to overrule my sense of honor.

What does it matter, Wil? He has his opinion and you have yours. Just apologize, and be done with it. Then you can eat!

But then before I could say a word, there was a loud thump down the hallway, like someone fallin' down. All three of us looked to see what it was, but there was no one there. Then I caught Joseph and Mrs. McDavitt exchangin' nervous glances again, and it suddenly occurred to me what was goin' on. In one brief moment, like an epiphany, it all made sense. I felt a flood of relief washin' over me, and my confidence came rushin' back. I finally had Joseph over a barrel, and I was holdin' the high ground for once. Now I just had to play my cards right.

I took a deep breath and let out a sigh of relief, then composed myself and pointed toward the noise down the hall. "I'm sorry. Is there someone else here? I don't mean to impose."

"No. No one else here," Mrs. McDavitt lied, but her eyes couldn't hide the truth. "Probably just my iron fell in the cabinet," she said.

But it was no iron. The look on Joseph's face told me that.

"Oh. Well, I reckon that makes sense." I did my best to reassure her with a smile, then sat down, picked up my spoon, and looked up at Joseph. "I heard tell of some folks who were tryin' to help a group of John Henrys not far from here," I lied, pausin' to take a sip of the soup. "I heard one of 'em up and robbed the good folks at knife point. Took all their money, they say, and their good silver too. I reckon it just goes to show you can never be too careful, even when you're tryin' to help someone."

Joseph sat down too, tryin' real hard to look like nothin' was wrong, but he couldn't disguise the look in his eyes. *He knows.*

"Is that so?" he asked, tryin' to sound incredulous.

"Yessirree." I took another sip of the soup and continued. "I'm s'posed to notify the Colonel if I find any runaways," I lied again. "You know, for the protection of the good citizens, of course. Some of 'em could be dangerous you know. Wouldn't want anyone to get hurt."

Now it was Joseph's turn to sigh, and the hard expression on his face melted away. He knew he was caught like a fox trapped in a hen house.

"What do you want, Wil?" he conceded, pickin' up his own spoon.

"I didn't come here to fight with you, Joseph. All I want is a little somethin' to eat, and maybe a bath. Whatever else happens in this house is none of my business. I was just hopin' we could be civil enough toward each other and maybe you could see your way clear to helpin' me out a little."

Then, for the first time since the war had started, I thought maybe I saw that look of brotherly love in his eyes like I always remembered seein'. He even smiled a little and said, "I reckon there's no harm in helpin' a man out when he's down."

Mrs. McDavitt still looked a mite confused, but Joseph gave her a reassurin' look. Her look turned to relief, and all was well again.

"Good. Finish your lunch and then we'll get you cleaned up," she brightened up. "Can you stay for dinner so I can wash your clothes? I'm sure Father McDavitt would like to meet you when he returns."

What a world of difference a hot bath and a couple of hot meals makes. We spoke no more about the war that night, or the so-called "underground railroad," but mostly talked about Joseph's studies. Father and Mrs. McDavitt were quite proud of him, and they were sure glad to have his help for the summer. He was just about to return to school for the next semester, but they'd already asked him if he'd consider comin' back again to intern again the next summer. They even encouraged him to attend the theological seminary there in Gettysburg after he graduated from the college. The subject of the new state came up briefly, but I mostly just held my tongue on account of not wantin' to start another argument.

Mrs. McDavitt washed my shirt and trousers and hung 'em out to dry. It was a hot and sunny afternoon so they didn't take long to dry. She even insisted on givin' me a clean pair of Father McDavitt's stockin's before she'd let me leave. The Good Lord knows I needed some.

It was gettin' late, and I didn't wanna be left behind, so I put my trousers and shirt back on and picked up my jacket, rifle, and packs, and made my courtesies to Father and Mrs. McDavitt. I shook Joseph's hand, then left to find the rest of the regiment. But as I walked, I could still hear Joseph's words echoin' through my mind.

'Why are *you fightin' this war?'*

Return to the Valley

We crossed over the Potomac and bivouacked on the Virginia side that night, not far from the site of that first battle at Falling Waters. Then we marched into the town of Martinsburg the next mornin'. By the time we arrived, the fed'ral garrison had already skedaddled, leavin' the town unguarded, and there was quite a welcome for the boys in gray that day.

We were delighted to get the news that the Innocent Second was to be detached from the brigade to remain there for provost guard duty and to keep watch on the river crossings. So we set up camp there on the outskirts of the town while the rest of the brigade marched on to Harpers Ferry with Ol' Jack.

Marchin' into Martinsburg was like a homecomin' for most of us, exceptin' those boys we'd added as new recruits earlier that year. Most of the Second Virginia were only a few hours ride from home there. But Capt'n Colston said there weren't enough of us left to authorize furloughs, so we were permitted to send for our loved ones to visit us as long as we stayed there in town and reported for duty on time.

Late in the mornin' on Sunday, September the fourteenth, a small group of wagons and carriages came into view on the road to Charles Town, and a good many of the boys gathered around to see who was comin'. My eyes caught sight of that familiar carriage, and I felt my heart poundin' in my chest like it might explode. I reckon there were several joyous reunions that mornin', but I didn't much notice. The only thing I could think of was the angelic form of my sweet Maribel as she stepped into view and was helped down out of the carriage. It was then I caught sight of the great rounded curve of her belly under the brown dress, and my heart leapt into my throat.

So captivated was I by the sight of my beautiful bride carryin' my unborn child that I barely even noticed that Tommy was there with her too! It was Arty's voice that finally caught my attention.

"Tommy?"

Before I even knew what happened, he'd already run past me to meet his brother who was hobblin' toward us with his crutch under one arm. Then the fog in my brain suddenly cleared and I realized that I'd been just standin' there like a dumb fool waitin' for her to come to me—and *she* was the one with child!

Finally my feet started runnin' like they had a mind of their own, straight toward Maribel. Her eyes lit up like the stars on a moonless mountain night and that beautiful smile spread across her face. I thought my heart would burst.

When I reached the place where she was standin', she threw her arms around my neck, pulled my face to hers, and kissed me long and sweet on the lips. Dear God in Heaven, how I'd missed the taste of her lips. Her kisses were sweeter than honey on a Sunday biscuit.

"I'm very glad to see you alive, Mr. Harleck, but you've been losing weight, I see," she said, tryin' to use her serious voice, but the sparkle in her eyes said otherwise. She was forever teasin' me, but it was one of the thousand little things that just made me love her more.

"Well aren't you a sight for sore eyes," I answered.

The mere sight of her was so intoxicatin' that I couldn't help but to just hold her hands and stare at her. I noted that the dress she was wearin' wasn't quite as fancy as the ones she usually wore, but I didn't much care. And the great bulge in her dress that reminded me she was carryin' my child, made me desire her all the more.

"But shouldn't you be home restin' in your condition?" I chastised, suddenly realizin' just how great with child she actually was. After all, a lady shouldn't oughta be strainin' herself like that.

"Oh, fiddlesticks!" she scolded back. "Why do men always think women are such frail and fragile creatures? I'm fine!" Then she smiled again, and I felt just a mite embarrassed.

It was then I finally realized that there was another person standin' there behind her. I looked up and saw a familiar face.

"Amos!"

"Hi, Wil!" the face said, smilin' with excitement at me.

My younger brother Amos was almost nineteen by then. He was as tall and slender and handsome a young man as ever there was, what with that headful of thick wavy blond hair and that boyish face, and a pair of bright green eyes that blazed out from under his thick brows. He had a charmin' smile too, with one crooked tooth in the top of his mouth that made him all the more lovable. He'd been chompin' at the bit to get into the war as soon as he was old enough, but Pa wouldn't have it. Until the draft, that is. Then Pa didn't have much choice in the matter.

I could feel the smile breakin' across my face. "How've you been, little brother?"

Amos always was a bit of a shy one, but his face beamed like the noonday sun on that day. I thought he was just about to burst with excitement.

"I'm enlistin' in the cavalry next month!" he blurted out, too excited to keep the news to himself any longer.

He was sure I'd be excited too, but it hit me right in the gut, and I felt the smile fadin' from my face. This war was gettin' more and more costly all the time, and the thought of my little brother fightin' in it made me feel more than a little uneasy. And then it hit me: I finally understood how Joseph must've felt about me.

"Well, isn't that just somethin'," I managed. I reached out and mussed up his thick hair with one hand, but I couldn't look him in the eye, or bring myself to say what I was really feelin'. That would've pretty much made me a hypocrite.

The look in his eyes told me that he was hopin' I'd be real excited. So I just hugged him tight to my chest so as he couldn't see the look on my face, on account of that was the best that I could do.

"It sure is good to see you, little brother."

"You too, Wil," he said, huggin' me back.

I thought maybe I'd somehow managed to avoid the subject, but then he stepped back and looked up at me again with that young innocent face and those bright eyes, and I knew it wasn't over yet.

"I knew you'd be real proud! That's why when I heard y'all were back here in the valley, I couldn't wait to come and tell you myself!"

I swallowed hard and looked for somethin' to say that wouldn't be a lie. "I *am* real proud of you . . . real proud of the man you've become."

His eyes beamed and he grinned wide, showin' off that silly crooked tooth like it was a shiner from a prize fight.

"And you're a real good horseman too," I went on. "The cavalry will be lucky to have you. You'll probably be ridin' with Gen'ral Stuart. He's the best God ever made."

Then I remembered that Maribel was still standin' there, so I turned and took her under one arm, then grabbed up Amos with the other arm so I could walk between 'em.

"Well let's not stand out here in the hot sun with a lady in your condition. Let's go find some shade and a place to sit."

"Wait!" Maribel's face lit up again. "I brought something for you."

We walked back to the carriage where she retrieved a basket full of goodies. Then we headed off to find a tall shade tree.

"How are Mama and Pa?" I asked Amos, so as to change the subject to somethin' else besides the army and the war.

"Mama wanted to come real bad, but Vanessa's sick so Ma stayed home to take care of her. Pa couldn't come on account of it bein' Sunday and all. Everyone sends their love."

Much as I hate to admit it, I wasn't as disappointed with the news as I should've been. Part of me was actually glad of it. I reckon if Mama'd seen me in my present thinner condition and with holes in my shoes, it would've only made her worry all the more.

We found a suitable tree, and I took the basket from Maribel's hand and helped her sit down in the green grass, then Amos and I sat down beside her. Maribel opened the basket and produced a fine picnic lunch with hard boiled eggs, carrots and radishes from her garden, and fresh cornbread with blueberry jam. I don't rightly recollect just how much time went by, but we sure did enjoy sittin' and eatin' and talkin' the afternoon away—until Maribel could sit no more that is.

Thing is, a woman who's in the family way can't go very long without visitin' the necessary. So I helped her to her feet and Amos and I walked her over to the johnny latrine, then stood guard so she could have privacy as a proper lady ought to.

Later, we strolled down the streets of the town passin' the windows of the stores and shops, but they were all closed, of course, seein' as how it was Sunday. In the window of one small shop, Maribel spied a beautiful ribbon bow which she fancied for the baby's hair, if it was a girl that is. So I made note of the place so I could return the next day and buy it for her. I thought perhaps I could mail it to her as a surprise for the baby. And if it turned out to be a boy, well then I reckoned Maribel could just wear it in her own hair. We spoke of names for the child as we walked.

"So, what will we name our child, Mr. Harleck?" she asked playfully.

"Hmmm," I thought aloud. "Let's see. What *shall* we name this child? How about Beauregard?" I teased.

"Oh, no. That'll never do!"

"You don't like Beauregard?" I asked with a chuckle.

"Oh, no! Beauregard is much too pretentious—and French!" she said, laughin'.

"Quite right, madam!" I said, laughin' myself as well and doin' my best to sound like a right proper aristocrat. "Very well, Beauregard it is not. How about—"

"Cornelius!" she blurted out.

"Good heavens no, woman! Do you want the boy to grow up at all?"

"That was my grandfather's name!" she said, smackin' me on the shoulder incredulously and laughin' again.

"I know! How about Chauncey?" I could scarce even get the name out without breakin' a smile.

"Oh, you horrible man, you!" she chided, smackin' me again in the shoulder, and we both laughed together.

"How about Andrew?" she countered, after the laughter subsided. "Andrew's a nice name, and Andrew was one of the Disciples,"

"Andrew, huh? Yeah. I like that. Andrew Robert Harleck. Now that's a fine name."

"Uh-huh," she smiled hopefully.

"And if it's a girl, we'll name it Maria Grace, after your grandmother and mother."

"Oh, that's beautiful!" Her face and eyes lit up, and she smiled even more brightly than before.

"Very well, done madam. Andrew Robert it is, or Maria Grace if it's a girl."

"Done, sir," she mocked in return.

"Aww. I was hopin' you'd name him after me!" Amos teased from just behind us.

"Sorry little brother!" I said, reachin' back to tossle his hair again. "Maybe next time."

The sun dropped low in the sky, and we knew it would soon be time for them to go, but none of us wanted the afternoon to end. It was the best day I'd had in . . . well, in eight months. We walked back to the carriages and wagons where most of the others were already waitin' to go. I hugged Amos once more and shared one last tender embrace with Maribel. She clung to me and laid her head on my shoulder, and I didn't wanna let her go.

"You be sure and come back to me, now Mr. Harleck. I have no desire to raise this child without you, you know."

I hesitated, not wantin' to promise somethin' I couldn't deliver, but I knew what she wanted to hear. "I promise, Mrs. Harleck," I said, half prayin'. Then I took her face in my hands and kissed her tenderly, wishin' that kiss would never end, and wonderin' when, if ever, I'd see her again.

Tommy and Amos helped her up into the carriage.

"Bye, Tommy," I said, wavin'. "Take good care of 'em, will ya?"

"Always do," he said smilin'. "Take care, Wil."

Then Amos took the reins and off they drove, back down the road toward Charles Town.

The next four days were filled with thoughts and memories of that visit from Maribel and Amos. I also did a lot of prayin' for Maribel and the child, and that the war would end soon. Maybe if ol' Granny Lee could whoop the Yankees in Maryland, we could finally march on Washington and force Lincoln to end the war . . . Maybe.

September the fifteenth brought the sound of artillery fire from somewhere off to the east. Then came the good news of the Yankee garrison's surrender at Harpers Ferry. But the news two days later was not as good. We heard the sound of distant cannon fire all day that day too, but it came from many miles away and bounced off the mountainsides, so there was no tellin' where the battle really was. The courier came that night with news of a terrible fight along the Antietam Creek near the town of Sharpsburg, not even a full day's march from where we were.

The courier told Capt'n Colston that Gen'ral Lee had held against strong Yankee attacks all day. Just when it looked like the Yankees were about to sweep our boys from the field, Gen'ral Hill's division arrived from Harpers Ferry just in time to push the Yankees back and save the day. But the cost had been great, and many a man and boy, both Johnny Reb and Billy Yank, lay on that field, never to see home again.

The next day brought another report, and Capt'n Colston gathered the regiment to break the news. "Looks like we're stayin' here for a few more days, boys. Gen'ral Lee's withdrawin' back into Virginia, and we're to hold the crossing here 'til all of our boys are safely back across the river."

My heart sank. Where was the final victory I'd been prayin' for? After all of the victories the Good Lord had given us, why hadn't He seen fit to finally let us win? Worse yet, it didn't look like the end of the war was comin' anytime soon either. Gen'ral Lee's withdrawal surely meant there was to be no marchin' on Washington this time.

"I have one more piece of bad news, gents." The Capt'n paused for a moment to make sure we were all lookin'. "We received a telegram this afternoon. Colonel Botts died yesterday."

I knew that his wound at Second Manassas was mortal, but I was still prayin' that somehow he might miraculously recover. Of all the colonels of the Second Virginia, he was the favorite of most of the men. Mine too.

We stayed there in Martinsburg for another week. Then we finally marched south toward Winchester to meet the rest of the brigade which was camped there. But our spirits were low on that march. Bad enough that we were marchin' away from the Yankees again, but then the weather turned gray and rainy to beat all, and sloggin' through the mud just made us even more miserable.

By the time we arrived, the telegraph wires were buzzin' hot with the news that Lincoln had issued a new proclamation. It said that all the slaves in any state found in rebellion to the United States on the first of January of the comin' year would be declared free. It sorta struck me as funny that ol' Lincoln was issuin' a proclamation for states where he didn't have any say in the matter, but I knew this was bound to stir up a new nest of hornets up north, and that sure as likely meant trouble for us. I didn't like the institution of slavery any more than the next fella, but it sure was becomin' a troublesome topic.

The plain truth was, the Confederacy was runnin' out of fightin' men. The Conscription Act told us that. It was also runnin' out of money. All we had to do was look at our feet to know that. Now it looked to be runnin' out of time too. With the Yankee Navy blockadin' most of our ports and this new proclamation stirrin' up a big fuss

A Frail Hope

October 1862

Following the humiliating defeat at Second Manassas in August, Lincoln relieves Pope of command and reluctantly restores George McClellan to overall command of the Union Army. In September, McClellan pursues Lee into Maryland, where his troops discover Lee's battle plan wrapped around three cigars and lying in a field. But although McClellan holds the key to Lee's undoing in his hand, still he is slow to act, allowing Lee precious time to reunite much of his scattered army near the small town of Sharpsburg, Maryland. It is here, on September 17, 1862, after slowly and meticulously maneuvering his army into position, that McClellan finally launches a series of savage and determined attacks across the Antietam Creek. In the heavy fighting on this single day, Lee's casualties include over 10,000 men killed, wounded, captured, or missing—more than one fourth of his forces engaged there. McClellan's losses number over 12,000. Their combined casualties on this one day outnumber all of the casualties from all previous American wars combined. It is the bloodiest single day in American history.

At the end of the day, the rebels still hold the field, but Lee is forced to withdraw his battered army across the Potomac and back into Virginia. McClellan's army is now twice the size of Lee's, but once again he does nothing, and Lee is allowed to escape. Two weeks later, Lincoln, exasperated at McClellan's refusal to pursue and destroy the depleted rebel army, visits his commander in camp. But McClellan still refuses to move, insisting that he must "rest and refit" the army.

The fall of 1862 provides a brief respite for Lee and the Army of Northern Virginia. While McClellan delays, Lee takes full advantage of his opponent's trepidatious nature to rest, replenish, and resupply his own army. By mid-October, the ranks of the army again begin to swell, owing largely to the return of many soldiers who were formerly wounded or missing, and an energetic recruiting effort. Although Lee's first invasion of the North has ended without success, the war is far from over.

Despite his general's refusal to move, Lincoln seizes the initiative. His Emancipation Proclamation is brilliant. In one stroke, he transforms the war. What before was largely viewed as a costly and bloody war to preserve the Union has now become a noble crusade to end slavery on the continent. At long last, the tide is beginning to turn, and the northern war machine is reenergized. But Lincoln, of all people, understands the fickle winds of political favor. He knows he cannot afford to squander his newfound momentum. Fed up with McClellan's insolence and lack of progress, Lincoln again relieves him of command—this time for good. In his place, Lincoln appoints General Ambrose Burnside to command of the army. Burnside is a modest but brave soldier who is perhaps best known for the distinctive configuration of thick whiskers on the sides of his face (hence the term, "side burns").

By November, Burnside is busily laying plans to win the war with a quick and decisive campaign. Using his vastly superior numbers, he hopes to deceive Lee into placing his defenses in the piedmont of central Virginia while he moves against Richmond via direct overland route. If successful, he plans to cross the Rappahannock River further east, near Fredericksburg, and march quickly south toward the Rebel capital before Lee can react. But the logistics of moving such a huge army prove to be considerably more daunting than expected, and Burnside is soon bogged down north of Fredericksburg, leaving Lee plenty of time to redeploy his own forces on the heights behind the town to block Burnside's path.

October 30, 1862

To: Private William Harleck
Second Virginia Infantry Regiment, First Brigade,
Second Corps, Army of Northern Virginia, C.S.A.

My Darling Wil,

I am writing this letter to inform you of the good news: You are a father, my love. Three days ago, on the twenty-seventh of October, our precious daughter was born. She has my hair, and bright blue eyes like her father, and we are both in good health. I think we should call her name Maria Grace, after my grandmother and mother, as you suggested.

Your mother knitted a beautiful new blanket for her with pink and yellow flowers on it, and I found some nice linen, which my father bought for us in Charles Town, with which to make the most adorable little dress and bonnet. I think it scandalous that the price of pins, needles, thread, and a yard of fabric for a dress has gone up nearly ten times over in only a single year. It is most disagreeable that our hard-earned profits should be gobbled up by taxation for the war, and the remainder paid in this pitiable Confederate paper money, while the Yankee greenbacks flow freely in the marketplace. It was most a humbling experience indeed to have the ladies from the church take up a collection to buy us a bassinette and some of the other things we needed, but these hard times shall not last forever.

It seems only last week that we picnicked under the tree in Martinsburg with Amos and strolled through the streets together, but oh, how I long for you to be home with us now. I do not mean to complain, my love. I know that you would be here if you could. Life here has been a great deal more difficult this year, thanks in no small part to frequent visits by the northern *soldiers, who made no apologies for simply taking whatever they needed. But we have been greatly relieved these past two months to have our own army so nearby to free us from the burden of constant occupation. We have been happy to share what little we have left with our brave soldiers, as they appear to be in such desperate need.*

Mr. Lincoln's audacious proclamation has certainly stirred things up here at home. Although Father is a fair and kind man, and never given to mistreating our negro slaves, one has only to glance in their direction to know that they must have had many discussions amongst themselves about the prospect of freedom. I don't know what we will do should many of them decide to flee across the border into Maryland. Without their help, Father could not possibly run the plantation alone, and I fear it would spell our certain ruin. I can only hope and pray that the Good Lord will bless us with victory and end this terrible war soon.

How greatly I desire to see you home and safe again, and to see your face when you first behold our precious angel with your own eyes for the first time. I continue to pray for your safety and that you may return to us quickly and all will be made right again.

Until then, my love, I remain,
Your devoted wife, Maribel

A Brief Respite

October of '62 was a good month for the Innocent Second, as months go in war time. After leavin' Martinsburg, we marched to Jefferson County and made our camp near the town of Rippon, just a few miles south of Charles Town on the road to Winchester. We called it Camp Allen in honor of our late Colonel. There were only thirty-six of us left in the whole regiment by then, but our spirits were lifted by bein' so close to home. We were permitted occasional visits home so long as we also took some time to persuade any able-bodied man or boy we should encounter to join up. But ever since the Conscription Act, most of the men of fightin' age had already either joined up or paid someone else to go fight for 'em. Things bein' as they were, I took notice that most of the new recruits were barely men at all, and gettin' younger by the day, it seemed. And I often thought about Amos and wondered how he was doin'.

At long last, the summer heat broke, and the days started growin' shorter. The weather turned moderate—even pleasant—for October in the Shenandoah, that is. The trees were all turnin' their beautiful fall colors, and the warm days and cool nights made life more tolerable all around.

Along about the middle of that month, we heard some distant musketry and cannonfire, but it was miles away, and we were never involved. We heard tell that Jeb Stuart's cavalry had skirmished with the Yankees when they tried crossin' the Potomac, then A.P. Hill's division attacked and drove the Yankees back across the river into Maryland. All of this, of course, was welcome news to us.

Throughout the month of October, the ranks of the regiment seemed to grow every day: men and boys who'd been gone for months straggled back into camp in a steady stream; others who'd been sick or wounded returned to duty; and every day brought new recruits, both young and old, from all around. I didn't see Amos among 'em, but I wondered if he'd made good on his promise and enlisted in the cavalry. If he had, he'd probably be with either Fitzhugh Lee's or Hampton's Cavalry Brigade. Both had seen action when the Yankees tried to cross the Potomac.

Life at Camp Allen reminded me of those early days at Harpers Ferry: all day long, drillin' and marchin', marchin' and drillin', trainin' all the "fresh fish" who were just musterin' in.

Capt'n Rowan came by one day early in October to make a special announcement. "Gather 'round, men," he said while the boys from Company A were preparin' to eat a bite of lunch.

"Private Willis, step forward," he ordered. Carlton looked suspicious of why the Capt'n was callin' him out, but he stepped forward anyway.

"Private Willis," the Capt'n continued, "I know you and I haven't always gotten along very well. Hell, I'll be honest, there were times I didn't like you much. But lately I'm beginning to think maybe I was wrong about you. I've watched you in battle, and you're a hell of a fightin' man, and a good leader . . . when you're not drunk, that is."

"Well, thank ya, Cap'n." Carlton said, lookin' a bit embarrassed.

"Now that Sergeant Robertson's been mustered out," the Capt'n went on, "and with all the new recruits comin' in every day, well, this company needs a proper sergeant to help keep good order and discipline. And seeing as how you're now the senior enlisted man in the Company, I'm hoping you'll take the job."

The Capt'n unfolded the cloth stripes, and held 'em out for Carlton.

Carlton was more than a mite shocked. He looked down at the stripes in the Capt'n's hand, then back up at the Capt'n. Now I can count on one hand the number of times I've seen Carlton Willis turn red with embarrassment, but none more than this.

"Of course," the Capt'n added, "this means you'll have to stay away from the booze now, if you think you can do the job, Sergeant."

Carlton hesitated for a moment, then answered. "I can do the job, sir," he said, takin' the stripes for his jacket.

"Hurrah!" Jim shouted.

"HURRAH!" the boys all hollered back. Then there was shoulder-pattin' and hand-shakin' all around.

"I hate to interrupt the celebration," the Capt'n hollered in the middle of all the congratulations, "but I've got one more announcement."

The fellas all got quiet again so the Capt'n could speak.

"Private Harleck, would you step forward, please?"

Me?

I was surprised to hear my name too, but I stepped forward.

"I should've given these to you long ago, son, when I asked you to serve as Lay Reader for the Company. You've been carryin' that extra responsibility for over a year now. I think it's high time you had the rank—and the pay—to go with it."

He held out his hand, and in it he held a new pair of Corporal stripes.

"Congratulations, Corporal Harleck."

I didn't know what to say, so I just said, "Thank you, sir!"

There was another round of hand-clappin' and then the Capt'n spoke up again.

"And now, Sergeant Willis, I believe it's time for you to form up the Company for afternoon rifle drills."

"Yes, sir," Carlton said, salutin' the Capt'n and holdin' his salute until the Capt'n returned it. Then he snapped his hand down and turned to the Company. "You heard the Cap'n. Form up for afternoon drill!"

Funny how a man with little use for authority can have a change of heart when he's given some authority of his own. Carlton's promotion made him nigh intolerable to the new recruits, but he had 'em whipped into shape in no time. He'd already all but given up the drinkin', but he could still be a blowhard when he wanted to be—a quality that made him just right for the job.

Still, he kept a special eye on Jim, Arty, and me, and took good care of us. Said he reckoned God was watchin' out for us, and he wanted to 'stay in good with the Man Upstairs.' He even took to callin' Jim "Uncle Jim," on account of him bein' the oldest man in the Company now. All the other fellas took right to it, and Jim didn't seem to mind at all.

By the thirty-first of October, the Innocent Second had grown from thirty-six men to 432—the largest since the Valley campaign. Company A alone grew from nine officers and men to fifty-four. There were sixty-seven new recruits, and quite a few fellas returned to duty after bein' sick or wounded. Turns out, there was also a good number of boys who'd gone to their farms on the "French leave" to feed their kinfolk for the summer, and now that the harvest was in, they were comin' back to do their duty again. Jim and I didn't feel too kindly about that, seein' as how Colonel Botts had threatened to have Jim shot if he tried the same. But I reckon the army had finally come to realize that havin' the men back was better than punishin' 'em for tryin' to feed their young-uns.

Our biggest problem that fall was not havin' a colonel for the regiment. It'd been more than two full months since Colonel Botts was shot, but the Innocent Second still didn't have a new colonel to replace him. L'tenant Colonel Nadenbousch was wounded, and Capt'n Rowan was lame from his wound at First Manassas and thought himself unfit for command. Capt'n Colston was the highest rankin' field officer left. He'd been doin' the job, but the new brigade commander, Gen'ral Paxton, still hadn't officially appointed him to command. So the Capt'n just did the best he could without the official title—or the pay. It was one thing for a capt'n to command fifty men, but leadin' 430 men was a horse of a different color.

The best day that fall was November the fourth. That's when I got the letter from my sweet Maribel informin' me of the birth of our daughter, Maria Grace Harleck. I had no earthly idea how to go about bein' the father of a newborn babe, but I sure was proud as a peacock to be one. Capt'n Rowan even said I could go home and visit my wife and daughter at the next opportune time. When that day finally came, I was so excited I could scarcely think straight.

"Easy there, Wil," Jim said, puttin' a hand on my shoulder. "You're more nervous than a fat chicken on a Saturday night!" he laughed with a big smile on his face. "You don't wanna drop that new baby of yours."

It was all I could do just to string words together and try to make some sense of 'em. "I don't know what I'm s'posed to do. I've never been a father before."

"You'll do fine. Just trust the good sense the Lord gave ya." Then he paused. "Besides, it's not so bad . . . " he added, but in his eyes I could see sadness, and I knew he must be thinkin' of his own little Dorothy.

I wanted to believe it was all gonna turn out alright, but I was still nervous and a little scared.

What will she be like? What if I'm not a good father? Or what if, God forbid, I should die and then she has no father at all? Or worst of all . . .

I remembered the look on Jim's face when Dorothy died. It was the worst pain I imagined a father could ever feel, and I knew I never wanted to drink from that cup. But then I looked up at Jim again, and he just leaned back with a grin on his face.

"It's gonna be just fine, Wil. Trust me. You'll see."

Capt'n Rowan even let me borrow his horse to ride into Charles Town, for which I was mighty grateful.

The very first time I ever laid eyes on Maria Grace, I could scarcely stand. It was a Sunday, but I was hopin' I might find both mother and child at home, what with the baby bein' so young and all. So I rode straight to the Nellis plantation.

Maribel met me with the child in her arms as I rode up to the house, but instead of runnin' up and throwin' her arms around my neck like before, she just stood quietly there on the porch holdin' the child. She was wearin' the same brown dress she'd worn at Martinsburg just a few weeks before, but it seemed more worn than I remembered, and it fit a tad more loosely. But then her smile caught my eye, and I saw her bright eyes gleamin' with joy like the mornin' sun, and I forgot all about the dress.

"Welcome home, Mr. Harleck," she said with joy in her voice. "Come and meet your daughter."

I don't much recollect gettin' down off the horse and walkin' up the steps to the house. All I remember is the sight of my very first child. Her tiny round face and bright blue eyes, the wisp of light brown hair that peeked out from under the soft blanket, the tiny hands with their tiny fingers so small and frail, and it all seemed like a miracle to me. I could scarcely take my eyes off of her.

"Would you like to hold her?"

I couldn't make myself say anything, so I just nodded, and my heart beat like a big drum when Maribel gently laid her in my arms and showed me how to cradle her softly. She made only one small sound when Maribel placed her in my arms, but then her bright eyes looked up at me, and we were both filled with wonder.

I don't rightly know how much time went by as we sat together on that porch and I held the tiny bundle in my arms. I only know I wished it would never end.

After a while, Maria Grace started fussin' and growin' restless, 'til finally Maribel said, "Well, I suppose I should feed her now and put her down for a nap."

Just about then it occurred to me that feedin' actually meant nursin'. I reckon my face must've turned red, seein' as how her whole face broke out in a big smile.

"Why, Wil Harleck, I do believe you're blushing," she said with delight in her voice.

I didn't rightly know what a man should do while his wife was nursin' a baby, but I should've known better than to ask a stupid question.

"What can I do?"

She took the child and stood up with a grin. "Thank you for your kind offer, sir," she mocked with a gleam in her eye, "but I don't believe your services will be required at this time. We ladies can handle this." Then she just smiled and went into the house.

When she finally returned, she sat down next to me.

"Did you hear the news about Amos?" Her voice was casual, so I knew it couldn't be bad news. I reckoned it had somethin' to do with his plans to join up.

"Not since Martinsburg in September. Did he enlist?"

"Yes, he did, and what a handsome young man he is in the gray uniform too."

I wanted to be proud of my little brother. We'd always been close, and I knew it was what he wanted most to do, but I couldn't shake the feeling that he was only doin' it to follow in my footsteps, and somethin' just didn't seem right. About four out of every five battles or skirmishes in the Charles Town area were fought by cavalry troopers, and the thought of Amos bein' one of 'em didn't make me feel any too good.

"Did he join the cavalry like he said he wanted to?"

"He sure did. Fifteenth Virginia Cavalry, General Lee's Brigade, I think he said. But I thought General Lee was in command of the whole army?"

"He is, darlin'. He means Gen'ral *Fitzhugh* Lee, Gen'ral Lee's nephew. He commands one of Gen'ral Stuart's cavalry brigades."

"I didn't know General Lee had a nephew who is also a general."

"Yep, and that's not all either. He's also got a son, *William Henry* Fitzhugh Lee, who's also a cavalry gen'ral! I heard he commands one of the regiments in his cousin 'Fitz's' brigade."

"My. I say, that is mighty confusing. How do you keep it all straight in your mind?"

"A man can learn a lot just sittin' around the bivouac fire at night and listenin' to the other fellas talk," I replied with a smile. "The *real* trick is sortin' out which is the truth, and which is just camp canard."

"Camp canard?" Her face looked puzzled, but I half thought she was just humorin' me by askin' questions she already knew the answer to, just to keep me talkin'.

"You know, camp stories—mostly balderdash, half-truths and made up rumors."

"Oh. Yes, I suppose that would be most difficult."

A little while later, William and Grace Nellis returned from church, whereupon Grace insisted that I stay for dinner. But dinner that day wasn't like the Sunday dinners I'd remembered from our childhood. We had enough to eat, to be sure, but it was somehow different. Instead of great piles of tender ham, fresh vegetables, hot rolls, and homemade pie, there was a small chicken, a small squash, and some cornbread.

"I'm sorry there isn't more, Wil," Grace said, tryin' her best to be dignified, but her voice gave away her embarrassment. "I'm afraid these hard times have left us with a little less these days."

"It's perfectly fine, ma'am. I'm just delighted not to be eatin' hard tack and salt horse—" The words came out almost without thinkin' about 'em, but one look at her face told me I should've thought more carefully. "It's not *really* horse," I tried to explain, hopin' to ease her mind. "That's just what we call the pork because it's so tough and salty you can't tell just exactly what kind of meat it really is."

"Oh, my," she managed, still a bit mortified.

Luckily, Maribel came to my rescue. "You know soldiers, Mama. They have such a colorful way of talking sometimes." Her smile somehow managed to put Grace at ease again.

"Well, we're just glad you could be home to visit with little Maria Grace," she said straightenin' her shoulders in that prim and proper way that gave away her family upbringin'.

We talked about all kinds of things during dinner, but mostly about the war, seein' as how it touched almost every part of our lives. But it wasn't until Grace brought up the Emancipation Proclamation while Samuel was still there in the room, that things started feelin' a mite awkward.

"Well, I just think it was hideously presumptive of Mr. Lincoln to say that all of our slaves are to be freed this January the first. I mean, who does he think he is, anyway?"

Then it was William Nellis' turn to speak up. "Well now, Grace, I suppose he thinks he can persuade more folks to support the war if he makes it a war to end slavery instead of just a war to put down a rebellion."

"Well, that may be so, but that doesn't give him the right to tell us what we can do and what we can't do. Besides, our slaves are well treated. We give them room and board, and treat them kindly. We don't whip or beat them . . . without good reason. What makes him think any of them would want to leave? Besides, what would they do anyway? Where would they go?"

"I'm sure—" he started, but it was no use. Grace was gettin' her dander up, and there was no stoppin' her once she got her dander up. Funny thing too: the more she got her dander up, the more her southern drawl came out.

"I mean, maybe there are some people who do mistreat their slaves, but that's a personal private matter, and not one that the gove'ment—least of all the fed'ral gove'ment of another country—should be stickin' its nose into!"

"Grace—"

"And now he's gone and planted this foolish notion of freedom into their heads, and what's to keep them from risin' up and killin' us in our sleep!?"

"GRACE!" He stood up to make his point, but she'd already said everything she wanted to say. He took a deep breath and let out a sigh. "No one's going to kill anyone in their sleep, isn't that right, Samuel?"

Samuel's eyes widened with surprise and he froze right where he stood for a spell. I reckon havin' Mr. Nellis suddenly draw him into the conversation was the last thing he was expectin'.

"N-n-no, suh! N-nobody gonna kill nobody!"

William Nellis heaved another sigh, like he was contemplatin' what he should say next. Then he continued, "Samuel, would you like to leave us?"

Samuel looked down at the floor and shifted quickly back and forth from one foot to the other. He tried to make himself look up, but couldn't. A blind mule could've seen he was nervous.

"No, suh, Mr. Nellis. We's happy here."

"There, you see? There's nothing to worry about," William said, sittin' back down at the table.

I was startin' to feel mighty uncomfortable with the whole conversation. The war had given me plenty of time to think on the matter of slavery, especially what with Joseph's newfound feelings on the matter and all, and I was already feelin' a mite convicted about the whole affair. Samuel was a kind and gentle man, and quiet too. I can't recollect ever hearin' him say more than three or four words strung together. He had dark eyes that were deep and thoughtful, and when he looked down I noticed the short black hair on his head was turnin' gray, which made his dark skin look even darker. But then I found myself feelin' ashamed for even noticin' his skin color after all the years I'd known him. He was almost like a member of the Nellis family to me, and he just had a way about him that made people wanna trust him. I found myself wonderin' what kind of man he might've been if he'd had the chance to go to school and live as a free man.

Grace didn't say anything else, but it was plain to see by the look on her face that the conversation was far from over. I could see Maribel was feelin' uncomfortable too, so I was mighty grateful when she tactfully changed the subject to the one thing she knew could get her mama off her political soap box.

"Mr. Cochrane at the tailor shop says he'll order some new fabric for baby clothes for me next week. Wouldn't little Maria Grace look just adorable in emerald green with lace?"

"Oh, she would be so beautiful!" Grace's face lit up. "And I'll make a new quilt for her for winter."

Easy as pie. I was so proud I wanted to chuckle out loud, but I didn't dare give it away, so I just smiled like a proud papa. I wasn't rightly sure even William and Grace could afford to buy that fancy fabric, but I reckon it didn't much matter, as long as Grace believed they could.

On the ride back to camp that afternoon, I marveled at what a wonderful wife the Good Lord had given me, and prayed that He'd keep her and our child safe and well.

A Sea of Blue

Not much happened for the next three weeks, but the days grew shorter and the nights grew colder, and there was no doubtin' that fall had settled into the Shenandoah. We were glad when the order finally came to march south up the valley early in the fourth week of November. The march was long and unpleasant, especially seein' as how it was the first forced march we'd done in at least two months, and our shoes were just about completely worn out. It was hardest on the new recruits though, on account of them havin' the most tender feet and not bein' accustomed to the long marches.

We marched up the west valley to New Market, then turned east through the Swift Run Gap to Orange Court House, and on to Spotsylvania. By the evenin' of November the twenty-ninth, we arrived at Guinea Station, just south of Fredericksburg. We'd marched an average of more than twenty miles each day, which had the effect of quickly sortin' out the bummers and no-accounts among us. I was surprised and a tad pleased to see that there weren't all that many.

The brigade bivouacked there at Guinea Station on the Richmond, Fredericksburg, and Potomac Railroad for about two weeks while we waited for the Yankees to make their next move. We didn't much care for sittin' around doin' nothin', but at least the weather was mild and altogether tolerable for December. Word around camp was that the whole Yankee army was comin' our way lookin' for a place to cross over the Rappahannock. But the river was mostly too high to ford, all the bridges near the town had been destroyed, and we were placed just right to keep 'em from slippin' around our flank. Nosirree, if those Yankees wanted to get to Richmond, they'd have to get through us first.

I was on sentry duty on the mornin' of December the twelfth when I saw a courier ride into camp in a big hurry. It wasn't long before Capt'n Rowan sent out word to the company to strike the tents and prepare to march. The worst thing about bein' on sentry duty when the marchin' orders came was not havin' time to get anything to eat before the march.

We formed up the regiment, and Capt'n Colston and a few of the officers stepped forward. "We're movin' out, men," he started in a loud crisp voice. "The Yankees are buildin' pontoon bridges across the river just up a little ways from here, and we're goin' to make 'em regret that idea."

I'd never even heard of a pontoon bridge before, and I had no earthly idea what a pontoon was, but I reckoned any bridge was still a bridge, so whatever it was, it meant the Yankees were up to no good. No matter anyway. We aimed to stop 'em no matter what kind of bridge it was.

The Second formed up with the rest of the brigade and marched north along the railroad to a place they called Hamilton's Crossing. But long before we got there we could hear the Union guns—a whole mess of 'em, from the sound of it—firin' on Fredericksburg town. And lots of musket fire too.

Some of Gen'ral Stuart's cavalry was guardin' the railroad crossing when we arrived there, and I looked for Amos but didn't see him. There could be no doubt that we were gatherin' the army for a battle, and I knew he'd be somewhere nearby. In my mind, I could see him there, sittin' up high in the saddle and wavin' his hat wildly in the air. It struck me what a winsome devil he must be in the gray uniform, his blond hair flyin' and green eyes blazin', and that smile wide enough that you could see every white tooth in his mouth—even the crooked one. That was my little brother, alright. The image was so real it was like he was right there in front of me. I tried to content myself with knowin' that at least there was less danger of him bein' killed or wounded in the cavalry than in the infantry, but that image in my mind still haunted me, and I knew I wouldn't sleep well until I knew that he was safe.

We turned and headed west up a road that ran along the back side of a big wooded hill. Then, after awhile, we turned onto a smaller dirt road that ran up the ridge to the right, then just ended in the middle of the woods. The brigade was posted there in a line that ran into the woods along the crest of the ridge, with the Twenty-seventh Virginia on the left, then the Thirty-third, Fifth, and Fourth. The Second was placed on the right of the brigade across the small road, and there we stayed for the night. About 400 yards in front of us, on the other side of the ridge, was A.P. Hill's division, so we knew that we were bein' held in reserve.

The night was cold and damp and generally miserable, and sometime before dawn the next mornin' a thick blanket of fog settled in so that each man could scarcely see the man next to him. There was to be no buildin' fires for cookin' either, so it was cold hard tack for breakfast and nothin' else. Hard to fight on an empty stomach, but fightin' on a full one was worse. Besides, what choice did we have?

But worse than havin' no food was havin' no shoes, or in my case, shoes that were fallin' apart and would scarce stay on my feet. Some of the boys had nothin' but strips of cloth wrapped around their feet to protect 'em while they marched and keep 'em warm at night. At least I still had my new stockin's, but even they were beginnin' to come apart. So the cold nights were especially hard on our feet, and I wondered how many good boys would have to fight the battle tomorrow with nothin' on their feet at all.

The fightin' started around ten o'clock the next mornin', after the fog started liftin'. Most of it seemed afar off, so we didn't concern ourselves much. But by around noontime, the fightin' was gettin' hot and heavy. We heard our own guns open fire just up the ridge a ways, and it wasn't long before the Yankee gunners started shootin' back. Along about one o'clock in the afternoon, the Yankee artillery went silent, and we heard the familiar sound of hundreds of muskets that could only mean they were a-comin' up the hill toward Hill's boys just below us. Walker's Brigade was placed somewhere off to our right, but there was a gap in the line between us and Walker's boys. Capt'n Nadenbousch was the first to notice the problem, but since we were in reserve behind Hill's boys, I reckon no one thought it was important enough to make a fuss about. But when the Yankees broke through Hill's lines, we were ordered to advance down the hill, and danged if those Yankees didn't drive right up into that gap!

It was a confused affair, to be sure, but we all lined up as best we could in the trees and somehow managed to advance down the hill and wheel to the right. This had the effect of turnin' the whole front of the brigade toward the oncomin' Yankees. Don't you know they were mighty surprised when they came up close, thinkin' they'd flanked us, and we fired full in their faces. Then a fierce fight broke out, but it wasn't long before the Blue-bellies started fallin' back, so we pushed forward and drove 'em right down off that hill. We stopped when we got to the road where Hill's boys had been dug in earlier, and we stayed there 'til the battle was over. But the boys from Walker's Brigade, they just kept right on pushin' forward 'til they drove the Yankees back to the railroad. Then another brigade pushed 'em back across the big field and nearly back to the river before they finally ran into Fed'ral reinforcements and had to fall back to reform in the safety of the trees.

The clouds finally cleared out, and the night was as clear and cold as any I can recollect—and deathly quiet too, exceptin' every now and then some poor fool picket would fire off his musket somewhere in the distance. The cold nights were becomin' especially hard on us, since mostly all we had to keep warm was our worn out jackets and oil cloths, most of which had holes in 'em. If a man was lucky, some loved one from home may've sent him a blanket and a pair of warm stockin's. The blanket my Mama had sent me in January had served me well, but it was long since worn out from the harsh uses of army life. So, for the most part, we just lay awake shiverin' in the shallow trenches Hill's men had dug the night before, and we hardly slept a wink. I never did like sleepin' in a trench. Too much like a shallow grave, and I'd seen a few too many of those.

By mornin' on the fourteenth, everything we owned was covered in frost, and we were glad to see the sun for the first time in days. Not much happened that whole day. I reckoned the Yankees must've been as tired and cold as we were. We could still hear musket fire off in the general direction of the town, but not like before. It was more like small handfuls of skirmishers firin' here and there, instead of whole regiments firin' in volley.

It wasn't 'til later that day that we really learned what a great victory we'd won. Stories spread like wildfire through the ranks of the battle at the "Slaughter Pen" and the wave upon wave of blue troops who'd tried gallantly to push Longstreet's boys off of Marye's Heights, like an angry sea against the immovable rocks of the shore. One thing was sure though: after that day, not a man among us doubted the courage of our foes.

Later that afternoon, the sun finally began to warm things up, and we saw signs that the Yankees were preparin' to withdraw back across the river, for which I was mighty grateful. As evenin' fell, the sky began to fill with strange and ghostly lights of brilliant colors the likes of which none of us had ever seen before, nor since either. It was a little like watchin' a lightnin' storm through a stained glass window, but there was no thunder—no sound at all. It was the darnedest thing we ever saw, like fireworks goin' off afar away in the heavens, and we took it as a good sign.

Good News and Bad

December the fifteenth was a Monday, and it was cold, gray, and wet again. But our spirits were lifted at the sight of the fed'ral army withdrawin' back across the pontoon bridges. A good many cheers went up from our lines, to be sure. We'd whooped the Yankees but good this time, and we wanted 'em to be good and sure to remember it.

It was almost enough to make a fella wonder if maybe, just maybe, they'd go back to Washington and stop all this fightin' and just let us be. But we'd whooped the Yankees plenty of times before, and still they just kept comin' back for more, so there was no reason to believe they'd change their minds this time either. Well, a fella can always hope.

"Do you s'pose the Yanks'll go back home now, so we can get some furlough to be with our kin for Christmas?" I asked Arty.

"Ha!" Carlton scoffed before Arty could answer. "Did you get knocked senseless or somethin'?" he grinned.

I knew Carlton was right, but it wasn't the answer I wanted to hear. I looked at Arty, hopin' to get a different opinion, but it was no use.

"'Fraid Carlton's right, Wil," he said. "Them Yankees aren't goin' anywhere, and neither are we, I reckon."

But oh how I longed to see my sweet Maribel and hold my precious child again.

So I resolved to have a good day anyway. We even built a fire so we could cook some sloosh for dinner. It wasn't much, really, but just about anything'll do on an empty stomach, and it was the first "hot meal" we'd had in three days.

It wasn't 'til after dinner, while I was sittin' on a log tryin' to write to Maribel by the firelight that Capt'n Rowan came by lookin' for me.

"Corporal Harleck . . . " he started.

"Yessir?" I said, standin' up and salutin'.

He returned my salute, but he had a grave look about him that was like a father who was about to give his child the switch, even though he didn't want to.

"You'd better come with me, son."

I felt my heart skip a beat, and my mind started racin' to think of what could be wrong. Whenever the Capt'n said somethin' like, "You'd better come with me, son," you can be sure that whatever's comin' next isn't good. But I stood up anyway, stowed my papers, and followed him to where he was camped just twenty yards or so into the woods. As we got closer, I could see another soldier there, standin' partly in the shadows near the Capt'n's tent. I reckoned he was likely cavalry, by the looks of the wide-brimmed hat with the big feather plume.

What would a cavalry—Amos!?

But as we got closer, I could see he didn't look like Amos. He was an older man with dark hair and a mustache and beard. He wore tall boots nearly up to his knees and a gold sash around his waist, and I could see a sword hangin' there just under the great gray capote which was left unbuttoned in front.

Officer?

My mind raced to find a reason why a cavalry officer would wanna talk to me.

"Corporal Harleck, this is Colonel William Ball, Fifteenth Virginia Cavalry," the Capt'n said, gesturin' toward the man.

Fifteenth Virginia—that's Amos' regiment! But why . . . ?

I saluted the Colonel, and he returned my salute with the ridin' crop he was carryin'.

"Pleased to meet you, sir," I said, tryin' hard not to sound too nervous.

"The pleasure is mine, Corporal," the Colonel replied politely, shiftin' the ridin' crop to his left hand and shakin' my hand with his right. "Captain Rowan here speaks highly of you."

Seems friendly enough. Maybe it's not bad news. Maybe he wants me to join the cavalry and serve in the same regiment with my brother!

But then the Capt'n pointed to a small stool.

"You'd better have a seat, son," he said flatly.

It seemed mighty strange that he'd want an enlisted man to sit while the officers stood, but I saw the look on his face was serious, so I took off my hat and sat down.

"I'm afraid I have some bad news for you," the Colonel said gently.

Dear God, not Amos!

I tried to swallow, but my mouth was too dry, and my heart was already up in the back of my throat, so all I could do was sit there like an idiot schoolboy and wait for him to go on.

"It's about your brother, Amos," he went on.

No!

I couldn't breathe. It was like bein' kicked in the gut by an angry mule.

"I'm real sorry . . . " He paused for a minute, like he was searchin' for somethin' else to say. I don't rightly know how long it was, but it seemed like forever. Then he finally spoke again. "He was wounded in battle while guarding the river crossing near Falmouth on the seventeenth of November. We didn't think his wound mortal, but he died this Tuesday last."

No! It can't be possible! There must be a mistake. He only just enlisted three months ago, and he was so young. It should've been me, not him.

I just sat there, stunned, and couldn't speak a word. My eyes welled up full of tears until I could scarcely see, and my throat choked up until I could scarcely breathe.

What're you doin', Wil, you darned fool?! Don't go gettin' all soft and sentimental in front of them. You're a soldier, not a child. Act like a man.

But this was my kid brother Amos, and no matter how much I tried to look like I was in control, I felt my body betrayin' me. It was like a battle ragin' inside my head and my lines were beginnin' to break. I felt a tear run down my cheek. I took a deep breath and sat up as straight as I could, tryin' my best to rally and reform my lines by bitin' down on my tongue.

"I was with him in the hospital when he died," the Colonel went on. "He asked me to give you this." He reached into his jacket and pulled out a letter which he handed to me. "He wrote it a few weeks ago, on the day he was wounded, but never sent it. I don't know why."

I don't remember takin' the letter from his hand. My whole body and mind were numb as I read it.

November 17, 1862
Falmouth, Virginia

To Private William Harleck
Co. A., 2nd Va. Inf. Regt., 1st Va. Inf. Bgde., 2nd Corps, A.N.V.

Dearest brother, Wil,

I am writing to you today to inform you that I have enlisted in the 15th Virginia Cavalry Regt, Col. W. B. Ball, commanding. It is a fine regiment, and I am proud to be serving my country as you are. I know you would be proud as well.

I am sorry that I have not written to you sooner. I have been quite busy these last few weeks learning the fine skills of cavalry soldiering. It is difficult, but I am learning quickly from some of the finest cavalry officers in all the South. Col. Ball is a most excellent horseman and a fine officer.

I m told we may be riding near the enemy today, so I must go now. I am only a little nervous about fighting in my first battle, but I am confident that I have learned much, and we are ready to show the Yankees how Virginia cavalrymen fight. I will write you again upon our return, and tell you of our glorious victory.

Until then, may the Lord keep us, and bless our cause.

Your brother,
Amos

"I'm real sorry, son," the Colonel's words were like echoes—almost like he was far away or somethin'. The only thing I could hear were Amos' words ringin' again and again in my mind, almost like I could hear him sayin' the very words he wrote.

"I will write you again upon our return, and tell you of our glorious victory."

Amos . . . So young and innocent . . . Why? Why didn't you tell him, Wil? You should've told him there's no such thing as a glorious victory. Only horror and blood and pain and death. And now it's too late.

I still can't rightly put into words my feelings of utter despair on that day. I can assure you that I'd rather have spent an eternity in Hell than to get the news that my little brother was never goin' home again, and I began to wonder how Mama was takin' the news. I knew it would be especially hard on her.

Does she even know? Has anyone told them yet?

I looked up at the Colonel, but my voice was weak and shaky, and I could only get out two words: "Our folks . . . ?"

I reckon he saw all the questions in my eyes. "We buried him Thursday by the old Salem Church, just west of here. I sent your daddy a letter," he said kindly. "I would've come to find you sooner, but the Yankees've been keepin' us pretty busy these last few days."

God . . . I don't understand . . . Why Amos and not me?

I felt hollow inside as I walked back to where the rest of the company was bivouacked that night. Jim and Arty and Carlton must've seen the look on my face and knew somethin' wasn't right.

"What's wrong, Wil?" Arty asked.

But I was in no mood for talkin'. I handed him the letter and walked off into the woods to find a place where I could be alone. It was hard findin' a solitary place. The roads were jammed with horses and wagons and people comin' and goin' everywhere, and even the woods seemed to be alive with soldiers. But eventually, I found a fallen tree out in the woods where I could just sit and think.

After a little while, they came lookin' for me. But I was surprised when Jim and Arty just stood nearby and didn't say a word. Instead, it was Carlton that did the talkin' first.

"Arty showed me the letter. Did somethin' happen to yer brother, kid?" he asked straight out. But his voice wasn't like it usually sounded. There was kindness there.

I couldn't make myself talk about it, so I just nodded, lookin' down at the ground.

"Killed?" he asked, sittin' down beside me on the tree.

I nodded again.

"Were you close, you and him?"

I still didn't wanna talk, but I knew Carlton wasn't goin' away until I did.

"Yeah . . . " I nodded, swallowin' hard. "Real close."

I'd hoped he might see that talkin' about it was upsettin' me, but he didn't seem to notice, or else he just didn't much care if he was upsettin' me anyways.

"You were lucky, ya know," he said, "ta have a brother that close."

He took a deep breath and let out a sigh, lookin' up at the bare trees all around. I thought it was ironic that they looked as dead as I was feelin' inside.

"My brother and me, we ain't that close," he went on finally. "If'n I was to be killed today, he wouldn't shed a single tear."

Maybe he was right about me and Amos, but it was still too painful to talk about. So we just sat there in silence for a while.

"Well, anyway," he said finally, "you know where to find us." Then he stood up and patted me on the back.

Then Arty stepped up and put a hand on my shoulder. "Real sorry about Amos, Wil . . . " He looked like he wanted to say more, but I reckon he saw the look on my face and decided better of it, so he just said, "Real sorry," and let it go at that.

"We're here if ya need us, Wil," Jim said quietly. And the three of them walked back toward where the regiment was camped.

Me, I just sat there in the woods on that fallen tree 'til I got so cold I was shiverin', then I finally went back to camp to get warm by the fire before turnin' in for the night.

For the whole next week I prayed that I'd be able to go home. What with it bein' nearly Christmas and all, and with Amos' death, I wanted to be with my folks and see my wife and daughter in the worst way. But the blasted Yankees weren't leavin'. They'd crossed back over to the other side of the Rappahannock, sure enough, but then they just stopped. And since it looked like they weren't plannin' on goin' anywhere, we were stuck there too. Turns out all that prayin' was for nothin'. So I just stopped prayin'.

Christmas day came and Gen'ral Jackson made arrangements for special Christmas mornin' services. There was a Catholic mass early in the mornin'. Then Arty and I attended the Protestant service with Jim, Carlton, and a good many of the other fellas. The services were a mite bigger than usual, but I didn't take the Eucharist. I still felt dead inside, and I hadn't prayed for over a week, seein' as how I was still a might angry with the Almighty, on account of Amos' death and all.

I'd had just about a bellyful of this war, and I wanted to go home worse than ever. I even thought about desertin' just for Christmas like some of the other boys had done, but then I thought of what would happen if I was caught. Bad enough Mama had already lost one son. I couldn't bear the thought of her losin' another one too. And even if by some miracle I managed not to get myself shot tryin' to desert, how could I dishonor Maribel and Maria Grace by turnin' yellow like that?

Christmas in camp sure was a far cry from Christmas back home. The commissary had managed to round up some extra livestock and potatoes so we could cook meat and potatoes for Christmas dinner. But it was nothin' like Mama made back home. I missed her tender ham roast with string beans and sweet potato pie. There was music and singin' and laughter all around the camp that night in spite of the bitter cold. The bivouac fires were stoked up high, and the boys all sat around close to the fires, each one doin' whatever he could to make the best of it. Capt'n Rowan even bought a bottle of cheer and shared a toast to Gen'ral Lee, which the boys were only too happy to oblige. But I didn't feel much like celebratin', so I just turned in early.

Another week went by and still the Yankees showed no signs of movin', so the arrival of the New Year was celebrated in much the same way. Gen'ral Lee gave strict orders that there was to be no firin' of the rifles into the air on account of the Yankees bein' so near. I reckon that was wise, seein' as how half the army was 'celebratin'' by drinkin' John Barleycorn or Oh Be Joyful or whatever kind of libations they could otherwise find or make.

It snowed that night. It was a warm, wet, heavy kind of snow, and I woke early the mornin' of January first to find everything covered with a blanket of white two inches thick. It was 1863 now, and accordin' to Mr. Lincoln, all the slaves in the Confederacy were officially free. I knew I should've been worried about the Nellises: wonderin' if they'd suddenly find themselves without many of their slaves, but I couldn't get past my own grief and misery. So I just sat there shiverin' and cursin' the weather and wishin' I was back home.

The snow turned into a cold rain, which turned everything I owned wet and muddy. By the end of the first week of January, things were fast goin' from bad to worse. For me and a good many other fellas, our old brogans had more holes than a woodpecker's favorite tree. Some of the boys had no shoes at all, and no way of keepin' our feet warm and dry in the harsh winter weather. But Richmond had no new shoes to send. And shoes weren't the only things we needed that Richmond didn't have. Gen'ral Lee had to have the commissary gen'ral round up coats and blankets and food from the farms and villages for miles around to keep the army warm and fed—all 65,000 of us. He promised to pay the good citizens for their generosity, but Confederate money was fast becomin' less and less valuable on account of the danged Yankee blockade.

Then, if that didn't beat all, we got word that Gen'ral Bragg's Army of Tennessee had been defeated somewhere out west at a place called Nashville, on the eve of the New Year. I didn't know much about Tennessee, but I reckoned the news meant that most of it was now in Union hands. One thing sure seemed clear: if we didn't win this God-forsaken war soon, the Yankees would have no need to defeat us in battle. All they'd have to do is wait 'til we starved or froze to death.

A Bitter Pill

May 1863

After his epic failure at Fredericksburg, Burnside makes one more attempt to outmaneuver and defeat Lee, but he is thwarted by bad weather, and his engineers are once again unable to deliver the badly needed pontoons for crossing the rising Rappahannock River on time. To make matters worse, his subordinates have lost confidence in their commanding general. Some have even gone directly to Lincoln with their concerns.

Reluctantly, Lincoln relieves Burnside and places General Joseph Hooker at the head of the Army of the Potomac. Hooker is a hard-fighting West Pointer with a reputation for gambling, hard drinking, and fast women. To Lincoln's great displeasure, Hooker is also known for his insubordination, remarking that "nothing would go right until we had a dictator, and the sooner the better." Nevertheless, Lincoln, banking on Hooker's reputation as "Fighting Joe," appoints him anyway, saying, "Only those generals who gain success can set up dictators. What I ask of you now is military success, and I will risk the dictatorship."

In late April, Hooker leaves nearly 40,000 men to threaten Fredericksburg from the east and moves west with 75,000 more. His goal is to cross the Rappahannock and Rapidan Rivers further upstream, where there are shallow fords for crossing. Then he plans to approach Lee from the rear, surprising him and trapping him between the two halves of his huge army. But when Lee learns that his flank is turned, he defies all convention and divides his force in the face of a superior enemy. Leaving only 11,000 men to hold the heights behind Fredericksburg against nearly four times as many Federals, Lee and Jackson race west on the Orange Plank Road with 50,000 men to meet the oncoming threat.

In the three days that follow, Lee and Jackson will once again astound and bewilder a superior foe, dividing their smaller force yet a second time and, with a rapid flanking movement, striking the unprepared Federals from behind. The battle at Chancellorsville will become Lee's greatest triumph, but the cost of victory will prove to be catastrophic. In an ironic twist of fate, Jackson is mistakenly shot by his own men while returning to his lines after a night reconnaissance. Although the wounds themselves are not mortal, his left arm must be amputated, and he will succumb to pneumonia. Within a week, the famous "Stonewall" is forever lost to the South.

March 27, 1863

To: Corporal William Harleck,
Second Virginia Infantry Regiment, First Brigade, Second Corps, Army of Northern Virginia, C.S.A., near Fredericksburg

My Darling Wil,

It has been many days since I received your last letter, and I desire that I might hear from you again soon. I pray that you are well and that the Lord may keep you in good health and spirits.

Please pray for our darling Maria Grace, as she has taken ill two days ago with a dreadful fever and has become nearly inconsolable. I pray it is not serious, but she is so small and delicate, and I fear the worst for her. Evelyn Harkesson's baby died of fever last week, and I read in the papers that there is an outbreak of Typhoid in the valley.

The winter here has been long and harsh, and the presence of northern soldiers in the valley has made life difficult to bear. The Yankees have made it their business to go about enforcing that detestable proclamation wherever they go, and many of the Negroes have taken flight, leaving the hard work to be done mostly by the women and children and older men. Only Samuel and his wife Hannah remain here with us now, as they are advancing in age and have no desire to begin a new life somewhere else. Father is concerned that without all of our Negro help in the field we will not be able to plant the spring crop in time.

We remain hopeful that the Northerners' taste for war shall continue to wane, and this war may soon come to an end. Dare we hold out hope that France or England, in their insatiable lust for cotton and tobacco, may soon apply pressure on Mr.

Lincoln to end his reprehensible blockade? Yes, that would be most agreeable indeed. But I fear they will not, or that they will wait until the war is already won before declaring an alliance with the Confederacy.

Joseph returned home for a visit again last week, and it did your mother good to see him. She took Amos' death very hard indeed, and although it has been three months now, she still has not returned to her former cheerful self. In my last letter I wrote that your father had slipped on the ice and hurt his back. I am pleased to tell you that he is recovering well, and is able to walk again, though more slowly than before. You would be quite proud of Vanessa, my love. She has become a strong and responsible young woman and a great help to your mother and father during these difficult times.

I am sending you a new pair of stockings which I knitted for you from what little yarn could be found. I dearly wanted to send some of your favorite macaroons, but the Yankee blockade has made it impossible for us to buy coconut and many other things which are badly needed. We are even lacking even such common necessities as flour for bread and meat for our table,

Pray for us often and write when you are able. I greatly long to see you again soon and pray that it may be under more agreeable circumstances. Take care, my darling, and come home to us soon.

Until then, I remain,
Your Loving Wife, Maribel

Lee and Hooker at Fredericksburg and Chancellorsville—May 1863

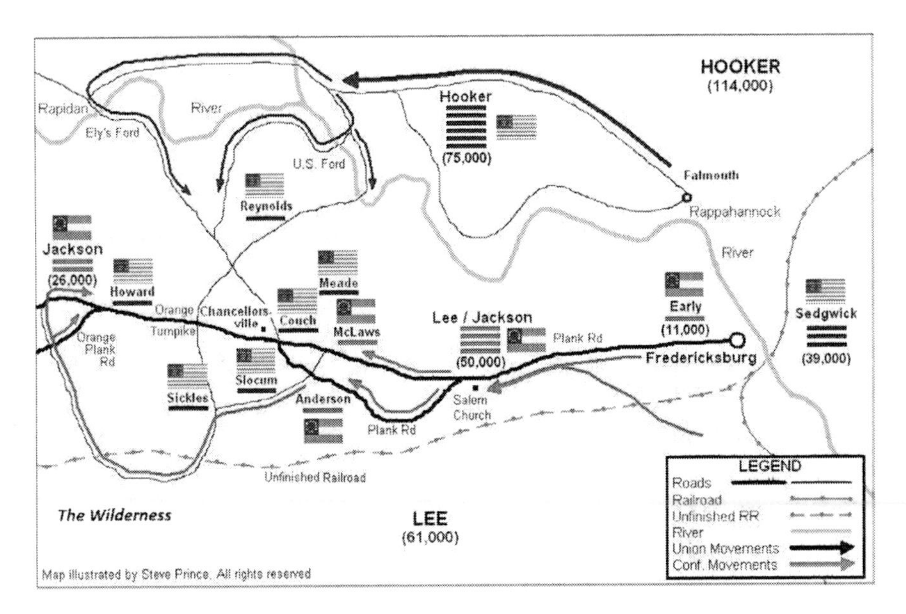

The Mud March

Winter of '63 found the Stonewall Brigade camped just to the southeast of Fredericksburg near a little place called Corbin's Neck, though some folks called it Moss Neck. The winter weather arrived in early January, and we were well motivated to build some sort of decent shelter against the disagreeable weather. A fella might've even called it severe if it hadn't been so irregular: one day it was cold and bright and clear with bitter wind; the next it was damp and gray; and the next it was all snow and ice. And all the time the ground stayed just warm enough so that all the rain and snow and ice just turned into mud. And the mud was everywhere.

We built some good log huts there, and they were a far sight better than sleepin' on the ground, with or without tents. Gen'ral Paxton called the place Camp Winder, after our departed Gen'ral, God rest his soul. Most of the boys didn't take too kindly to the name, seein' as how Gen'ral Winder hadn't particularly been the most popular gen'ral we ever had. But I thought it was a fitting name, seein' as how it wasn't exactly the best camp we ever had either. Besides, it really didn't matter much what they called it, as long as it kept us warm and dry. Funny thing though: some of the old-timers took to callin' it "Camp Whiner," on account of all the bellyachin', complainin', and carryin'-on by some of the draftees who'd never been in a winter camp before.

Word came that the Yankees were on the move again, and we wondered if we might have to abandon our new camp after we'd just completed it. But no order came to march. Likely the Yankees were just as much stuck in the mud as we were. Maybe more, seein' as how the plank roads on our side of the Rappahannock were a far sight better than most of the roads on the Yankee side. Accordin' to our cavalry scouts, the whole Yank army was bogged down in the mud near Falmouth, just across the river north of Fredericksburg town. After a while, I reckoned they finally just gave up tryin' and settled in to camp for the winter.

We read in the paper that Lincoln had gone and relieved another gen'ral, seein' as how he couldn't lick the Reb army. I couldn't even recollect how many gen'rals there'd been. Heck, I could barely recollect the name of the last one. Anyway, the paper said the new gen'ral's name was Hooker, and he was makin' some mighty big changes: better food, better hospitals, and more furlough for the soldiers. They already had better shoes, better uniforms, better equipment, and better guns too, for the most part. It was almost enough to make a man jealous. But then I started thinkin': the Billy Yanks had always had it better than us, but it hadn't helped 'em so far, leastwise when it came to whoopin' us anyway. Maybe we were just tougher in battle on account of havin' it tougher all around.

By the time March arrived, we'd gotten pretty well accustomed to not havin' a colonel for the Innocent Second. So when the news came that L'tenant Colonel Nadenbousch was recovered well enough from his wounds so as to be promoted to colonel of the regiment, and Capt'n Colston was promoted to l'tenant colonel, well, nary a man even shrugged. Except for Capt'n Rowan, that is. He was none too happy at bein' passed over, but it was hardly a surprise. After all, he'd already turned down the chance to command twice on account of his bad foot. I liked Capt'n Rowan. He was a good officer and a good man, but a fella could hardly complain about not gettin' promoted after that.

It'd been four months since Amos' death, but I was still findin' it hard to be happy about anything. I hadn't seen my wife and child in five months, the weather was miserable, and the news from home wasn't much help for cheerin' a fella up. Mama wrote me a letter in March sayin' that my Pa had hurt his back and couldn't get around much. Then she said that the Yankees were back in the lower valley causin' all kinds of trouble for the folks back home.

In early April I got a package and a letter from Maribel. It said that our little Maria Grace was ill with fever. Few things can unsettle a man more than hearin' that his child is ailin'. The letter also said the Yankees had freed most of Mr. Nellis' slaves, leavin' him without enough help to run the plantation. The package contained a new pair of thick stockin's to help keep my feet warm and dry in the confounded winter mud, for which my feet were grateful, but which did little to ease my troubled mind.

Jim came over and sat down on a log by the fire next to me to get warm. He didn't look at me; just stared at the fire for a while, then finally he piped up.

"What's on your mind, Wil?" he asked. "You haven't been yerself lately."

I reckon he figured I'd had enough time to get used to Amos bein' gone, and it was high time I talked about it. But I still didn't feel much like talkin'.

"Still feelin' down about Amos?" he pressed.

His words still struck like a dagger into my heart. I tried hard to swallow the lump that was risin' up into my throat, but all of the feelings came rushin' to the surface, and I couldn't hide 'em anymore. But the words still wouldn't come. I didn't want anyone to see me cryin' or think me weak, so I wiped my eyes and leaned back, wavin' my hands and arms at the smoke from the fire so as to hide the tears. But Jim knew the truth.

"You miss him, huh?" he asked.

I stared down at the ground and picked up a stick that was layin' in the mud at my feet. "Yeah," I said, tossin' the stick into the dyin' flames. "Reckon so."

Then I remembered that it hadn't even been a year since Jim lost his daughter, and it was like someone had reached out a hand to keep me from sinkin' down into the bottomless bog of sorrow.

"You miss Dorothy?"

Then it was Jim's turn to just sit there quietly, and for a moment, neither of us said anything. We just sat there starin' into the dyin' fire and watchin' to see if the stick I'd thrown in would catch fire.

"More than I can say," he finally answered tearfully.

Just hearin' Jim say how much he missed his little girl gave me the courage to finally admit how I was feelin' about Amos. "I just didn't think it would hurt so much."

"Reckon I didn't either," he agreed, still watchin' the fire as the stick began to burn.

"It just doesn't make a lick of sense," I objected. "I thought the cavalry'd be safer."

But he didn't say a word. He just sat there listenin'.

"Look at you and me. We've been through more battles than I care to count, and we're still here," I went on. "Why would God take Amos the first time he ever saw battle?"

Jim just looked down and shook his head.

"He was so young and innocent . . . " my voice trailed off.

Then I thought about Maria Grace bein' sick, and my stomach got all tied up in knots. *So young and innocent . . .* I must've had a worried look on my face too, seein' as how Jim got that concerned look in his eye.

"Somethin' else botherin' ya?"

I nodded, half glad he'd asked. "Maribel says Maria Grace has come down with the fever too," I heard myself sayin'.

"Oh . . . " The look of concern got even deeper.

There was another moment of silence between us, but I reckon we both knew what the other one was thinkin'.

He's thinkin' about how his little girl died of the fever, and he's gotta know I'm thinkin' it too.

"Been a while since I've seen you pray," he noted.

Truth be told, I was feelin' a tad convicted about that. But how's a man s'posed to pray when he's feelin' like God is so far away?

"Yep," I confessed. It was the truth, so I might as well just say so.

I wanted to pray for Maria Grace and all the things Maribel had put in her letter, but I didn't even know where to start. Part of me was still angry at God for lettin' Amos die. I wasn't rightly sure God would be in a mood to listen to my prayers now anyhow.

"Would ya like me to pray with ya? We could pray together?" he offered.

"What good will *that* do?" I shot back. "God ain't listenin' anyway!" I couldn't choke back the words any more. It was like they all came gushin' out at once, like a river breakin' through a dam. "I HATE this war! Why is God torturin' us like this? Why does He let us win battles, but He won't let us win the war? Why don't the danged Yankees just quit and go home already? Why'd they have to go and kill Amos?! Why?! He was just a boy! Just a young innocent boy! He didn't deserve to die! Why did God let him die?!"

Jim took in a breath and heaved a big sigh. "Well, now I reckon we're gettin' somewhere," he said, glad to finally get me talkin'. "We all hate the war, Wil," he said quietly. "And all of us have lost loved ones . . . " There was a tear streakin' down his face now. "But I don't think it was God who started it."

Finally he turned his head and looked at me. "Truth is, Wil, I ain't rightly sure if God's on either side. I've been thinkin' on it, and even if He was to take sides—now that Lincoln's turned it into a war to end slavery—what makes us so sure God'd be on *our* side?"

"Well I wish He'd hurry up and make up His mind. I've seen just about enough killin' and sufferin', and I don't wanna see any more! I just want it to be over!"

"I reckon we all do," he said with sadness in his voice.

"Well then why doesn't God do somethin' about it?" I asked, fightin' back the tears.

"Maybe He is," he said, lookin' far away. But there was pain in his face, and I knew there must be some truth to what he was sayin'.

"I got a feelin', when all this is over," he went on, "none of us, Reb nor Yank, will ever wanna fight another war like this again . . . Nosir . . . Not as long as we live."

I didn't rightly know what to say. I'd never thought of it that way before.

I watched as his eyes fell to the ground. "God knows we've paid a high enough price," his voice trailed off.

About that time, Arty and Carlton walked up.

"Hey, Wil, Jim," Arty nodded.

"Well, I gotta go," Jim sighed. "I gotta report for sentry duty in half an hour." He stood up, put a hand on my shoulder, then walked away.

"Mind if we join ya?" Arty asked.

"Suit yourselves," I said, soundin' a mite less pleasant than I should've.

"Who pissed in your grits?" Carlton asked.

"It's nothin'."

"You upset about somethin'?" Arty asked.

"I said it's nothin'," I insisted. "I don't feel much like talkin' about it."

"Don't sound like nothin' to me," Carlton challenged.

"I've just had a bellyful of this war, that's all," I tried to explain. But they exchanged a look that told me they knew there was more to it than I was sayin'.

"Thinkin' about Amos?" Arty pried.

"That, and other things," I replied, pickin' up another stick and tossin' it into the bed of hot coals that the fire had become.

Carlton sat down on the log next to me and stared into the embers. "Had me a boil once," he said. "Hurt too, 'til I finally cut it open and drained it."

I couldn't help myself. I looked at him like a cow lookin' at a new gate. I wasn't rightly sure if it was wise words he was sayin', or just plain crazy talk. But he just kept lookin' at the coals.

"After that, it healed up and went away," he added, with a hint of a grin.

That's when I finally understood what he was sayin'. Who would've ever thought that Carlton was such a deep well?

"It's Maria Grace too," I finally admitted. "Maribel says she's down with the fever. I'm just worried, that's all."

"Would it help if we prayed about it?" Arty asked. "It's been awhile since we prayed together."

"I don't feel much like prayin' right now," I said, tryin' to look away and feelin' ashamed.

"Well now, it seems to me you ain't felt much like prayin' for awhile now," Carlton pointed out. "As I recollect, you ain't led Company Prayer in over three months now. But I seem to recall the Cap'n makin' you a Corporal for that there exact reason."

I felt my face turnin' red with embarrassment.

"So, the way I see it, Corporal," he went on, puttin' on his sergeant voice and pointin' at the stripes on my jacket sleeves, "you got a job to do. So either you'd best work it out with the Man upstairs, or else you need to give them there stripes to someone else who's willin' to do the job."

What could I say? He was right. But how could I pray, in the mind I was in?

"I can do the job," I said. "I just need a little time, that's all. I can't pray 'til I get my heart right."

"Well, if you're mad at the Almighty, alright then, but doesn't the Good Book say somethin' about not lettin' the sun go down on yer anger?"

"Yeah . . . " Since when did Carlton know anything about what the Bible said?

"So I reckon you'd best get started," he went on, lookin' up at the sky. "It'll be gettin' dark soon."

I prayed that night for the first time since December.

Still, I couldn't get Jim's words out of my mind.

"I reckon when all this is over, none of us, Reb nor Yank, will ever wanna fight another war like this again . . . "

I thought long and hard on the matter that cold evening. It was almost like I could hear my Pa's words echoin' in my head. But it wasn't his voice. It was mine.

"There's more to this life than fightin' and dyin' for a cause, Wil, or even bein' a father and raisin' a family. God's ways are higher than our ways. Maybe what He really wants is just for people to love Him, and maybe learn to love each other more too. Those are the two greatest commandments."

Mind the Flank

By the middle of April, the weather broke and things were startin' to look a mite brighter. And not just the weather either. For a couple of weeks, it seemed like the whole world was all suddenly comin' together just right.

I got letters from Maribel and Mama with news from home. Maribel said that Maria Grace was doin' much better and things were lookin' up. Mr. Nellis had even managed to hire a couple of boys as hands to help with the plantin'. Mama said Pa's back was mostly healed, and she was bakin' and sellin' pies to help bring in some extra money for the family, seein' as how the war was takin' its toll on Pa's offerings. People gave what they could, but there just wasn't as much to go around as there used to be. She even saved enough to buy me a new pair of shoes, which she sent right away, along with a loaf of bread she'd baked for me. It wasn't fresh anymore by the time it arrived at Camp Winder, but I didn't mind. I ate it anyway, and even shared some with Arty and Jim. We were just thankful to have somethin' other than the poor excuse for vittles the army was handin' out.

Of course the spring weather brought more rain, but it wasn't too bad, and we didn't mind it so much. At least it was warmer than the freezin' rain and snow we'd had the month before. It made things muddy again for a few days, but we figured if it was muddy for us, it was muddy for the Yankees too, which would sure as likely slow 'em down if they had any ideas about goin' somewhere.

By late April, it was clear the Yankees were plannin' to cross the Rappahannock at Fredericksburg again. But after the whoopin' we gave 'em the last time, we couldn't figure out why they'd try comin' back for more. They had to be up to somethin', and it didn't figure to be somethin' good.

We marched out of Camp Winder and back up to the Prospect Hill, where we placed our lines along the same roads and earthworks we'd held before. There we waited. Then, on the night of April the thirtieth, the order came that we were movin' out early in the mornin'. The next day we marched west with most of Gen'ral Jackson's Corps—all exceptin' Gen'ral Early's Division, that is, which we left there in Fredericksburg to keep any Yankees that might try and cross the river from makin' any trouble for us.

By late that afternoon, we reached a small church beside the plank road, and there we saw Gen'ral Paxton sittin' on his horse by the road with Gen'ral Lee and his staff. There was a band there and they were playin' some grand music for marchin'. The sign in front of the church said, "Salem Church."

Salem Church? I recollect I've heard that name before . . . Right about then I recalled where I'd heard the name. *Amos . . . That's where the colonel said they buried Amos!*

I wanted to see my brother's grave more than life itself, but how could I just fall out of the column right there in front of all the gen'rals? *After this is all over, I must come back to this place. But how will I even find him? Did they mark the grave with his name?*

I had to admit it didn't seem very likely. If he was lucky, maybe they tied two sticks together as a cross and hung somethin' he owned over it. But a good many boys were just buried with no markers at all, on account of those doin' the buryin' not knowin' who the departed souls were.

Gen'ral Paxton's voice broke through and brought my mind back to the plank road as he sat up on the horse and called out as we marched by. "Keep movin', boys! If those Yankees think they can get 'round our flank, they've never met the Stonewall Brigade!"

We could hear the sounds of battle not far ahead, but we never saw any fightin' that day. We marched down the plank road 'til we found the place where the Yankees had built their first line of defenses, but they were long gone by the time we got there. That night we bivouacked behind the lines and rose early the next day. All Colonel Nadenbousch would say was, "We're movin' out, men." But no one seemed to know *where* we were movin' out *to*. Wherever it was, we reckoned we must be goin' to the ball. For the life of me, I never could figure why anyone would call it "the ball." Maybe some poor deluded fella with an overactive imagination thought that battles were like dances—big, bloody, murderous, horrifyin' dances.

Anyway, we knew we were likely goin' into the fight, seein' as how we had mornin' prayers and it was only Saturday mornin'. The gen'rals always liked to hold mornin' prayers on the day we were goin' into battle: one last chance to beseech the Good Lord's mercy and commend our spirits to Him and all.

I didn't feel much like goin' to mornin' prayer, but I went along anyway. Jim and Arty and Carlton were there too, along with Capt'n Rowan and several other boys from the company. I don't recollect much of what the Chaplain said. It was the usual standard prayer, but I wasn't really payin' all that much attention. I was still a mite unsure of just exactly where I stood with the Almighty at the time, and where He stood with me.

After mornin' prayers, some of the boys cooked sloosh for the march, but it was mostly half raw and a bit doughy on account of there not bein' much time for cookin'. Before long, the bugler sounded the march call, and we formed up to march.

And march we did too—quick and quiet-like—no drums, no music, nor even the usual chatter between soldiers. Just the shuffle of hundreds of feet on the dirt road and the sounds of the forest. We marched down the plank road and across an unfinished railroad bed, then turned up a narrow dirt road that seemed to wind endlessly through the dense forest of the Virginia wilderness.

Along about midday it was startin' to get mighty hot. We heard some shootin' a ways behind us, and I thought perhaps we were goin' the wrong way, but we never slowed for a moment. Matter of fact, we hardly stopped marchin' all day that day. We just kept on marchin', quick and quiet, like the march of the dead.

After we'd gone about twelve miles or so by my reckonin', we came across another plank road, and the Stonewall Brigade turned east, back toward Fredericksburg. But the rest of the division just kept on goin' northward up that narrow road.

About ten minutes after we started up the plank road, we came to a small farmhouse, and there we stopped. Gen'ral Paxton deployed the brigade across the road, but the forest there was so thick and dense with underbrush a 'possum couldn't crawl through it, much less an army.

By around six o'clock in the afternoon, we were beginnin' to wonder if we were gonna fight at all that day. Then all of the sudden, we heard shouts and musket fire off to our left, just through the woods a ways. Not long afterwards, we heard the unmistakable shrill sound of the rebel yell, like all Hell was breakin' loose on earth.

It didn't take long to figure out that the attack was underway, and from the sound of it, our boys were winnin'. We were gettin' mighty hungry, but there was no time to eat. We were ordered back onto the plank road, and we advanced up the road to support the attack. When we finally got there, we found a whole camp where the Yankees had been so surprised they just up and left everything behind when they fled—even the food cookin' on the fires—which was a mighty big shame, seein' as how we had nothin' to eat, but had to just go on by and let it all go to waste!

We were held in reserve that evenin', and spent most of our time movin' the line back and forth across that road, first this a-way then that a-way, like a big drunken snake. But the Yankees kept fallin' back, so we kept on advancin'. Our boys pressed the attack 'til shortly after nightfall, then the sounds of the battle started dyin' down a bit. We heard the sporadic firin' of a few pickets up ahead just a little ways, but aside from that, there wasn't much action that night. We finally got some time to eat, but couldn't cook anything, seein' as how we couldn't build our bivouack fires. The woods were too dense and dry, and we were too close to the fed'ral lines. So we ate whatever else we could find, which wasn't much.

It was late that night when the courier came lookin' for the colonel. That's when we first heard that Gen'ral Jackson had been shot. The news hit us like a bayonet in the belly. No one seemed to know if his wounds were mortal, but even if they weren't, we'd never fought a battle without "Stonewall" in command. It just wasn't right, and we were mad as hornets about it, and a mite concerned too.

The courier said that A. P. Hill had also been wounded by Yankee artillery, so Gen'ral Stuart was in command of the Corps and Gen'ral Heth had Hill's Division. We were glad to hear that Gen'ral Stuart's orders were to renew the attack at first light and Gen'ral Heth's Division was leadin' the attack. Colston's Division, with the Stonewall Brigade, was to support Heth.

It was a strange feelin' for a man, knowin' he was likely goin' into a fight, and both wishin' for the fight and not wishin' to fight, all at the same time. The thing was, we had no love for fightin', but the thought of *not* fightin' and givin' the ground back to the Yankees was a far sight more distasteful—especially seein' as how they'd shot our beloved "Stonewall." We didn't find out 'til later that Ol' Jack had actually been shot by our own pickets, who mistook him for Yankee cavalry while he was ridin' back to our lines after sundown.

It was dark that night, and there was a mist hangin' in the air that made it hard to see very far. We were tired as dogs, but couldn't sleep much: never could on a battlefield anyway. Carlton and some of the other fellas were sure the Billy Yanks would try and sneak up on us in the night to try and retake the ground, so I mostly just tried to find a comfortable place to rest my eyes and my weary feet. Every now and then there would come a shout or a rifle shot from a picket somewhere off in the darkness, or the sound of horses' hooves passin' by, or some other noise—just in case we had any notions about accidentally fallin' asleep.

Before sunrise we were roused up and got ourselves as ready as we could for the day's fightin' ahead. Of course it would've been a mite more tolerable if there'd been somethin' to eat. Although I usually preferred not to eat on the mornin' of a battle, we'd marched clean around the enemy's flank the day before without even stoppin' for a meal. There'd been no time to bring up the supply train, and we were plum out of the rations we'd brought with us from Fredericksburg.

Sure enough, the Yankee's opened up a terrible storm of cannon fire at first light. There were shells clippin' through the dense trees and burstin' all around, but we just hunkered down and let 'em come. If they were gonna hit us, there wasn't much to be done about it, so might as well just stay put.

The next thing we knew, the bugler was playin' and officers were shoutin' to form the brigade. Capt'n Rowan stood up quick as you please and drew out his sword.

"Company!"

Another shell burst about fifty yards behind us, but the Capt'n was steady as a rock. He looked around and saw the rest of the regiment formin' up too.

"On me, boys! Form up on me!" He waived his sword in the air, and the men started movin' out from behind the trees and the hasty breastworks we'd piled up during the night. Formin' up in the trees was different than formin' up in the open field. By the time all the boys got into line of battle, the line snaked around trees and shrubs, and up and down gullies and ridges in both directions. It wasn't a pretty sight, to be sure, but it served the purpose.

The whole regiment advanced, but the thick trees and brush slowed us down better than any breastworks or fortifications the Yanks could've built. To our left was the Orange Turnpike, and off to the right, somewhere nearby, the sound of the cannon fire was reachin' a fever pitch. The Blue-bellies had fallen back to a stretch of high ground somewhere just up ahead of us, and they'd done us the very great service of leavin' a gorgeous empty hilltop for our guns to be placed—whereupon a tree-mendous artillery duel shortly ensued.

We pressed on through brush and bog, and soon began the climb up toward the high ground. It wasn't long 'til we came into range of their muskets, which they were obliged to inform us thusly by way of demonstration. From where I stood, it sure seemed to me like the Yankees had all but forgotten that we'd pushed 'em back yesterday, seein' as how they were dug in like ticks on a hound dog and shootin' like they aimed to fight.

We came to a halt and fired a volley, then reloaded and kept advancin'. But the Yankee fire seemed to be gettin' hotter with every step we took. Several times each minute the air would come alive with the deadly sounds of speedin' Minie balls as they spun past nearby, strikin' tree or ground or worse. And then the line faltered and stopped again.

It was just about then that Gen'ral Paxton appeared on foot just ahead of the brigade. He had his sword drawn out and held it up high. I could tell it was Gen'ral Paxton on account of how he looked a mite like Jackson himself from a short distance.

"Remember Jackson, men!" he shouted.

"For Jackson!" came a chorus of responses.

Then it was like the whole brigade joined in. "JACKSON! JACKSON! JACKSON!" The whole woods echoed with the shouts of southern pride, and the line—such as it was, all tangled and twisted like a briar patch—surged forward again.

Not ten minutes later, Gen'ral Paxton went down—shot square in the chest—and everything started goin' crazy. A thick smoke was risin' up through the woods, and we could hear the cracklin' sounds of flames even over the sounds of the battle. But with all the smoke and confusion, it was hard to tell just where the fire was.

The Second Virginia was placed on the right of the brigade, and we got separated from the other regiments in all the marshes and thick smoke and underbrush. The sounds of battle further off to the right told us we were closin' in on the Yankee center, but the smoke and confusion was so thick we could barely tell friend from foe. Then, somehow, as if by the hand of God himself, we ended up on a high wooded knoll just in the edge of the woods near a cabin. And there we were, lookin' right down on the Yankee breastworks.

Colonel Nadenbousch was shoutin' and runnin' back and forth frantically to get the regiment back into line.

"SECOND VIRGINIA! MAKE READY!"

We fell into line and reloaded.

"TAKE AIM!"

Three hundred fifty rifles found their targets.

"FIRE!"

The forest exploded in a wall of smoke and the smell of powder filled the air. Then we saw another regiment advancin' on the Yankee position to our left, and the Billy Yanks gave up the ground and fell back into the open field that lay directly behind 'em.

But just as our boys reached the abandoned fed'ral breastworks, the Yanks reformed and fired, and the line surged back again. The air was filled with deadly hot lead and thick smoke from the brush fire, but they kept on a-comin', and we kept on firin' down on 'em.

The thud sounded close by, but I didn't think the ball hit me 'til I felt my body twist, and everything went sideways. I found myself lyin' on the ground lookin' up at the smoke-filled sky, followed presently by a wave of searin'-hot pain. It shot up from my right leg all up through my body like lightnin' had struck me from the ground up, and I cried out in pain. My hands grabbed for my leg, and I was greatly relieved to find it still in place.

It was the strangest sensation I ever had, lyin' there lookin' up at the battle still goin' on all around me, but the sounds all jumbled together in a dull roar, like I was under water or somethin'. I saw Jim's face leanin' over me and saw his mouth movin', but I could just barely hear what he was sayin'.

"You okay, Wil?" His voice sounded like he was talkin' through a bushel of cotton.

Then his eyes went to my leg and I saw the look on his face change. I pulled my hands back and saw they were covered with blood, and I felt that familiar sick feelin' risin' up in my belly, but there was nothin' in there to vomit. So I just laid there and retched 'til the strong flavor of bile filled my mouth.

There was more commotion above me, and I saw Carlton step up quickly. He tried to lift me up, but Jim grabbed him by the shoulder.

"Here they come!" he shouted.

Jim stood up and shouted somethin' else, but there was too much noise, and everything was startin' to get hazy. Carlton grabbed me by the arm, pulled me back a few steps behind the fightin', and leaned me up against a tree. I couldn't understand his next words to me. Then they turned and rejoined the fight. I reached out toward them.

Wait! Don't leave me here to die!

I tried to call out, but I was too weak, and no one could hear my cries. Soon the fightin' moved further away, and I found myself leanin' against that tree all alone. My hearin' was comin' back, but my head was swimmin' and the pain was gettin' worse. The smoke from the fire filled my lungs and nostrils and made me cough and choke 'til I could scarcely breathe, and I could feel the heat of the flames gettin' closer.

I rolled over and tried to pull myself along with my hands and arms toward the fightin' and away from the fire, but it was no use. I was too weak and the fire was catchin' up quick. I looked up and reached out my hand again and tried to call out to my friends, but I could barely even breathe. My whole world was goin' dim, and I knew I was about to pass out. The last thing I remember, through the smoke in the distance, was seein' Carlton fall.

Death of a Hero

I can vaguely recollect bein' carried to the hospital later that night, but I have no idea how long I was there before the surgeon came to take my leg. I can tell you without hesitation that I would not wish such an experience on anyone, be he friend or foe. I would've much preferred to just take my chances, but the surgeon wouldn't have it, and I was in no condition to argue.

The worst part was before the actual cuttin' took place. First there was the godawful realization that some surgeon I'd probably never met was fixin' to tie me down and take a bloody saw and cut off part of my leg. Next came the horror of bein' carried into that room with the basket of arms and legs there on the ground, and the stench and stain of blood everywhere—and knowin' that many a man who'd had a limb amputated didn't survive. I begged and pleaded with anyone who would listen.

Then came the cloth soaked with chloroform, and the strange sensation of losin' all feelin' in my body. The cuttin' was like a nightmare. The chloroform filled my head with strange, ghastly sounds and images and made me so groggy I could scarcely feel any pain—only a dull feelin' like my leg was bein' crushed. Then I went out.

I woke some time after dark in the worst agony imaginable and begged for relief, but there was no one there to hear and no relief to be had. So I spent the rest of the night driftin' in and out of sleep and tryin' my best to block out the pain, but it was no use.

Monday came and I began to recollect things more clearly. That's when I remembered that I hadn't had a decent meal in more than three days. I was so weak and hungry I was beyond hunger.

Jim and Arty came by later that afternoon. Arty had a sling around his arm and his hand was wrapped up in bandages, but aside from that he looked fit as a fiddle.

"Hey, Wil, how you doin?" he asked.

I tried to sit up to talk but didn't have the strength for it and fell back down.

"Not . . . too good . . . "

"Rest easy, Wil. We'll come back again later," Jim added.

"H . . . hungry . . . "

"You hungry?" Arty asked, leanin' in so he could hear me better.

I managed to nod weakly, but that was all I could muster.

"We'll see that you get somethin' to eat," Jim replied.

I closed my eyes for just a moment to regain my strength, but when I opened 'em again they were gone. But I do seem to recall them comin' back later to bring me some bread and jam.

"Here ya go, Wil," Arty said with a grin. "Found this in one of the officers' tents in the Yankee camp we captured."

I managed to eat it with much gratitude, but the pain made it hard.

It was several days before most of the wounded were moved from the battlefield into homes around Fredericksburg, and I was left in the care of an older couple, along with four other wounded fellas. The woman said her name was Elsa Kleber, and her husband's name was Joseph, like my brother's. They were kind and made us feel most honored and welcomed in their home, and they took good care of us. They didn't have much, but they happily shared what they had.

By the followin' week, my body was feelin' much stronger, and the pain in my leg was far more tolerable. But I couldn't get used to lookin' down and seein' nothin' below my right knee. I knew I should be grateful to God for savin' my life, but I was feelin' none too thankful.

Then my thoughts turned to matters of practicality.

How's a one-legged man s'posed to make a livin'? I'll be about as useless to Maribel and her folks on the plantation as a three-legged mule.

I remembered Tommy, and suddenly I had a great deal more respect for him. I wondered how he was gettin' along with only one leg, but I knew life would never be the same for him—or me—again. The life of a cripple was a pitiable thing, and detestable to my very soul. I couldn't abide livin' off the charity of others, and even if I was lucky enough to find work in a trade shop somewhere that didn't require me movin' around too much, I doubted I could earn as much as a whole man could. It was becomin' painfully clear that providin' for my family was about to get a whole lot harder. And gettin' around on one leg—well, that was another matter entirely.

The war was over for me, of that much I was sure. I tried to console myself with thoughts of goin' home to see my family. But how could I face Maribel as a cripple? How could I take care of my family like a proper man ought, all the while knowin' that my wife would just be lookin' on me with pity? I could scarcely bear the thought. All day long, my thoughts tortured me, and all night long, the images of the battle still burned hot in my memory, and I didn't sleep well at all.

By Monday, May the eleventh, only three of us still remained at the Kleber house. Mr. Kleber came into the parlor that afternoon lookin' like he'd just lost his prize pig. He held a newspaper in his hand, but he didn't look at it. He took a deep breath, and with sadness in his voice, informed us of the news.

"I haf sad news for the Confederacy," he said in his Dutch accent.

He paused, lookin' downcast, then around the room at each of us. "General Jackson iss daid . . . " He paused reverently for a moment, then continued, "Died yesterday uff pneumonia." Then he shook his head slowly and almost whispered. "God help us oll."

But it sure didn't feel like God was helpin' us. Come to think of it, I wondered if the Almighty had just up and decided to switch sides. Or maybe He was just off somewhere sleepin', instead of doin' His part. It just didn't reckon.

What kind of cruel God would support our battle, and yet prevent us from victory? How are we s'posed to win the war without Stonewall?

The Klebers had told us how the battle at Chancellorsville—that's what they called it in the papers—had been a miraculous victory for the South, and how our boys had driven the Yankee hordes back across the river in utter defeat. Yet still the war went on. The danged Yankees just wouldn't admit they were licked.

It was two days later, on May the thirteenth, that Jim and Arty came to visit me again. When I first saw 'em come in the door, my spirit was lifted, but they didn't smile much. Then I saw Capt'n Rowan come in behind 'em, and I felt my heart stop beatin', and a lump rose up in my throat.

What news is bad enough to bring the Capt'n out here personally . . . again?

"Good to see you alive, son," the Capt'n started in. "How're you feeling?"

"Alright, I guess, sir," I lied. I swallowed hard and tried to stand up, but when he saw me strugglin' with the crutch, he waved his hand as if to push me back down.

"Don't get up."

I knew the Capt'n was just tryin' to be polite, but I wasn't sure how I felt about him givin' me special treatment. *I may be missin' part of my leg, but I can still stand in the presence of an officer as well as the next man!*

But it was clear that gettin' up wasn't gonna be as easy as I thought. Finally I saw the look on his face and stopped strugglin'. I threw the crutch down on the floor in anger, then just collapsed back into the chair.

"It's alright, son," he said. But it wasn't alright.

"I have some news for you," he continued, pickin' up the crutch and leanin' it against the wall behind me. It was the same tone of voice he'd used when he and Colonel Ball told me the news about Amos. I felt the lump in my throat grow. "You're going home. Full discharge, effective immediately. Soon as you can travel."

I reckon that part wasn't a great surprise. After all, what good is a one-legged soldier? But the look on his face told me there was more.

"And there's one more thing." He produced a piece of paper from his pocket and cleared his throat before continuin'. "I have a letter here from Mr. William Nellis of Charles Town. It's addressed to the Colonel." He looked up at me and hesitated for just a moment while he read the expression of bewilderment on my face, then he went on.

"It reads: 'Dear sir, I humbly beseech you to grant a leave of absence for my son-in-law, Corporal William Harleck, on the regrettable occasion of the untimely death . . . '" He hesitated just long enough to glance up at me, then read on, "'of his infant daughter on this 27th of April past . . . '"

I tried to breathe, but couldn't. My lungs refused to draw a breath. I was paralyzed with shock, but I could still feel the blood drainin' from my face. It was like a cannon shell had gone off inside my head. I could barely think at all.

The Capt'n went on. "'There will be a memorial service for the family at the Zion Episcopal Church in Charles Town on . . . " He paused again and looked up from the paper long enough as if to say he didn't wanna read the next part, then his eyes went quickly back to the page, "'on Friday, the 8th of May . . . at six o'clock in the afternoon.'"

He looked back up at me again like he was tryin' to figure out what to say, but there was nothin' to be said. "'If it is within your power to grant a furlough,'" he read on, "'so that Corporal Harleck may attend the memorial with his wife and family, I would be most grateful and humbly obliged to your service. Your most humble servant, William Nellis'."

The Capt'n stood upright as tall as he could and took a deep breath, lettin' the hand with the letter fall to his side. I could tell he was doin' his best to be strong, but I knew it was all just on my account. He looked mighty uncomfortable at havin' to deliver bad news to me twice in just six months.

I tried to be strong too, as a man should be, but it was no use. The weight of it all just overcame me.

"Nnoooo!" I cried out, tryin' my best to make his words go away. I tried to stand up, but fell to the floor on my face, and all thoughts about bein' strong and dignified and manly vanished like vapors. I just laid there on that floor makin' a pitiful spectacle and sayin', "No . . . No . . . " over and over again.

After a few minutes—I reckon that's how long it was, anyway—Arty and Jim helped me back up into the chair, and I wiped my eyes on my shirt sleeve. They didn't say much but just sat there next to me. Arty put a hand on my shoulder like he was tryin' to lend me some of his own strength, or maybe just to let me know he was there. But as I looked up at him, I saw in his eyes that his own heart was breakin' too.

"I'm real sorry, Wil," he said softly. "I'm sure it was a real nice service."

"I'm sorry, son," the Capt'n added. "I know this news must be hard for you, but the letter only just arrived yesterday—probably because of the battle. Colonel Nadenbousch asked me to come by and deliver it in person."

He stepped forward and held out the letter in his hand. I saw my hand reach out and take it, but I couldn't feel it, like it was some kind of strange dream. I was still too overwhelmed to talk, but by the look on his face I could tell he understood.

"I'll make arrangements to have your things packed up and brought here. You can go and be with your family as soon as you feel well enough to travel."

Battle of Faith

I'd heard my Pa say many times that "God will not suffer you to be tempted above that ye are able." I reckon maybe the Almighty was fixin' to test me and see just how much I was able, seein' as how just when I was sure things couldn't get any worse, they did.

After the Capt'n left, Jim came over and put his hand on my other shoulder, across from Arty.

"Is there anything we can do, Wil?" he asked.

But there was nothin' they could do or say to bring back my precious child, or my little brother, or my leg. I held that letter in my hand and tried to read it again, hopin' somehow maybe the Capt'n had read it wrong, but my eyes filled up again 'til I could no longer see straight, and the parlor of the Kleber house dissolved into a dark sea of bitter tears.

WHY, God? Why are you doin' this to me? My child . . . So young and innocent—like Amos . . . WHY? Just when she was gettin' better?!

My mind desperately searched for the memory of her tiny face, but in that moment I couldn't even recollect what she looked like. The memory of holdin' her in my arms and gazin' upon her face was just too painful. And now, never again to hold her and look upon her with joy . . . I tried to think of somethin' else—anything else—that would make it stop, but my thoughts raced like a twister against my will, leavin' a path of destruction in my soul. In my mind I could see Maribel weepin' with inconsolable grief over the lifeless body of our infant child, and it burned in my mind and brought a wave of terrible guilt and sorrow and anger beyond my meager ability to describe. The pain was more than I could bear. I felt it wellin' up inside me like a ragin' river overflowin' its banks in the rainy season, and I knew I was losin' control. Out of control and drownin': that's exactly how it felt. It was like I was bein' swept away by that ragin' river, and I was goin' under. And the harder I fought, the harder it was to keep my head above the water. In the back of my mind I could hear my Pa's words again, but they only seemed to make it worse.

Where are You, God?! You said you'd never give me more than I could bear! Why do you hate me?! Why are you doin' this to me?!

My mind raced like it was reachin' out desperately to grab onto anything that might keep me from drownin'. I looked down and saw the letter clenched tightly in my fist, all crumpled into a ball.

I couldn't even be there for the funeral to comfort her . . . How painful this must be for her. If I'm feelin' this much pain and sorrow, she must be in utter despair.

Arty and Jim just looked at each other, like neither one had any idea what to do or say next.

"We're real sorry about your little girl, Wil," Jim finally said. But he wasn't just sayin' it just because he felt bad. There was genu-ine compassion in his voice and in his eyes. Then I remembered Dorothy.

Jim knows just how I feel . . . I couldn't understand until now, but he's known since that day last August.

I looked up at him and wanted to tell him that I finally understood, but I couldn't make the words come out. All I could do was hope that he knew.

I don't even recollect how long they sat there with me—perhaps an hour or so—but it seemed like a long time. Finally, it was Arty who turned his chair so he was facin' me.

"Wil . . . " he started. "It'll be gettin' dark soon, and we've gotta be gettin' back."

All I could do was nod my head.

He leaned forward, puttin' his elbows on his knees and lacin' his fingers together. "Wil, there's somethin' else," he said.

But I couldn't comprehend what he was sayin'. My soul was dyin' and my mind couldn't conceive of even one more thing.

"We can't stay long, but we knew you'd wanna know," he said in a soft voice.

Whatever the news was, it couldn't be any worse than I'd already heard, so I just sat there and stared at them.

Arty went on. "It's Carlton, Wil . . . "

Right away my mind flashed back to the battle. I remembered seein' Carlton through the smoke. He was wavin' his arm and callin' the men to press forward. And then I saw him fall . . . and I knew what was comin' next.

I didn't wanna hear it. I couldn't . . . I held out my hand.

NO MORE . . . PLEASE! I can't take anymore!

It felt like a shell explodin' in my heart. I grabbed the crutch leanin' up against the wall behind me and threw it across the room with all my might, ventin' the full fury of my soul on that despised instrument, and screamin' like a madman as I watched it bounce off the brick fire-place and fall to the floor. Whatever tiny scrap of constitution and dignity I had left, abandoned me, and I could hold back the tears no longer. I found myself bent over in that chair with my head in my hands weepin' as a child might weep into the folds of his mother's dress, overwrought with grief, betrayed by my own strength, and drownin' in the deep swift river of sorrow.

"I can't bear any more . . . " I pleaded through the tears. "The pain's too much . . . No more, please!"

Arty glanced down, then back up at me, without sayin' a word, like he knew that I'd already figured out what he was gonna say.

It took awhile before I could rally any bit of self respect, but eventually I was able to regain my composure enough to ask. "How?" I breathed. There was just somethin' inside of me that needed to know.

"Shot twice—in the arm and stomach," Jim said gently. "But he died a hero, Wil," he went on. "He kept the Yankees from retakin' the ground."

I couldn't say a word. I just sat there with my head in my hands for quite some time. But then, bit by bit, the deep sorrow that was stranglin' me began to fade, and in its place I began to feel somethin' I never expected: I felt proud. One thing I knew about Carlton best of all: he'd wanna die fightin'—a soldier's death—a hero's death.

"I was with him when he died," Arty said. "He asked me to give you this."

Arty reached into his shoulder bag and pulled out a Bible and handed it to me.

Carlton had a Bible?

I reached out to take the Bible from Arty's hand. It was smaller than my Pa's, with a new black leather cover that felt cool and smooth in my hands. Holdin' that Bible had a strange effect on me. It was like an unexplainable peace came over my soul.

"How long has he had this?"

"Bought it in Martinsburg, after Second Manassas," Jim said.

I suddenly remembered all the times when we'd prayed for Carlton just before the battle. Had he finally stopped runnin' away from God?

Then it struck me like lightnin' on a hot summer night: *Runnin' away . . . Isn't that just what you've been doin', Wil Harleck?*

I opened the book and found a small piece of paper stuck between the pages. The paper had Carlton's handwriting on it. All it said was:

April 10, 1863
Fredericksburg

At first, I thought maybe it was a letter he was fixin' to write, but the words were right in the middle of the paper, so that didn't rightly figure.

"What *is* this?"

"That's the day he was baptized," Jim answered with a smile.

"Baptized?" I couldn't hide the shock in my voice.

"Yep," Jim laughed. "Right there in the Rappahannock! Darnedest thing ya ever saw!"

"And look," Arty pointed to the open page.

There, underlined in Carlton's pen, were these words:

"He that believeth and is baptized shall be saved"

"He knew you'd be real proud, seein' as how it was you that helped him get right with the Lord in the first place," Arty said with pride.

"Me? What . . . ? When?"

"Yep. Said he reckoned the Good Lord was tryin' to get his attention after all those close calls at Winchester and Port Republic and Second Manassas, so he went and bought himself a Bible and started readin' it." Arty sat back in the chair and smiled for the first time that day. "He woulda told you himself, but he said somethin' about waitin' 'til you were done feudin' with the 'Man Upstairs'."

At first I felt a mite put out at the notion, but there was no denyin' he was right: I *had* been feudin' with God. And I reckoned if anyone could spot a man who was feudin' with the Almighty, it'd be someone who'd done his share of feudin' himself—someone like Carlton.

"He even gave up drinkin'!" Jim chimed in. "Woulda got baptized sooner too, but the river was too cold!"

The whole thing was like a breath of fresh air. I felt like Carlton had thrown me a rope in that ragin' river of sorrow, and I could finally hold my head above water. It didn't make the pain of losin' Maria Grace go away, or bring back my leg, but it felt like a weight was lifted off my chest, and I could finally breathe again.

Then Jim leaned forward. "You just never know when somethin' you do or say might make all the difference in the world to someone else."

His words pierced my heart like a knife. I'd been blamin' God for all my troubles, but even in my darkest time—even when I was mad at God—He was still workin' out His plan. Then the words of my Pa came floodin' back:

"We're not guaranteed an easy life, son. War or no war, hard times come on us all, and life is full of disappointments. But God's love; now that's something you can always count on."

Turns out the heavy load I'd been carryin' around was all my own doin'. In all my pain and anger, I'd never stopped to think that maybe I might be lookin' at it all wrong. In that moment, it was like a lamp bein' lit in the darkness.

God . . . I think maybe I'm finally beginnin' to understand . . . Help me. I know I've been a stubborn mule lately . . . and I'm sorry.

I still didn't understand why Amos and Maria Grace had to die, but then I remembered the words Pa used to read from the Good Book: *"O death, where is thy sting? O grave, where is thy victory?"* And it all came together in that moment.

"We really haven't lost 'em," I said almost in a whisper. "We'll see 'em again in Glory."

"And we *have* gained a brother," Arty added hopefully.

Then Jim sat back and smiled thoughtfully. "It's true, the Good Lord did take Dorothy, Maria Grace, and Amos home before we'd've liked," he said with peace in his voice, "but maybe he also took Carlton—and even ol' Stonewall himself—to keep watch over 'em."

Farewell the Innocent

June 1863

The stunning victory at Chancellorsville provides Lee with a much needed opportunity. President Jefferson Davis and the Confederate government are becoming increasingly concerned about the South's chances of victory. The Union naval blockade has taken a heavy toll on the southern economy, and the sheer industrial might and dense population of the North is beginning to crush the South. To make matters worse, Lincoln's Emancipation Proclamation has all but smashed any realistic hope of European nations coming to the aid of the South. Any nation which now allies itself with the Confederacy will, in effect, be declaring its support of slavery. The South's only hope now rides on the shoulders of General Robert E. Lee. The Confederacy needs a decisive military victory, and soon.

Seizing the momentum from his triumph at Chancellorsville, Lee gathers the Army of Northern Virginia, 70,000 strong, and slips quietly through the Blue Ridge and into the Shenandoah Valley. Using the mountains to screen his movements, he moves north, crossing the Potomac into Maryland and Pennsylvania. His objective is the Union railroad center at Harrisburg. There he hopes to draw out the Union Army of the Potomac and defeat it on the ground of his choosing, then march against Washington, DC. If all goes as planned, Jefferson Davis is to send a letter offering an end to the hostilities, to be placed on the desk of Abraham Lincoln the day after Lee has destroyed the Union army.

Back in Washington, reports of a large Confederate force moving northward begin to arrive. Lincoln orders Hooker to begin pursuit of Lee's army, but Hooker is reluctant and slow to respond. So, on June 28, Lincoln replaces him with Major General George G. Meade. Meade, with over 90,000 men, presses the march into Pennsylvania, anxious to throw the invaders out of his home state.

Unaware that a large federal force is approaching dangerously close to his flank, Lee has allowed his force to become spread out over a distance of more than sixty miles, trusting that his cavalry commander, Jeb Stuart, will warn him of any approaching danger. But instead of screening the Rebel army and keeping an eye on Meade's movements, Stuart has committed the balance of his troopers to raiding towns north and east of Lee's main body. When Lee finally realizes the danger, he moves quickly to unite his army at the only suitable crossroads: a sleepy little town in southern Pennsylvania called Gettysburg.

May 18, 1863

To Cpl. William Harleck,
2nd Virginia Inf. Rgt, 1st Brig., 2nd Corps, A.N.V.
near Fredericksburg

My dear son,

I pray this letter reaches you in time. I read in the paper this past week that you were injured by the leg in the recent battle, and I received a letter from your friend, Artimus, that you are to be discharged soon. Please send word if you are able. I shall arrange to meet you when you arrive in the valley and see that you have a ride home.

I should be most cruel indeed were I not to mention that your mother also greatly desires to see you returned safely to us, although the news of your injury has not been easy for her so soon after the deaths of Amos and little Maria Grace. I have no doubt that Maribel also desires to see you home soon, as she has been most distressed over the loss of her child these last few weeks. We held a fitting memorial service for the child, but it was quite difficult for Maribel. I am quite certain that your presence may yet provide some small solace for her in these most trying times and entreat you to hasten your returning with all possible speed.

I await your reply.

Your Father,
Elias B. Harleck

Mustering Out

I didn't rightly know just what to think about the whole musterin' out business. It was a well-known fact that there were some fellas who'd do just about anything they could to see the cashier and get mustered out: some because they were needed at home; some because they reckoned they'd seen enough of the war and done their part; and others because they were just plain yellow and wanted to get out the army. I surely didn't want anyone thinkin' I was a yella-belly, but a one-legged soldier is about as much use in a fight as a two-legged stool.

I was paid in Confederate greenbacks—little good as they were—and whatever rations I could carry. I was allowed to keep my rifle too, but it was more burden than help, seein' as how I only had one arm to use for carryin' things. Ironic how the only way a one-legged man could walk like he had two legs was to give up the use of one arm as well, for workin' the crutch.

I couldn't go by train on account of the Yankee cavalry, and I hadn't learned to ride a horse with only one good leg yet, so I had to go by wagon. It was a slow and painful way to travel, and over a hundred twenty miles it was too, so as to steer clear of the Yankee army. Six days it took us to get from Fredericksburg to Winchester carryin' a wagonload of flour and beans, dried salt pork, and a cask of wine, to be delivered to the commissary major there. Four of us—the driver, me, and two other boys who were also headin' home to the Valley—traveled by the plank road to Culpeper on the first day. I persuaded the driver to stop at the Salem Church as we passed by so as I could try and find Amos' grave, but found nothin' that I could be sure of. We traveled on through Boston town the next day, then on to Fletcher Mill, then across the mountains through the Thornton Gap to Luray, and up the east valley to Front Royal, and finally to Winchester. The other two boys and me, we took turns ridin' up front with the driver and layin' in the back on the sacks of flour. By the third day, I reckon even the hard floor of a rail car would've been greatly preferred to that wagon for travelin'. The railroad would've been much faster, leastwise. But the long trip gave me plenty of time to think about what I might say to my Pa when I saw him, and what he might say to me.

How am I ever gonna explain Amos' death to him? If I know Pa, he won't be any too happy that his son was buried in some unmarked grave behind a little church in the middle of no place, instead of in the church cemetery in Charles Town, where he belongs. But will Pa blame me for encouragin' him to join up in the first place? Or will he just be glad I'm home? What should I say?

I reckoned that seein' my Pa for the first time since Amos' death was gonna be about like comin' across a black bear in the woods: you just never know which way it's gonna go. But there was no avoidin' it, so I just had to pray for the best and prepare for the worst.

Pa was there waitin' for me in Winchester when we arrived. He wore a serious look on his face as he watched me climb down out of the wagon. But then again, that's the way he usually looked anyway. I thanked the driver and he tossed me my pack. I said good-bye to the other fellas and they wished me well, then they drove off. When I turned around, Pa was standin' just a few feet away waitin' to help me with my pack.

"A-afternoon, Pa," I said, tryin' to stand up straight, but soundin' a mite too much like that 16-year-old boy I remembered.

He coulda knocked me over with a feather when he stepped up to me, hugged me, and kissed my face, which—I can assure you—my Pa rarely ever did.

"It's good to see you, son," he said, steppin' back and pattin' me on both shoulders.

"Thanks, Pa," I said, greatly relieved that he wasn't angry.

He looked down at my legs again, and I wondered what he might say. It was plain that one leg was a full cubit shorter than the other, and even though the bandage was covered by the leg of my army trousers now—which were tied off just below the right knee—I reckon it was still quite a shockin' sight for him to behold. But the look on his face told me he wasn't all that worried about it, and I hoped maybe it was because he was just glad to have me home alive.

He took my pack, tossed it up in the wagon, and helped me up into the seat next to him.

"Have you had anything to eat today?" he asked. "Your mother sent a basket with some bread and cheese if you're hungry," he added, jerkin' his head around toward the back of the wagon.

"Thanks," I answered, reachin' around behind me to get the small basket Mama had packed. "I'm starvin'! I haven't had anything to eat since last night in Front Royal."

"Thought as much," he said, snappin' the reins, and the horse began the slow trot home.

The first part of the journey to Charles Town was just like I expected: quiet. Even though Pa didn't seem angry, it still took me a while to get up the courage to talk to him about Amos. I thought if I ate the bread and cheese Mama'd sent first, maybe he'd just think I was bein' polite. But after the food was gone, I had to come up with another plan. So I reckoned the best way to go about it was to start by talkin' about somethin' else first, and then work up to it.

"Seen Maribel lately?" I asked.

"Mm-hmm," he nodded. "She wanted to come with me to meet you, but her mother wouldn't hear of it."

"Why not?" I had to ask.

"Too dangerous," he said with a grave look. "There's federal cavalry all over this end of the valley."

"Oh, yeah," I said. "I reckon that's as good a reason as any." But I couldn't help wonderin' if maybe there was another reason too.

"How's she doin'?" I asked, lookin' to see if I could find the answer in his face. I half thought I might be steppin' right into a hornet's nest just askin' the question, but all I could see was the gentle smile under those deep eyes.

"Well, you know this war's been hard on her—especially the death of Maria Grace . . . " he trailed off, still lookin' at the road ahead.

"Yeah. Me too, I reckon."

Then he turned his head to look at me. "She's not the same young schoolgirl you used to know, Wil," he said. It was the same tone of voice he always used when he was warnin' me to watch my step around Mama, when she was in a mood.

"Whadaya mean?" I asked.

"I mean when a woman loses a child, it changes her," he said. Then he turned to watch the road again. "She's grown up a bit."

I thought about what he'd said for a minute. Then I remembered.

Mama's lost a child too, and so has Pa.

"I reckon this war's been hard on all of us, huh?" I asked.

"Afraid it has . . . " he said thoughtfully.

With all my heart I wanted to avoid talkin' to my Pa about Amos, but somethin' deep down inside wouldn't let me leave it alone. I knew it was gonna come up, and when it did, I'd probably get one of Pa's sermons about settin' a good example for others, or some such thing. But then I heard Carlton's voice echoin' in my mind, "*The way I see it Corporal, you got a job to do* . . . " and I knew I had to do what needed to be done. So I resolved to take the blame for Amos' death, come what may. I took a deep breath and got up my courage.

"I'm really sorry about Amos, Pa," I said in a low voice, lookin' down at my legs. I suddenly realized that I felt more like a man than I'd ever felt around my Pa before.

"Mmm-hmm," he nodded like he already knew what I was gonna say. "I know, son, but there was nothin' you could've done."

I looked up at him in amazement, and maybe just a tad bit of relief.

Does he really mean that? No sermon? No guilt?

But I wasn't convinced that was all there was to it. "If it wasn't for me," I argued, "maybe he wouldn't've signed up in the first place."

But Pa just kept his cool. "He was of conscription age, Wil. If he hadn't signed up on his own, he would've been drafted anyway."

I had to admit, Pa was right, but I still couldn't help feelin' guilty.

"I thought he'd be safer in the cavalry . . . " I tried to explain. But he just looked at me, and for the first time since before the war began, I saw grace in my Pa's eyes.

"Cavalry, infantry, artillery, or civilian, does it really matter?" he asked calmly. "Is there any safe place in war, son?"

I felt the lump in my throat, and my eyes watered up at the feeling of great relief that came gushin' up out of my soul like a mountain spring. I tried to answer, but I was too moved to speak.

"You didn't start this war, Wil," he looked up at me again with that deep thoughtful look on his wrinkled brow, "it was thrust upon all of us."

I took a good honest look at his face. It was the first time I noticed how the traces of gray in his brown hair framed his deep eyes and gave his thin face a deep, wise look about it.

"You and Amos might've been the ones wearin' the uniform," he went on, "but all of us have fought the war." Then he paused and fixed his gaze back on the horse. "No, son," he said, his voice soundin' suddenly far off, "You didn't kill Amos. The war did that . . . and blamin' yourself won't bring him back."

That was the best day I ever had with my Pa. There was more healin' in those words than he could ever know.

More than a few tears were shed when we arrived in Charles Town to find Maribel, Mama and Vanessa, and William and Grace Nellis, there at the courthouse to meet us. Tommy was there too, and even a few of the folks from the church had come out to welcome me home.

Just the sight of Maribel, standin' there with her folks and wavin' at us as we rode up, made my heart stand still. But even though she was smilin', I could see Pa was right, even before I got down off the wagon. There was just somethin' different about her. The special glow she'd had the last time I saw her with the baby, was gone. And her smile, well, it just wasn't as bright as I remembered. She wore a plain linen blouse with a slim tan skirt, and her hair was all up in a bonnet, instead of hangin' down about her shoulders like before.

Then again, when it came to appearances, I wasn't exactly lookin' like the prize hog at the fair that day either. I hadn't had the chance to prepare for a proper homecomin'. If I had, I'd've got myself a shave and a haircut at the barber, had a bath, and put on a nice, clean, pressed uniform. But things bein' as they were, I must've been quite the sight to behold after that long ride home, all filthy and unkempt and covered with dust like I was. I reckon I didn't smell any too good either. I surely must've been a far cry from lookin' like that innocent wide-eyed boy goin' off to war only just a couple of years before.

I climbed down off the wagon as best I could with only one foot and grabbed the crutch from behind the seat. But when I turned around, Maribel had a worried look on her face, and Mama was just outright cryin'. Both ladies came rushin' up to hug me, but they were obviously both distressed about my leg. Mama stopped just a few feet short and looked me up and down again with both hands over her mouth. She looked a smidgen older than I remembered, and more thin and tired too.

"Oh . . . dear," she said through her hands, tryin' to fight off the tears.

"It's alright, Mama," I tried to reassure her. "It doesn't hurt much anymore." But I knew she wasn't buyin' what I was sellin', even if it was the truth.

But Maribel didn't stop.

"Oh, Wil . . . " she said with her voice full of sadness, and she threw her arms around my neck. She didn't kiss me, but just laid her head on my shoulder and held me there for the longest time. It was strange, standin' there on one foot and tryin' to hold her in my one free arm while I steadied myself on the crutch with the other. But it felt so good just havin' her there in my arms again, that everything else just didn't seem to matter much. And knowin' that I never had to leave her and go back to that cursed war again—well, that was the best part of all.

After a minute, I let go of the crutch—leavin' it under my arm to keep it from fallin'—and took her face in my hands so as I could gaze upon her again. There was deep sadness in her eyes, but I could still see a glimmer of hope there too. I wiped the tears from her cheeks with my hands and kissed her on the lips as tender as I could. Then I looked in her eyes again.

"I'm sorry, Maribel . . . " I tried to speak, but the words got caught in my throat, and she teared up again. "I'm so sorry I couldn't be here for you," I managed. Then we just stood there and held each other without sayin' a word.

Finally, after a good long while, she stepped back and looked up at me and wiped the tear from her own cheek with the back of her hand. "You kept your promise," she said, workin' hard to smile. "Welcome home, Mr. Harleck." Then, for just the briefest of moments, I thought I saw that familiar sparkle in her eye, and she kissed me back.

Mama was next. We hugged and she smothered my face with tearful kisses of joy, and then she remembered that others were waitin' to greet me too. "Well, would you look at me," she said, blushin' and wipin' the tears from her eyes. "I'm a terrible mess. And I've gone and forgotten all of my manners too."

She turned around and took my arm, and she, Pa, and Maribel walked with me over to where Vanessa, Tommy, and the Nellises had been waitin'. There were quite a few hugs and handshakes, and many a healing word was exchanged that day.

After all of the welcomin' was done, we set about findin' a place for me to stay. Mama and Pa had only one spare room in their house, and it was hard to imagine Maribel and me stayin' in the tiny room where Joseph and Amos and I grew up. So we took Maribel's folks up on their generous offer to stay in their home while I finished healin'—just 'til we could find a place of our own.

But that turned out to be harder than I thought. The war had pretty much done-in the economy in the Shenandoah. What with the shortage of young men to work the land; and many of the slaves havin' made their way to freedom; and what with the cost of feedin' and supplyin' both armies; and the frequent lootin' and pillagin' done by the Yankees; and the collapse of the Confederate dollar; well, there wasn't much left.

I tried to find work, but no one had much use for a one-legged former preacher's boy turned soldier. So I did what I could to help Mr. Nellis on the plantation, but as rich as he'd been when the war started, just about all he had left was his house, his land, and his good name, and that was worth a mite less than it used to be at the bank.

Now William Nellis was a resourceful man. After the death of Maria Grace, well, Grace and Maribel, they were nigh inconsolable. So I reckon he thought maybe havin' a memorial photograph of the child might help ease their grief, so he went and commissioned one of those photographers with their new-fangled cameras to take a photograph of little Maria Grace all in her pretty little burial gown. Then he went and had a real nice grave marker made for her. But when it came time to pay for all these things he couldn't afford 'em. Turns out, he just happened to have a pair of nice big oxen for which he had no use anymore, seein' as how the Yankee army had sent most of the slaves north to freedom and there weren't enough left to work the fields. So he took the oxen across the Potomac to Williamsport and sold 'em there for fed'ral greenbacks, which he used to pay for the funeral and the photograph, and even had some left over which he kept to make sure there was food on the table for the summer.

When I first laid eyes on that photograph, it felt mighty strange indeed. I'd seen photographs before—mostly of live soldiers before the battle, and dead ones after, and the likes. Heck, a few of the fellas in the Innocent Second had even gone and had photographs taken of themselves. But it was different seein' my own departed child dressed in that white gown and lyin' there as if she was just sleepin'. Still, it was good to have somethin' to remember her by, but it couldn't heal the emptiness in our hearts.

We also found some comfort in prayin' together, and even readin' some passages from the Bible together at night before we went to sleep. But I reckon there'll always be a scar on our hearts left by our precious little one. It's just the way of things, and there's nothin' anyone can do to change it. Life goes on, but the pain never truly goes away.

The month of June brought two memorable occurrences. The first was the passin' of Gen'ral Lee's army through the lower valley on its way north. This came as a great relief to a lot of folks in Charles Town who were rightly concerned about what would become of the town if the war continued on. The Yankee cavalry had already withdrawn on back across the river when Gen'ral Stuart's boys rode through, so everyone came out to see the boys in gray as they marched through the town. They weren't a pretty sight, to be sure, lookin' all tattered and worn like they did, but it still did the heart good. A band played "Dixie" and "Bonnie Blue Flag" and the like, as the boys marched by, regiment after regiment. They were all dressed differently: some in full uniform and some not; some with jackets buttoned up, some unbuttoned, and some with no jackets at all; some with new shoes, some with old worn-out shoes, and some with nothin' but cloth wrapped around their feet; and all nature of different hats. But they had high spirits. We didn't see the Stonewall Brigade, but Gen'ral Hill's new corps came through town on the thirteenth, and Gen'ral Longstreet's First Corps passed through the next day. It felt very strange indeed to be standin' on the side of the road lookin' on, instead of marchin' with the boys.

The second occurrence was the news that the Yankee Congress had voted to admit the proposed new state of West Virginia to the Union on June the twentieth. And even though most folks in Charles Town wanted nothin' to do with it, Jefferson County was to be included in the new state. This had the unfortunate effect of renderin' our already mostly worthless Confederate money even more worthless, seein' as how the Yankees had no use for it at all. We did think it ironic, though, that for about a month—from June the twentieth until right around July the twentieth—turns out Charles Town was actually a fed'ral town under Confederate occupation, instead of the other way around.

By early July, though, we read the horrible news about the disaster at Gettysburg, and the fall of Vicksburg on the Mississippi, which gave us all great cause for concern. In the weeks that followed, it seemed like there was an endless steady stream of southern boys, all foot sore and covered with dust as they marched back through town again on their way south. But they didn't look like the same soldiers who'd passed by just weeks before. These boys had a defeated look about 'em that I'd never seen before.

In the Service of the South

By mid-July, I knew I needed to find work on my own. My leg was healin' up nicely by then, and livin' with the Nellises and bein' an extra mouth to feed was startin' to weigh on the family's purse a mite more than I'd've liked. And it didn't do my self-esteem any good either.

Without the help needed to farm the land, the Nellises had all but given up on plantin' the big fields that were once filled with wheat and corn. I'd tried workin' in the smaller field where they'd managed to plant some corn, tomatoes, and beans to feed the family, but it was too late in the season to plant many new crops and too early to harvest what little crops we'd managed to get in the ground.

I showed Maribel how to weed the sweet corn, peas, and string beans, but she wasn't used to workin' the field and struggled greatly to accomplish little. And with only one good foot, I wasn't much good in the field either.

"I can't get this hoe to work!" she complained, choppin' at the dirt. "The soil is too hard and dry."

"Did you try usin' the corner of the blade to break up the clay, like I showed you?" I asked.

But the scornful look in her eyes told me she was in no mood for my advice. Still, I know she wasn't the only one feelin' frustrated.

"I feel as useless as tits on a boar," I grumbled, "just sittin' here on the ground pullin' out weeds a few at a time and makin' you do all the man's work."

Well, that only brought another scornful look.

"It is not just *man's* work, Mr. Harleck," she scoffed. "I can manage just fine if you don't mind," she said swingin' the hoe down even harder like she was determined to prove it.

I could see that her delicate hands were gettin' caloused and blistered, and she was sufferin' noticeably from the brutal heat. But seein' as how she was in no mood to be trifled with, I decided it might be best just to let the matter drop.

"Beg pardon, my darling," I said as sincerely as I could. "I didn't mean to imply that you couldn't do the work." I forced a smile to try and reassure her, which seemed to help some. But I knew I was gonna have to do somethin' soon to start earnin' my keep and helpin' the Nellises pay more hands to work the field. One thing was sure: if the work was left to Maribel and me, we'd surely starve by winter, sure as the day was long.

With Gen'ral Lee's army gone, the fed'ral cavalry soon returned to the lower valley. Seein' as how they knew the Nellises were loyal to the Confederacy, they made no apologies about stoppin' by the plantation whenever they were in town, to take what little we had for themselves. It was clear things were gettin' worse instead of better, and I knew I had to find work—and soon. I went down to Mr. Jennings' wheelright and blacksmith shop, but found it closed. A neighbor saw me there and came to see what I was lookin' for. He was an old-timer with a white beard and tufts of white hair stickin' out from under the felt hat he wore.

"Lookin' fer someone, stranger?" he asked.

"Yeah. I came to see Mr. Jennings."

"Gone," he scoffed. "Closed up shop and moved out west somewheres. Kansas, I think he said. Last summer, it was."

"Oh . . . "

"He had two young fellers workin' for him, but they went off to the war. Heard they was both killed. Sad . . . 'Bout yer age, they were too." Then he pointed at my leg. "That how you lost that?"

"Yessir."

"Anyways, after that, Jennings said he'd had enough, so he up and sold his house and moved out west."

I reckon it didn't matter much that the old-timer didn't know I was one of the two boys he was talkin' about, so I didn't bother tryin' to explain it. What mattered was that Jennings was gone and I still needed work.

"Whatchu lookin' fer Jennings fer, anyways?" he asked.

"I was hopin' he might have work I could do."

"'Fraid yer about a year too late, young feller."

Then he cocked his head and looked up out of the corner of his eye, like he was rememberin' somethin'.

"Seem to recall some army feller came here lookin' fer wheelwrights, though."

"When?"

"Few weeks back."

I thanked him and hobbled back to the wagon. I was gettin' better at gettin' around on my own by then. I spent the ride back into town thinkin' about what the old-timer had said. It just made sense. If I couldn't be a soldier, maybe I could help in another way. It was the only other skill I really had. The army was long gone from the valley, but I had a good idea where I might find 'em.

That night at the dinner table, I decided to make my plans known.

"I went down to Mr. Jennings' shop today," I announced, matter-of-factly.

"Oh?" William asked. "I thought that place was closed up."

"It is, but there was an older fella there who told me the army was lookin' for wheelrights when they came through a few weeks back."

"But hasn't the army moved on?" Maribel asked. "How can you . . . "

But then the look on her face changed, and I knew she'd figured out what I was thinkin'.

"No!" she insisted, standin' up.

"Maribel—" I started to argue, standin' up and bracin' myself up with the chair, seein' as how that's what even a one-legged man's s'posed to do when a lady stands up. But she wanted none of what I was about to say.

"You are *not* leavin' me again, Wil Harleck!" she shouted, her face turnin' red.

"Maribel, be reasonable—" I tried again.

"No, Wil!" she argued, fightin' back the tears. "You *can't* go back . . . There must be *something* else you can do here at home—"

"There is no other way, Maribel!" I shouted. "Look at me!"

But she turned away and wouldn't look at me.

"Look at me, Maribel!" I shouted again, motionin' toward my short leg with one hand. But she couldn't make herself do it.

"Who wants to hire a one-legged cripple like me?!" I ranted on. "What else can I do?! Wheelrightin' and soldierin' are the only things I know, and if I don't find work soon, we're—!" I was just about to say 'we're gonna starve,' but then I remembered that her folks were right there next to her, and I didn't wanna offend their generosity by incinuatin' that they couldn't provide for their own family. " . . . well, beggin' your pardon, sir, ma'am," I said more calmly, noddin' at William and Grace-Anne, then lookin' back at Maribel again, "but we can't keep freeloadin' off your folks forever," I went on. "It just wouldn't be right. I . . . I just wouldn't feel like a man."

Maribel huffed and threw her napkin down on the chair, then turned and rushed out of the room.

William was standin' up by then too, but he didn't say a word. He just watched her leave. Then he shook his head and looked at me. Finally he spoke. "She's *your* wife, son. You'd better go talk to her."

I grabbed my crutch, followed her up the stairs to the bedroom, and knocked on the door.

"Maribel?" I called.

"Go away!" she said through the door.

I could tell she was cryin'. I turned the porcelain knob, opened the door, and hobbled in.

"I said, go away!" she insisted again, her face buried in her hands.

The sight of her standin' there by the window cryin', bathed in the soft twilight of evenin', tore at my heart. I started again more gently, "Maribel—"

"It's not fair!" she tiraded, turnin' and lookin' up at me. "Why do you have to go back to that awful war again? Haven't you sacrificed enough already?"

"Maribel, I *have* to do this," I insisted softly.

She swallowed hard. "Isn't there *any* other way?" she tried. But she already knew the answer.

I moved over to where she stood and took her hand in mine.

"It's not like I'm goin' off to fight like before," I said, tryin' to reassure her. "It's just wheelright work . . . in the rear, with the supply train."

She looked up at me with tears in her eyes, and I could see that my words alone were not enough.

"I don't want you to go," she pleaded.

As we stood there together and my eyes beheld the woman before me, I found myself captivated by her again. Maybe her clothes were not as fancy as before; maybe her hair looked a bit more grown up now; and maybe her hands were a bit rougher and her face betrayed the toll the war had taken on her; but I saw the light of inner beauty in her eyes that reminded me why I'd fallen in love with her in the first place. This was not the same playful young girl I'd known before. But then I wasn't the same wide-eyed boy either.

I wiped the tears from her cheeks and she looked up at me, her eyes still wet.

"Lay with me tonight?" she asked tenderly.

We hadn't yet been together since I'd returned home. I'd been afraid of what I might find in her eyes when she first saw my leg. Truth is, I was still havin' a hard time lookin' at it myself. But there was longing in her eyes that night. It reminded me that perhaps I'd been a mite selfish of late. In my own fears of bein' less than a whole man, I'd forgotten that she was a woman, and she had needs of her own.

She laid her hands on my chest and lowered her gaze. Then her hands moved slowly down across my stomach to the buttons of my trousers, and I began to feel powerful uneasy.

I took hold of her wrists and tried to step back. "Maribel, I'm not—" I started.

"Hushhh," she whispered gently, steppin' in close again and givin' me a look that said she wasn't takin' no for an answer. "I've been missing you, Mr. Harleck. It's been a long time . . . "

She led me to the bed. I couldn't speak at all, but neither could I look away as she turned her attention back to my clothing. The plain brown fabric of her dress couldn't hide the shapely form of her bosom or the soft curves of her waist. And havin' her hair all up like she did only made me wanna kiss the delicate curve of her neck.

She gently lowered my trousers, and I found myself holdin' my breath. My thoughts turned back to my fear. But instead, I saw the strong woman my Pa had talked about. She set her face, drew in a quiet breath, and looked down slowly.

I felt my heart would stop while I waited there wonderin' and fearin' what Maribel must be thinkin' of that sight. When she first laid eyes on my amputated leg, she made a small gasping sound that I can't recollect ever hearin' her make before.

She reached out like she wanted to touch the scar tissue where my limb came to an end, but then stopped.

"Does it still hurt?" she looked up at me and asked, almost in a whisper.

"Sometimes a little," I confessed, "but not like it used to."

Her tender fingers explored the wound softly. Finally, when her eyes again met my own, it wasn't disappointment or pity I beheld there. It was tenderness and love. And in that moment I felt whole again.

Maribel reached out for the crutch and I offered it up. She took it and leaned it against the footboard while I sat down on the edge of the bed. After she reached down to take off my shoe, she stood and loosened the laces of her dress, lettin' it drop to the floor. Then she reached her hands inside my unbuttoned shirt and gently pushed me back on the bed, whereupon she proceeded to remind me of the wonder that I'd been missin' for so long. No need to say, I never wanted that night to end.

I woke to the bright rays of sunlight floodin' in through the window and Maribel asleep, her head on my shoulder and her warm breath on my chest. After awhile, she stirred and looked up at me.

"Good morning, handsome," she said with that sweet smile.

It occurred to me just then that there was nowhere else I'd wanna be. "You, madam, are a flatterer," I chided.

"Perhaps so, sir, but it is the truth nonetheless," she smiled even more brightly. "Besides, it remains to be seen whether I am a *good* flatterer or a *bad* one."

"Rest assured, Maribel, you are most definitely a *good* one."

"Are you sure I can't persuade you to stay, then?" she asked, bitin' her bottom lip and lookin' up at me out of the top of her eyes. "Hasn't the army had you long enough, Wil?" Her voice was becommin' more sincere now.

Now it hadn't escaped me that I'd married a resourceful woman. I knew that she wanted another child. The loss of Maria Grace had left a mighty big hole in our hearts, and I had to admit that another child would have been like a balm to our souls. Maribel had done her best to make sure this was a night I wouldn't soon forget. She knew I'd be sure not to stay away for long if she was in the family way again. Wise woman.

"If there's another way, darling . . . well, I'm just not seein' it."

She sighed against my chest and offered no words, though I wasn't sure if she was givin' up the ground or just reformin' for another attack. Either way, I thought it best to take the offensive by way of a rapid flankin' movement.

"I'll send for you as soon as I can," I reassured.

She looked up again out of the top of her eyes. "Promise?"

"I promise."

I reckon Gen'ral Jackson would've been proud of my military solution for handlin' a strong Southern woman. Of course, somethin' tells me that Maribel still had command of the field, thruth be told.

I set out the next day, and within a week found Gen'ral Lee's headquarters near Culpeper, just where I thought it'd be. The Gen'ral's adjutant was a young major; handsome, well groomed, and well dressed, with light brown hair and a well-trimmed mustache that couldn't hide the kindness in his eyes and face. And polite he was too. I reckon he must've been quite popular with the womenfolk.

"May I be of some assistance to you, sir?" His question struck me dumb for a spell. I don't seem to recall ever bein' called 'sir' before. Leastwise not by an officer. Maybe it was on account of me not bein' in a uniform, or maybe it was on account of me havin' only one good leg. But whatever the reason, it was plain to see he was a true southern gentleman.

"William Harleck, sir—" I had to clear my throat to get the rest to come out. "I came to inquire if the army has any need for a one-legged wheelwright."

He was only too happy to oblige. "Why I do believe you would be of great service to the army, Mr. Harleck," he smiled. Whereupon he proceeded to send me straight to the supply train. There I was introduced to a man named John McCormack, who promptly put me to work fixin' wagon and cannon wheels. John was the master wheelwright in the First Corps, Army of Northern Virginia—Longstreet's Corps. Before the war, he had a shop in Warrenton, where he lived with his family. He was a temperamental fella, with all the personality of a badger, and not to be trifled with. But for some reason, he was always kind enough to me—as long as I worked hard and didn't make too many mistakes.

The work was long and tiresome, and we still moved around quite a bit, but the food and the livin' conditions were a mite better than camp life in the infantry, to be sure. And imagine my surprise when the first of September came and I was paid the handsome sum of twenty eight dollars for a month's work! Nearly three times what I'd made as a private! So I worked hard, wrote to Maribel often, and saved every penny I could.

September of '63 was a good month. Gen'ral Longstreet took two divisions of the First Corps and loaded 'em on trains headed south. We had no idea where they were goin', and they didn't take us with 'em, but we were bustin' with pride when we heard later on that they'd arrived in Georgia in time to help Gen'ral Bragg whoop the Yankees at a place called Chickamauga. At a time when everything seemed to be goin' wrong for the south, every victory was like a ray of warm sunlight on a cold and cloudy day. Then I got a letter from Maribel sayin' that she was expectin' our second child, and I became rather more excited than I'd been in quite some time. I was more anxious than ever to start makin' a new life with Maribel, and I hoped that maybe things were gettin' better.

But hope always seemed too short-lived. Gen'ral Lee couldn't spare Gen'ral Longstreet for long, so he brought his two divisions back to Virginia in October. But then, late in November, we got word that Gen'ral Bragg's army had been routed at Chattanooga, and it was becomin' clear to us that it was really just a matter of time now after all.

I was doin' my best to save money while still sendin' a little home each month to help Maribel, Mama, Pa, and Vanessa keep food on their tables. There were times I wondered if I'd ever be able to save enough to find a new place for Maribel and me to live, but all I could do was work and save and pray, so these I did as best I could.

I visited home for Christmas, and I was delighted to see that Maribel was beginnin' to show by then, even though she tried not to make it too obvious. The glow had begun to return to her face, and her eyes sparkled again for the first time since before Maria Grace had passed, and I began to feel like maybe things might just turn out alright.

"Tell me we'll be together soon," she said in her most persuasive voice.

"We're together now, aren't we?" I answered, hopin' that it might be enough.

"You know what I mean, Wil Harleck," she said, scoldin' me playfully.

"Soon," I assured her. "I've been savin' money, and I almost have enough for a place for us to live, but it needs to be someplace safe for you and our child."

"Can't you take me with you?" she asked. "I could work to help earn money." But she already knew I'd never agree to that, leastwise not while she was with child anyway.

"The best place for you is right here until after the child is born."

But I wasn't convinced that was really true either. The war loomed over us all like a dark storm cloud. The economy in Jefferson County was bad, and gettin' worse all the time, and Yankee soldiers seemed to be forever lurkin' about. Truth be told, there wasn't really a safe place to have a child within a hundred miles—south of the Mason-Dixon, that is—but there was no need worry Maribel about that.

It felt good to be home with loved ones, but Christmas was a mite lean that year. Most of the good folk in the Shenandoah had lost almost everything they had to the war, and many were in need of food, medicine, clothing, and the other basic necessities of life. But our two families shared what little we had and somehow managed to fill the Nellis' table with food.

The winter of '64 was cold but fairly quiet, and not much happened in the way of fightin'. On April the fourteenth, our second child was born—a boy—and we decided that Carl Amos might make a fine name. I visited with Maribel and the child again that same week, and as I held my son in my arms on that bright spring day, I felt young and innocent again for the first time in nearly three years.

But my visit was cut short by rumors that the new Yankee gen'ral, Gen'ral Grant, was on the move in northern Virginia. I was growin' restless for the end of the war to come and wishin' that it could all just be over, so as we could just stop all the fightin' and get back to livin'. But I reckon it had to run its course. Gen'ral Lee won a battle in the Wilderness in May, almost exactly one year after Chancellorsville, and in almost exactly the same place. But this time, the Yankees didn't retreat. They just turned and tried to get around our flank near Spottsylvania, but the ol' "Gray Fox" was too quick.

The Second Virginia was engaged there, at a place called the "Bloody Angle." Arty was wounded in that battle, and Jim was captured when the Yankees surprised our boys by stormin' over the breastworks in a dense fog. By the end of May, the lines shifted to a small town northeast of Richmond called Cold Harbor. Gen'ral Lee bloodied Grant's nose there too, but it didn't stop him. He just kept right on movin' by the flank. By June our lines had shifted again, this time to the southeast of Richmond, around Petersburg.

The Shenandoah Valley changed hands four times in the summer and fall of '64, but Sheridan's Union cavalry finally drove Gen'ral Ewell's boys out of the valley, then burned nigh on everything. There were two battles near Charles Town which gave me cause for some great concern, but none of my family was hurt. But everywhere, the truth was becomin' painfully obvious. In spite of all the bravery and valor of our boys, the Confederacy was crumblin' apart, piece by piece.

From June of '64 until April of '65, I stayed and worked mostly in the town of Petersburg. It was not a pleasant ordeal for the boys in gray there, to be sure. They spent day and night in the muddy trenches, come rain or shine, heat of summer or dead of winter, and all the supplies a fella needed for the basic necessities of life were becomin' mighty scarce.

The army finally stopped movin' around so much, which made my job easier, but it was more than a week's journey from Petersburg to Charles Town, so I could no longer visit my family anymore. Mr. McCormack had a wife, Candace, and three children, who lived in Warrenton. But by July, Warrenton was mostly occupied by the Fed'rals too, so he sent for them to come and stay in Petersburg. There he rented a house and invited me to send for Maribel and little Carl Amos to come and live with his family in exchange for sharin' the rent.

By August, Sheridan was makin' life nigh intolerable for the folks back in the Valley. William and Grace-Anne Nellis left their plantation and moved to a small farm in Lynchburg. They begged Maribel to stay with them there, but Maribel wouldn't have it. She insisted on comin' to Petersburg with the baby to be with me. Turns out, Candace and Maribel got along famously together. Maribel said Candace was like a big sister to her, and her children were only too happy to help look after little Carl Amos.

As the summer of '64 drew to a close, only the slimmest hope for a southern victory remained, and that depended entirely on our northern brethren. We hoped and prayed that somehow, by some miracle of God, Lincoln might lose the election and a new president would sign a truce. But when November came and the votes were counted, Lincoln had won again.

By the winter of '65, it was as plain as the broad side of a barn that the South couldn't last much longer. Sherman had broken our back in Georgia, and Grant was stretchin' his lines further and further west to cut off Richmond. Gen'ral Lee just didn't have enough men left to keep up the fight.

By April, the Yankees were nigh to cuttin' off our last supply routes, and Maribel had to take Carl Amos and flee to her folks' home in Lynchburg for fear the Yankees would take the city and burn it. Finally, Gen'ral Lee had no choice but to abandon Richmond and try to escape to meet up with what was left of Johnston's army somewhere down in North Carolina. But ol' Grant, he proved to be a mite smarter than most folks gave him credit for. He cut off all our escape routes and pinned our boys down at a place called Appomatox. I was there with the supply train on the ninth of April, 1865, when Gen'ral Lee decided the only honorable thing left to do was to surrender. Of the more than twelve hundred men and boys who'd once served in the Innocent Second, only seventy-one were there to witness the surrender, and only seven were from Company A. I heard tell that Capt'n Rowan and L'tenant Davenport both survived the war, but neither of them was present at Appomatox that day.

Five days later, some danged fool went and shot Lincoln in the head. I may not've cared much for the man, but I reckon that was downright uncalled for. Like it or not, the war was finally over. There was no need for more killin'.

Forlorn Hopes and New Beginnings

Now that all the fightin' was finally over, John McCormack talked about goin' back home to Warrenton and rebuildin' his business there. He offered me a job and even said he'd help me find a new place to live. Well, seein' as how Lynchburg was just down the road a little ways from Appomatox, I reckoned I'd stop by the Nellis farm to visit with Maribel and my son, who was nearly a year old by then, before headin' up to Warrenton. I promised to send for them as soon as I could find a place for us to live there. Turns out there was plenty of work for wheelrights in Warrenton, and by late July, I'd saved up enough money to buy a small house that had been empty since the war, where we could start our new lives together. It wasn't long before Maribel had that old house lookin' like a right proper home, with a little help from Candace and John of course. That Christmas, Maribel surprised me with news that she was carryin' our third child, and it filled me with hope for brighter days to come.

In the spring of '66, the Good Lord called my Pa home at the young age of 52. It goes without sayin' that it took us all by surprise.

When we got the telegram, my first thoughts were of Mama, seein' as how she'd already lost so much. But all of us had had our share of heartbreak and tragedy, yet somehow God had sustained us through it all. And I was real thankful for that talk I'd had with Pa on that ride back home from Winchester.

We returned to Charles Town for the funeral. Mama's face lit up like the full moon when she saw little Carl Amos for the first time since just after he was born. Then, when she saw that Maribel was in the family way again, she got even more excited, and insisted on waitin' on Maribel hand and foot while we were in her home. It was good to see Mama and Vanessa again, and I even got to see Tommy and Arty too. They said they were fixin' to go up north to Pittsburg to look for work in the big city, where the economy was better. I can't say as I blame 'em though. There wasn't much sense in tryin' to find work in Jefferson County, to be sure.

Mama asked Joseph and me to say a few words at Pa's funeral service. Joseph seemed right at home speakin' in front of all those people, but it felt mighty strange for me. I'd heard my Pa give a dozen eulogies, but I'd never dreamt I'd be helpin' to give his. But when the time came, I knew just what to say. Funny thing is, all those sermons and wise words I'd remembered him sayin' my whole life, well, they all suddenly made more sense then, and I was thankful for the strong faith he'd planted in me. So I just said 'thank you' for all those things.

Now my Mama was a strong woman, thank the Lord. Still, she took Pa's death pretty hard. And even though Vanessa had grown up to be a strong and capable young lady herself—even had herself a fine young suiter named Matthew—I was still a little worried about their well-bein', seein' as how all the men in the family were gone now, and they'd have to look after themselves.

But after the funeral, Joseph surprised us all by announcin' that he'd accepted Pa's parish. He even offered to move into our old room in the parish house, so as Mama could stay in her home—and Vanessa too, leastwise until she married. We all sat in the parlor for hours that night and talked of better times and fond memories.

For Joseph and me, it was like nothin' had ever come between us. I reckon it was a time for healin' old wounds for a good many folks, and we were no different. We didn't speak much of the war. Turns out, we had plenty of other things to talk about. After he'd graduated from the seminary, Joseph had returned to Williamsport and met a young lady named Anna, and they were fixin' to be married soon. So we mostly kept Joseph talkin' about his new bride-to-be, which wasn't hard to do.

Maribel, Carl Amos, and I returned to Warrenton later that week. It was there, our second daughter, Amanda Maye, was born in July—the first of our children to be born in our own home. She had her mama's hair and eyes, and the same sweet spirit as Maria Grace. Of course nothin' or no one can ever replace a child who was lost to this world, but holdin' Amanda in our arms and gazin' upon her cherubic face sure did help to fill our hearts with new hopes and dreams.

Maribel and I and the children attended Joseph's wedding in October that same year, where we met Anna for the first time. She was strong and clever—just the kind for Joseph—and quite beautiful in her wedding dress too. Yessirree, Joseph had gone and found himself a fine woman. It was a nice wedding, though a bit modest. Of course when Mama wasn't busy cookin' and servin' the banquet meal, Maribel kept her busy with the children, which, needless to say, thrilled Mama to no end.

It's been twelve years now since the war, and Maribel and I have been blessed with a fine healthy family of our own. Carl and Amanda have two younger sisters, Ellie and Emily. But I often sit alone on the front porch in the twilight and think back on my days in the Innocent Second. I still remember all the good times and all the bad times we had. I think of all the friends made, and all the friends lost. So many battles fought; so many sacrificed. And was it really worth fightin' for in the end?

Sometimes I read from Carlton's Bible to remind me of how God brought me through it all, and made me a better man for it. And I pray He'll do the same for the country. I think on how the war changed this nation, and I reckon maybe ol' Abe Lincoln had at least one thing right: all that blood on our hands oughta be for some good reason. If we can't be an innocent nation anymore, at least we can be a free one—for all men.

Glossary of Military Unit Structure in the Civil War

Company—The most basic infantry or cavalry unit, typically composed of up to 100 men at full strength, but usually much less due to attrition from combat, desertion, and illness. Most companies were commanded by captains and composed entirely of men from the same town or county when first formed. A company could also be divided into platoons and squads for functions requiring smaller unit structures.

Battalion—Usually composed of four or more companies, normally ranging from 400 to 800 men at full strength. (Southern artillery units were organized into guns, batteries, and battalions, but rarely larger. Northern artillery battalions were sometimes called brigades instead of battalions.)

Regiment—Typically composed of ten companies (or sometimes two battalions) usually ranging from 1,000 to 1,600 men at full strength (though some were larger). Usually commanded by a colonel, the regiment was the primary infantry or cavalry unit of organization employed in the war.

Brigade—Normally composed of three or more regiments, typically ranging from 3,000 to 6,000 men at full strength and commanded by a brigadier general.

Division—Usually composed of two to six brigades, normally ranging from 6,000 to 12,000 men or more at full strength and commanded by a major general. Confederate divisions were typically larger than Union divisions.

Corps—Usually commanded by a major general (or sometimes a lieutenant general in the south), and composed of two or three divisions, normally ranging from 20,000 to 35,000 men or more at full strength. Again, Confederate corps were frequently larger than Union corps. (Singular and plural are both spelled 'corps' and pronounced with a silent 'ps'.)

Army—Usually composed of two or more corps, but army structures varied greatly from army to army, depending mostly upon the commanding general's preferences, and sizes varied greatly depending on availability of troops and the mission of that particular army. Likewise, the rank of the commanding general varied from north to south, and from army to army.

About the Author

Steve is a retired U.S. Navy Master Chief whose love for American history was inspired by teachers who brought history to life with passion and a flair for the dramatic. A graduate of Liberty University and a licensed minister, Steve has written many technical directives and professional curricula, and his article, "Keeping the Hook Moving" was published in the July/August 2009 edition of Navy Supply Corps Newsletter. *Farewell the Innocent* is Steve's first work of historical fiction, culminating ten years of research on the Second Virginia Infantry Regiment, C.S.A.

Steve and his wife currently live in historic Williamsburg, Virginia with their children and their Siberian Huskies. In his spare time, he volunteers with Siberian Husky rescue, and is a member of the Frontiersmen Camping Fellowship. His great desire is to share his love of history with others in much the same way he first became inspired.